We'll Always Have Paris

Kate Penney is the co-author of seven novels for young adults, including the *House of Shadows* and *Throne of Swans* duologies, which she wrote with her sister as Katharine Corr. Kate read history at Sidney Sussex College, Cambridge, and worked in London before becoming a full-time mother and writer. A hopeful romantic, she's a Jane Austen superfan and can't resist a happy ending. Kate lives in Surrey with her husband, daughters and cats.

We'll Always Have Paris

Kate Penney

HODDER &
STOUGHTON

First published in Great Britain in 2026 by Hodder & Stoughton Limited
An Hachette UK company

The authorised representative in the EEA is Hachette Ireland, 8 Castlecourt Centre, Dublin 15, D15 XTP3, Ireland (email: info@hbgi.ie)

1

Copyright © Kate Penney 2026

The right of Kate Penney to be identified as the Author of the Work has been asserted by her in accordance with the Copyright, Designs and Patents Act 1988.

All rights reserved. No part of this publication may be reproduced, stored in a retrieval system, or transmitted, in any form or by any means without the prior written permission of the publisher, nor be otherwise circulated in any form of binding or cover other than that in which it is published and without a similar condition being imposed on the subsequent purchaser.

All characters in this publication are fictitious and any resemblance to real persons, living or dead, is purely coincidental.

A CIP catalogue record for this title is available from the British Library

Paperback ISBN 978 1 399 74592 5
ebook ISBN 978 1 399 74593 2

Typeset in Plantin MT by Hewer Text UK Ltd, Edinburgh
Printed and bound in Great Britain by Clays Ltd, Elcograf S.p.A.

Hodder & Stoughton policy is to use papers that are natural, renewable and recyclable products and made from wood grown in sustainable forests. The logging and manufacturing processes are expected to conform to the environmental regulations of the country of origin.

Hodder & Stoughton Limited
Carmelite House
50 Victoria Embankment
London EC4Y 0DZ

www.hodder.co.uk

To my sister, Elizabeth

PART ONE

Summer

Chapter One

Emma

Thirty minutes is the same as 1,800 seconds, or 1,800,000 milliseconds. I know this because I collect random facts the way other people collect shoes, or Christmas tree decorations. Thirty minutes is more than enough time for everything to go horribly wrong. Or for things to get even worse. It's only half past ten and I've already got a mental list of things I definitely shouldn't have done this morning, including sleeping through my phone alarm, taking a taxi instead of the metro to the Gare du Nord – the road was blocked by a protest, so I had to get out and walk – stopping to buy postcards, and wearing my Mary Janes instead of my trainers. I love them to bits, and they looked right for the event I was coerced into attending yesterday evening, but they are definitely *not* designed for running in.

My trenchcoat was another mistake: far too heavy for the suddenly warm weather: the thirty-first of May is still officially spring. Meteorological summer doesn't start until tomorrow. Astronomical summer, three weeks after that. I was going for elegant and Parisian when I got dressed. What I've ended up with – as far as I can tell from my reflection in the shop window I've just sprinted past – is sweaty and demented. The scuffed, overstuffed suitcase skittering along behind me definitely doesn't help.

What if I've somehow managed to drop my ticket since the last time I checked it was in my bag? What if there's not enough time left for me to get through passport control? What if I can't find the right carriage? What if—

Shut up, Emma. The catastrophising stresses me out. Then I feel bad for getting stressed out. *Shut up. It isn't helpful.* As if I don't know that already.

If only I'd said no to my super-persuasive best friend and housemate, Daisy.

'Please, please do this one thing for me, Ems. It's the last favour, I promise!'

'Yeah, I've heard that before.'

'But where's the down side? All you have to do is go there and enjoy yourself. And just show up to this one teeny, tiny event on Thursday evening. And tell them you're my assistant. And take some photos, using my good camera. And spend maximum ten minutes taking texture shots when the exhibition opens to the public on the Friday. Otherwise, it's basically a free mini-break in Paris, the City of Love.'

The way she said it, it sounded like 'lurve'.

'But I'm not your assistant, Daisy! You don't have an assistant. And I don't want to spend three hours taking photos of . . .' I consulted the email she was showing me on her phone. '". . . Paris and the Printing Press: a Celebration." 'I mean, seriously? Why did you even apply for this job?'

'It's a long story, okay? But pleeeease, Ems! If I don't take the make-up gig in Bath, I may never get another chance. This could be a really big thing for me. And I can't blow off the photo gig because it's sponsored by the biggest-selling newspaper in France, and you never want to piss off the media.'

I remember groaning at this point.

'I really can't, Daisy. I've got an important meeting with the editor first thing on Monday morning about the next ghostwriting project, and I have to prepare. Besides, it's too short notice. It's not what I was planning to do. There's no time for me to get organised or book restaurants or anything. No time to figure out a schedule.'

'It's Paris – you don't need a schedule! And you'll be back by Friday afternoon; you'll have the whole weekend to work. I reckon it will be good for you to do something spur-of-the-moment. Maybe it will give you inspiration. Or maybe you'll meet someone. After all, it's been nine months since you finally dumped that awful, self-obsessed Simon.'

'I don't want to meet someone. I'm focusing on my career right now.'

'But this is about *my* career, Ems. I can't afford to turn down this job, so I can't go away next week. But you could. Everything's paid for: the travel, the hotel. There's even a meal allowance for the day of the event. When else will you get to explore Paris basically for free? Come on, Ems. Please. For me.'

It went on like that for a while. For long enough.

Finally, in the distance I spot the front of the Gare du Nord, all pale stone and statues. I speed up, slaloming around slower pedestrians. Shove my way through a meandering American tour group. Scatter a crowd of teenagers on a school trip, even though there's only half an hour left for me to get on the Eurostar back to London. Even though I know – I just *know* – that I'm never going to make it on time.

Daisy messaged me this morning.

You've not posted any pictures.
Hoping this means you met a hot
French guy at the printing press thing
and have been otherwise entertained!

Her Instagram is already full of photos and selfies from the event she was working at this weekend. *Hashtag dreamlife. Hashtag smashingit. Hashtag bestjobever.* What if I took a selfie right now? An honest one? *Hashtag anxious. Hashtag hotmess. Hashtag nofuckingclue.* I won't, because no one wants some stranger's disappointing reality cluttering up their social media feed, but the thought makes me smile slightly even as I strain to make out the time on the clock that sits in the centre of the station's towering façade.

I'm going to miss my train.

This is what comes of taking risks.

Kieran

Thirty minutes is no time at all. Barely enough time to make and enjoy a decent cappuccino. And yet, thirty minutes in Paris this morning has just changed my life. I took a risk, and it paid off. I knew it would. Still, I close my eyes, tilt my face up to the unexpected spring sunshine and *grin*.

I'd taken a huge risk in the first place, of course. Contacting René Arnaud, superstar chef-owner of La Reine de la Nuit, telling him I was the best chef in the Lille metropolitan area and inviting him to the restaurant where I work ... He said I was arrogant. But he did come. And he liked my cooking enough to allow me to work in his kitchen for three days. He liked the results of that enough to invite me back this morning for a final test. I went in expecting to be asked to make something complicated – some dish so utterly French that it would be bound to trip up a half-Québécois, half-Irish immigrant who learnt to cook on the fly rather than at a fancy Parisian culinary school. Instead, he told me to surprise him. So, I took a chance. I made him an omelette. One of those dishes where you can showcase your incompetence in plenty of ways: rubbery texture, too much filling, unbalanced seasoning, etc., etc. Perfection, on the other hand, doesn't draw attention to itself. Monsieur Arnaud ate the omelette, and drank the wine I'd paired it with, in silence. Then he glanced up at me.

'Hand your notice in to your employer. I'll expect you here by the end of next month.' He shook my hand. 'We can deal with your contract at that point.'

No mention of the salary: we both knew I'd take the job whatever he offered. La Reine lost its Michelin star a year ago, Arnaud is hungry to get it back, and he didn't need me to tell him that I'd do anything to be part of that success story. Barely thirty minutes after I'd walked into La Reine, I was headed back to the Gare du Nord, stopping briefly at one of the *bouquinistes* along the Seine to buy a few more second-hand cookery books by way of celebration.

I check the clock above the station entrance; there's only a few minutes until my train back to Roubaix. I don't want to miss it. I want my new life to start as soon as possible. But I also want to fix this moment in my memory. Trying to get a better look at the statues ranged along the station façade, I step backwards—

Emma

Nearly there. I push myself to run even faster, glancing up at the clock above the entrance to the station—

The force of the impact sends me reeling – I've run smack into someone. He drops the stack of books he's carrying. Swears and grabs my shoulders as I start to fall.

'Steady! Are you okay?'

The tall stranger is looking down at me with concern.

All I can do is stare back up at him. I seem to have lost the power of speech. And movement. Deep brown eyes, framed with long, dark lashes. A slight curl in the shock of golden-brown hair. A boyish, uncertain, lopsided smile. I drink the stranger in, and my insides start fizzing.

'*Madame – ça va?*' he asks.

'Er – *oui*. I mean, yes. I mean . . .' I blink at him. '*Mademoiselle*. Not *madame*.' It seems very important, suddenly, that he knows I'm not married. He's still gripping my upper arms, but it doesn't make me anxious, or affronted. Instead, I'm imagining how his strong hands might feel against my bare skin. A hot blush rises up my neck and floods my cheeks. 'Oh – my – my train . . .'

The words seem to snap him out of a spell. He lets go of me just as my precariously balanced suitcase tips over. We both reach down for it, and as our fingers brush something jolts through me, an electric shock of desire and recognition and – and *rightness*.

Did he feel it too?

He's staring at me as if he might have done. Our gazes are locked. I can't look away.

'Um . . .' he mutters, 'um – train – I mean – sorry.' He starts to scrabble for his scattered books, but his eyes are still fixed on me, and now he's blushing too. 'Damn. Hold on.' From somewhere he produces a pen and a scrap of paper and writes on it before thrusting it into my hand. 'Call me.' The stranger dashes into the station, but before he's swallowed by the shadows he turns once more. 'Please! It might be fate!'

I take a quick look at the paper – *Kieran*, and a mobile number – and clutch it tight in my fist. The escalator to the Eurostar check-in is just ahead. I move forward automatically, my focus on the piece of paper and the instant his fingers brushed against mine.

Nonsense, of course. I don't believe in fate. Stuff just happens, and most of it is bad.

So why is every fibre of my being screaming that he might be The One?

Get a grip, Emma. You can't actually call a complete stranger you literally ran into.

Can I?

Kieran

What just happened?

I ask the question over and over until I'm on the train and in my seat.

What just happened? Did she feel it too? That sudden, breathtaking moment of connection. That sense of *haven't I met you somewhere before*? The hairs on the back of my neck stand up. Even though I'm sitting down, my pulse is still racing.

Green eyes. Wide green eyes, the colour of mint, and ebony-dark hair. That's all I remember. But I know I'll never forget her face.

Panic rises in my throat. I should have written down my surname too. The panic increases when I notice the corner of a paper bag sticking out from between my stack of books.

Postcards. Postcards I didn't buy. Postcards she must have dropped.

I half-rise from my seat, seized by the impulse to run after her, as the train jerks into motion.

Stay calm. She's got your number.

It's a new number, but I definitely wrote it down correctly.

I did, didn't I?

Fuck.

Chapter Two

Emma

Unlike Paris, London has apparently decided not to bother with the whole 'change of seasons' thing this year. Although it's now almost the middle of June, the sky outside is grey and disapproving and a cold wind is rattling the window panes aggressively. Daisy and I even talked about turning the heating on last night. We didn't, obviously – the cost! the planet! – but we both agreed it might as well still be March. I tilt my head, scrutinising the coffee table in front of me: it still looks streaky. I spray on some more polish and give it another vigorous rub. Mrs Farrell, whose house I'm currently cleaning, has an eagle eye for dust. Not that I'm complaining. Cleaning other people's houses one and a half days a week pretty much doubles my income, and means I can afford to live in London – just – and put away the princely sum of £50 a month for emergencies, and still have the very occasional nice thing.

I glance at my phone as I start dusting the mantelpiece and the knick-knacks crowded on to the mahogany surface. Forty-five minutes left. I run through the rest of the day in my head: bus home, Lidl – Daisy's given me a list, and we've run out of bread; put some washing on while Daisy cooks – curry, given what she's asked me to buy. And then . . .

Should I call him?

Yes.

No.

Yes.

Maybe?

'Argh!' My outburst disturbs the cat that's dozing on the sofa; it lifts its head and glares at me. It's been ten days since he gave me his number. The stranger. Kieran. The man who probably accidentally ran off with my postcards. I still can't decide what to do about it. About him. But I can't stop thinking about him, either. Imagining all the details about him that I don't know, which is basically everything.

The cat miaows and looks at me expectantly.

Which is pretty much the way Daisy is going to look at me the moment I get in.

The bus is packed. Once I've squeezed on, I'm crammed between a man who badly needs a shower and a woman – definitely old enough to know better – watching TikTok videos on her phone with the volume turned up full. I spend the first part of the journey planning ways to silence the noise. Stamp on the phone? Throw it out of the window? Stuff it down the smelly man's sweatpants? Luckily for my sanity she gets out at Kilburn and I snag a seat. Leaning my head against the rain-streaked window, I try to imagine myself back in Paris, reliving the day I spent sightseeing. In my mind's eye I retrace my steps, repeating the route I'd plotted out for myself like a mantra. The Eiffel Tower, the Champ de Mars, the Hôtel des Invalides, the Jardin des Tuileries, the Louvre, the Sainte-Chapelle, Notre-Dame, Shakespeare & Co., the Panthéon, the Jardin du Luxembourg. I'd walked until my feet hurt through beautiful parks and along elegant boulevards and had taken in the outsides of one stunning building after another. It was all a long way from the number 31 bus on a damp Monday evening.

The supermarket's not too busy. I pick up one of the little wheely baskets and wander through the relatively peaceful aisles, debating with myself.

There's no point in calling him. He probably lives in France.

But he might not live in France. You were in Paris, but you don't live in France. He might live in London.

That's even worse. If he lives in London, and he's a psycho, he'll be able to find you.

Why is he suddenly a psycho? He didn't look like a psycho. He looked like a dreamboat.

I give a loud, gushy sigh. The woman standing next to me in front of the frozen peas gives me an odd look.

Dreamboat? What is this, a 1960s sitcom? Of course he doesn't look like a psycho. They never do. Ooh, those chocolate cookies are massively reduced!

Can we focus? We don't need more biscuits. What if I get a burner phone? Then he won't have my real number, and if he is a psycho I can just throw the phone away.

A burner phone? That's a bit much. Besides, if he turns out not to be a psycho, then you'll have to explain to him at some point that he doesn't have your actual number. Though of course he might be using a burner phone too.

Why would he use a burner phone? That's not very honest.

Maybe he's engaged. Maybe he's married. Maybe he's the head of an international dark web organisation that—

'Oh, for heaven's sake, will you shut up!' The guy ahead of me in the queue spins around. He looks upset. 'Sorry – not you – I'm, um . . .' I gesture to my left ear, hoping he'll think I'm on a call, and that he won't notice that I've not got any earbuds in.

When it's my turn, I canvass the opinion of the checkout person.

'This guy I bumped into at a train station gave me his number. Do you think I should call him?'

She looks surprised at the question, which is fair enough. 'Er, dunno. Is he hot?'

'Yeah. Definitely. I think so. Thought so. I mean, we only spent two minutes together, if that, and—'

'Well, if you liked the look of him . . . That'll be £46.50, please.'

£46.50? I only bought a few things. I pay, and she turns – with something like relief – to the next customer.

* * *

Daisy and I have been renting a tiny, two-bedroom Victorian terrace house on the western edge of London for the last two and a half years. Our landlord owns five houses around here. He's a nice enough guy – at least he's a human rather than an offshore property fund – but his general attitude to maintenance can be summed up as 'if it's broke, don't fix it – unless legally obliged to'. As a result, our house has seen better decades, let alone better days. Even the woodworm have given up on the rotting wooden window frames as a bad job. As for the interiors, they're incoherent enough to induce a headache in anyone who wanders in unprepared. The décor veers wildly from 1980s florals through aggressively bland magnolia to rag-rolled feature walls and lurid polyester carpets. The furniture is a mix of Swedish flat-pack and undateable, moth-eaten things that can only have been picked up from probate house clearance sales. But at least it's home.

Daisy's making some tea in the little galley kitchen; she grabs the shopping bags as soon as I walk in and dumps them on the water-stained wooden work surface. 'Thank God, I'm starving. How was your day?'

'Peaceful enough. I had a nice chat with Mrs Singh about the operation she's having next week, and Mrs Farrell was out. What about you?'

'Frantic, as per. Spent all day planning a TikTok campaign for my mum's friend's daughter's hairdressing salon. I wouldn't mind, but she keeps asking for a bigger discount on account of having apparently babysat me one time, when I was five.' Daisy huffs. 'I need to get out of the social media gig. It's brutal.'

Daisy's career is one long series of gigs. Currently, as well as organising social media campaigns, she's also an event photographer – hence the job in Paris – and a make-up artist. She had to give up doing magic at children's parties because her tricks – highlights of her act included fake-guillotining a rabbit and pretending to chop her own arm off – literally reduced her small clients to tears.

She finishes unpacking and shoves the last couple of things into the dated oak-veneered cupboards before returning to the now empty shopping bags.

'Hold on – where's the bread?'

'Huh?'

'Bread. We've run out. You said you'd get some. And why do we have yet another packet of chocolate biscuits?'

I peer into the bags. Shake them, as if the bread might somehow magically appear. It does not.

'Oh, hell. Sorry. I'll get some tomorrow. I guess I got distracted.'

'Distracted?' Daisy narrows her eyes and shakes her head. 'Oh, I see what's happened, Emma Carol Christmas.'

My full name. Now I know I'm in trouble.

Daisy points at me. 'You need to bloody well call him. Or not. Just make a decision.' She says the last line louder, for emphasis.

'But it's so hard . . .'

She tsks at me. 'It's really not. Did he look normal enough to have a second conversation with? That's the only decision to be made, and it's not that difficult. And you don't need to go round asking everyone's opinion as a delaying tactic.'

I open a bag of salt and vinegar crisps and shove a handful into my mouth. 'I do not ask everyone's opinion!'

'Yes, you do.' She starts counting off on her fingers. 'Me. Your editor. The women you clean for. Susie.' Daisy waves her hand, indicating our neighbour who lives next door. 'Mel from the corner shop. Even the plumber who came to fix the tap.' Her gaze grows even more suspicious. 'You asked someone in Lidl, didn't you? Another customer. Own up.'

Ha, she guessed wrong.

'No,' I say, drawing myself up and trying to look righteously offended. 'I did not ask another customer.'

'You asked someone though, I bet.' Daisy huffs and gets out the huge and ancient Le Creuset casserole dish she inherited from her mum. 'Seriously, Ems. Just call him, for crying out loud. Or throw the piece of paper in the recycling and have done with it.'

She's right. I know she's right. I go and fetch the sheet of paper from my bag where I've been keeping it, folded up in my purse, and return to the kitchen. My hand hovers over the wicker basket jammed with magazines, empty milk bottles, junk mail and cardboard. But I can't quite bring myself to drop his phone number on top. Instead, I groan and snatch my phone from the counter. 'Fine. I'll phone him.'

'Great.' Daisy gives me a thumbs-up. 'Just be chill. And keep it short.'

'Chill. Short. Right.' I can feel my breath quickening. I key the number in before I can change my mind and press dial. It rings. And rings. And goes to voicemail.

'Hey, this is Kieran. Sorry to miss your call, but I'll get back to you.'

I'd forgotten how sexy his voice is. His accent kicks my heartbeat up another notch.

'Voicemail!' I mouth at Daisy as the automated voice tells me to leave a message after the tone. Panic rises in my chest. I could just finish the call, but he'll still see the number. The tone ends. Silence.

'Er . . . um . . . this is Emma. Hi, Kieran!' My voice has gone weirdly high-pitched. 'Um, you don't know me. I mean . . . we bumped into each other at the station, the other day. In Paris. You've probably forgotten, 'cos I know it's been a while, but, um, I couldn't decide, and then . . .'

Daisy is making frantic hand signs for me to wrap it up.

'Um, anyway, you gave me your number. And you asked me to call you. So, this is me. Calling you. Um—'

The dial tone cuts me off. I put my phone in my pocket and press the heels of my hands to my eyes.

'What just happened?' Daisy demands. 'I thought we'd agreed you would keep it short. And chill.' Her voice is disbelieving. 'That, Emma, was the opposite of chill.'

'I know, I know! It was – it was—'

'Cringe,' Daisy supplies.

'*So* cringe.' I move my hands to my burning cheeks. 'He's going to think I'm crazy.'

After a moment, she shrugs.

'Look at it this way: if he never calls you back, at least you don't have to fret about it any more. You can pretend it never happened.'

'He's never going to call me back,' I assert.

But I want him to, I realise. Hearing his voice again took me instantly back to that moment when our fingers touched. I close my eyes and try to recapture the thrill that shot through me.

The harsh buzz of my phone vibrating against the countertop makes me jump. Daisy snatches up the paper and compares the number.

'It's him,' she breathes.

'Uh-uh.' I shake my head and back away. 'I can't talk to him. I'm just going to ramble again, and—'

My flatmate thrusts the phone towards me. 'Answer it. Or I will.'

She's serious. I slide my thumb across the screen and swallow hard.

'Er, hello?'

Chapter Three

Kieran

Her breath hitches slightly just before she speaks.

'Hello?'

'Emma – it's Kieran. Kieran Landry. Otherwise known as train station guy, I expect.' Why did I say that? 'Not that I make a habit of hanging out at train stations giving my number to beautiful women,' I add quickly. I take a deep breath – I can feel I'm on the brink of rambling – as Marianne, our *chef de garde-manger*, sticks her head into the break room and raises her eyebrows enquiringly. *C'est elle*, I mouth, and point to the phone. 'I'm so delighted you called.'

'Really?' Emma asks. She sounds surprised.

'Of course. There's no way I would have forgotten you, even if I hadn't accidentally ended up with your postcards.'

'Ah, I guessed you might have them.'

'Yeah, I'm sorry. They must have got mixed up with my books.'

'Don't worry. It was my fault for barging into you. I only bought them because I didn't actually have time to see much of Paris and, well, you know, why does anyone buy postcards?'

Marianne has returned, bringing with her François, the pastry chef. Great, an audience. I decide I need to steer the conversation away from the postcards.

'Every day, I've been wondering whether you'd phone,' I say. 'I normally ignore calls from unknown numbers, but I've answered every single one in the past ten days; you'd be amazed how many people want to offer me an amazing broadband deal.

Honestly, I've been driving all of my colleagues here bananas, talking about you.'

'*C'est vrai,*' François yells out. 'He has!'

I give him the finger and make a *shoo go away* motion with my free hand. Both of them completely ignore me. Unfortunately for me, the restaurant is closed on a Monday, and we're only here working out the menu for the next week; there are no waiters with orders demanding my colleagues' attention.

'I'm sorry I couldn't pick up when you first called, by the way.'

'Was that someone speaking French?' she asks. 'Do you live in Paris?'

'I will do, soon. I'm moving there at the end of the month.' The words make my stomach swoop. Excitement about what's next, but sadness, too, creeping in around the edges. Especially when I look at Marianne and François. 'At the moment I live in Roubaix. It's in northern France, just inside the border with Belgium. What about you?'

'London,' she replies. 'White City, to be precise. Famous for the BBC Television Centre as was, and Wormwood Scrubs. That's a prison.' A pause. 'There's also a large hospital nearby. And Westfield, of course. That's a shopping centre. Like, a huge shopping centre. With a cinema, and lots of great shops and loads of restaurants, and—'

I hear someone interrupting her in the background, and Emma breaks off.

'Sorry,' she says after a moment. 'I don't actually work for the Westfield publicity department.'

'No need to apologise. And I know Westfield. I worked in London for a bit.'

'What kind of work?'

'Restaurants. I'm a chef. I spent some time in a couple of French restaurants in London, learning the craft, as it were.'

'Oh, that's amazing. I'd love to be able to cook.'

'What about you? What's your day-to-day?'

'Um, I'm a writer.' There's a slight rising inflection at the end of her voice, as if she's uncertain.

'Wow, impressive!'

'Oh, I'm not published. Well, I am, but not as myself. I'm a ghostwriter, at the moment. I'm working on the whole six-figure book deal thing, but so far . . .' She laughs nervously.

'I'm sure you'll get there. It's good to have a dream. That's why I'm moving to Paris, actually.' I grin, still delighted by every memory associated with that morning. 'When we bumped into each other, I'd just landed my dream job in a restaurant there. Everything's falling into place, and I know it's going to be completely—' I choke back the word *brilliant*, suddenly hearing how it might sound when Emma's literally just told me that she hasn't made it as a writer yet. Marianne covers her face with her hand, and she's right. 'Sorry. That came out wrong – I'm not really a huge show-off who's massively up himself, honest. It's just that it's a big thing for me, and—'

'And you're excited, and you don't want it to go wrong,' Emma says. Her voice sounds warm, as if she's smiling. I close my eyes and I can see her as she was that day at the station, gazing up at me, eyes wide, a tentative smile playing on her lips. 'I understand,' she adds.

'Yeah.' I smile too. 'You're exactly right.'

There's a beat, and we both start talking at once.

'So what else—'

'What kind of—'

Cue more nervous laughter on both sides.

'Please,' I say, 'after you.'

'Okay . . . so, I was just going to ask what else I should know about you. You know, like, if we'd met through online dating I'd have already checked out your profile.'

That makes me laugh again, properly this time.

'I guess that's true. Well . . .' I try to recall the various dating profiles I've added – and usually, after a few weeks, deleted. 'I'm single – that's important to know. Half French-Canadian, half Irish, and I was brought up in Cork. I'm thirty-two. My favourite TV show is *MasterChef* and my favourite book is *Perfume*, by Patrick Süskind – I prefer reading or fun, episodic TV shows to those long-drawn-out dramas where you either have to watch eight episodes in one go or try to keep five impossibly complicated plotlines separate in your head.' What else? For a moment, my mind is terrifyingly blank. What the hell have I done with my life, other than cook? 'I collect old film posters. I've an older brother and my parents are both alive. And if I'm comfort-eating, it has to be *velouté de châtaignes*. That's creamy chestnut soup to the rest of us.'

Marianne is covering her face in embarrassment, *again*, and François is biting his lip, trying to keep from laughing out loud, while holding up a piece of paper on which he's scrawled *BORING!!!*

I panic.

'Oh, and in my spare time, if I ever get any, I like to free-climb.' The words just pop out as if my brain has given up and my mouth is out of control. 'And parkour. I love parkour.'

I hate parkour. I tried it once for about five minutes and nearly killed myself. And I've never free-climbed in my life. I've never done any sort of climbing, free or otherwise. I'm scared of heights, for one thing. Oh, God, please don't let her be some sort of world-class climbing athlete who can clamber up sheer rock armed with nothing but a paperclip and a small nail file.

'What about you, Emma?'

'Me? Well – sorry, hold on a moment.'

I guess she's trying to cover the phone with her hand, but she's not doing a great job of it. Though her voice is muffled, I can still hear her: *No, I'm not going to say that! Don't be ridiculous!*

'Sorry about that,' she says to me. 'What can I tell you? Um, I'm single too. Born and raised in London. Um.' Emma pauses. 'My mum died a few years ago, so I've no parents and no siblings, but, you know, it's okay.' She pauses again. I don't offer her any sympathy; I'm guessing from the bright and brittle tone of her voice that she doesn't want any, at least not from me. 'I'm twenty-nine,' she continues, 'and I live with my housemate, Daisy, who's also my best friend. My favourite TV show is *Bridgerton*, my favourite book . . . I've too many to list. Comfort food ... My comfort food is chocolate. I love chocolate. Sometimes I go for a run. And if I've got any other spare time, um, I mostly like to do jigsaws. That sounds very boring, doesn't it? Especially compared to free-climbing.'

There's a defiant note in her voice, and I wish again that I hadn't mentioned the bloody free-climbing.

'Not at all – it sounds grand. Jigsaws can be very ... meditative.'

François and Marianne leave, though not before Marianne has tapped her watch. She's right. Pierre, the restaurant owner, will be here soon, wanting to check the week's menu, and he'll definitely be looking for any excuse to give me a hard time. He wasn't exactly happy when I handed in my notice.

'Listen, I know this whole thing is a bit crazy – or at the very least, impulsive – but you seem . . . really nice.' I close my eyes in horror as my lagging brain catches up with my mouth. Nice? What am I, a thirteen-year-old boy? I was raised in the land of Joyce and Yeats and all I can come up with is 'really nice'?

Luckily for me, Emma laughs. 'You do too.'

I sigh.

'So, there's just the small matter of the English Channel between us. How's your swimming?'

'Good enough for a swimming pool, but not much more, sadly.'

'That's too bad. Mine's no better, if I'm honest. Of course, if this were a film, one of us would definitely be an Olympic swimmer. Scorning the cold to find the one they glimpsed across a crowded room, slathered with grease, using the stars to navigate international shipping lanes . . .'

'And battling sharks, of course,' she adds. 'Films are always better with sharks. Most films, anyway. Not period drama, I suppose, and maybe not sci-fi, but you know, lots of films. Some films.' I hear her mutter something under her breath. 'Sorry. I'm just a bit of a fan when it comes to sharks. Did you know that the basking shark that lives around the UK can filter up to 450 tonnes of water an hour?'

'No, I didn't know that.' *Sharks?* Whatever – I've a feeling she's worth it. 'But I think you're on to something though. *Pride and Prejudice and Sharks. 2001, a Space Shark Odyssey.* Genius.'

Marianne appears in the doorway and points – even more pointedly – at her watch. I decide to go for broke.

'Look, I've to go, I'm afraid – I'm actually at work, but can we maybe chat at the weekend? Or maybe even a Zoom call, or a FaceTime, or something like that.' I hesitate, then add, 'I'd really like to see you again, Emma, even if it is only on a screen.'

She doesn't reply.

'What do you think?' I prompt. 'Of course, if you'd rather not, I—'

'No – I mean, yes. We can have a video call. That would be lovely.'

I grin.

'Brilliant. Would Sunday be good for you? 11 a.m. your time? And I'll call you.'

'11 a.m. Sounds good.'

'And about the postcards – I can send them back to you.'

'Oh, don't worry. It was great to talk to you, Kieran.'

'You too. Take care now.'

'And you. Bye.' She ends the call.

I stare at my phone for a moment, still grinning like an eejit, then add her name and number to my contacts.

Emma.

I don't need to write down any of the details she shared with me. I know I'll remember them.

I can only pray that she'll forget about the free-climbing.

Chapter Four

Emma

Daisy stalks back into the living room, where I'd gone to escape the running commentary she was offering while I'd been in the kitchen. I should have guessed she'd just listen from behind the door.

'Sharks?' She throws up her hands, her face a grimace of disbelief. 'Fun facts about *sharks*?' Her voice pitches even higher.

'I know, I know!' I grab one of the sofa cushions and hide behind it, though there isn't a cushion in the world big enough to smother my embarrassment. The sofa – ancient, sagging, and covered in an alarmingly psychedelic floral fabric – creaks as Daisy throws herself down next to me. She pushes the cushion down.

'On the other hand, he asked to talk again, right?'

I nod. 'We're going to FaceTime on Sunday. Maybe he's really into sharks.'

Daisy grins. 'He's really into you, more like. What does he sound like?'

'As cute as I remember. He grew up in Cork, hence the Irish accent.'

'Mmm,' Daisy murmurs appreciatively. 'Love an Irish accent.'

'Me too, as you know.' Daisy and I had first become friends in Year 10, bonding over our obsession with the TV show *Being Human*, and in particular with Aidan Turner's tortured-yet-sexy vampire.

'What else?' Daisy swings her legs up so we're facing each other.

'What about dinner?'

'It's simmering, so there's no excuse. Tell me everything.'

I relay all the information Kieran volunteered about himself. Daisy props her chin on her hand and frowns thoughtfully.

'Sounds promising. French and Irish is automatically off-the-scale hot. Can you imagine? You're in bed, and he tells you how gorgeous you are and what he wants to do to you in Irish-accented English, and then tells you all over again in French.'

We both stare into space, momentarily stunned by the image Daisy's conjured.

'However,' she continues, 'professional chefs have to work really antisocial hours. Maybe there'd be no time for linguistically fulfilling sex.'

'But you would get a lot of delicious food,' I counter.

'Possibly, possibly. Though all the delicious food might make you so fat he goes off you.'

'Hey, what about some body positivity here? He might have fallen for my scintillating personality.'

Daisy looks sceptical, which is fair enough. He can hardly have found out much about my personality in the two minutes we spent staring at each other at the Gare du Nord. But it wasn't just physical. At least, not for me. There was something else there. Some inexplicable connection. I feel the ghost of his hands on my arms again and shiver.

'What about that book he mentioned?' Daisy asks, jerking me back to the present. 'Any clues there?'

I pull a face. 'I read it once. Arresting, though not really my cup of tea. Ten-second summary: it's about a guy who has no smell himself, who becomes a *parfumier* and goes round killing virgins to capture their scent. As far as I remember. An outsider who tries but ultimately fails to find his place in humanity.'

Daisy is pulling a face too. 'Murdering virgins? Why would this Kieran pick that as his favourite book? That's giving me psycho vibes.'

'Just because he enjoyed the book, that doesn't mean he wants to emulate or even likes the protagonist. Anyway,' I add, lamely, 'Kieran seems really nice.'

'Well don't just go giving him our address yet,' Daisy counters. 'All that rock-climbing will have given him strong arms. Great for sweeping you off your feet but also probably very useful for crushing you to death.'

'You have a dark and twisted mind, Daisy Takahashi.'

I throw the cushion at her as she laughs, jumps off the sofa and whisks out of the room. Two seconds later, she's back.

'One more thing: do not text him or message him or contact him in any way before Sunday. Got it?' She points a warning finger at me.

'But what if he messages me?'

'Ignore it. Unless it's a message to confirm the FaceTime, in which case you reply with something quick like *Sure* and a thumbs-up emoji. No waffling, no kisses, no suggestion that you're looking forward to it, and definitely no sharks.'

'No sharks,' I repeat.

'There's no need to go full-on ice queen, but you want him to think that he's keener than you.' The finger wags again.

'But what if he messages about something else? Like, he just asks how my week is going?'

Daisy considers this possibility.

'Then you give a one-word reply. *Great*. And a smiley face emoji. But not too big a smile.' Daisy is as deeply attached to emojis, memes and gifs as she was when we were teenagers. 'But I don't think he will message you,' she adds. 'If your description is accurate, he's sexy AF. He knows he's own worth. Make sure you don't forget yours.'

I spend Tuesday morning cleaning another house and Tuesday afternoon trying, and failing, to make some progress on one of the many stalled writing projects tucked away on my laptop. Number of messages from Kieran: zero. It's still zero by Wednesday mid-morning, when I walk into my local coffee shop, Café Olay. I suspect Ron, owner of the shop and self-declared super-barista, was aiming for either Café Olé or Café au Lait, but I've never dared ask him. I'm here for a Zoom meeting with

Lauren. She's the editor who works for the celebrity I ghostwrite for, and one of the founders of Anchor & Hope, a boutique publishing company that shot to prominence on the back of the same celebrity's massive sales. Fortunately, before I can torture myself too much – *why hasn't Kieran texted me? WHY?* – James hurries over to the booth I've nabbed at the back of the café. One of my fellow ghostwriters and another west London local, he dumps his bag on the table and grabs both my hands.

'Emma, my fabulous friend, you are never going to guess what's just happened. Go on, guess!' He's bouncing up and down with so much excited energy that I can't help laughing.

'I will guess,' I reply, 'but coffee first. It's your turn, remember?'

James groans and sprints to the counter. Luckily for him there's no queue, and Ron has already started on our usual order. By the time I've booted up my laptop and clicked on the Zoom link for our editorial meeting, James is back. He sits next to me and pushes a skinny cappuccino in my direction.

'Thanks.' I take a sip, and feel my shoulders relax. 'Okay. So, I'm guessing that—'

'I finished my crime novel and I asked Lauren if she knew anyone who might be interested and she said to send it to her! And not even just the first three chapters, the whole manuscript!' James rushes the words out.

'Lauren? Are you sure that was a good idea? I didn't think A&H did crime. Wouldn't it have been better to—'

'But if Lauren likes it, I can bypass the whole agent thing. And she's so senior she can definitely get it through acquisitions!' He flings his arms around me and hugs me, almost sending the coffees flying. 'This could be it: no more ghostwriting! My crime novel might actually get published! And then it might get picked up by Netflix and turned into a show that's such a huge hit that me and Petros can retire to somewhere hot!' His face is a picture of bliss. In his head, the coffee shop has disappeared and he's already on the beach, holding a drink with an umbrella in it. 'Tell me you're happy for me.'

I hug him back tightly. 'Of course I'm happy for you, James.' And I am. Really happy. So happy that I want to rip out the tiny bit of me that suddenly feels sick with envy, that feels a wash of relief when my laptop chimes, closing down the conversation.

Mia pops up on my screen. James and I squish closer and wave at her.

'Hey, Mia, how's Cambridge today?' James asks.

'Flat and full of tourists, as per,' Mia replies. 'How are you, my co-ghostwriters? Loins girded? Protective charms at the ready? I've wiped down my screen with holy water, just to be on the safe side.'

Our meetings usually start like this, with Mia insisting that Paige Adams Pereira, the reality TV superstar in whose name we churn out three erotic novels a year, must be a witch. Or in league with the devil. Or the Mafia. What else, she argues, can explain the planet-wide success of someone so devoid of any discernible talent?

'Be careful what you wish for, Mia,' James counters. 'If someone manages to teach Paige how to use AI we'll be toast. She'll probably get rid of us by waving her wand and—'

Lauren pops up on the call.

'—and sprinkling some of her inimitable magic over our manuscripts. That's what makes them fly off the shelves.' James sighs wistfully. 'Paige is one of a kind. Oh, hey, Lauren.'

'Nice save,' I murmur.

'Morning, everyone.' Lauren's dressed in her usual black, with her blonde hair swept up. Maybe it's her red lipstick and red-rimmed reading glasses, but she looks so much more vibrant than the rest of us, as if the screen can barely contain her. I can see why James decided to send her his completed manuscript. Still, it feels like a risk. Paige is Lauren's meal ticket, and it's a relationship she won't risk. 'Paige will be here in a few minutes,' Lauren continues, 'so let's make sure we're ready. Mia?'

'I'm nearly done with the copy-edits for *Prince of Pain and Pleasure*,' Mia replies. None of us giggles; we're mostly immune to Paige's title choices by now. 'I should be able to send them to you by next Monday.'

Lauren nods. 'Great. And what about the summary for Paige and the question-and-answer sheet for events?'

Mia glances at her notes. 'I'll need another week for those.'

'No longer than that, okay?' Lauren looks away briefly, making a note. 'Paige has an interview lined up on the twelfth of next month. James?'

'The second draft of *Daydreams of a Busty Biologist* is nearly ready. I reckon three more weeks to finish the structural edits. It's shaping up well.'

Lauren peers over her glasses at James, but all she says is, 'I hope so.'

Then it's my turn.

'Emma, the sales of *Dare to Be Dirty* aren't as great as we'd hoped.'

I've been prepared for this, and my defence is ready.

'To be fair, I did say the concept was too literal. To set the entire thing in the servants' quarters of a stately home ... there was no glamour. If she'd only allowed me to tweak the idea a little—'

Lauren cuts me off.

'You know how this works, Emma. Paige has the concept; you just bring it to fruition. As she says, it's the sex that sells. The setting is window-dressing. You need to really lean hard into the sex for the next title.'

Mia titters, earning herself a glare from Lauren.

'And cut the social commentary.'

'It was only a couple of sentences on the terrible working conditions,' I protest. 'The characters had to have something else to talk about other than the footman's enormous—'

'Listen, the rights of man – and woman – are important, but they don't turn anyone on.' Lauren sighs. 'No one is having fun times with a vibrator and the complete works of Karl Marx.' She pauses. 'At least, not the same people who are queuing up for the latest Paige Adams Pereira, so—' Her expression changes to one of dismay. 'Fuck, she's early.'

The screen rearranges itself to accommodate Paige's face.

'Hey, guys!' she trills. 'How's my top team, my wonder wordsmiths?'

We all beam and answer cheerily, and I wonder if James and Mia loathe themselves as much as I do at that moment.

Lauren takes charge and brings Paige up to date on the next two books, *Prince of Pain and Pleasure* and *Daydreams of a Busty Biologist*. Paige seems pleased, and Mia and James look relieved. Paige turns her focus to me.

'So, Emma, babes, are you ready for the next book? It's going to blow your sexy socks off.'

'Absolutely.' I nod enthusiastically. 'Ready to get down to it.'

'Great. I know you tried really hard with *Dare to Be Dirty*, but it definitely needed more glamour. So, what I'm thinking is . . .' She closes her eyes. 'An orchestra. On tour. All those young, nubile musicians, away from home, controlled by a dark and brooding but incredibly hot conductor. And they're stuck with each other for months at a time in some exotic, erotic five-star resort . . .'

Nubile? And as for staying in five-star resorts . . . Daisy has a cousin who's a violinist in an orchestra – a great guy, but definitely not someone you'd describe as nubile – and he thinks he's hit the jackpot if he lands up at a Premier Inn.

Gazing at me again, Paige smiles and winks.

'I want to go big with this one, Emma. Orgytastic orchestral manoeuvres in the dark. Sex on the Steinway. Sex *in* the Steinway. All those phallic woodwind instruments. And string instruments.' Her eyes light up. 'Oooh, let's tie someone up with harp strings. And then beat them on the bottom with a pair of drumsticks.' Paige's voice deepens. 'I want to go dark. Dark and sexy and horny and – ooh—' she giggles '—horny! *French* horns.' She winks again. 'Pun definitely intended. I'll send you the plot summary later today, hun. Okay?'

My mouth takes over even as my brain is still recoiling in horror. 'Of course. And what's the title?'

'Um . . .' Paige's face scrunches in thought. '*My Summer of Symphonic Sexcapades.*'

'Brilliant, Paige.' Lauren applauds. 'Genius. As always.'

Sycophant. Next to me, James covers his snort of laughter with a pretend coughing fit.

'Emma,' Lauren continues, 'I'll expect the first draft in two months, as usual. Anything else before we wrap up?'

Everyone shakes their head and the meeting ends. I slam the laptop shut.

'"*Symphonic Sexcapades*"?' James mutters. 'She is definitely losing it.' He pats my hand. 'I'll get you another coffee. I'm thinking an extra shot and lashings of caramel syrup this time. Screw the diet.'

'Two extra shots.'

'You got it.'

As he gets up, I put my head in my hands. Maybe this is the final straw. Maybe this is my bridge too far. My line in the sand. Maybe I should tell Paige exactly what she can do with—

My phone buzzes, interrupting my pity party.

Kieran's messaged me.

Chapter Five

Kieran

> Late start today so I've been
> watching some TV, and I've
> realised you're definitely right. More
> sharks needed! All the sharks!

'What do you think?' I ask as I hit send. 'I want to come across as friendly. Flirty, but not in a creepy way. Entertaining, yet not frivolous.'

The question is directed at my brother, Brendan, who's on the other end of a video call. I'm currently stretched out on the bed in my cramped studio flat, part of a subdivided top-floor apartment not far from Roubaix station. Brendan, three years older than me, is in his house in Cork. He's sitting on the floor with my two-year-old niece, Roisin, in his lap, surrounded by a sea of brightly coloured plastic building blocks.

'You're asking a lot of a short text, Kieran,' he replies. Producing a tissue from somewhere, he wipes Roisin's nose. This temporarily banishes the thick green mucus that's the main symptom of the child's current cold, but to be honest Brendan is fighting a losing battle. The green goo is like a never-ending stream of biblical proportions. A tsunami of snot. If you were to drop the child behind enemy lines, you'd be done by the UN for breaching laws on germ warfare. Brendan is already reaching for another tissue as he adds, 'And it could come off as sarcastic.'

'Really? But I've already sent it.'

'So why did you bother to ask my opinion, you eejit?' Brendan shakes his head. 'Send a smiley face, quick.'

'I'm not sending a smiley face.' Instead, I add another text.

I think you'd have a great career
in TV production, honestly!

I catch my breath as three dots appear on the phone screen. 'Three dots. She's replying.'

'What does she say?' Brendan asks. His voice changes, becoming higher-pitched as he starts talking to Roisin. 'Daddy wants to know what Uncle Kieran's up to, doesn't he?' Brendan leans close to his daughter, scrunches up his face and blows a raspberry, and Roisin gurgles with laughter. 'Yes, he does! He wants to know! What's Uncle Kieran doing, trying to have a romantic relationship with someone in a different country?' Roisin is staring at her father, rapt. 'Hasn't Uncle Kieran gone through enough spur-of-the-moment relationships? Hasn't he realised that he is an impulsive, hopeless romantic, who gets swept up in the passion of it all and then almost inevitably gets his heart broken?'

Roisin sneezes, pebbledashing Brendan's face with bogie. I burst out laughing.

'Yeah, very funny,' my brother growls, reaching for the tissues. 'You know I'm right.'

'You are not. I'm not a hopeless romantic. Well, I'm not hopeless, at any rate. And who says this relationship has to be romantic? Maybe I just want to—'

My phone pings.

Too right. Whatever the question,
sharks are always the answer.
What TV show are you watching?

I grin.

'Well?' Brendan demands. 'Tell me what she said, then.' He gasps and puts his hands over his daughter's ears, sending

Roisin into hysterical laughter as she tries to prise her father's fingers away. 'Is it something raunchy? I bet it's something raunchy.'

'It's not raunchy. And the fact that you're even asking means you've been watching way too much daytime TV with Mum and Dad.'

'Nothing wrong with that. Honestly, single people are so sensible nowadays! Where's the sexting? How am I going to vicariously enjoy an adventurous sex life if my own brother won't even play ball?' He releases Roisin. 'Go on, then, read it to me.'

I obey.

'Ah, that's a good sign,' he opines. 'She's a sense of humour, then.'

'I think she does, yes.' I turn back to my phone to reply.

> Something with vampires. I switched it on while I was doing some packing and got sucked in, haha. Got me thinking: what about . . . vampire sharks?!?

'Maybe you just want to what?' Brendan asks, frowning at me. 'Have a casual fling? I hope for your sake that's not what you're planning, Kieran Landry. If I tell Niamh that's what you're planning . . .' He draws his forefinger slowly across his throat.

I replay the last two minutes of our conversation in my head; fortunately I'm used to my brother's conversational gymnastics.

'No, I'm not after a casual fling, and I'm well aware that my darling sister-in-law will kill me if I ever attempt one. Maybe I just want to be friends with Emma.'

The three dots reappear on the screen.

> Yes! Vampire sharks who bite people and turn them into more sharks. I'm

also very much here for were-sharks.
Those are the ones who turn into
sharks whenever there's a full moon.

I text back instantly.

> Yes!! They'd have to live near the coast, mind, so they don't get caught short and end up flopping about on the pavement.

Or they could live in houses
with shark-sized water tanks
in the basement . . .

> That's how you'll hunt them down: look on the property listings for houses with indoor swimming pools in areas with suspiciously high rates of inexplicable shark-related deaths.

I have to go now, I'm afraid, but
I'll definitely get on to that later.

> Looking forward to an update!

I put the phone down. Brendan, still waiting patiently on the other end of our video call, has moved his laptop and is now sitting on the sofa, though this too is covered in primary-coloured plastic cubes. One thing Roisin definitely doesn't need for her next birthday is more Duplo. Now he's sitting next to a window, I notice the dark shadows under my brother's eyes. He's thinner, as well. Too thin, for someone with a physique like his. While I'm tall and wiry like my father, Brendan takes after his dad, who died before he was even born, right at the start of what looked to be a promising career as a professional rugby player. Brendan is built like the father he never met, and bears his surname, but otherwise he is just as much a Landry as I am.

'You're looking tired,' I say. 'Are you getting enough exercise? Are you eating healthily?'

'Thanks so much,' he replies, scowling. 'Way to boost a man's confidence.' With a sigh, he rubs a hand over the dark stubble on his chin. 'It's a lot, you know? Especially since Roisin's not sleeping properly with this damn cold, and Niamh's working all hours on a big case.'

'Remind me: when is Dad's next hospital appointment?'

'Five weeks. We'll get the latest set of results at that point. Niamh is taking a couple of days off, so I'll be able to drive Mum and Dad and be there to hear the doctor, and I can stay over that night if I need to. Mum gets so flustered. Niamh's taking her out shopping at the weekend as a distraction.'

'Poor Mum. I'll give her a call later. Niamh's a good woman.'

'She is.'

I hesitate. The guilt, that never quite stops whispering in my ear, prickles along my spine. 'I could come back, you know. For a few days, at least.'

'Get away with you. You'll have barely started at the new place. We can manage.'

'Thanks, Brendan.'

He shrugs, then smiles. 'Next time you're over, you can spend the entire week cooking for me. I'm already planning the menu.'

'I'll cook whatever you like, that's a promise.' My glance strays to the packing boxes strewn, in various states, around my living room. 'I suppose I'd better get on.'

'Not so fast. I want to—' He gasps and dives out of view, though I can still hear him. 'Oh, no, that does not belong in your mouth, young lady. Spit it out. No, that's – okay, that's better. Have some water.' Brendan reappears. 'Sorry, she was trying to eat a crayon. Kids, eh? Where was I? Oh – that was it. I want to know what your plan is, Kieran. You said you felt a kind of spark when you met this woman, but as your big brother I have to ask you: is it really wise to pursue any kind of relationship when you're in different countries, and with you so busy with your career? Isn't it going to make you miserable, in the long run?'

It's a question I've asked myself several times over the last couple of days. Still, I shake my head.

'I don't think so. Maybe I'll end up back in London. Maybe she might decide she wants to move to Paris. But even if that doesn't happen, even if I do end up miserable, I know I'd regret it more if I didn't try. You know me. Seize the moment. Who dares, wins.'

Brendan huffs, shakes his head and laughs. 'As I said before: impulsive. I hope for your sake this whole escapade doesn't come back and bite you on the arse.' He picks up a piece of Duplo and turns it over in his fingers. 'I suppose it's useless to point out that you don't know anything about this Emma, and that she might turn out to be completely different from whatever image you're building up in your head.'

'She might,' I agree. 'But then what? I'll have wasted a few hours of my time. I think it's worth the risk.' Turning over my phone, I look back at the handful of text messages Emma and I exchanged this morning, and they make me smile all over again. 'She's worth the risk. Just don't ask me how I know that.'

'Fair enough. Let me know how it goes on Sunday, okay?'

'Will do. Say hi to Niamh for me. And give my nephew a hug when you fetch him from school. Love you.'

'Love you too.'

For the next three days, Emma and I end up exchanging at least a couple of dozen text messages each day. Nothing of consequence. It's more 'have you read *Dracula*, and don't you agree it's bloody terrifying?' than 'let's discuss the geopolitical crises of the twenty-first century and what might be done to avert the approaching climate disaster.' And thank fuck, because, although I try to do my bit, it's all frankly far too depressing to discuss in depth with someone you're just trying to get to know. Especially as a string of text messages. Instead, Emma's texts about vampires and books and the publishing industry – and sharks, of course; she told me that sharks have eyelids, which was news to me – make me laugh. A couple of times I play back the voicemail she left me, then I read the texts again and try to imagine her speaking them. I like the way she sounds. Her accent is generic London, at least to my ear, but there's a warmth to it. As if, beneath the surface-level nervousness, there's someone bubbly trying to get out.

Not that she can be more nervous than me by the time Sunday morning rolls around. I know very well France is one hour ahead of the UK and Ireland, but I still keep checking the 'world clock' function on my phone to make sure it hasn't sneakily changed while I wasn't looking. I tidy the flat as much as possible, given the ongoing packing situation, and try to artfully arrange a few books behind where I'll be sitting. I dither over whether to take down the film poster I've stuck on the wall. On the one hand it's advertising James Bond, which might have certain connotations for a modern, independent woman. On the other hand, it's in French, so maybe that sort of . . . balances it out? Having discussed it all with Niamh – there's not a single member of my family who knows the meaning of the word 'boundaries' – Brendan passes on a suggestion that I should use a fake background, like Versailles, or some other fancy French place. I think Niamh thinks I've delusions of grandeur. But I decide against it: I don't want Emma to get the idea that I'm hiding something.

The cleaning and tidying takes me to eleven o'clock. One hour to go. My stomach lurches, stuck somewhere unpleasant between nervousness and excitement.

All I have to do now is figure out what to wear.

Chapter Six

Emma

'Calm down, Emma!'

'I am calm!'

'No, you're not. If you don't stop fretting, you're going to get all sweaty and ruin your make-up. It's just a video call!'

'If it's just a video call then why did you insist on me washing all of my make-up off and letting you redo my entire face?'

'Well . . .' Daisy stops, temporarily silenced.

'Hm?' I raise an eyebrow, pressing my advantage.

'Well – well, you want to look like you've made an effort *without* looking like you've made an effort, and, let's face it, I'm just better at that than you are. Effortless elegance, that's what we're going for. Chic, and glamorous, and – and *fabulous*, but at the same time looking like you've just thrown something on because you don't really care.'

I swear, defeated by the clasp of the necklace I'm trying to take off. Daisy turns me round, sweeps my hair out of the way and does it for me and I swing back to face her.

'This is another power play, isn't it?' I say. We've had several conversations on this topic since I called Kieran on Monday evening. Variations on the theme of 'romantic relationships are like a cold war, but with more exchange of bodily fluids'.

'Obviously.' Daisy nods. 'As I've said before —'

'And will no doubt say again—'

'—the power balance is established at the start of a relationship. You want to be the one with the power. Whatever this ends up being.'

'But it's all so pointless.' I survey the pile of clothes on my bed with something like disgust. 'We live in different countries. Why am I so worried about having nothing to wear when there can never be anything between us?'

'Oh, spare me the dramatics!' Daisy exclaims as she sifts through the pile. 'You've got some nice pieces here. Which is more than I can say about your underwear. Girl, those pants are passion-killers.' She looks me up and down despairingly then bursts into laughter. 'Erection-erasers. If you decide to get down and dirty with him, I'm taking you to buy some proper lingerie first.'

'Hey!' I protest, tugging the waistband of my M&S knickers a little higher. 'Just because I'd rather be comfortable . . .'

Ignoring Daisy's muttering, I drag a summer dress from the pile, flatten it against my body and survey my appearance in the mirror that's screwed inside my wardrobe door. The white cotton is printed all over with black letters in different fonts and sizes. When I bought it from one of the local charity shops I thought it would make me seem cool and writerly, but now . . .

'Ugh. I look like a walking eye test.'

My flatmate takes the dress and holds it out at arm's length.

'It's not so bad. You've already got those lovely poppy flower earrings, so if we added a red belt, and a chunky necklace . . .' She tosses the dress back to me. 'I'll see what I've got in my wardrobe. Put it on.'

Clothed, I sit down on the edge of the bed. God knows I'd love to get down and dirty with Kieran. I go tingly all over at the mere thought of it. I whisper my name over to myself, trying to match his intonation and accent.

Daisy reappears with three red belts and several necklaces over her arm. And some bracelets. How many accessories does the woman own?

'Here: try . . . this, and this, and this.'

I loop the belt around my waist, put the necklace over my head and clasp the bracelet around my wrist.

'Perfect. And you can wear it to Louisa's baby's christening later, too.' She nods her head. 'I am, without a doubt, a genius.'

She's not wrong. The extra touches she's added turn what I'm wearing from a dress I've just thrown on into an *outfit* – something pulled together and stylish and carefully curated. I give her a hug.

'Thank you. And I'm not trying to be dramatic, honestly.'

'I know.' She looks at her phone. 'Ten minutes. I'm going to make some tea; it'll give you something to do with your hands.'

I follow her downstairs and head into the back room: our combined workspace-slash-dining room, where I've already set up my laptop. It's looking pretty good, and no wonder: I spent an hour or more cleaning and tidying earlier this morning. I straighten the books on the bookshelf – I think they'll just be in view – as Daisy calls out, 'Five minutes!' My stomach growls loudly, as it tends to do when I'm nervous. I wrap my arms around my middle in a doomed attempt to stifle the sound. Daisy walks in a moment later with a tray on which is a glass of water, a steaming mug of tea and a chocolate biscuit.

'I could hear your stomach from the kitchen. Now don't forget, we need to leave by one to get to the church.'

'Don't worry,' I reply, stuffing the biscuit in my mouth, 'we probably won't talk for long, and I—'

My laptop starts ringing. I hurry to sit down, nearly choking on the end of the biscuit.

'Wait . . .' Daisy whispers, as my finger hovers over the 'accept call' button. 'Wait . . . and . . .'

I hit the answer button before she gets to 'now'. She rolls her eyes but gives me a thumbs-up and hurries out of the room.

Kieran appears on the screen.

He's just as arresting as I remember. He's wearing a slightly rumpled azure-blue shirt which brings out the blue of his eyes. I have to swallow hard before I speak.

'Hey!'

'Hey, Emma!' His eyes crinkle as he smiles at me and gives a little wave. 'It's so lovely to see you again.'

'You too.'

Silence.

Oh, God, an awkward silence twenty seconds in! Quick, say something. Do something!

I take a mouthful of tea. Big mistake.

With a strangled cry I spit the scalding liquid back into the mug – 'Fuck!' – grab the glass of water and take a gulp, holding it in my cheeks like some chipmunk-human hybrid until the pain subsides a little.

Kieran's eyes are wide with shock. Or horror. Or possibly disgust.

'Are you okay?' he asks, his voice unsteady.

'Yes – sorry.' I glug some more water. 'The tea was really hot.'

'I could tell. That's horribly painful. I've burned and scalded myself plenty of times in the kitchen – more times than I can remember – but mouth burns are the worst.'

'Sorry.' Why do I keep apologising? What is wrong with me? 'I'm just – I'm just really nervous. I know it's ridiculous, but—'

'It's not ridiculous at all. I'm nervous myself. You should have seen me this morning, cleaning and tidying. And I'm not even going to tell you how many shirts I tried on before I got to this one.' He pauses. 'How about – how about we pretend we met on a dating app, like normal people?'

His grin makes me smile. 'I guess that would work. Though I should let you know that I hate social media, and especially dating apps. I had Insta until recently, but it just made me depressed. And the number of times I've downloaded a dating app, only to delete it again a week later . . .'

'Me too. It all just feels so – so—'

'Contrived?' I suggest.

'Exactly so. Contrived and fake. Whereas running into someone at a train station is spontaneous and natural.'

Talking to Kieran does feel natural. My nerves begin to ebb away.

'To be fair,' I say, 'I was the one running. You were just standing there minding your own business when I charged into you.'

'You knocked me for six, literally and figuratively.' He leans closer to the camera and props his chin on his hand. The way he's looking at me ... a sensuous wave of heat surges through my body, and it has nothing to do with the tea.

In fact, the next time I take a sip of tea, it's stone-cold. It doesn't feel as if we've been talking for long, but my phone says it's been over an hour and a half. And we've not struggled for conversation. Recalling our meeting prompts us to share what we were doing in Paris that May morning. Kieran tells me about his interview, which leads him to talk about the restaurant he's moving to and the restaurant he's leaving. He tells me about his colleagues – who are also his friends – and what they get up to on a Friday night after the restaurant has closed; karaoke seems to feature heavily. I tell him about Daisy and the exhibition I went to photograph, and about James and Mia and our existence as badly paid cogs in the Paige Adams Pereira publicity machine – though I spare him the details of the books. Frankly, there's no way I could describe the stuff that Paige insists her characters get up to without ending up a bright red, incoherent blob of embarrassment. Especially since I'd quite like to try some of it out with Kieran. By contrast, his most shocking revelation is that he never eats dessert and hates chocolate.

'You're kidding me,' I insist. 'How can you dislike chocolate? What's not to like?' I consider the question for a moment and come up with nothing.

He shrugs.

'Not just dislike, Emma. Loathe. I can't stand the stuff.' He pulls a face and shudders. 'Can't even bear the thought of it.'

I smile sweetly. 'Is there maybe something wrong with your tastebuds?'

He reacts with mock outrage. 'And me a chef? You just come over here and say that to my face!'

Is that an invitation? Sidestepping, I shake my head.

'I don't know. I'm not sure I can be friends with someone who doesn't like chocolate.'

'Well, in that case I love the stuff.' He grins. 'Can't get enough of it. Just don't ever buy me any, because I'm actually very picky.

A complete chocolate connoisseur.' He hesitates. 'Seriously, though. I wish you would come over here, even if it was to insult me. Just get on a train, or a plane, say.'

He makes it sound so easy: don't think, or plan, just do! An insidious tendril of panic combines with my desire to kiss him, quickening my breathing. I sidestep again.

'Will you have time for a holiday before you start your new job? Your family must miss you.'

For the first time since we started chatting he seems to close up, looking away and leaning back on his sofa and fiddling with something out of sight of the camera.

'I don't get back much, to be honest. Time off is a problem in my industry. What about you? Do you travel much? I guess you can write anywhere, right?'

'In theory.' I've not told him about the one-and-a-half-day-a-week cleaning jobs. Or about the writer's block. 'In practice, not so much. I need absolute silence. And a properly supportive chair. And an ergonomic keyboard.'

A blush creeps up my neck. *Way to make yourself sound super middle-aged and undesirable, Ems!*

'But that's only because I've got a slight scoliosis. It's not an age thing; I was born with it. Not that it's genetic, or degenerative, or anything. Nothing I need to worry about passing on to the next generation!'

Oh, God, he's going to think you're already talking about having kids! Instant death to any new relationship! Distract him, quick!

I take refuge in honesty.

'And I just can't afford it, unfortunately. Travel, I mean. Money is a problem in my industry.' I take another sip of cold tea. 'As I said, the trip to Paris in May was free.'

He rubs a hand over his face.

'And there's me suggesting you should jump on a plane. Sorry. I didn't think.'

'That's okay. I would if I could. Given enough notice.' My turn to shrug. 'I need a good run-up to get used to the idea of something. I had a therapist once who suggested I take a day off and fill it with spontaneous activities. I did take the day off, but...'

'The spontaneous activities?'

'I just couldn't. I ended up planning the entire day with military detail. Unleashed evil mastermind levels of organisation, if I'm being honest.'

For the second time in our conversation, silence falls. Then we both start talking at once.

'Maybe things will—'

'Perhaps we could—'

We laugh, and the tension ebbs.

'You first,' I say.

'I hope things get easier for both of us,' Kieran says. 'I hope good things happen. Maybe I'll enter *MasterChef* and win it. Then I'll write a bestselling cookbook, off the back of which I get a TV show. And a film. Scratch that: an entire film franchise.'

'Dreaming big.' I nod approvingly. 'And maybe I'll write a novel that instantly wins the Booker Prize – in fact, all the prizes. Everywhere. And it also gets turned into a movie franchise.'

'And would there be sharks in these films?'

'Obviously.' I sigh, trying not to think about the number of unfinished novels currently squatting on my hard drive. 'Or maybe we'll both win the lottery. Though I'd have to actually start playing it first.'

'Yeah,' Kieran agrees, 'me too.'

Daisy sticks her head round the doorway and waves at me then points to her wrist. I check the time on my phone.

'I'm so sorry, I've got to dash – I've got a christening to go to.'

'Oh, of course – God, where has the time gone? I've really enjoyed this, Emma.'

'Me too.'

Daisy reappears. She's got her coat on now.

'I really have to run.' Panic forces my hand. 'Listen, I know we're stuck in different countries, but can we still be friends, in the meantime? While we wait for the *MasterChef* win and the Booker Prize and all the film franchises?'

'Yes,' Kieran nods slowly. 'I'd love that. I was hoping you'd say that. Same time next week?'

'Same time next week.'

Chapter Seven

Kieran

'Morning, Emma, hope the writing went well yesterday. I'm just building myself up for my third Saturday in Paris. Lunch service and dinner service today, and the busiest day of the week in the restaurant. I'm still working my way around the different kitchen stations at the moment, getting used to the team, under the watchful eye of Monsieur Arnaud, the owner and executive chef, and Paul Fabier, the guy I'm replacing as sous chef.'

I pause and take a sip of my extra strong coffee. It's 9.20 on a late July morning, and I'm sitting on a chair in the Luxembourg Gardens in the fashionable sixth *arrondissement* of Paris, recording a voice memo.

I've discovered several things about Emma in the past few weeks. She twirls one lock of dark hair around her index finger when she's thinking, and when she laughs – *really* laughs – she snorts. She likes order and organisation; one morning, when I video called her out of the blue and she was just finishing off some work, I watched her arrange her things on her desk with almost mathematical precision, like some hot female version of Hercule Poirot. She keeps an old Oxford dictionary next to her laptop, because she prefers to look up words in a real book than online – she said that flipping through the pages means there's always a chance you'll stumble upon an amazing new word at the same time. And she loves audiobooks just as much as I do. After making this particular discovery, we decided to try sending each other these recordings as another way to keep in touch. More relaxed than an email and better for longer messages than texting. A way to tell each other the story of our lives. That's the theory, anyway. I think for a moment, trying to figure out what story I want to tell today.

'It's been thirty-five degrees and humid ever since I arrived here, nearly a month ago now. Perhaps the cooking gods have taken against my interpretation of classic French cuisine and are trying to roast me alive in a fine jus of my own sweat. Or perhaps the city just loathes me. I'm sure my colleagues at La Reine loathe me, Paul Fabier in particular, but I'm trying not to take it personally. After all, it's not just me that Parisians treat with utter disdain. It's everyone who isn't Parisian. And as far as I can tell, they're not even that keen on one another.'

Another sip of coffee. What would a writer say next? What might Emma say? Something about the setting, perhaps.

'The city is full of tourists, but lots of locals are away on holiday. Those who aren't will take themselves off next month instead. I'm currently drinking my coffee beneath the shade of a tree in the Jardin du Luxembourg. I'm not sure exactly what kind of a tree – I never did go in for trees much – but it's maybe a …' I glance up uncertainly at the canopy above me and squint at the leaves. *'Maybe a plane tree? I don't know. It's beautiful here. There's a serenity to the place. Unlike the area around my flat, which is noisy, grimy, and smells as ripe as a teenage boy's PE kit bag. And I was a teenage boy, so I speak with authority. Overall, though, I'd say that Paris reminds me of my grandmother on my mum's side. Ancient, messy, aggravating, and liable to piss someone off as soon as she opens her mouth. But somehow still beautiful, and on the whole, I have to admit, fabulous.'* Is this turning into too much of a travelogue? *'Hope you get the postcard I sent you – it's one of the postcards I accidentally stole from you, and I thought I should start returning them.'* I'm running out of time, so I decide to wrap things up. *'We've not talked really about the weekend you spent here just before we met – what did you think of the city? And by the way, good news – it looks like I should be able to take a few days off in early October. Hopefully I'll be able to spend a couple of days in London. Maybe you can reacquaint me with the joys of the Westfield shopping centre. I'm keeping my fingers crossed!'*

I send the memo and start wheeling my bike along the path leading out of the gardens, but I don't get on it and I don't put my phone away. There's a call I need to make before I get to work.

My father's voice is thick with sleep. 'Hello?'

'Hey, it's me. I'm so sorry – I didn't mean to wake you. I'll call back—'

'No, no. Just – just give me a moment.' There's the sound of creaking springs – my dad getting out of bed – and a rattle as the curtains are pushed open. More creaking. I guess he's sat back down on the bed. 'Okay. Right.' Even that small exertion has left him breathless. 'Now, we're good to go.' Dad has lived in Ireland since he was fifteen, but there's still a ghost of his Canadian accent. 'How are you, son?'

'I'm grand. I'm on my way to work. But Brendan said he'd call me yesterday after you got your results, and he didn't. And I can't call him now 'cos he'll be getting the kids up and out. Did you not go to the hospital? Did they cancel the appointment?'

'No. I had the appointment alright.'

My chest tightens.

'So why didn't Brendan call me?' It's easier to focus on being annoyed with my brother than what's happening with our dad.

'Because I told him not to. It was late by the time we got home, and I knew you'd be at work. I told Brendan I'd talk to you today.'

The tone of his voice tells me everything I need to know. Still, I have to ask.

'And?'

'Well, it's not terrible, but it's not great. Not as good as we'd hoped. The damn thing is still there. Smaller than it was, for sure, but not gone.' He sighs. 'And they reckon now the chemo is done it'll probably start to grow again. After all the sickness, and exhaustion, I really thought that—' He cuts himself short. 'Well. There it is.'

'Christ.' My throat is dry. I stop walking to get my water bottle from my bag and take a swig, and another, hoping to drown the sudden nausea that's blooming in the pit of my stomach. 'Dad, I'm so sorry. I . . . I . . .' Words fail me. Literally.

'Hey, I'm not dead yet. Not by a long stretch.'

'But it's so unfair!' I smack the side of my fist against the wall next to me. 'They should have tested you earlier; they should have—'

'Enough of that,' Dad interrupts me. 'You've no call to be angry with the hospital. They're doing their best.' He pauses, then chuckles. 'Besides, your mother is angry enough for the entire family right now. She's furious. Like a one-woman rampaging horde.'

'Furious with whom?'

'Oh, with everyone and everything, as far as I can tell. The cancer – which is fair enough. The ultra-processed food industry. The media. The Irish government. The Taoiseach, the Prime Minister of Canada, most of my relatives, and God. And Ed Sheeran, apparently.'

'Ed Sheeran? Why in the name of all that's sacred has she taken against Ed Sheeran?'

'I've no idea, Kieran. Your guess is as good as mine.' My father sighs again. 'I doubt she knows why she's angry with him, either. You know how she is.'

'Yeah. I can imagine. Poor Mum.' I force myself to ask the next question. 'So, what did the doctors say, after they gave you the results? What's next?' *Please God*, I say to myself, *let there be a next. Let this not be the end of the line*.

'Well, that's the good news. There is another potential option. They want to try immunotherapy.'

I grab at the word the way your stereotypical Irishman might snatch at a Guinness.

'Oh, I've heard good things about that. Really good things. Why the hell didn't they try that in the first place?'

'Because for this type of cancer it's not been properly tested up until now. However, there's a trial just finished, and the results are promising.' There's just a beat as he adds, 'Really, very promising,' as if trying to convince himself as much as me.

'Brendan will give you all the details. He spent nearly an hour last night grilling the doctor about statistics, and probabilities, and treatment windows, and interim care and all that jazz.'

It's easy for me to forget about all the hard work that comes with caring for someone who's suffering from cancer. The drug regime; the hospital trips; the physical and emotional support. All the nitty-gritty that Brendan and Mum have had to get used to dealing with on a daily basis over the last few months. My guilt roars in my ears. *You should be there. You should be at home, helping.*

'Kieran, love,' Dad says, weariness creeping into his tone, 'are you still there?'

'Yes, I'm here.' But I'm not *there*, though, and isn't that the point? 'One year, Dad. I need a year in Paris, that's all. In one year, I can learn what I need to learn. I can make it count. Then I'll come back, I promise. I'll open a restaurant in Cork and settle down.'

For a moment, there's silence on the other end of the line. Is he going to remind me that he might not have a year?

'Settle down? You?' He laughs a little. 'I'll believe that when I see it. Honestly, Kieran, you don't need to feel bad. We all know how important this job is to you. And we're all so proud of you. *I'm* so proud of you.'

I don't know what to say, so I don't say anything.

'However,' Dad continues, 'if you can come for a visit, that would be fantastic. Your mother and I miss you.'

'Of course I'll come. I can likely take a few days at the start of October.'

In October I'll still be able to get one of the seasonal direct flights from Paris to Cork. There'll be no need to stop off in London. No excuse, either. I suppress the stab of disappointment that accompanies this thought; I've no right to such self-pity.

'I'll come over then. And that is a promise.'

'I'll look forward to it. Now you'd better go. I can hear your mother coming up the stairs, and if she catches you she'll keep you chatting until lunchtime.'

'Okay, Dad. Tell her I'll call on Monday.'
'Will do. Love you.'
'Love you too.'

Dad puts the phone down. I've reached the back door of the restaurant now, and in another minute, I'll be officially late, but I want to text Emma again before work takes over.

Hope you got my voice memo – I
can't wait for our video call tomorrow.
In the meantime, please send
me some fun facts as a matter of
urgency. I could really do with a laugh.

I chain up my bike, push open the door and hurry into the kitchen. Of course, everyone else is already there. Monsieur Arnaud glances up from the order book he's studying.

'Monsieur Landry, I'm so glad you could join us. You are with Claudette on the fish station this morning. She is waiting for you.'

The lunch and dinner services pass in a blur. I've worked in six professional kitchens before La Reine, but, although Arnaud sticks broadly to the traditional Escoffier method of the *brigade de cuisine*, he still has his own way of doing and organising things. I've just not been here long enough yet to absorb everything. By half past midnight, when the restaurant and kitchen have been thoroughly cleaned, and everything is put away ready for the next service on Tuesday evening, I'm almost asleep on my feet.

'Kieran.' Arnaud beckons me over as I'm heading towards the locker room.

'Yes, chef?'

'You did well this evening.' There's a large balloon glass in his hand: cognac. He swirls the deep amber liquid and takes a sip. 'Your *filet de thon meunière avec oignons rôtis et sauce vierge* was quite excellent.'

'Thank you, chef. I—'

'But you need to react quicker to the – the ...' he pauses to search for a phrase '... the cut-and-thrust of the kitchen. Your French is good, but it needs to be better. And you need to be more assertive with the rest of the staff. You are not their friend. You are their sous chef. Or you will be. You must be free of doubt. You must know your own mind, and command them accordingly. Are you confident in your abilities?'

His words sting.

'Yes, chef. Very confident.'

'Then the rest of the staff must see this confidence too. Get some sleep. I'll see you on Tuesday. And on time, please.'

'Of course, chef.'

Dismissed, I finally make it into the locker room, change out of my whites and check my phone for the first time in nearly eight hours.

The battery is dead.

As I now know – because Emma knows, and she told me – Paris is 213 miles from London. And it's 521 miles from Cork.

At this precise moment, the distances feel much further. I might as well be stuck on the moon.

Chapter Eight

Emma

'You're late.' I check my watch. 'An hour and twenty minutes late. Even for you, that is something of a record. You were meant to be here at nine so we could get an "early start", in your words.' Thunder booms overhead and the gentle shower that started five minutes ago dials up to a deluge. It's the middle of August, and the great British summer seems to be already over.

James manoeuvres past me into the hallway and shakes himself like a wet dog. 'That's not fair! I did text.'

'Texting "be there in 10" over an hour ago does not count.' I pick up my phone and show him the evidence.

'I know, I know. I'm sorry.' He holds out a dripping carrier bag. 'I got distracted by something urgent on my way out of the house.'

I'm unappeased – James's 'urgent distractions' usually turn out to be TikTok videos of Jane Austen spoofs or people dressed up as characters from *Lord of the Rings*.

'But I brought a peace offering,' he says. 'Look in the bag.'

Inside the bag is a box bearing the logo of a high-end Danish bakery that has an outlet in the Westfield centre. A bakery I'd happily visit on a daily basis if I could afford to. I'll say this for James: he knows the way to a woman's heart. This woman, at least.

I give in and smile at him. 'Not bad, as peace offerings go. Come on, I'll put the kettle on.'

He follows me through to the kitchen and I get out two mugs and – eventually, once I've wrestled it from the back of the cupboard and rinsed the dust off – drop two teabags into my mum's old teapot. Given the cost of the baked goods, it seems worth the effort.

'Daisy not around today?' James asks, extracting the milk from the fridge.

'No. She's at some kind of shoot over in Bloomsbury. That one-off make-up artist job she landed in May seems to be turning into something more full time.'

'Oh, that's amazing. Well done her. And how's it going with that new boyfriend of hers, the divine Daniel?'

'Good, I think.' I hesitate over the selection of cakes and pastries that James has provided and just about manage to resist the urge to instantly start stuffing them in my face. Instead, I very carefully cut each of them in half, select four halves and arrange them neatly on the plates. 'She's started spending quite a lot of time at his flat, which is not surprising because it's about a thousand times nicer than here, but it does mean my diet has got a lot more limited.'

'You should really learn to cook a few more things. You can come to mine for dinner this evening if you like.'

'That's kind, but Daisy is definitely here tonight.' She would never leave me on my own on this particular day. And dinner is already planned. I'm going to make my signature dish. My only dish, if I'm honest: tuna pasta bake, made using a Colman's sachet and store cupboard ingredients. I honestly don't know what I'll do if they ever stop selling the sachets. 'Let's go and sit down. And bring the rest of the cakes.'

James doesn't mention Kieran until we're in the back room, sitting at the battered dining/work table that dominates the space.

'And what about your chef friend. How are things with him?'

Friend, I notice. Not boyfriend. I'm glad James isn't making assumptions. There's definitely something between Kieran and me, aside from the variable width of the English Channel – between 21 miles and 150 miles, depending on where you're standing – but I don't want to pin it down. It feels too fragile at the moment. An action as definite as naming it might destroy it altogether.

'Kieran and I are good, I think. He's not Simon, for one thing.' I grimace as I remember; Simon used to keep track of exactly who had called whom and how long for, as if our romance had to be translated into a bar chart and plotted on to a spreadsheet. 'Somehow it's easier, even though Kieran is in Paris.' I sigh. 'Though it's also hard, because he's in Paris.' It's hard because all I can do is imagine what it would be like to have Kieran hold my hand, or kiss me, or take me to bed. My imagination is good – it's *really* good – but it's not the same.

'Maybe it's easier *because* he's in Paris,' James says – though he seems to be directing his comment at the sugar-encrusted cinnamon bun in his hand rather than at me.

'What do you mean?' I ask.

'Oh – nothing. Just want to make sure you're doing the right thing, that's all.' James pats my hand. 'I don't want you to get hurt, Ems.'

'I know. But Kieran is just . . .' I shrug. 'I really like him. A lot.'

There's so much more I could say. I could describe to James the habit Kieran has of stroking his thumb along his jaw when he's thinking about something. Or the way his long, expressive fingers swoop around the screen when he's talking about something that excites him. But I don't want to share these things, not yet, not even with my friend. I want to hug the threads of this new thing to me and keep them just for myself, for now.

'Anyway, we're sending each other voice messages, and texting. And we have a video call every Sunday.'

'That's nice.'

Is there an undertone of pity in James's voice? I take a forkful of the chocolate and caramel confection in front of me and start trying out phrases in my head, imagining myself into a less complicated future. *You must meet my boyfriend, Kieran. He's a chef. Have you met my fiancé, Kieran? He owns his own restaurant.* We've got married and I'm working out what our children might look like when James brings me back to reality.

'So, shall we get down to business? Time to bring out the PAPs?' That's what we call our Paige Adams Pereira books. 'Do you want to go first, or shall I?'

Irritation sours my final mouthful of cake, but he's not wrong. Our plan today – before James and the weather derailed it – was to walk, then write. Most of the time I like to write alone, in absolute silence, but sometimes it's good to have someone else around for moral support. Especially when things aren't going so well. Which at the moment they're definitely not.

'You go first,' I suggest.

James gets out his laptop and a selection of vibrantly coloured notebooks.

'So, I got Lauren's line edits back on *Daydreams*, and they're mostly okay. But Paige has asked her to add in a scene where our busty heroine and her love interest are in the biology lab, and . . .' He claps his hands to his cheeks and shakes his head. 'It's just too much.'

I'm surprised; James isn't easily shocked.

'What do you mean? Too explicit?'

'It's not even that, exactly – it's the health and safety implications.' He tilts the laptop towards me so I can see the email from Paige that Lauren's forwarded. 'I mean, tearing off the lab coats and having it away on the wooden work benches is all fine, though I'd be worried about splinters. And getting up close and personal with a utility clamp? Also fine, if that's your cup of tea. But this section here, with the Bunsen burners . . .' His finger runs along the relevant line. 'It just sounds dangerous. And as for this next bit . . .' He huffs. 'I had to look up what a retort was, and it's made of glass, and, even if it wasn't, I just don't see how it would fit. It's like—' He makes a shape with his hands to indicate some sort of large, spherical object with, at a guess, two tubes sticking out of the top. Definitely not something that's meant for any sort of contact with any part of the human anatomy.

For a moment, we're both silent.

'Well, do you think Paige actually knows what a retort is? Maybe she's confusing it with a . . . a test tube.'

'Still . . .' James sighs. 'What should I do?'

I think for a moment, trying to banish from my head the images Paige's email has conjured. 'I'd do all the other edits,' I say, 'then send them back to Lauren with a note, asking if they've considered the legal implications if anyone is daft enough to try what Paige is suggesting these characters get up to. The thought of litigation might be enough to dissuade her.'

'Good plan,' he replies. Yet he's still hesitating, chewing on his bottom lip.

'What else are you worried about?'

'My crime novel. Lauren's had the full manuscript for nearly nine weeks, and I've asked her about it a couple of times, but she's kind of brushed me off.'

I take James's hand. 'You know what publishing's like. There are glaciers that move more quickly. And it's holiday season. I'm sure she's just waiting for the right people from acquisitions to all be back in the office.'

'Yeah, I guess you're right.' He squeezes my fingers. 'Have you heard what Mia's been landed with as her next PAP?'

'Yes! I couldn't believe it when she told me the title. *Deep Space Dominatrix*.'

'You have to hand it to Paige. Who else would decide to set an erotic novel on the International Space Station? Speaking of unlikely settings, how are the orchestral sexcapades coming along?'

I groan and drop my head into my hands.

'It's a disaster, James. I am *so* far behind schedule. I thought I had it all down to a fine art. Write the sex scenes, since that's what Paige is mostly concerned about, then fill in the gaps with as much plot and characterisation and as many cliff-hanger moments as I can cram in. But with this . . .' I sigh and flip open my notebook to show James all the outlines that I've worked out then deleted. 'I just can't make it work. It's as if the writer's block that's been stymieing all my own projects has now infected the ghostwriting. I've barely written a third of the book, and my deadline is in two weeks. I'm screwed.'

James nods as he looks through the notebook.

'Screwed with some inappropriately shaped musical instrument, I'd say. There's nothing else for it. If you can't get it done in time, you'll have to ask for an extension.'

'Bugger.' I pick up a cinnamon bun and stuff it into my mouth, imagining Lauren's expression if I ask for my deadline to be moved by two weeks. The three-books-a-year schedule doesn't leave anyone much wiggle room. If I'm late, it impacts the copy-editors, and the proofreaders, and the cover designers, all of whom work on James and Mia's books too. Worst case scenario: I miss my deadline, and the entirety of next year's Paige Adams Pereira publishing schedule goes tits-up.

'Look,' James says, 'why don't you stick to your plan as much as you can? Let's mind-map the sex scenes, make them really stupendous, and then the rest of it can be a bit crap, or even a lot crap, and Lauren still won't really mind.'

'Okay. I have been thinking about the pivotal scene at the end of the second act. Paige says in her outline she wants an orgy late on, so I thought, maybe the crazy conductor makes them all start performing some symphony in the nude, and everyone starts off tense and angry, and then it all gets extremely ... graphic.'

'That's good,' James nods, picking up a felt tip pen and turning to the pile of A3 sheets I've got ready at the end of the table. 'And don't ask me why, but I'm envisaging xylophones being in the mix somewhere.'

'Ooh – we could hang a triangle off someone's anatomy.'

'Yes! See? This is the power of baked goods. Let's get some more cake down you. We'll have the whole book wrapped up by teatime.'

'So, I obviously didn't get the whole book done, but James helped me feel a lot better about it. I reckon I can go a couple of days over deadline without Lauren going completely Cruella de Vil, and hopefully that will give me enough time to churn out some sort of more or less complete draft.'

I press pause and take a sip of tea. It's nearly ten-thirty at night, now. Daisy's downstairs watching *First Dates* and probably talking to Daniel at the same time. I'm in my bedroom recording a voice memo to send to Kieran. He's been having a difficult time the past few weeks, struggling to get used to the new restaurant and worrying about his dad. In an attempt to cheer him up, I've already recounted the discussions I had with James today about alternative uses for lab equipment and orchestral instruments, and I've described my 'signature dish' in detail, challenging him to improve upon it. But I want to be truthful, too. Especially since he opened up to me about his father.

I press the resume button and continue.

'*After James left, I went down to the Thames. It's my mum's birthday today – she would have been fifty-four – and I always buy some flowers and throw them on to the water. We used to live near the eastern end of the Thames, and Mum loved the river so much. She thought being buried or cremated was boring. She wanted a Viking funeral instead. She wanted to float down the Thames between fire and water.*'

Mum always was one for crazy ideas. *Let's buy an old ice cream van but sell cake instead! Let's stencil all our furniture and try to make a business out of selling it! Let's forget school and work and take a train without knowing the destination!* The ice cream van rusted to bits on the drive. Mum stencilled one chest of drawers, and I thought it was beautiful, but she wasn't disciplined enough to take it any further. We did take the impromptu train journey, though. It was fun. Until we got separated, and I ended up in Portsmouth. I was the most scared I'd been in my life. Happy memories, sad memories. I've written them all down, terrified that I'll forget.

I press the record button again.

'*Of course, I couldn't actually organise a Viking funeral. It's illegal, for starters. But I did throw her ashes into the river. Probably also illegal, but a lot less obvious. It's where I go now, when I want to remember her.*' What else can I tell him? '*Mum didn't cook much*

– I think she found the organising a bit overwhelming. Easier to bung something in a microwave. But she did make tuna pasta bake, which is why I still make it. And Queen of Puddings, which is why it's my favourite dessert.'

I pause the recording as a huge yawn overtakes me.

'I need to go to bed. I've got a lot of words to write tomorrow. I think James is right, though. Maybe I should learn to cook some more things. And maybe ... maybe you could teach me.'

I hesitate for a heartbeat or two, then plough on.

'This is going to sound odd, since we've only actually spent two minutes together, but I miss you, Kieran. Night.'

I send the recording.

'Night, Kieran,' I say out loud. 'Night, Mum. Happy birthday!'

Maybe, somehow, they can both hear me.

Chapter Nine

Emma

'Fuck – the croissants!'

I race downstairs to the kitchen, turn the oven off, grab the tea towel, wrench open the oven door, fling open the back door and start flapping the tea towel furiously in the air just beneath the smoke alarm. The croissants have only been in a few extra minutes, but our ancient oven does a passable impression of a volcano. It belches carbonised fumes if anyone dares use it for more than twenty minutes at a time. At least all the tea-towel-flapping has to be good exercise. When I'm sure the danger has passed, I put the kettle on, rescue the only very slightly overdone croissants and arrange a cafetière, plates and mugs on a tray.

'Daisy – breakfast!' I call up from the bottom of the stairs.

After a few moments she appears, wearing some ancient Disney-themed pyjamas and a pair of dark glasses and groaning, softly.

'Just leave me in my bedroom and let me die. It's the kindest thing to do.'

'How much did you drink last night? You didn't seem that bad when you got in.'

'That's because I'm a brilliant actress. 'Specially when it comes to acting sober.'

'Come and sit in the garden. I've made coffee – the good stuff – and *pain au chocolat*. It's lovely and sunny outside.'

'Argh . . .'

'Come on,' I urge. 'It's a gorgeous Sunday morning. You can't spend all day in bed. You'll just regret it later.'

Daisy lowers the glasses slightly and glares at me. 'You sound like my mum.' Still, she does come down the stairs, and shuffles after me into the garden. We settle ourselves at the wobbly cast-iron table, clinging to the shade cast by our neighbour's laurel hedge, and I pour her some coffee.

'At least you don't have to work tomorrow.'

I don't either, in theory. Tomorrow is the last Monday in August, which means it's also a bank holiday, and neither of my Monday cleaning clients wants me there. In practice, unfortunately, I'll have to spend all day working on the dreaded *Symphonic Sexcapades*. I reckon, if I put in a lot of hours, and try not to mind that it's basically word vomit, I should get it done by the middle of next week, just a few days past the deadline. But today I'm taking a day off. I close my eyes and soak in the Sunday morning music of west London: percussion (the staccato chug of a lawn mower from next door), melody line (someone nearby singing along to Taylor Swift), and bass (the constant rumbling traffic on the A40). Bliss.

'Haven't you got your thing tonight?' Daisy asks. She's removed the sunglasses and is looking a little less corpse-like. 'Your cooking thing?'

'Yeah.' I grin. The anticipation is like a happy little spark in the centre of my chest. 'You're at Dan's tonight, right?'

'Don't worry, I won't be here to cramp your style.' She gives me a sly look and winks. 'If you and Kieran end up virtually sleeping together after your virtual first date, you can be as noisy as you like.'

'It's not a date,' I retort. 'He's teaching me to cook something. And as for virtually sleeping together, I can't imagine how that would even work.'

'And you a porno writer,' Daisy replies, snagging another croissant.

'It's erotic fiction, thank you very much.'

Daisy laughs, and I know I'm not fooling her. In my head this evening's video call is very much a first date, given that it will involve eating a candlelit meal at the same time as each other, even if not in the same geographical location. Assuming I manage the cooking bit. And I've definitely spent time imagining what might virtually come afterwards. A lot of time. But, although that's been fun, I can't help feeling that virtual anything is a poor substitute for the real thing.

'You know,' Daisy says, sounding cautious, 'I still think you could—'

'I'm not using my emergency fund, Daisy. It's for emergencies.' I sigh. 'Besides, after having to fork out for a new laptop in February and getting my phone screen repaired in May, there's hardly any money in it. It's not so much an emergency fund as a minor inconvenience fund at the moment.' I laugh despite myself. 'I can maybe afford an emergency manicure, but that's about it. And no,' I add as Daisy opens her mouth, 'I'm not going to let you lend me money, either.'

'Okay, okay.' Daisy raises her hands in defeat. 'When do you get your next chunk of money from the books?'

'Some time after they've accepted the manuscript, which in practice is always the second draft I send them, so probably . . .' I shrug '. . . November or December. So maybe then I'll visit, if I have time to plan it out. But I still hope he'll be in London in October.'

The sun has risen further, eating away at the shade. Daisy, shorter than me, scrunches her legs up in her chair to keep them out of the heat.

'Does it make you happy?' she asks.

I know she means the thing – whatever it is – with Kieran. I take the last *pain au chocolat* and eat it slowly as I think.

I love talking to him. I look forward to every video call. Often, I see something or hear something and think, *oh, I need to tell Kieran about that, he'll find it funny too*. His tales of growing up with a sibling fascinate me. His spontaneity terrifies and excites me in equal measure. He never seems to worry about what might go wrong. I'm not even sure it occurs to him as a possibility. He's like a window into an unimagined world. And, so far, I'm enjoying the view.

'Yes. It makes me happy.' Happy enough for now, at least. To say I'm not fretting about the future would be a lie.

My phone vibrates.
'A text from Kieran?' Daisy asks. 'Is it sexy?'
'Nope. It's a shopping list.'

Kieran

I text her.

> Is that all okay? Only ten ingredients
> – nothing expensive – and your
> flatmate might have chilli and garlic
> already. And it's all stovetop, so no
> need to worry about your crazy oven.

The three dots appear, disappear, and appear again.

> This is just a main course, right?

> Yes. I picked up some cheese and
> crackers for my second course, so
> you get whatever you fancy. And
> wine. I'd recommend a chardonnay.

I hesitate for a moment, then add:

> At the risk of sounding like
> a patronising arse, you have
> some equipment, right? Like,
> a pan, a frying pan, a knife, a
> wooden spoon, etc etc.

> Yes, I have all of those. Or Daisy does.

There's a pause, and then a photo of Emma appears, holding a large knife, wearing a saucepan on her head as if it was a helmet, and grinning maniacally at the screen.

> I mostly use them for medieval tournament cosplay, but understand they are multi-purpose.

She always says she's not spontaneous, but she's wrong. In some ways, she's more spontaneous than any other woman I know.

First time I've seen someone look hot in a saucepan!

> Bet you say that to all your kitchen flunkies! Off to shops now, wish me luck.

Text me or call if you get into difficulties!

Emma sends me a thumbs-up emoji. I stash my phone and head out.

It's a fine day. I rescue my bike from the crowded rack and head south, aiming for the Bois de Vincennes, the largest public park in Paris. As I cycle, my mind drifts back to yesterday's scene at the restaurant. I still can't quite believe it happened, though maybe I shouldn't have been shocked. Everyone told me that Arnaud had a temper. A lot of men in his position do. Something to do with the way an executive chef is treated as a king in his own kitchen, perhaps. Even as a sous chef, I've felt the danger. The instant, unquestioning obedience goes to our heads. Or maybe our dicks; Niamh sometimes tells both Brendan and me that's what we think with. An innocent mistake gets interpreted as a challenge, and suddenly we go all aggressive alpha male on some other poor fucker's arse. And I thought I'd already seen Arnaud at his worst.

By the time I'm in the park and wheeling my bike around the crowded shore of Lac de Saint-Mandé, whatever is bugging me about what happened is still bugging me, and I'm no nearer to figuring out exactly what it is. I sit on a bench and text Marianne, my mate from Roubaix, describing what happened and asking her opinion. The message has just sent when another arrives from Emma – a photo with a caption. She's holding up a bulb of fennel in front of what looks like a sports centre entrance with a huge advert for a climbing wall.

> Visit White City! We have exotic vegetables, it turns out, AND places to climb! Fennel does count as exotic, right?

I laugh out loud, drawing curious glances from the French family picnicking nearby, though I'm also simultaneously thinking, *fuck, she's not forgotten about the whole free-climbing thing, then.* I text her back.

> How did I get to be this old and only now be discovering the treasures of west London? And yes, you're definitely allowed to think of fennel as exotic. Looking forward to initiating you into its delights later on . . .

I've not told her yet that I'm not going to be able to spend any of my holiday in London, but I need to. And soon. Tonight, maybe. I should have told her immediately I found out about my dad's results. But what can I say – I'm selfish. I want her in my life, and I don't want to give her a reason to decide that our relationship, such as it is, is more aggro than it's worth.

Should I tell her she haunts my dreams, or would that just make everything worse?

Emma

Right. I survey the table one more time – the clean end of it, not the end covered with pens, scraps of paper and peeling yellow sticky notes. *I think we've got everything.* Place mat. Cutlery. Napkin – square of kitchen towel masquerading as a napkin, actually, but hopefully he won't notice. Wine glass. Water glass. Single deep pink dahlia cut from the garden and placed in a vase. Candle.

Not bad, Emma Christmas. I catch a glimpse of myself in the mirror that hangs over the boarded-up fireplace. Daisy did my make-up before she left, and I've pinned my hair up, and put on a gingham summer dress I found in a charity shop last week. Second-hand, but could be vintage. *Not bad at all.*

The cooking trial is still to come, though. I hurry back into the kitchen. The ingredients are on the side, and I've got out the pans and stuff he mentioned earlier. The wine is in the fridge and my laptop, balanced on a chair in the corner, is plugged in and ready. I glance at the time. 19.44. One minute to go.

Kieran

'Hi, Emma!' I wave as she appears. Nearly three months after we first met, and just seeing her on a screen is enough to make my heart beat faster. 'You look amazing.' She does, too. Between her dark hair, her red lipstick and the black and white check dress, she looks like a fifties film star.

'You're looking pretty good yourself. Are those chef's whites you're wearing?'

I bow. 'In honour of the occasion. Though, given the temperature outside, I might strip down to a sleeveless tee in a bit. If you've no objection.'

'No objection at all.'

She smiles, and it's so sexy I almost pull my jacket off that instant. But I force myself to focus. I want her to do well at this dish, so she'll get some confidence to try other things.

'Alright, then. What we're going to do first is prep our fennel.' I angle my laptop screen so she'll be able to see what I'm doing. 'Take a firm grip on the knife, and cut the fennel bulb into quarters, like so . . .'

Emma

I take a deep breath, inhaling the aroma of the bowl of pasta that's sitting in front of me. I've moved the laptop into the back room and propped it up on a stack of books, so it's almost as though Kieran is sitting across the table from me. He's taken off his chef's jacket, and, as much as I love a man in uniform, he's also looking pretty damn fine in the sleeveless tee, so much so that I have to wrench my gaze away from his biceps. Still, I've controlled myself enough to light the candle, and I've poured myself a glass of wine. Now for the moment of truth.

Almost.

'What's wrong?' he asks.

'Well, this is going to sound daft, but we've never eaten in front of each other. What if you look at me shovelling pasta into my mouth and think, *ew*?'

He chuckles. 'What if you decide I chew like a pig with a sinus problem?'

'Exactly.'

'Then let's take a mouthful together. On three. One, two, three . . .'

I take a forkful of pasta and immediately stop caring about how I might look. 'Oh, my God, this is delicious! Fuck!'

'Told you it would be.' Kieran, looking just a little bit smug, grins and raises his wine glass. I mimic his action. 'To the chef.'

'To the chef. And thank you. I would never have tried a recipe like this on my own.'

'Ah, this is just the beginning. I've been writing a list of recipes that I reckon would be perfect for beginners, and that work within the limitations of your kitchen. We can cook our way through them.'

'I'd like that. I even enjoyed the food shopping today. I did what you suggested and spent some time looking at the different fruits and vegetables, and smelling things, and reading some recipe cards.'

'And you found everything okay?'

'Yes. And, even better, I came up with a new idea for a book. The first workable new idea I've had in months.' I pause, so I can savour the pasta I'm eating and relive the dawning realisation I'd had in the middle of the tinned goods section that yes, this idea was solid. This idea would actually work. This might be something I can – finally – get published under my own name. I start talking through the idea. He seems genuinely interested. Excited for me.

Kieran

Her eyes sparkled when she mentioned this new book idea she's had. I love that about her – that she can be so enthusiastic. I've noticed it before: beneath the anxious, plan-everything-out Emma, there's definitely another much bubblier Emma trying to get out.

I tell her about what happened on Saturday night at the restaurant: the discovery of the missing case of vintage wine, Arnaud losing his shit at the waiting staff, accusing the sommelier of fraud and then finally sacking one of the kitchen porters on the spot.

'Can he do that?' Emma asks. 'Just get rid of someone like that?'

I shrug. 'In this case, I suspect yes. I'm still considered an outsider by some of the staff, but someone let slip that the guy is an illegal immigrant that Arnaud was paying in cash. No status, no protection under the law.'

'That's awful. The poor man.'

'The worst thing is, it just doesn't add up. Porters don't have anything to do with the wine deliveries, and it's all locked away, and the number of people with access to the keys is really small. And would he be likely to know which wine to steal?' I pull the cheeseboard towards me and cut off a slice of Comté. 'I don't know. Arnaud is not turning out exactly as I expected.'

'You should bond with the other staff by giving him a nickname,' Emma suggests. 'Like Mia always referring to Paige as the Mistress of Evil, or something.'

'I like that idea.' I take another sip of wine, resolutely not letting my gaze drift down to Emma's distractingly magnificent cleavage. God, but she's a fine-looking woman. 'And how are the *Sexcapades* coming along, or shouldn't I ask?'

Emma

There's a definite glint in his eye. I take a spoonful of chocolate mousse and try to eat it in what I hope is an alluring manner.

'I'm approaching the end. I've written the big orgy scene, but I still have to do the passionate tryst on top of the piano that comes after that. Did you know a Steinway Model D concert grand is almost two and a half metres long and weighs five hundred kilos?'

'So definitely hefty enough to support at least a couple of people, by the sound of it.' Kieran leans closer to the screen, propping his chin on one hand and holding his wine glass in the other and looking at me with those 'come to bed' eyes of his. 'And the orgy scene sounds fun. Do you fancy sharing the details?'

The blood rushes into my face. 'Definitely not while we're eating. But, I suppose I could email you the relevant scene later. Just so you can get a flavour of my work.' I really want to rip his clothes off. 'And if you like it, I'll give you copies of the other books I've written for Paige, when you come to London.'

Kieran

London. Shite. Shite, shite, shite.

I've got to tell her. Now.

'Emma – I'm so sorry. Really sorry. I should have told you before, when I first realised, but – I'm not going to make it to London in October.'

She blushes fiercely, pulling away from the screen. 'Oh. Of course. Don't worry about it.'

'But I have been worrying. That's why I didn't tell you earlier. I'd come if I possibly could, and the last thing I want is to mess *this* up.' I gesture to indicate the two of us. 'But with my dad's results the way they were, and my mum and my brother taking all the burden ... I have to give them a break, even if it is only for a week. And I need to see my dad. I'd never forgive myself if he suddenly got worse and—' I break off, almost overwhelmed by a surge of panic, and take a deep breath. 'Sorry. But I can get a direct flight to Cork in October. I'll have no call to be in London at all.'

'You don't need to apologise. And don't worry,' Emma repeats, more gently. 'I know how brutal it can be when someone you love has an illness like that.'

She does, of course. She's not talked a lot about what happened to her mum, but she's told me enough.

'Hopefully I can come to London next time I get a break. Maybe after Christmas. Or maybe I'll just pitch up and surprise you.' She seems to tense up, and I wonder if I've said the wrong thing. 'But in the meantime, shall we keep going with the cooking lessons?'

'Yes.' Emma smiles, but then adds, 'It's getting late, and I've got to get up early to write, but thank you for this. It was fun.'

'I'll text you tomorrow. Sleep well.'

'You too. Goodnight.'

'Night.'

She's gone. And out of my mouth come words that I guess I wanted to say, even if I didn't realise it.

'I think I love you.'

Emma

I touch the blank screen where his image was, refusing to even think the words that are trying to make me hear them.

I don't want to. If anything is a risk, it's falling in love.

PART TWO

Winter

Chapter Ten

Kieran

'*Monsieur Giroux, ils ont presque fini leur fromage.*'

Having told Marcel that the guests are nearly done with their cheese course, the waiter lingers, hanging around near the door that separates the kitchen from the dining room and looking pathetic, like the last banana in the fruit bowl. Not a proper waiter: a skinny seventeen-year-old in a poorly fitting suit, hired in for the day – the clothing as well as the boy, at a guess.

'*Alors, débarrassez les tables! Vite!*' Marcel, *maître d'hôtel* of La Reine de la Nuit, shoos the boy out of the kitchen. 'Imbecile,' he growls, switching to English. 'A proper waiter would not need to be told to clear the tables! I am surrounded by—'

Just as I think the throbbing vein in Marcel's head might explode, Ettore, the sommelier, grabs his shoulder.

'Just remember how much they are paying us, hmm?' His grin draws a slight answering smile from Marcel. Ettore glances at the two teenagers who've been given the job of loading and unloading the dishwashers and leans closer to Marcel. 'Though I can see your point. My grandmother moved faster than those two, even before her hip replacements.' Marcel laughs, and Ettore moves away, satisfied.

As well as the two in here, there are four more teenagers currently in the dining room, each one a schoolkid with the grand total of zero hours' experience of a professional kitchen. But then, we're not in the restaurant today. Marcel, Ettore, Alex – the pastry chef – and I are in the kitchen of an event space, catering for a private Christmas lunch party for fifty people.

A kitchen that somehow manages to be vast and industrial yet way too basic at the same time. There's not enough ventilation, and the room smells of bleach layered over the ground-in stench of old school dinners, as though it's showcasing some sort of disgusting perfume combination. Outside, it's cold enough for snow. In here, between the ovens and the dishwashers and the waves of panic coming off the temp staff, it's practically tropical.

I gulp down some water and return to helping Alex plate the *bûche de Noël*.

'I still can't believe how much we're being paid,' Alex murmurs, glancing up from her work for long enough to wink at me and smile. 'Thank you for asking me to join you.'

'*Je vous en prie*,' I reply. 'I could hardly manage all of this without the three of you. And sure, it's not that much money.'

It *is* that much money, even divided by four, and even after taking out the cost of ingredients and the wages of the temp staff. When the client first got in touch, I was stunned by how much the guy was willing to fork out for two Sundays of my time. The amount I'll end up making is totally worth all the annoyances, including preparing Christmas dishes even though today is only the first Sunday in December and last Sunday, when we did our first lunch for him, we were still in November. I talked about it with Emma. She agreed that it was far too much money for me to turn down, though it means we've now missed two of our weekly video chats. At least she has some social thing to go to later. At least we've been texting during the day.

The last swirl, drizzle and decoration has been added to the plates. I take advantage of the pause while Marcel marshals the waiters to pick up my phone and text her again.

> Dessert is ready to serve. You'd like it: chocolate, chestnut and caramel Yule log with raspberry coulis, candied berries and spun sugar holly leaves. Alex's, our pastry chef's, speciality.

> You had me at chocolate – I am literally drooling right now. I hope Alex will make it for me if – when – I manage to get back to Paris. He sounds very talented!

I'm about to correct her assumption that Alex is a bloke when one of the waiters returning from the dining room crashes into one of the waiters carrying a tray of desserts. There's an explosion of *bûche de Noël* and dirty crockery. Alex and Marcel both explode into fast, angry French.

> Dessert disaster! Speak later. X

I'll text her later, or call. I want to tell her how much I miss her, anyway. I can clarify then.

Emma

'I don't know, Daisy,' I say, peering out of the window. 'It looks like it might rain. And it's so cold. It might even snow, according to the forecast. Maybe I'll just stay here.'

'Oh, no, you don't,' Daisy replies, turning on the lamps and closing the curtains. It's almost half past five, which – fun fact – means it's currently nautical twilight in London. Not as dark as astronomical twilight, apparently, but dark enough. 'You're not chickening out now.'

'But I don't know any of Dan's friends.'

'So? I've only known them for six months; that's why I want you there too. Moral support. And it will do you good, as well. Otherwise, you're just going to sit here and stew over that bloody email. You know I'm right.'

'Yeah, I guess.'

'Good. We'll leave shortly, yeah? We can help him set up.'

'Yeah.'

Daisy whisks out and I sit back at my laptop, but I can't bring myself to open the manuscript I'm supposed to be working on.

Instead, I pick up my phone and scroll back through the texts from Kieran. He sent me a photo of the menu he's been serving at the event today. *Gougères au gruyère, verrines de cappuccino glacé carottes et cumin, coquilles Saint-Jacques gratinées, terrine de saumon, dinde de Noël, bœuf en croûte, pommes de terre à la dauphinoise* ... I don't know what some of them are, but they all sound delicious. The kind of food that might easily be better than sex. And as for the pudding he described ... my stomach growls. I send another text.

> Leaving in a little for Dan's 'potluck supper club' and worrying now about what I've let myself in for. I'm bringing after-dinner chocolates and Daisy has made a vegetarian chilli, but no idea what the rest of the guests are offering. Very much doubt any of it will live up to cappuccino carrots, whatever they are! At least there will be wine. If we all die of experimental cookery – unfortunately, Dan has developed a thing about offal – this has been fun! Xx

I want to say more. Something about missing him today. Today's the second Sunday we've not had a video call since we first started ... I want to say dating, but I can't kid myself that Kieran and I are actually, properly, dating. Since we first started corresponding? Too Victorian. Since we became pen-pals, perhaps. Twenty-first century, digital pen-pals. If I were in one of Paige's novels right now, I'd be groaning with frustration and heading for the nearest bedroom without being too fussy who was in the bed. Since I'm not, I'll probably just eat my own body weight in carbs. Assuming carbs are on offer.

'Ems, time to go.' Daisy already has her coat on and the casserole dish – wrapped in a towel and a bin bag – in her arms. 'Don't want to miss the bus.'

I slip my phone into my bag. Whatever I'm trying to say, it will have to wait.

Kieran

'*C'est tout?*' Alex asks. Despite the long hours of work, and the heat, she still looks immaculate, not a strand of her blonde hair out of place.

'*Oui, c'est tout,*' I reply, flipping the tea towel over my shoulder. Everything has been tidied up. Marcel has returned the catering supplies to their crates, and he and Ettore are moving them and the remaining wine downstairs to Ettore's van. '*On peut se détendre, maintenant.*' Though right now, I'm feeling the opposite of relaxed. Keyed-up. Jumpy. Perhaps it's because I've not talked to Emma today.

Being a private chef for the past two Sundays has certainly been exhilarating. My contract with Monsieur Arnàud forbids me from cooking outside La Reine, but he's been pissing me off; for the chance to take a risk, to secretly defy him, I would have said yes even if the money on offer hadn't been so good. I guess the others felt the same. But now the excitement of the day is over, and the adrenaline is fading, and I'm starting to regret agreeing to this second private event. My virtual Sunday dates with Emma have become part of my life. So has she. Missing one date felt okay. Missing a second feels as though we're on the cusp of losing something.

I glance at the clock on the wall: seven in the evening here, six in the UK. The supper club she's attending will just be getting going. Too late for me to call her now.

Marcel reappears, grabs his coat from the stand and raises an eyebrow at Ettore, who is checking the contents of the last case of wine against a list.

'Ready?'

'A moment.'

Marcel smiles at me. 'We have a quiet evening planned. Just the two of us, and Ettore has already made dinner.'

'Lasagne, just as my mother used to make it,' Ettore says, 'followed by Pecorino Toscano matched with an aged *vin santo*.' He kisses his fingers at Marcel and winks. 'I am still educating him about the excellence of Italian cuisine.'

The Ettore-Marcel vibe has been a revelation over the past two Sundays, and the main benefit of me taking this gig – aside from the enormous pay packet. From working with him at La Reine, I would have described Ettore as a serious man with strongly held views on the correct pairing of wine to food. Friendly – we're both outsiders, being the only non-French restaurant staff – but reserved. Relaxed, joky Ettore, who sings Puccini while he's decanting the wine, was entirely unexpected. And though I'd realised he and Marcel were mates – Marcel's attitude to me started off pretty sub-zero, and he only defrosted once I got to know Ettore – I had no idea they were engaged. Their flirty banter has been an eye-opener as well as a delight.

Ettore sticks his clipboard into the box of wine and picks up a bottle he's put to one side. 'Here. This has been opened, but the idiots didn't drink it. It's too good to waste.'

I study the label – Domaine Perrot-Minot, Chambertin-Clos de Bèze – and give a low whistle. 'Far too good to waste. Thanks, Ettore.'

He grins. 'You get any more catering invitations, you let us know, *si*?'

'I definitely will. See you both on Tuesday.'

As Marcel and Ettore leave, I pull a couple of plastic cups from the water dispenser in the corner of the kitchen and offer one to Alex. 'Fancy sharing some wine before you head off? I can't drink it on my own.'

'But of course.' She smiles, then wrinkles her nose and gestures at the grotty kitchen. 'Not in here, though.'

'The dining room?'

'I have a better idea. Get your coat.'

A minute later and we're on a balcony that opens off the dining room, overlooking Quai de la Tournelle and the left bank of the Seine. Opposite, across the tops of the trees, I can see the

Christmas lights on Île Saint-Louis and along Rue Saint-Paul on the *rive droite*, and a little to the left is the glowing jewel of the restored Notre-Dame. The view reminds me why Paris is called the city of light: the whole place glitters as if it's been dipped in stardust. Alex and I stand next to each other, huddled in our coats, sipping the Grand Cru wine and taking in the spectacle.

'*C'est un belle ville, non?*' she asks after a while.

'Yes. Yes, it's very beautiful.'

I wish I could show Emma this view.

'Kieran . . .'

As I turn, Alex puts her arm around my neck and kisses me. The shock of it makes me tense up and pull back a little. But her lips are soft and sweet: mingled notes of red plum, black cherry, rose, ginger. And the warmth of her body as it's pressed against mine is almost as intoxicating as the wine.

I close my eyes and kiss her back.

Emma

'What? I can't hear you. The music.' I point to my ears, and the guy I'm talking to – well, miming at – smiles and nods as he bops along, dad-dancing to Little Mix. Hugo, I think he's called. Or Hugh. Something like that. Posh. A barrister. Dan met him last month at some work thing; polo, or golf, or rugby, or some other event involving balls. The supper club has turned into an impromptu disco, and thank God because most of the food, with the exception of Daisy's chilli, was pretty inedible. Three plates of tripe – they all follow the same online recipe blog, and apparently tripe is very 'in'. Some undercooked chicken drumsticks served with a garlic sauce strong enough to drop a healthy man at twenty paces. A completely unseasoned mushroom soup that might as well have been tepid water. A home-made chocolate ice cream cake that had partially collapsed under its own weight and was so full of ice crystals that even I couldn't eat it. Seriously, who looks at the weather in December and thinks, *you know what we need right now? An ice-cream-based dessert*.

However, there is, thankfully, an ongoing abundance of wine and vodka, and everyone has been partaking pretty liberally. We've pushed back the furniture in Dan's massive warehouse conversion living room and now we're all dancing to hits from ten years ago. Dan spent the first twenty minutes rushing around with coasters and reminding people to be careful not to spill any red, but he seems to have finally relaxed, or maybe he's just been distracted by Daisy. They're currently grinding up against each other, kissing in a way that suggests they're trying to make up for the lack of dinner – one pot of chilli doesn't go far between ten ravenous people – by eating each other's faces instead.

Hugo, or possibly Hugh, leans closer and yells in my ear.

'I said, are you seeing anyone?'

'Oh. Yes. Well, no. Not as such.' I shrug, as James Bay starts trying to Hold Back The River. 'It's complicated.'

'Ah.' Hugo/Hugh does a self-conscious little twirl complete with arm-pump action, almost sending my wine glass flying. 'So that's not a definite yes.'

The wine is making me sleepy now. I wish I were dancing with Kieran. For a moment I close my eyes and sway and imagine I'm in his arms, leaning my head against his chest. When I blink my eyes open, the man in front of me is still looking at me expectantly, waiting for an answer.

'Yes. I mean, no. I mean, I guess?'

I drain my glass just in time: whatever his name is takes my empty hand and now he's twirling me around.

'In that case, Emma Christmas, would you have lunch with me next Saturday?'

And maybe it's because he's quite good-looking or maybe it's just the wine or maybe it's because I'm at someone else's home and this guy is one of his friends and I don't want to make things awkward and I've always been terrible at saying no in any case, but I find myself nodding.

'Yes,' I say. 'Yes. Why not?'

Chapter Eleven

Emma

I throw off the duvet, wait until I'm absolutely freezing then drag it back on top of me and try to snuggle up in the bed and think meditative, sleep-inducing thoughts.

That's right, you're nice and relaxed. So relaxed and sleepy.
Really relaxed.
Long, slow breaths.
Relaxed.
Sleepy.
Slow breath in, slow breath out.
In, and out.
In, out.
In, out.
Shake it all about.
You do the hokey-cokey and you turn around, that's what it's all about. Oh ...

'Oh, for fuck's sake!' I push myself upright and turn on the bedside light. Three-bloody-thirty in the morning and I've been lying here for five hours without a wink of sleep. I'd done all the right things, too. Light, early dinner. Limited screen time. Nice warm bath with a lavender bath bomb I'd treated myself to last week. Reading a relaxing book by lamplight before turning the light off at ten-thirty.

And had any of it worked?

'Hah!'

Daisy stayed at Dan's after the so-called supper club on Sunday, and she's still there tonight, so I don't need to worry about my hollow laugh waking her up. The book on my bedside table claims to give you perfect sleep if you stick to its rules – and predicts unmitigated horrors if you don't. I pick up the book and start to yell at it.

'As for you, you can take your good sleep hygiene practices and shove them up your – up your – dust jacket!'

Hurling the book into the corner of the room makes me feel a little better. I push my pillow into a more comfortable position against the headboard, take a sip of water and pick up my phone. Hesitate for a moment, then open the texting app.

You awake? X

We've progressed to kisses at the ends of some of our messages, though I can't remember who started it, or exactly what they mean, given the ongoing . . . situation.

There's no reply.

Probably because he's asleep. At least that makes one of you.

Though I might just have woken him up. And he's not replying because he is awake, but he's also now annoyed.

Hey, if he leaves his phone on and unsilenced, that's on him.

Or maybe he's awake but ignoring the message because he's actually having amazing sex with some gorgeous Parisian who—

Yeah, I'm awake. Can't sleep.
Hate not being able to sleep. X

I text back instantly, of course.

Me too. I keep veering between
too hot and too cold. My
room is like an ice box.

My room is like an industrial walk-in
freezer. And I should know, I've
spent enough time in them!

> Did you know that the spread
> of domestic refrigeration led
> to the final collapse of the
> international natural ice trade?

I regret the text as soon as it's sent. I could have sent something flirty. *Sorry you're freezing, wish I were there to warm you up!* Or, *If only we were together, we'd send the temperature up to sizzling!* Something like that, but better. Instead, I go and bring up the ice trade.

> I didn't even know there
> was an ice trade.

> Oh, yes. They had magazines
> and everything. *The Ice Trade
> Journal*, for example.

> I just can't stop myself.

> Though apparently it later changed
> its name to *Refrigerating World*.
> Maybe I should get a copy, it
> might help me doze off!

> I don't know, it sounds pretty gripping
> to me! Why are you awake, though? X

I consider my options. *Because I can't stop thinking about you?* Cheesy, a little desperate-sounding and also, at least tonight, not the entire truth. *Because I miss you?* Is it technically possible to miss someone you've only spent two actual, physical minutes with, those minutes being nearly six months ago now?

I do miss him, though. We communicate almost every day, even if it's just a throwaway, how's-your-day-going one-liner.

But, increasingly, I'm worried that I shouldn't miss him. That this is all going to end badly.

Tell him that you're lying awake because—

Er, partly because, I think you'll find—

Okay, tell him you're lying awake partly because you've somehow agreed to have lunch with a random posh guy you met yesterday, but at the same time you think you've fallen in the L-word with him, Kieran, and, given there seems to be no possibility of your ever actually being in the same country, let alone the same room, maybe it would just hurt less to stop now.

Maybe that's what I should do. Tell him I want to end it. But the thought of never speaking to him again hurts even worse.

The L-word? What is wrong with you? Can't you even say, in the privacy of your own head, that you might be – that you feel you could be—

'Oh, bugger.'

But that you can say out loud?

I decide not to mention any of the relationship-related stuff. Or the lunch date thing. It doesn't feel like the right conversation for the middle of the night, and I'm also mindful of Daisy's continued lectures about power dynamics within relationships, etc., etc., etc. Though since she always stays at Dan's place, and he never stays here, I'm not sure she's really picked the right hill to die on.

Worried about work. And I've
missed our Sunday video calls. X

I said I didn't mind – what else could I do? The client was offering so much money. And if Kieran had said no, it would have affected the pastry chef guy, Alex, or whatever he's called, and Ettore and Marcel. But in the aftermath of Dan's stupid supper club I've realised that I did mind. I minded very much.

> Video call now?

Sure. Hold on.

The faded, oversized band T-shirt I'm sleeping in can't be helped, but I try to wipe the worst of the grease off my face with my fingers, thankful for the low lighting. At least Kieran's face, when it appears on my screen, looks as bleary as I feel. His hair is sticking up at odd angles and his chin is shadowed with stubble, though he's wearing one of his seemingly endless supply of pristine white V-necked T-shirts. He rubs his eyes with the inside of his wrist, an oddly childlike gesture.

'Hey, Emma.' His smile is sleepy, lazy, and almost melts me into a hot, steamy puddle, despite the room temperature. 'I've missed our chats too. And I'm not missing any more of them. The client called today and asked us to do next Sunday as well, but I've said no.'

'Are you sure? What about the money? What about your friends from La Reine?'

He shrugs.

'It's no problem. There'll be other opportunities. Now, what's going on with your work?' His eyes widen. 'Is this to do with toilet-gate?'

Toilet-gate. My latest, and worst – to date – work disaster.

Last week, Mia, James and I had one of our rare invitations to Lauren's actual office to bask in the glory of Paige's physical presence for half an hour. We mainly go for the free biscuits. Mia and I were discussing the new idea that James has been given to write when we went into the ladies' loos. I was being quite . . . honest with my opinion. What I didn't realise was that Paige was in there too.

I knew she'd overheard. I could tell by the way she smiled at me. She looked like a particularly toothy shark (some species have up to 300 teeth at a time) that's just spotted its next meal.

'Yes, it is to do with toilet-gate: I had an email yesterday from Lauren. I'll try and get it up on my laptop and read it to you.'

I prop the phone against my water glass and pick my laptop off the floor.

'Is that . . . Robbie Williams, on your nightie?' Kieran asks. I can tell he's trying not to laugh.

'It's not a nightie, it's a T-shirt,' I say, pulling the duvet higher and strategically positioning my laptop in front of Robbie's face. 'Merch, actually. My mum went to one of his gigs and brought it back for me.' I clear my throat. 'Okay. Ready?'

'Lay it on me.'

'Bear in mind that Lauren emailed me the day before this, saying that the second draft of *Sexcapades* is in great shape and she was ready to trigger the first part of the advance payment.'

'Got it.'

I take a deep breath and start reading.

Hey, Emma,

Just a further update on *Sexcapades*. As you know, Mia was meant to be working on a book set on the International Space Station, but Paige has had another one of her totally brilliant ideas, which is to combine your book with the space station idea: the first orchestra on tour in space! With sex! When aliens make contact, the orchestra is sent to meet them as a sort of cultural exchange, and, of course, culture isn't the only thing that gets exchanged!! So basically, what you've done now but set in space instead of in the five-star resort, and with aliens to increase the spice level up to eleven. ALL THE SPICE. Since we're back to first draft status I won't now be able to accept the draft you sent me two weeks ago, so I won't be able to trigger the initial advance payment, unfortunately, but I promise I will trigger it on receipt of the first draft of the updated book. I'm sure it won't take you long, you superstar! We need the new draft before Christmas if the schedule isn't to be totally screwed.

PS This has absolutely nothing to do with Paige overhearing your comment about her newest idea being 'utterly ridiculous' and 'fifty shades of totally fucking mental,' so don't stress about it. She's a very forgiving person!

I shut the laptop and turn to look at Kieran.

'It's obvious what happened. Paige sent the email to Lauren and told her to pretend it was from her. All those exclamation marks and writing in capitals – it's pure Paige. "Very forgiving", my arse.'

'And is she allowed to do that? Delay the payment?'

'I think so. I'm going to have to dig out my contract again; I've not looked at it since I signed it, and that was three years ago now. No, four years.' Nearer five, if I'm being honest. Where the hell has my life gone? 'I might need to get some advice. The whole thing sucks.' Rage-tinged panic condenses into a hard, painful lump in my throat. 'It's a huge rewrite. I just don't know how I can possibly get it done in time. It's less than a month until Christmas.' In vain, I grope under my pillow for a tissue. 'Shit.'

'Hey,' Kieran says gently, 'don't cry, Ems. It'll be okay, I'm sure. You'll figure something out. And I'll help you any way I can.' He swears under his breath. 'But right now, I just wish that I could give you a hug. And maybe a handkerchief.'

'Found one.' Luckily, I've unearthed a wodge of crumpled tissues that had slipped down behind the mattress. 'I'd take the hug, though.' In a heartbeat. The thought of being enfolded in Kieran's arms threatens to reduce me to a bawling wreck – especially since I'm struggling to remember how his hands felt after all this time – so I take refuge in my extremely dusty tissues.

'I really wish someone would hurry up and invent that thing,' Kieran says.

'What thing?' I ask, emerging from the tissues.

'You know, the thing.' He groans and stifles a yawn. 'My brain is giving up. That thing that dissolves you into little floating granules and zips you across to another place and then reassembles you. That would solve all our problems. *Star Wars* thing.'

Light dawns.

'*Star Trek*, not *Star Wars*. You mean a transporter. And yes,' I sigh, 'it would be really handy.' My eyelids are growing heavy. 'But you haven't told me about what happened after the lunch event yesterday.'

'After?' he asks, frowning.

'The dessert disaster. Was the client angry?'

'Oh – yeah. No, it was fine.' Kieran grins suddenly, and even in the gloom of his apartment his face seems to light up. 'Alex was furious – making those spun sugar holly leaves is a pain in the arse – but we had extra. And one of the teenage waiters was a snotty little jerk, so seeing him covered in cake gave us all a laugh.'

I put both hands over my face to cover an enormous yawn.

'Poor Emma.' His voice is so gentle. 'You're tired.'

I can't help myself. I immediately imagine him holding me and murmuring those words into my hair.

'You'll feel better after some sleep. Perhaps we should say goodnight,' Kieran suggests.

'Not yet. You haven't told me why you can't sleep. We can't just talk about my problems.'

'I've no problems, not really. Just . . .' He pauses. 'Just worried about my dad, as usual. Not that there's been any change. Honestly, now, we should both try to get some sleep, or we'll feel shite in the morning.'

'It is the morning,' I remind him.

He groans.

'I mean proper morning, not middle of the night masquerading as morning.' He tilts his head as he looks at me. 'You needn't worry about me. Go to sleep; you must be exhausted.'

'Alright.' I dither: should I blow him a kiss, or not? I decide not. If he didn't blow one back, I don't think I could cope. 'Thanks for chatting, Kieran. Night.'

'Night, Ems.'

I lie back down in the bed and reach for my phone to turn it off. The three dots have shown up, as if Kieran is texting me now. But they disappear, and don't return.

I start to message him. *What were you going to say?* But I hit delete instead of send. He's right. I am exhausted.

Kieran

Three dots.

What was she going to text me?

I put my phone down. Pick it up again. Put it down. It's too late to tell her now. I still don't even know if I should. I turn out the light and pray for sleep.

Chapter Twelve

Kieran

'*Dear Emma, good afternoon from the Arctic wasteland that is currently Paris in December. I enjoyed the text messages yesterday very much. Your description of a typical day in the life of an erotic novelist reduced me to tears-running-down-my-face, unable-to-breathe, hysterical laughter. Seriously, I almost wet myself. Your messages should come with a warning label: not recommended for reading on a packed metro. Though on the other hand, people were keen to get as far away from the clearly deranged* étranger, *so maybe I should read the next instalment on the metro too.*'

I pause the voice memo recording, trying to work out how to phrase the next bit.

There's something I need to tell you.

Something happened that I want to tell you about.

I never did tell you why I couldn't sleep the other night, and I want to.

My phone flashes up a notification: my brother wants to video chat. Caught between relief and the sudden ratcheting-up of tension that comes with every call from home, I answer.

'Brendan. Everything okay?'

'Don't worry – no emergency. Dad's at home. Now a good time?' he asks.

'Sure,' I reply, relaxing a little. 'No lunch shift today, so I've a later start. I've been doing a bit of sightseeing.' Montmartre this morning; I've done my tourism, and eaten my packed lunch, and sent a couple of photos to Marianne and François, my old colleagues from Roubaix. Now I'm sitting on a stone step just below the Sacré-Cœur basilica, the cold beating through my jeans and numbing my arse and the backs of my thighs, the city spread out before me, rain-washed and glinting in the pale December sunshine. I squint at my phone screen and take in my brother's appearance. 'You know someone's crayoned a goatee and moustache on your face, right?'

'It's pirate day at Colm's school. I'm a parent helper, and the fake beard I bought gave me a rash, so I improvised. I've an eye patch too—' he holds up a square of black plastic '—but it's break time at the moment, so I've been allowed to take the bloody thing off.' He briefly swivels his phone around to give me a view of the empty classroom: it's been lavishly decorated with skull-and-crossbones flags and printed-out images of pirate ships, inexpertly coloured-in.

I wince at the sound of children shrieking and squealing in the playground outside.

'How many of them are out there? It sounds like a bloodbath.'

Brendan glances out of the window. 'Letting them bring plastic cutlasses was probably a mistake. Not my problem, though, thank—' He catches himself just before swearing. 'Thank goodness. So, I've good news, and not so good news. The good news is, we've been given a date for Dad to start the immunotherapy. End of January.'

'That's great. And the not so good news?'

'Dad's losing a lot of weight. He's no appetite. Won't eat anything Mum cooks. Though, you know, that's hardly surprising.' He pulls a face.

'I understand. Poor Dad.'

Our father was always the cook when we were growing up – I got my passion from him. Mum's cooking, if she *had* to cook for some reason, was utilitarian. It kept us alive. That was about the best you could say of it.

'It's pretty common for people to lose their appetite with all the drugs and so on, isn't it?' I ask. 'Have you talked to the doctors?'

'I'm always talking to the bloody doctors,' Brendan says loudly. He looks around, guilty, and lowers his voice. 'They've given us some powder to make up into a drink for him, but it's horrible. He won't drink that either. And he's getting so thin, Kieran. Even since you saw him in October, he looks like an old man—'

My brother, my built-like-a-tank, rugby-playing, one-of-the-lads brother, turns his face away so I won't see the tears in his eyes. The train-track rattle of my guilt forces its way to the front of my mind. *You shouldn't be here, you shouldn't be here, you shouldn't be here...*

But I don't want to be there. That's the truth, even if I can barely admit it to myself. Whenever I think about the situation back home, I'm sick with shame and disgust. Shame at my dad for being so shrunken and weak, for smelling of illness and medication. Disgust at myself for not being able to cope with seeing him like that.

You're a thirty-two-year-old man, Kieran. Will you grow a pair of balls, for fuck's sake?

'Bren—' I begin.

He interrupts me, his voice falsely bright, and my impulse to confess dissolves.

'So, I've been meaning to ask,' he says, 'have you some simple recipes I can follow? I want to make something delicious that might tempt him.'

'I have, actually. I've been teaching Emma to cook, so I came up with a few things that would be easy for her to do. I'll email them to you.'

'Grand. And how is it going with her? You're still talking?'

'Every day, in some shape or form.'

'It must be frustrating, though,' he observes.

'You have no idea.'

'How long can it go on, with the two of you never actually seeing each other? Zero chance of a kiss, let alone a—'

'You're in a classroom, remember!'

My brother grins as someone in the school playground rings a bell.

'Do you need to go?' I ask.

'I've a few minutes yet. They all have to go to the bathroom after break.'

'I need your advice, then.' I take a deep breath. 'Sunday night, someone kissed me. Just put her arm around my neck and kissed me.'

'What?' Brendan's eyes open wide. 'Who? How? Did you kiss her back?'

'Maybe, a little bit.'

He shakes his head. 'Kieran, you can't kiss someone a little bit. You either kissed her or you didn't.'

I scowl at him. 'Fine. I kissed her. But only for a moment, only until I came to my senses. It was Alex, the pastry chef that works at La Reine. The last two Sundays we've catered these private Christmas lunches, together with a couple of the other guys from the restaurant, and then last Sunday, after we'd got everything finally cleaned up and the others had gone, we went out on to the balcony to have a glass of wine.'

The memory is still vivid. The city, glittering with a thousand points of light. The damp, freezing air. The warmth of Alex's body after she'd pulled me towards her. The woody fragrance of her perfume.

'I did kiss her back. I was tired, and I'd been drinking, and Paris is so damned romantic . . .' I break off, swearing softly. 'But then suddenly I was imagining that I was kissing Emma. I pulled away and told her it wasn't happening. I told her about Emma. And she was, you know, okay with it. She didn't get angry or anything. Just said that she thought we'd be good together, and pointed out that she was in Paris and Emma wasn't. And might never be.' I sigh. 'Then she said goodnight and left.' I try to think back over the four months or so Alex and I have been cooking together. 'I mean, I asked her if she wanted to share the wine with me, so maybe she got the wrong idea.'

Brendan is shaking his head.

'What?'

'She probably thinks you've been flirting with her.'

I give an outraged scoff. 'I do not flirt.'

'You do so flirt. You can't help it.' My brother laughs at my expression. 'Kieran, I love you, but you're a charming fucking bastard. Too charming for your own good. When you let your guard down with people, there's a way that you have of looking at them. You've probably been smouldering at the poor woman without even realising it.'

'I do not smoulder.'

Brendan just gazes at me, one eyebrow raised.

'Fuck. Well, should I tell Emma that I kissed Alex?'

'Do you want to end things with her?'

'No!'

'Then don't tell her. It was an accident. A misunderstanding. You're in the situation you're in, and there's no point making Emma miserable just to salve your own conscience.' Brendan gives me a look that makes me wonder if he's more perceptive than I give him credit for, then glances away. 'I've got to go. The little—' he catches himself again '—the little darlings are coming back. Hey, sweetheart!' My nephew, Colm, cannons into his father. 'Wave to Uncle Kieran.' As Colm waves, Brendan adds hurriedly, 'I think you need to figure out what's going on with the two of you, though. Call me when you can. We need to talk about Christmas – holidays, and such. Me and Niamh could really do with a break.'

'Okay, I'll call you, but—'

He's gone.

Damn.

I stand and stamp my feet to get some life into them, sling my bag over my shoulder and get on my bike. I'll have to call him back, and sooner rather than later. My own fault. I'd talked in October about returning home again just after Christmas, assuming the restaurant would close as usual for a week or so at the beginning of January. But that was before Monsieur Arnaud had become quite so ... erratic, is that the word? Effusive one moment, irritable the next. Staying at the restaurant all hours or turning up late. Despairing about the future of La Reine, or cocky as the cock on the proverbial dunghill. He questioned my commitment when I asked him about taking a holiday in January, more or less threatening to replace me with someone who doesn't ever take a break.

I have a sudden brainwave: use the money I've earned from the lunches to fund some respite care for Dad, so that Mum and Brendan and Niamh will be able to take some time off. It's a great idea, and I'd feel better about myself if I hadn't been hoping to use the cash to pay for Emma to visit me in Paris.

I weave my way in and out of the traffic, following the route almost automatically, heading south so I'll end up crossing the Seine at Pont Neuf. In my head I continue composing the voice message I'd started earlier.

I miss you, Emma. Sometimes I think something magical happened, that moment outside the Gare du Nord. Somehow, we got bound together, and there's an invisible cord, and – and – no, *a – a special bond, which keeps us –* no. *Something magical happened, and there was a spark,* yes, *a spark of like, intense, intense – like, a flame, that burns even brighter now that we're – that we're . . .*

Ah, bollocks.

Why is this so hard?

Soon enough, I'm pushing open the back door of the restaurant. I'm expecting the usual anxiety-tinged atmosphere – everyone is walking on eggshells around our executive chef, and I'm nervous about seeing Alex again. To my surprise, the staff – there's no Arnaud so far – are gathered around the long table at one side of the room, craning their necks to peer at a newspaper spread out across the surface.

'Kieran, *viens ici*!' Alex beckons me over. The others make space, and I bend over to study and translate the restaurant review she's pointing at.

It's full of praise for La Reine. The reviewer compliments everything, from the front of house to the cleanliness of the toilets, but he is ecstatic about the food. In particular, he is rendered speechless with delight by the fresh take on the classic chicken supreme: the morel- and herb-infused cream, the stuffing that has been added to the chicken breast, the roasted seasonal vegetables that dress the plate, the presentation – everything is superb, delicious, exquisite.

'*C'est ton plat,*' Marcel says, slapping me on the back. '*Félicitations!*' It's your dish. Congratulations. My name might not have made the paper – everything is credited to Monsieur Arnaud, as it should be – but my food has. I have to tell Emma.

After taking a photo of the review, I escape from my colleagues, duck out into the small courtyard behind La Reine and pull my phone out of my pocket.

There's a text from Emma waiting for me. Texts.

> Hey, K! Hope you're having a lovely day. Still raining and freezing here in London but the forecast for Paris is sunny, so hope it's accurate. No fun descriptions of my disastrous work life for you today, but a question. You remember on Sunday I went to Dan's absolute car crash of a supper club? You must remember the terrible food I described. However, there was one thing I didn't mention. There was a guy at there, and we started talking, and he wants to take me for lunch.

I sit down heavily on the steps that lead into the courtyard as my exhilaration evaporates.

> I love this thing between us. You know I do. But I don't know what it is, other than something I can't properly name. I'd like it to be more, and yet, and yet, and yet.

> So what do you think? Should
> I go? I don't want to hurt you,
> Kieran. Not for the world.

I hesitate with my thumbs poised over the screen, envisaging different responses, different futures.

Don't go. I love you.

Don't go. I've decided to quit and come back to London.

I'm moving back to Ireland, so don't go on a date – come and live with me in Cork instead. I love you.

The slam of a taxi door makes me jump. Arnaud is making his way down the stairs into the courtyard. I text back hurriedly.

> I want you to be happy, Em.
> If you think he might make
> you happy, then go. Xx

Chapter Thirteen

Emma

I wanted him to say no.

Actually, what I really wanted was for him to say, *No, you mustn't go on that date, because I love you, Emma Christmas, in fact I'd willingly die for you, and if I have to fight for you, like,* physically *fight for you, maybe with a sword, or by duelling at dawn, then I will.*

Unlikely, I suppose. And duelling has been out of fashion for nearly two hundred years. Still, he could have said *No, please don't do it.*

We've not communicated much since then. He texted me this morning, to be fair. Said he hoped it goes well. I texted back, one word. *Cheers.*

Such a way with words. It's lucky I'm a writer.

The bedroom door swings wide and Daisy appears, bearing two cups of tea. 'Knock knock!'

I make space in the bed. She hands me a tea and gets under the duvet next to me and sticks her icy, frozen feet on top of my legs, making me flinch.

'Bloody hell, Daze!' I exclaim, dabbing at the tea I've just spilt on the duvet. 'You've got no circulation, you know that, right? I'm amazed your feet don't just fall off. Also, saying "knock knock" when you're already in the room is not the same as knocking before you come in.'

Daisy dismisses my concerns with a wave of her hand. 'You've got nothing I've not seen before. God, it is so cold.'

'Too cold. I think I might cancel this lunch. I've got both

literal cold feet – though not as cold as yours, clearly – and metaphorical cold feet.'

I'm not exaggerating. The tension in my stomach is beginning to build into a tight knot of nausea and I've started to panic-poo. It's only nine-thirty in the morning, I've not eaten anything since last night, but I've already been to the loo twice.

'You'll enjoy it when you get there,' Daisy says. It's one of her favourite sayings, and she always wheels it out when I'm trying to get out of some social event or other. She'll probably have it inscribed on my tombstone. *Heaven. You'll enjoy it when you get there.*

'Yeah, maybe. What time are you and Dan off on your mini-break?'

She sighs happily. 'Couple of hours. I'm so excited. Can you believe it? Me, on a mini-break, like an actual grown-up.'

'We are grown-ups. A few more months and we'll both be thirty.' That's a depressing thought. For me, at least. Daisy seems more focused on her weekend away.

'Look at this.' She thrusts her phone in front of my face and starts swiping through images. 'It's the hotel website. It's so posh. Marble bathrooms with rain showers and artisanal toiletries. A tasting menu in the restaurant. A spa. A turn-down service.' She squeals with excitement. 'Ooh – they probably leave little chocolates on your pillow. If they do, I'll save them up and bring them back for you.'

An unwelcome thought flits through my mind.

'Dan's going to a lot of effort. Do you think he's going to propose?'

'Propose? Don't be ridiculous. Yes, it's a five-star hotel, and yes, he's booked me a holistic wellness ritual at the spa tomorrow afternoon, but that's just Dan. Besides, we've only been going out for a few months.' Daisy's words say one thing, but her face ... She looks self-conscious. Flushed with anticipation, as Paige Adams Pereira might say. 'But I didn't come in here to talk about Dan. We need to focus on you, and your lunch with Hugo.'

Hugo. The name sets my teeth on edge. But perhaps that's unfair. Perhaps he is as charming and intelligent as he seemed the other night, when I was slightly drunk. Quite drunk, if I'm being honest. Okay, extremely drunk. Still, this reluctance might just be my nerves talking. Though my nerves struggle to get a word in with Daisy.

'... and I think that electric-blue dress will look amazing, casual but also sexy, and I'll do your make-up, obviously, but first, your hair, I reckon—' She breaks off as I clamber out of bed. 'You okay, Ems?'

'Yeah, just need the toilet. Back in a sec.'

I glance at my watch again. 12.50. Hugo is twenty minutes late now, and there's only so much longer I can look at the menu. I can't face another complimentary breadstick. I take a sip of tap water, brush the crumbs from the paper tablecloth and try to stay calm. He's probably just running late. Maybe there's some screw-up on the Underground?

I check the Transport for London app: good service on all lines.

So, not a problem with the tube. Suddenly too hot, I pull off my cardi and push up the sleeves of my dress, subtly checking myself out in the mirrored wall panel. Daisy was right: the dress looks great. Clingy in all the right places, and cut low enough to make my boobs look good without offering them up on a plate. I'd want to date me, if I were Hugo. So why isn't he here?

It's 12.55 now. There could be lots of other reasons he's late. Maybe he's had an urgent phone call. Maybe he's had an accident. Maybe he's dead. Is it too much to expect him to text me? I check the settings on my phone. Wifi on. Bluetooth on. 5G with plenty of signal.

One of the waiters looks as though he's thinking about heading my way. I bend over the menu again as if lost in thought. Maybe I should phone a friend? I could call James. Even if he's not in, I can pretend he's there and have a conversation with his voicemail.

It's nearly one p.m.

Shit. Have I been stood up?

Feeling my face flush, I'm starting to gather my things when I hear my name.

'Emma, I'm so sorry.' Hugo, looking red and sweaty in head-to-toe Lycra, dumps his backpack and cycle helmet next to the table and sits down. 'Traffic is absolutely insane, bloody nightmare.'

'Oh. I'm guessing you cycled?'

'Only thing to do, coming out here to the back of beyond,' he says with a laugh.

It's White City, I want to reply, *not Mars. It's Zone 2.* But he's still talking.

'. . . and given the distance I didn't want to shell out for a taxi, and have you *seen* the price of Underground tickets recently? Daylight bloody robbery. Not that it matters: we'll go to a restaurant in central, next time. You look great, by the way. Really hot.'

I almost say 'not as hot as you' – he's started fanning himself with the menu – but I'm not sure he'll get the joke.

'Thank you. I—'

'What wine shall we have?' Hugo scans the drinks menu, his lips gradually pursing into a look of disapproval. 'Not a great list.'

'That's okay, I generally don't drink in the day, apart from special occasions. It sends me to sleep.'

'God, how puritanical of you!' Hugo smiles and pats my hand. 'Besides, this is a special occasion, so I insist.'

'Um, okay. I prefer red, then.'

'Hmm.' He examines the wine list some more, flipping back and forth, then turns to look for the waiter. For a horrible moment I think he's about to click his fingers. Instead, he waves. 'Excuse me!' His voice is penetrating, especially since there's hardly anyone here.

I shoot an apologetic glance at the waiter.

'Yes, sir?'

'A bottle of the Monte Tondo Soave Classico.' Hugo turns back to me as the waiter disappears. 'Now, let's have a look at the menu. Ooh, grilled sardines – I think we should have those as a starter. I do love grilled sardines. Though they have calamari, too. Mmm. Tricky.'

He's still studying the menu when the waiter returns.

With a bottle of what is clearly *white* wine.

What the hell? I decide I'm going to drink it anyway. I've a feeling I'm going to need it.

'Bugger! You stupid – arse!' The car that's just sped through a puddle, drenching me with freezing rainwater, continues on its way oblivious to my outrage.

I feel as if I might cry.

It's dark, and freezing, and I'm already sodden because I'm walking home from my stupid lunch date and I forgot to bring an umbrella. And now my beloved Mary Janes are full of puddle.

Westfield is open. The bright lights spill across the wet pavements, blurring, beckoning. I can window-shop, at least. Sniffing back tears, I turn towards the shopping centre, but as soon as I'm inside I realise it was a mistake. Yes, it's warm. And yes, the Christmas decorations are beautiful. But it's crammed full of happy families happily buying things, or happily eating and drinking together, all soundtracked to the same Christmas songs that seem to have been playing on a continuous loop since October. Noddy Holder and Slade warble about how Christmas is here.

Everybody's having fun, are they, Noddy? *Everybody?*

And then Elvis starts crooning about how he's going to have a blue, blue Christmas, and I'm thinking, you and me both, Elvis, and then my phone buzzes: a text from Kieran.

How did it go this afternoon? xx

I sit down on the end of a bench and stare at my screen.

If Daisy were here, she'd probably tell me that being angry, sad, hungry and tipsy is not the right state in which to call anyone, let alone someone you've recently decided you're probably in love with, and who you've wanted to sleep with for even longer. But she isn't here. She's off on a mini-break at a luxury spa hotel, most likely drinking champagne in a bubble bath by now. Besides, I really want to hear his voice.

George Michael's dulcet tones drift across the crowds of shoppers. He's going to give his heart to somebody special.

I bring up Kieran's number and hit the call button.

He answers instantly.

'Emma. I was really hoping you'd phone.'

'Is now a good time?'

'Fifty minutes until we open for dinner, so I can take a little bit of a break. Hold on.' He pauses, and I can hear noise of the kitchen receding. 'Right, I'm in the courtyard now. How are you? How was the, um, lunch?'

'Horrible.'

'Horrible food,' he asks, 'or—'

'Horrible everything.'

There's no reply.

'Kieran? Are you still there?'

'Sorry – I mean, I'm so sorry it didn't go well.'

'It was an unmitigated disaster. Nearly three hours of my life I won't get back. Not to mention the money.'

'He made you pay?' Kieran sounds incredulous.

'We split it. Which I wouldn't have minded if I'd had any say in what we ate or drank, but he just picked what he liked. I said I didn't like drinking much at lunch and preferred red; he ordered a bottle of white. And an Irish coffee, even though he had to cycle home. I said I wasn't that hungry, and I wasn't because I got so nervous this morning and my stomach—' I break off. Even in my frazzled state, I recognise that regaling the object of my desire with a description of my panic-poo episodes might not be a good idea. 'Well, that doesn't matter, but the point is, he ordered three courses. All really heavy things, or things I don't like, or things I don't want to eat, like calamari. I barely ate anything. Do you know how intelligent squid and octopuses are? Octopodes, I mean.'

'Octopodes?'

'It's the correct plural of octopus. People think it's octopi, but it isn't, because it's – it's – it's thingy.' My brain, fogged with rage and alcohol, complains as I rummage for the correct term. 'Ancient Greek. They like to play.'

'The ancient Greeks?'

'No, the octopodes. And squids are as clever as dogs. I wouldn't eat a dog. Would you eat a dog?'

There's a sound on the other end of the line as if Kieran is stifling a laugh.

'Dogs don't figure much in French cuisine,' he says. 'But what about this fella's conversation? Was he entertaining, at least?'

'Only if you count listening to someone talk about themselves the entire time as entertainment. I could probably write his biography now. I know all about his family – apparently he's descended from someone who once slept with someone who slept with Henry VIII.'

'That's probably a pretty wide field. Still, impressive.' Kieran gives a low whistle. 'Hope you curtseyed.'

'Oh, he would have loved that. Anyway, we had his whole family history for starters. Then, for our main course, we moved on to a list of how he's been hard done by in various ways. He didn't get into Oxford, even though his parents forked out for one of the most expensive schools in the country. He didn't get a first, because the university he did end up at failed to recognise his genius. He didn't get into any of his top choice of barristers' chambers, because they discriminated against him for being too posh, or too tall, or too hairy, or something like that. To be honest, I'd tuned out a bit by then.'

'Can't say I blame you. What did he follow up with for the dessert course?'

'Possessions. What he has, and what it cost. His flat, his sports car, his top-of-the-range bike, his enormous ultra-high-definition television. He kept referring to it as "sixty-five inches of pure pleasure".'

Kieran bursts out laughing. 'I'm sorry, but this guy is clearly compensating for something. I reckon you've dodged a bullet, seriously. He is a knob, but he obviously doesn't have much of a—'

'No. Probably not.' I laugh too. Kieran always makes me feel better about stuff. 'Dan's such a nice guy, I don't know how he's friends with someone like that.'

In the background, Wham! have given way to Mariah Carey. All she wants for Christmas is you.

'But even if he had been perfect,' I blurt out, 'even if he'd been kind and generous and interesting and looked like a male model, it wouldn't have made any difference, because – because—'

Part of my brain is screaming at me to shut up, but the rest of me is too confused by wine and lack of food and raging sexual desire to listen.

'—because I really wanted it to be you, Kieran. I wanted it to be you, sitting opposite me this afternoon. I wanted it to be you.'

There's a beat. A silence.

Oh, no. Oh no oh no oh no. He doesn't feel the same and now I've made it awkward.

Blood flames into my face. Maybe I can recover the situation. Make it seem like a joke.

'Obviously, I still wouldn't have wanted the calamari, or the Lycra, or the little patches of sweat that his elbows left on the table,' I say quickly, 'and that whole Henry VIII thing was a bit of a turn-off to be honest; I mean, the guy chopped off the heads of two of his wives, plus a lot of other people's heads, and—'

'I wish I'd been there too, Emma,' Kieran interrupts me.

It's my turn to pause.

'You do?'

'Of course I do. This long-distance thing . . . it's killing me. But if that's all we can manage right now, I'll take it, because the alternative is far worse.' I hear him sigh. 'When I said I didn't mind about you going on this lunch date, I lied.'

My heart leaps, and, suddenly, it feels like Christmas.

Chapter Fourteen

Kieran

'Kieran, may we speak for a moment?'

It's nearly eleven-thirty at night, and we're only just getting the kitchen back to its normal state of perfection after an exceptionally busy dinner service. I'm about to say no – whatever it is, surely it can wait? – but a glance at Ettore's face changes my mind. I've seen serious Ettore, happy Ettore and drunk-sexy-dancing Ettore – a few of us ended up at a nightclub the other evening and his interpretation of Prince's *Kiss* drew quite the audience – but this is the first time I've ever seen him anxious.

'Sure.'

We move together into Monsieur Arnaud's office; empty, since he's already left.

'What's on your mind?'

He shuts the door of the office.

'I might be wrong. I hope I am, but I think not. The stock – it is not right. I have counted and counted again, but there are bottles missing. Just like before.'

He means the theft a few months back that ended up with one of the kitchen porters being sacked.

'Which bottles?'

'No whole case, this time, but . . .' He makes a gesture, like someone picking flowers: one from over here, another from over there, a third from a different location entirely. 'He takes one bottle from this case. Two from that case. But altogether . . .' Ettore shrugs. 'He knows the good stuff, our thief.'

'What's been taken exactly?'

Nothing if not methodical, Ettore brings a list out of his pocket. I scan the carefully written details. He's not wrong. Vintage, all of it: wine, champagne, cognac.

'Ah, bollocks,' I murmur. 'We're going to need to replace this, especially the champagne. This week of all weeks.' The week running up to Christmas. One of the busiest weeks in our calendar. 'Shite.'

'Exactly,' agrees Ettore. '*Merda.*'

'And there's no possibility that the bottles have just been misplaced, or stored somewhere else?'

'*Assolutamente, no.* You know me: everything has its place, because I put it there myself. Even so, to be sure, I have scoured the cellar. These bottles—' he flicks the list I'm still holding with one finger '—have been taken.'

'Have you told Monsieur Arnaud?'

For the first time, Ettore hesitates.

'No,' he says eventually. 'You remember the way he was before. Blaming the porter – it was wrong. The porter could not steal the wine. He is not—' he huffs, searching for the phrase, and switches to French '—*il n'y avait pas accès.*'

'No,' I agree. 'I didn't see how he could have had access either. Not to the wine cellar.'

We both stare at the list for a bit.

'Okay,' I say. 'Okay, here's what we're going to do. You're going to go to the wine merchant and replace the champagne with the same, or similar. And see what cognac he's got. If he has something particularly interesting, tell him we're thinking of stocking it. See if he'll give us a bottle on the cheap.' Ettore looks confused, so I clarify. 'For a good price. We need to bait our trap.'

'Ah . . .' The sommelier nods.

'And I, in the meantime, will go shopping for a miniature camera.' I fold up the list and give it back to him. 'Keep hold of this but don't tell anyone else about it. Well,' I add, 'you can tell Marcel, obviously, but otherwise . . .'

Ettore taps his nose

'I understand. Mother is the word. I go to the *caviste* in the morning. Between us, we catch the thief.' He nods at me. 'The right one, this time. *Bonne nuit*, Kieran.'

'Thanks, Ettore. *Bonne nuit*.'

***

Dear Emma,

I'm back home now, it's just after half past midnight, and I'm sitting on the couch writing you an email, because my eyes are too tired to look at the little letters on my phone keyboard, and my throat is sore from shouting in a noisy kitchen. Hopefully you'll decide an email is cool and retro and 'old-skool', and not a sign of me getting middle-aged – though spelling school with a k might well be. Maybe I shouldn't tell you I'm drinking Fervex, the French equivalent of Lemsip, right now.

I break off to take a sip of the hot liquid and pick up the Christmas card that arrived from Emma this morning and reread it, even though I know what it says pretty much by heart.

To Kieran,
Merry Christmas / Joyeux Noël!
Our first Christmas 'together' –
the first of many, I hope.
With love,
(it feels so strange writing that –
strange, but exciting too!)
Emma xoxoxo

PS the 'o's are hugs, not sure if that's a
thing in Ireland/France/Canada

She's included a photo of herself. A snap from one of those self-printing cameras by the looks of it; a Polaroid, or something similar. A small rectangle, slightly grainy, showing Emma in an emerald-green coat somewhere outside, laughing, glancing back at the camera as if she is just on the point of turning away. The breeze has caught her ebony hair and she's got one hand raised, tucking a loose strand behind her ear. She looks so . . . so completely *alive*. If the photo started talking to me, I'd be no more than mildly surprised. The same tug is there, the same fizz of excitement I felt nearly six months ago now, that morning at the Gare du Nord. I drink some more Fervex and pick up the laptop again.

Thank you for the photo – I love it! Best Christmas present I'm going to get this year, I'm sure. My family have given up trying to find gifts I like – I'm impossible to buy for, apparently! – and usually resort to book tokens. Or socks. Or puncture repair kits. As for my colleagues . . . the atmosphere at La Reine isn't very festive right now. In fact, I've started writing a poem about it. Or knocking off someone else's poem, if I'm being honest. Please imagine me clearing my throat and standing up to declaim:

'Twas the week before Christmas, and down at La Reine,
Some bottles of booze have gone missing again.
And who is the culprit? I haven't a clue,
But me and Ettore know just what to do.

What do you think? It took me long enough to write four fairly crap lines; I've no idea how you manage to produce entire books. Ettore is our sommelier, by the way – one of the mates I went to that club with the other night. I'm sure I've mentioned him before. He discovered the missing bottles. Champagne and brandy mostly – our thief is a connoisseur. More on our cognac conundrum when I have something to report.

My brother, who has to stick his oar in whether he's been asked to or not, texted me photos of a magazine article yesterday entitled 'How to Keep Long-Distance Love Alive'. Suggestions include:

– Checking in each day.
– Virtual dates.
– Telling your partner you miss him or her.

Just for the record, and in case you don't know already: I miss you, Emma.

One of the other suggestions was to send each other flirty or dirty texts, or sexting, as I believe the youngsters call it. Therefore, please find below a close-up photo of my jaw, which one previous girlfriend described as 'kind of hot, given the right lighting'.

I break off to look in my photos for a shot of my face. After cropping it, until it's only showing about an inch of my jaw, I attach it to the email.

Play your cards right and I might send you a portrait of my earlobe next time.

I drain the Fervex, pull a face – it's grown cold – and yawn widely. I really do need to get some sleep.

Have to go to bed before I faceplant the laptop. I'll call you tomorrow, at some more civilised hour. I really do miss you, Emma. Love, Kieran.

I bring the cursor above the 'send' and my finger hovers over the mouse pad button, but I don't click.

PS. One of the other tips for a long-distance relationship is to dream about the future. So I may as well tell you now: my dream is for us to live together in the same country. Actually, my dream is for you to move to Paris, right now. I want to show you the city. I want to walk hand in hand with you along the Seine, and climb the Eiffel Tower, and visit Notre-Dame and do all the tourist things. I want to watch you light up in delight at the Christmas decorations in Galeries

Lafayette and the Christmas trees in Place Vendôme. Then I want to show you my Paris, the city I've discovered in the last few months. Then I want to cook for you. Then I want to take you to bed, Emma Christmas. I want to tear your clothes off and explore every inch of your body and make you sigh with pleasure. And then I want to wake up the next morning and do it all over again. That's my dream. Love you.

I pause again.

PPS. Seriously, don't just come and visit. Especially now, after Daisy's news. Move here instead. I know it feels like a risk, and I know you're not big on risk, but you can trust me. I promise. Still love you. Night night. Xx

I hit 'send' and shut the laptop and push myself up off the couch. But I've barely taken three steps when the entryphone buzzes.

I ignore it and head to the bathroom. It buzzes again, insistent.

'Oh, for fuck's sake . . . *Qui est là?*' I bark into the phone.

'*C'est moi, Arnaud.*' His voice is gravelly.

Fuck.

'Chef? Are you okay?'

'Can I come up?'

I check my watch. 'It's nearly one in the morning . . .'

'Just for a moment. I just need to ask you something.'

Left with no option, I buzz him in, unlatch the door and make for the coffee machine. It takes my boss a few minutes to climb the stairs; when he pushes open the front door, I hand him an espresso.

'What can I do for you, chef?'

'May I . . . ?' He gestures towards the armchair.

'Sure.' I sit opposite him, balanced on the edge of the couch, trying to convey through my body language that I'm not in the mood for a long chat.

'Are we alone?' Arnaud asks.

'Completely.' I gesture to my tiny apartment.

Despite my reassurance, his gaze darts around the

open-plan, minimally furnished living and kitchen area as if he's expecting someone to leap out. From inside the fridge-freezer, perhaps. The whites of his eyes are bloodshot.

'Are you okay, chef?' I ask.

'*Oui. Oui, bien sûr. Mais* . . .' He leans closer, and for the first time I smell the alcohol on his breath. 'I think someone is trying to steal from me.'

I'm about to ask whether he's talking about the missing champagne when he adds, 'Steal my recipes. My genius. Steal them and sell them to another chef.' He leans closer still and drops his voice almost to a whisper. 'I think there is a spy in the kitchen. I need you to help me, *tu comprends*? To watch. To listen.'

What can I say?

'Yes, I understand. I'll keep an eye out.'

I stand. To my relief, so does he. '*Merci, merci*.'

I manage to usher him towards the front door, but at the threshold he turns back to me. 'And we will talk again, yes?'

'Yes, of course. And I'll see you tomorrow.'

For an instant, he looks vague. 'Tomorrow . . .?'

'At the restaurant.'

'Yes. Yes, of course. Thank you.' He clutches my hand. '*Bonne nuit*.'

'Goodnight, chef.'

I watch from the landing as he makes his way unsteadily down the stairs. When I can't hear the sound of his tread any more, I retreat to my flat and bolt the door, then pick up the coffee cups from the table and put them in the sink. Pause for a minute, leaning on the countertop, eyes closed, thinking about how good my bed is going to feel.

But misgivings assail me. Grabbing my keys, I race down the stairs after him.

The street is empty. Hopefully he found a taxi. I hope to God he didn't drive here.

The frigid air makes me shiver and wakes me up a bit. I'm still going to order that mini-camera for the cellar.

I've a feeling, though, that it's going to confirm what I'm just starting to suspect.

Chapter Fifteen

Emma

'Good morning, chief bridesmaid,' Daisy trills, dumping an armful of wedding magazines on her side of our big work/dining table and making a beeline for one of the two chocolate-filled advent calendars propped up on the mantelpiece. 'Aw, it's a little reindeer today!' She holds the chocolate out for inspection briefly before popping it into her mouth and closing her eyes. 'Mmm. God, I love Christmas.'

'Not Christmas yet,' I remind her. 'Advent. Hence advent calendar. The clue is in the name.' I add a few more words to the sentence I'm typing and hit full stop. 'The Holly and the Ivy' floats in from the radio in the kitchen; I love Christmas music enough not to mind it even when I'm trying to write. 'Any chance of a tea? I've been working since seven.'

Daisy presses her hands together in supplication. 'Anything, if you promise not to start complaining again about people who celebrate Christmas in October and then take down the decorations on Boxing Day!'

She grins and heads to the kitchen and I crane my neck to peruse her latest stash of magazines. *Your Big Day. Wonderful Weddings. Wow! Weddings. Beautiful Brides. Bride & Home. Bride & Horse* – niche. *Bridal Hair, Dream Bridal Dresses, Everything Bride*. There's another pile of very similar-sounding titles upstairs in her bedroom. She's only been engaged for a couple of weeks; I wonder how long she's secretly been wanting to fill the house with a tsunami of articles on 'elegant table topiary' and 'gift list etiquette'.

Daisy puts a mug of tea down next to my laptop.

'Lovely, thanks, Daze. Do they have groom equivalents of these magazines? Like, *Groom & Home*? Or *Gorgeous Grooms*? Or *Groomal Hair*?'

Her face scrunches up as she thinks about this. 'Is "groomal" even a word?'

'Well, it should be, surely? If something can be bridal, why not groomal?'

'Fair point.' She sits down in front of her magazines. 'I didn't see any groom magazines in Smith's. Maybe they're not a thing.'

'Maybe we should start one. We could call it *Everything Groom*. Corner the market. There must be some grooms who want to buy magazines full of pictures of—' I pull *Wow!Weddings* towards me and flip it open '—floral arrangements and multi-tiered cakes. Or who want to read articles on "seating arrangements for fractious families".'

Daisy giggles. 'If Dan is anything to go by, then I'm guessing *Everything Groom* is going to have a really small readership. He seems to think a wedding is no different from inviting your best mates to the pub, and that the whole day will basically organise itself.' She stretches out her left hand and admires the enormous diamond that's now adorning the fourth finger. 'He does have excellent taste in jewellery, though.'

'And in women.' I link my fingers into hers across the table. 'I'm so happy for you, Daisy. Really.'

'You don't think I'm making a mistake?'

'Definitely not. Dan's lovely. And you've been going round in a little glow of delight ever since you got back from the mini-break.'

Her smile fades. 'I just wish you could move in with us too.'

'I don't. It would be weird. Besides, give it another couple of months and you'll probably have turned into a total Bridezilla. I'll be quite happy to go home after a day of wedding planning and leave Dan to deal with you.'

'Bridezilla, *moi*?' Daisy exclaims in mock outrage before bursting into a gurgle of laughter. 'Honestly, though, if I go off the deep end, I'm relying on you to rein me in. Mum's so happy that I'm "finally" getting married that she'd book Westminster Abbey for the service and Buckingham Palace for the reception if she thought she could swing it.' She takes a sip of her tea. 'Did I tell you she wants to invite all the mums of all the kids we were at primary school with, even though she's not seen most of them for nearly twenty years?'

I shrug. 'I get it. She wants to show off about her brilliant daughter, who's now a full-time make-up artist—' Daisy bows her head in acknowledgement '—marrying a hot-shot lawyer. In her head, she's probably like, *eat my shorts, bitches*. Even if she wouldn't phrase it like that.'

'You're right. I do think she might end up being quite . . . difficult, though, about wedding stuff.' She sighs loudly. 'Speaking of difficult people, how is it going with the book?'

I groan.

'I'm getting there, if "there" is a steaming pile of poo. There's no time for me to make it even halfway decent. I'm just vomiting words on to the page and hoping they make some sort of sense.'

'What's happening at the moment?'

I wake up my laptop and study the screen.

'So. Our heroine, who is also first violin and leader of the orchestra, having fallen in lust with the domineering conductor, has been having fun times in the orchestra pit with him and the entire percussion section. But now the aliens, even though they claimed to be coming in peace—'

'*Coming* in peace.' Daisy sniggers. 'Geddit?'

I shoot her a withering glance.

'But now the aliens—' I pause, waiting for Daisy to add another comment, but she just stifles a laugh '—reveal their true aim, which is to inject the orchestra with some sort of alien virus – I've not worked out the details yet – which will turn them all into ravenous sex maniacs who are constantly gagging for the slightest touch of alien flesh.'

'Why?' Daisy asks, her eyebrows raised.

'Why what?' I query.

'Why do they want to turn the orchestra into sex maniacs?'

'Er ... it's part of their plan to take over the Earth. If the earthlings can't think of anything but shagging around with aliens, they're not going to be able to mount an effective defence when the alien fleet turns up.'

Daisy frowns. 'So how quickly does this virus spread? Surely, as soon as the authorities realise that the orchestra is behaving weirdly, they'll just put them in quarantine. And is it really likely that an alien virus would attack a human immune system, if—'

I interrupt quickly.

'The whole alien invasion thing doesn't really matter that much. Trust me: Paige's readers are not going to be worried about the scientific likelihood of cross-species contamination. They're going to be far more interested in the fact that the alien leader, though looking suspiciously like a super-buff human male, also has two willies, a flexible tongue, and can sprout extra arms from his back if he needs additional ... appendages.'

Daisy's eyes open wide. 'Two willies ...?'

'Yes.'

'Hm. Well, based on that alone I'd buy a copy. I think it sounds brilliant.'

'I'll give you one of the author copies when I get them. It can be a wedding present.'

Daisy grins and checks her phone. 'We've got forty-five minutes before that woman arrives, so I think I'll do some more packing. Dan's coming round with a van later to take some of the boxes.'

That woman is someone I'm interviewing to take Daisy's place – a new tenant who can take over her portion of the rental contract. A new housemate. Exactly what I didn't want for Christmas.

Daisy walks round to my side of the table and stands behind me, crouching to slip her arm around my neck and lean her head against mine. 'You'll be okay, yeah?'

'Of course I will! Go.' I push her away gently. 'Pack.'

Only when she's left the room do I sink my head into my hands. Daisy's known me for long enough to know how hard I find change, but not for the world would I let her know exactly how terrified I am. There's a sheet of paper folded up in my jeans pocket: notes I took from the six weeks of state-funded therapy I somehow ended up with after Mum died. I've not looked at them for years, but I dug them out last week and have been carrying them around with me like a talisman since then. I unfold the paper now and reread the first few lines.

Welcome anxiety in; it's just your brain trying to keep you safe!
Change can be growth.
Do you want a small life?
Return library books.

The therapist must have been making a point about controlling the controllable with that last one. Either that, or I was just reminding myself to return my library books.

Change can be growth. Wish I'd remembered that one when I'd kept going out with Simon for a full nine months after I'd realised that his sophistication and erudition was actually just a gift for bullshitting. And that he mostly talked about himself. And that he was strangely obsessed with his mother. Perhaps 'familiar' isn't the most important quality in a life partner. But even *thinking* about Kieran's suggestion that I should just up and move to France sends a shiver of panic through my core. He makes it sound like it's so easy.

The doorbell rings. I go to answer as Daisy comes running down the stairs.

'Can't be her, surely?' I ask.

'She's very early if it is.'

We both put on welcoming smiles and open the door.

'Hi.' The woman on the doorstep smiles brightly and steps into the hallway. 'I'm Melissa. We did say eleven, didn't we?'

I glance at Daisy.

'Er, eleven-thirty, I think, but—'

'Oh, yes, how silly of me.' Melissa hands Daisy her faux fur coat. At least, I hope it's faux. 'Still, I'm here now. Can I see the room first? Up here?' She starts up the stairs.

For maybe only the fifth time since I've known her, Daisy is lost for words. She hurries after Melissa.

'Shall I make some tea?' I call after them.

'Not for me, thanks,' Melissa replies. 'I don't really like tea.'

Not like tea? Who doesn't like tea? I'd tell her to leave, only the thought of that amount of confrontation makes me want to hide behind the sofa. Plus, so far, she's the only applicant we've had.

They come downstairs. As Daisy shows Melissa the kitchen and the garden and the dining/work room, I sit on the violently floral sofa and try to at least look like someone who's in charge.

Okay. Who's the boss woman?
I'm the boss woman.
This is your home.
Yep.
And we're not going to put up with any shit, are we?
Nope.
Because you're an independent nearly-thirty-year-old with a successful-ish career.
Right. Successful. Ish.

I take a deep breath. And another.

Bugger, I need the toilet.

'How was the potential new housemate,' Kieran asks. His voice through my headphones sounds so close I can almost imagine he's standing next to me.

'Oh, you know. Okay. Doesn't smoke and is gainfully employed. Very ... clean. Ooh, hold on, they've got brandy butter on special offer.' I stretch past the overladen trolley of another shopper, snag a tub, and resume my wandering. I generally find pottering about the supermarket quite restful, but it's the twenty-third of December, the Christmas food frenzy is in full swing, and the aisles are as congested as my nasal passages at the height of hay fever season.

'Brandy butter?' Kieran makes an 'ugh' of disgust. 'How can you eat that stuff?'

'With Christmas pudding. Or straight from the tub in case of emergency.' As he laughs, I study my trolley. 'Right. So I've got the pudding, the brandy butter, a chicken, potatoes, carrots, celery, cream, chestnuts and Brussels sprouts, though I'm still not convinced I'm ever going to be able to make them taste nice.' I eye the small green bullets suspiciously. Mum only ever bought sprouts for Christmas dinner, and her only method of cooking was to boil them until they were snot-coloured and inedible. My recollection is that they sat on the plate as yellow-green garnish then ended up in the bin; I don't think either of us ever actually ate them.

'Once I've shown you how to cook the sprouts with the cream and the chestnuts, you'll be converted, I promise you.'

'Hmm.' Unconvinced, I pause in front of a display of seasonings and herbs. 'And you're sure I don't need the gravy granules? Just in case?'

'No, it'll be fine. We'll make the gravy from scratch. You'll be grand. Trust me.'

Trust me. Mum used to say that a lot. And I did. I pick up a tub of chicken gravy granules and pop it in the trolley. Just in case.

'Okay, I think I've got everything, then.' I head towards the checkouts and get into a queue.

'Some wine?' Kieran asks.

'Daisy's given me a fancy bottle of something French. It looks fancy, at any rate. It's from her and Dan.'

'When does she leave?'

'Tomorrow morning. They're going to her parents for Christmas and his parents for Boxing Day.'

'I wish you weren't alone.'

'I'm used to it. And to be fair, Daisy did invite me to join her, and I've spent Christmas at her parents' house plenty of times, but I didn't want to third-wheel it with her and Dan. And this way I get to virtually spend Christmas Day with you.' I start unloading my trolley on to the conveyor belt. The man in front of me, waiting to pay, pulls a bunch of vouchers and some cash out of his pocket, including a large handful of loose change. 'If I ever escape the supermarket.'

'I'm looking forward to it,' Kieran says. 'We can do a bit of cooking, eat a late lunch and watch a film together. Or watch the same film at the same time. Damn – I'm sorry, Emma – I need to head to the restaurant.'

There's a note of despondency in his voice that I'm not used to hearing.

'Is everything okay?"

There's a moment of silence.

'Yeah, it's okay. More or less. I'll tell you tomorrow. But I've decided – I'm doing six more months, then I'm out of here. I still want you to move to Paris sooner than that, but if you can't – next summer, Emma. Next summer, things will be different. And we can figure the future out together as we go along.' He laughs. 'God, it feels good to have a plan.'

Figuring things out as we go along is not what I'd call a plan. Still, six months . . . I can cope with another six months. As long as everything else stays the same.

Voucher man finally stops arguing about whether his 'BOGOF' discount applies to branded as well as own-brand loo roll and – still muttering – pays the bill.

'I have to go too. Text me this evening?'

'Will do. Love you.'

'You too.'

I end the call and smile at the checkout assistant.

You too. That's how I always answer.

I think I love him. I told him I did in my Christmas card. So why the hell can't I just say the words?

Chapter Sixteen

Kieran

I know as soon as I arrive at La Reine that something is seriously wrong. This time of the afternoon, the kitchen should be a hive of activity, with everyone prepping for this evening's dinner service. Instead, both kitchen and waiting staff are gathered in a loose knot: low voices, anxious expressions. Alex, her brow knitted into a frown, is drumming her fingernails over and over on the stainless steel work surface. Catching sight of me, she looks relieved and beckons me over.

'Kieran, *Dieu merci tu es là.*'

'What's happened?'

She gestures towards the stairs that lead down to the wine cellar. 'Go and see.'

More thefts, that's what I'm expecting. Either my secret camera's picked up the culprit, or someone has been caught red-handed. But the sight that greets me when I get down into the cellar pulls me up short.

Marcel is standing there with one hand on his hip, the other clutching a handkerchief to his face. Crouching next to him is Ettore. And lying on the floor between them, turned on his side, his head resting on a rolled-up apron, is Monsieur Arnaud.

I gasp and hurry over, fearing the worst. A heart attack, that's my guess. I'm about to ask whether someone has called an ambulance when the smell hits me. Vomit and alcohol and sour air.

'Oh, Christ . . .' The reek makes me gag. No wonder Marcel is covering his nose and mouth. Ettore must have turned Arnaud on to his side and thank God, because there's a pool of sick on the floor next to the man's head. He'd have surely choked otherwise. Looks like he's pissed himself, too.

Revolted, I look away and spot the empty bottles – also resting on their sides – in the corner of the room. Six or seven, maybe; there's some broken glass scattered around too, and a puddle of dark red wine that's already discolouring the flagstones. One of the empty bottles used to hold the 42% proof, sixty-year-old Armagnac that Ettore acquired to tempt our thief.

Arnaud stirs and snorts and farts loudly. I'm really surprised, given the amount of booze he's put away in what must have been an epic binge, that he's not actually dead. Just dead drunk.

'Fuck.' It's all I can think to say.

'*Exactement*,' replies Marcel. '*Et aujourd'hui en plus.*'

Today of all days. He's not wrong. We've had a tip-off from a good source: the booking we've got in the name of Lavigne for dinner tonight is supposedly Kobe Lavigne, the well-known American-French restaurateur. Arnaud has been planning a menu for the past three weeks in the hope of persuading the guy – if he shows up – to give him funding for a second restaurant. He wants to call it Arnaud's. A second restaurant means a second shot at regaining his Michelin star.

'Fuck,' I repeat. 'Is he in danger? Should we get him to hospital?'

'He's sleeping, I think, not unconscious.' Ettore stands up. 'Perhaps we should let him sleep. He would not wish this to be known. Better to keep the silence.'

'There's more,' Marcel says. He casts a look of disgust at Arnaud. 'He cancelled the order for the lamb.'

'Cancelled?' I look from Marcel to Ettore and back. 'But – but why?' I exclaim. 'How am I supposed to cook *côtelettes d'agneau grillées au porto, ail confit et sauce vierge persillade* with no lamb? It's meant to be this evening's star dish, for fuck's sake.'

Marcel shrugs. '*Je ne sais pas*. All I know is that Claude called *the boucher*, and asked why the lamb hadn't been delivered and he said Arnaud had cancelled the order yesterday. He must have been drunk.'

'Aargh!' All I want to do this instant is kick the snoring chef in the backside.

'Perhaps we should close the restaurant,' Ettore suggests. 'Say there is a power cut . . .'

'No. Definitely not. Even if the Lavigne who's got the booking isn't Kobe, think of all the business we'll lose if we're shut tonight. Margins are tight enough without kissing goodbye to that amount of cash.' Tonight is also our final night before the restaurant closes — for all of three days — until the twenty-seventh. 'Think of how it would look, too.'

The stench is making me nauseous; I press my fingers to my temples and try to think. What would Emma do right now? Write a happy ending. Cast me as the hero — I hope — and find a way for me to save the day.

'Okay,' I say, more to myself than the others. 'Okay. We need two things: a new star dish for this evening's menu, and to deal with this.' I indicate Arnaud with a jerk of my chin. Monsieur Arnaud is not exactly waif-like — even together, I don't think Ettore and I can haul him up the steep stairs until he's awake enough to give us at least a little bit of help. 'Ettore, do you mind staying down here with him for another half-hour? Marcel, would you go and fetch the new kitchen boy?'

'Chip?'

He pronounces it like 'ship.' Poor Chip. He's a clean-living American college kid on a gap year, eager to please, yet some of the staff have taken to calling him 'Frites'. And he's only been here a week. Well, he said he wanted to get some experience of the wider world.

'Yes, Chip. Send him to the chemist to get some headache pills — you'd better write it down so he can just show the pharmacist what he needs — then he can take over from Ettore. Let's get some drinking water down here for when Arnaud wakes up.

And a dustpan and brush too; Chip can clean up the glass. Tell him we'll pay him double time. No – triple time. This is not exactly in his job description.'

'*Et l'agneau alors?*' he asks.

'Don't worry about the lamb – I'll sort the food with the rest of the kitchen staff. You two just make sure the service and the wine are impeccable as always.' I laugh, surprising both myself and the others. Maybe it's the lack of air flow messing with my head. Maybe it's the unexpected injection of risk into what had looked like being just another day, when I'm already counting the hours until I've learned enough to escape this place altogether. Either way, I suddenly feel twice as alive as I did before. I wink at Marcel and Ettore. 'I'm going to look in the fridge. We must have something on hand that I can turn into a dish as delicious as the lamb . . .'

'*C'est lui?*' Xavier, who's in charge of the fish, calls out to one of the waiters who's just returned from the dining room.

He wants to find out if the male diner at table fourteen is in fact Kobe Lavigne, or just one of the many other Lavignes milling around Paris. We'd all like to know. I've absolutely forbidden anyone to look the guy up on their phones – we're under enough pressure this evening as it is – but still, they're all behaving like starstruck fans at a red-carpet event. I clap my hands for silence.

'Listen up, people,' I say, looking around the kitchen. 'It doesn't matter who the guy is. He could be Santa Claus, the president of France or the reincarnation of Napoleon for all I care. We're going to do what we always do, which is to produce the best food possible for all our guests.' There are a couple of laughs, but everyone murmurs their assent. I glance at the order slips stuck above the pass. 'Xavier, I'm still waiting on the *quenelles de brochet* for table seven.'

'*Oui, chef.*'

Arnaud chooses this moment, supported by Chip, to make an appearance. Most of the staff pretend not to see him. He has the decency to look embarrassed, at least. He also looks as if he's about to chuck up in what is currently my kitchen. I hurry over and herd them both into the adjacent office. Arnaud sinks into the chair and blinks at me hazily.

'Kieran . . .'

'Everything's under control. Go home.' I turn to Chip. 'Make sure he's got his keys and his wallet and get him into a taxi, would you?' Arnaud's face is glistening and slightly green under the stark office lighting. 'On second thoughts, go with him, get him inside and then get another taxi back. Bring me back the receipts so I can refund you.' There's a pile of letters on the desk; I riffle through until I find one with Arnaud's home address, tear off the corner of the letter and give it to Chip. 'That's where he lives.' The boy looks anxious, and I'm not surprised. 'I really appreciate this, Chip. You think you'll be able to manage?'

He squares his shoulders and nods. 'Yes, chef.'

'Good lad.'

Without a second glance, I return to the kitchen. A waiter hands me the order he's just taken. A glance at the table number makes me gulp and sends my heartbeat rocketing, but I've no time to panic. Taking a deep breath, I channel my inner Chip and force myself to lower my shoulders.

I can do this.

I raise my voice to be heard above the noise.

'Table fourteen. *Entrées: velouté de courgette, et bouchées à la reine. Plats de résistance: blanquette de veau maison, et pavé de bœuf sur son lit de champignons sauvages caramélisées avec crème, neige au gingembre, et calvados.*' Pavé of beef, cut from the heart of the rump, served rare on a bed of caramelised wild mushrooms with cream, ginger snow, and calvados. That's the star dish I've created to replace Arnaud's missing lamb cutlets. And our mystery Lavigne has just ordered it.

***

Hey Ems, texting as promised. Just home. Thank you btw for the very sexy photo of your ankle – totally

> here for Victorian erogenous zones,
> and it helped me get through an
> utterly CRAZY evening at La Reine.
> Turned up to work to discover Arnaud
> drunk as a lord, all but passed out.
> Bad sight of the month. Also, he'd
> cancelled the lamb I'd ordered. Yours
> truly had to come up with a new star
> dish on the fly, which went down a
> storm. It was even enjoyed by a guy
> who we suspect is a major player
> in the restaurant world, though it
> may have been someone entirely
> insignificant who just had the same
> surname and similar facial hair. Either
> way, I'm still high on adrenaline and
> public appreciation, unless the waiters
> were just lying about how much the
> diners enjoyed my dish to make
> me feel better – unlikely, since they
> are a) Parisian and b) not my mum.
> Though come to think of it my mum
> has a thing for brutal honesty too.

I hit send and take another deep breath, trying to calm down, though even throwing open the windows and letting in the freezing night air and the drizzle hasn't really helped with that.

> I meant what I said earlier. Six
> more months. Despite everything,
> I'm learning so much. And I'll
> have more say in what we cook if
> Arnaud, as I hope, decides to go to
> rehab. God knows the guy needs
> some help. I feel bad for him. Still,
> can't deny it's an opportunity.

I take my decaf coffee and go and stand by the window. The panes here are full length, opening on to a tiny Juliet balcony. There's a run-down office block opposite that takes up a good chunk of the view, but the bits of Paris I can see beyond that twinkle like a dream, presided over by the distant, glowing beacon of the Eiffel Tower. Someone in one of the flats below me is playing Christmas music: international hits interspersed with French songs that I don't know.

> Did I tell you I dreamed about you
> last night, Ems? You were standing
> outside the Gare du Nord, and I met
> you and held you in my arms. I'm
> going to bed now – maybe I'll get
> lucky and dream about you again.
> Merry Christmas Eve-Eve. Xx

Six more months. I can do that. When I think about Emma, about us finally being together, I feel as if I can do almost anything.

Chapter Seventeen

Emma

Happy Christmas Eve, Kieran! Maybe my favourite day of the year – your anticipation is at maximum, and you can pretend everything about the 25th is going to actually live up to your super-high expectations. You will absolutely be able to eat an enormous Christmas dinner with no ill effects! Father Xmas is real and definitely travels by reindeer! There will finally be peace on earth and goodwill to all!

I hit send, then read over my text again.

Well, apart from bloody Lauren and bloody Paige. Not sure they deserve any goodwill. Still, I reckon with a good chunk of undisturbed time today I will finish this car crash of a first draft and send it to L BEFORE CHRISTMAS as she requested. GO ME! Daisy and I had a fun breakfast – muffins and mimosas, because it is Christmas Eve after all – and she's now upstairs packing her suitcase. She's back

after Christmas to move the last of
her things out, but I'm telling myself
it will all be fine. She's not moving
to Mars after all. Or France.

My laptop is waiting for me on the table, the final chapter of *Alien Arousal* – the new title for *Symphonic Sexcapades* – up on the screen. Apparently, Paige has also come up with a tagline: 'In space, he wants to make you scream'. I look at the open page with loathing.

Very excited to hear about your
triumph last night! Does the restaurant
guy know it was you who cooked
him dinner and not Arnaud? I hope
so! If not you should definitely tell
him. Also glad you enjoyed my
ankle. I will send you a photo of
my bare shoulder next, if you think
you can handle the sexiness . . .

A postcard arrived this morning. The picture is a moonlit image of the Arc de Triomphe. '*Dear Emma,*' the other side reads, '*another of the postcards I stole from you – does it sound cheesy to tell you that since that fateful morning you've stolen my heart? Merry Christmas! Love, Kieran.*' Happiness wells up in my heart and makes me laugh. I tuck the card into my dictionary.

Got the postcard by the way. 100%
cheese, but then I LOVE cheese.
Have you noticed that there are
no lane markings around the A de
T even though 12 lanes of traffic
converge there? It seems completely
bonkers and very French! Fun fact:
accidents that happen there are

automatically treated as if both
drivers are equally to blame. Guess
that means there must be a lot of
accidents . . . Seriously, I hope you
never cycle there. Even imagining
the chaos makes me hyperventilate.
Better go finish my draft, but I can't
wait to do some kitchen prep with
you tomorrow, and that is not a
sentence I ever thought I'd use! E xx

Reluctantly, I put my phone away and turn to *Alien*.
Right, Emma. Focus. Where were we?
I begin to type.

The doors of Carly's cell whooshed open, and Xaphos strode in. Carly rose to her feet to confront him. 'How long are you planning to keep me locked up in here?' she hissed, all the while trying not to focus on the perfect planes of his face and the rippling muscles of his torso and the way his mane of long copper hair made her fingers itch – she just wanted to run her hands through his luscious locks and all over his hard, gorgeous body, right here, right now.

Xaphos smiled as if he could read her thoughts. 'You object to the comforts I've provided?' He gestured to the huge bed, piled with luxurious throws and silken pillows. 'Or the clothing?'

Carly was suddenly very aware of how naked she felt: the gossamer-thin bra top and skirt, decorated with fine gold chains, revealed far more than they concealed. She lifted her chin. 'I'm kept here against my will. That makes it a prison, however many pillows you provide.'

With a growl Xaphos pushed her back on to the bed and pinned her there as his extra arms appeared, and his extra hands began to undress her. 'You'll stay here until you give me what I want.'

Carly shuddered. The smouldering heat in the alien's eyes pierced her, scorching her soul.

'*Everything that I want,*' *Xaphos added. He extended his long, flexible tongue and began to . . .*

The doorbell rings, derailing my sentence.

'Bugger.'

I find Dan on the doorstep. 'Hey, Emma, merry Christmas!'

'Merry Christmas!' Dan and I exchange a chaste peck on the cheek. 'Come in. She must be nearly ready.' I yell up the stairs, trying to compete with the Christmas music Daisy's got blasting on her speaker. 'Daisy!' No response. 'Daisy, Dan's here!' Still no response. 'Why don't you go up? She'll probably need you to sit on her suitcase.'

'Suitcases, surely?' Dan suggests with a grin. Daisy doesn't do travelling light.

As he disappears upstairs, I head to the kitchen and put the kettle on. No point in returning to Xaphos and his extendable tongue until Daisy's got all her stuff in Dan's car, which is going to take at least ten minutes. True to form, I hear her and Dan bumping heavy somethings down the stairs a few moments later: one massive suitcase and two overstuffed, oversized duffel bags.

'Ems, can you run up and get my vanity case off my bed?' Daisy asks. 'Oh, and the Kindle from my bedside table. And the bag of magazines under the bed.' I'm heading towards the stairs when she exclaims, 'Fuck, the Christmas presents!' and dashes into the sitting room.

The vanity case is distended; it looks as if it contains enough products and appliances to make over a small army. I slip the Kindle into the carrier bag, heave the case off the bed – praying the lock doesn't give way – and struggle downstairs, dumping them with relief on the pavement outside, where Dan is trying to make Daisy's luggage fit into his smallish sports car. His eyes widen.

'Seriously, Daisy, do you really need all this—'

He breaks off, flustered, as Daisy stops arranging her Christmas presents in the footwell and gives him a look. He holds up his hands. 'Sorry. Stupid question.' As Daisy returns to the house, he pulls out one of the duffel bags and picks up the vanity case. 'Okay. Let's start again.'

It's so cold I can see my breath in front of my face. Definitely too cold to be standing around without a coat.

'I'm going to head back indoors, Dan.'

'Of course.' Dan stops wrestling with the luggage for a moment. 'Have a lovely Christmas, Emma. And we'll see you on New Year's Eve, right?'

'Of course. Wouldn't miss it.' I hurry back inside.

Daisy is waiting in the hallway, one hand on the banister, looking around. 'I guess we'd better get going,' she says, making no move to leave.

'Have a wonderful Christmas,' I reply. 'I'm going to miss you.'

She knows what I mean. That I'm not just talking about Christmas. Her eyes go glassy as I blink away my own tears.

'I'll be back on the twenty-eighth to get the last boxes and we'll have a girls' night, yeah?'

'Yeah. That'll be nice.' Despite my best efforts, a tear tracks down my cheek, hot against my chilled skin.

Daisy sniffs and drags the back of her hand across her nose.

'Fuck. Now I'm crying too. I'm going to ruin my eye make-up.'

'Don't worry.' I manage a smile. 'That vanity case must contain industrial quantities of mascara.'

She laughs as we both lean in and hug tightly. 'Best friends forever, right, Ems?'

'Best friends forever. Let me know you've got there safe, won't you? And say hi to your mum and dad.'

'Will do. Enjoy yourself with Kieran. And don't stress about the book stuff. It will all sort itself out.'

Dan lets out a shout of triumph as he forces the car boot shut.

'I'll call you tomorrow,' Daisy says, giving me a kiss on the cheek. I shut the front door behind her.

Around me, the house settles into silence.

I wander back into the kitchen, re-boil the kettle, make a mug of tea and turn the radio on. It's lunchtime now, so I make some toast too and slather it in butter and, since I'm having a break, eat a mince pie and do a little bit of my new jigsaw. It's an early Christmas present to myself: a map of France in five hundred pieces. Finally, I sit back down in front of my laptop.

Right, Emma. Time to focus. Two or three more hours and you can knock this baby out of the park and send it speeding over to Lauren. With any luck, it will give her concussion.

My fingers hover over the keyboard.

Xaphos and his extendable tongue. What's he going to do next? Lick her? Yes. Lick her like an ice cream.

'Everything that I want,' Xaphos added. He extended his long, flexible tongue and began to lick Carly's now naked torso with long, firm strokes, just as if she were nothing more than a soft, melting ice cream and he wanted to devour her. She gasped and moaned with pleasure, willing his tongue to explore the heat between her legs even as she fought to free herself from his grasp.

My mind wanders. I quite fancy an ice cream right now. Chocolate. Or chocolate and caramel. Maybe Xaphos should compare Carly to a flavour, but what flavour? Do aliens even have ice cream in this world? Could they bond when she introduces him to ice cream, or teaches him how to make it? I drift further, to Kieran, and our online cooking lessons, and I realise I don't know if he ever eats ice cream, and then I'm imagining him licking ice cream off my bare stomach, or just licking me all over, with or without the ice cream, frankly, and then the doorbell rings and I realise that somehow an hour has passed and I've only written fifty-four extra words.

The doorbell rings again. I press my hands to my flushed cheeks and go to answer it.

'James.' I blink at him. He's wearing a reindeer antler headband on top of his woolly hat. 'What are you—'

'Hello, my darling Emma, I was just on my way back from buying Petros's Chrissie pressie at Westfield and I thought to myself, you know what would be awesome? Chris-Evie drinks!' He holds up a bottle of Baileys and grins maniacally.

'Chris-Evie?'

James shrugs. 'It might catch on.'

'Well, it's a nice thought, but I'm on a deadline and—'

'Also,' he interrupts, 'I'm panicking.' The grin fades. 'I need advice. And Petros is no good, he's all calm and sensible and he's not a writer and he just doesn't get it.' James's voice has risen an entire octave.

''Kay.' I sigh and gesture him inside. 'But a quick drink, that's all.'

'Scout's honour.'

In the kitchen, James cracks open the Baileys while I find a couple of vaguely matching glasses. He pours a generous slug into each.

'So, what's worrying you?'

'My crime novel.'

I frown. 'But Lauren finally sent you back a load of edits, didn't she? I thought you said that she said that once the edits were done, she'd take it to acquisitions.'

'She did. And I have. I did the edits, and I sent the new manuscript in, and it wasn't easy, I can tell you, not while I was working on the first draft of my new PAP at the same time. Lauren said I'd hear back in a couple of weeks.' James takes a gulp of his drink. 'But that was the beginning of November. *November*, Ems. And now, every time I try to bring it up, she just finds a way to get out of the conversation. She's not replying to my emails about it; she isn't returning my calls.' His tone is getting more and more stressed, so I top up his Baileys. 'I don't know what to do.'

'What about *Harem Heat*?' James's new project for Paige is set in a generic and unspecified desert area, though due to her terrible spelling the initial email suggested that the characters were going to spend a lot of time 'rolling around in the dessert'. Given it was Paige, James had to check she wasn't actually expecting them to be making out in the frozen pudding section of the local Waitrose.

'Oh, she'll talk to me about *that*,' he replies bitterly. 'It's all "I need the new draft, James", and "do something sexy with the tent poles, James". But otherwise, she won't engage at all. I thought I was about to achieve my dream, and now it's just slipping away.'

I know that feeling, I'm about to say. But do I? It suddenly occurs to me that, in all the time I've been writing for Paige, I've never actually finished a book under my own name, let alone tried to get it published. *It's not good enough, it's not the right time* – I've told myself that for years. I've put it down to perfectionism, but what if – what if that's a lie? What if it's really something else?

James starts fidgeting around the kitchen, opening cupboard doors and examining the fairy lights and sending my thoughts skittering sideways. He pops a mini-mince pie in his mouth, but his shoulders just slump a little further.

'I should go,' he says. 'Petros's mum is arriving soon.'

'You and Petros are still coming over on Boxing Day, right?' I put my arm around him. 'We can stuff ourselves with leftovers and talk it all through.'

'I will be here with bells on.'

Knowing James, he's probably speaking literally. He makes me a present of the rest of the Baileys, and I'm left alone again. The alcohol has made me sleepy; I fix myself a strong coffee, sit back down at the laptop and give myself a pep talk.

Okay, Emma. Last scene with Xaphos: they have amazing sex, Carly subdues him with virtuoso violin-playing and the sheer force of her orgasmic attractiveness, he agrees to spare the earth if she will stay with him forever, end of story. Let's get this done.

'And what is it that you want?' Carly shuddered as she felt Xaphos's tongue snake across her inner thigh.

'I want power,' he replied, grinning at her wickedly. 'Power over the Earth. But mostly, power over you.' He kissed her deeply, nuzzling her breast and sucking on ...

The doorbell rings *again*.

'Oh, for fuck's sake!' I exclaim. If this is a delivery, and if the delivery guy makes some stupid comment like *oh, a Christmas present for Emma Christmas, what a coincidence!* I swear I'm going to deck him.

I stomp to the front door and fling it open.

The man on the doorstep is in his late fifties, muffled up in a heavy coat and scarf, his hands shoved in his pockets. Grey hair is just visible beneath his flat cap. Green eyes stare at me from behind a pair of dark-framed glasses.

I've not seen him for over sixteen years, but I recognise him instantly.

'Hello, Emma,' he says. His voice is different: softened into something more northerly.

'Hello,' I reply. I don't call him dad. After all this time, I don't think he deserves it.

Chapter Eighteen

Kieran

Christmas morning, and I'm woken by the sound of church bells floating across the city, summoning the faithful to Mass. For a moment I feel guilty: if I were at home, I'd probably be going too. But today, with no work other than making my own Christmas lunch while advising Emma on hers, I'm enjoying what I decide is a well-earned lie-in. A fat morning, as they say over here: *une grasse matinée*.

I stretch out in my bed, luxuriating, until my stomach growls and prods me into movement. I picked up some croissants from a nearby pâtisserie yesterday; I decide to fill a couple of them with Gruyère cheese, warm them in the oven and serve with sautéed mushrooms. While I'm eating, I read a battered copy of *A Christmas Carol*. A family tradition that started with my mum reading it to Brendan and me and continued with us both re-reading it every Christmas. I take a photo of the cover and send it to Emma, along with a question – *what's your favourite Christmas book?* – but I don't want to call her, not yet. I don't want to risk waking her. But Brendan, with two small children, will no doubt have been up since the crack of dawn, if not before. Once I've licked every last delicious morsel of the croissants from my fingers, I make myself a coffee and video call my brother.

'Merry Christmas, Bren!'

Brendan is knee-deep in wrapping paper, and I can hear both the kids shrieking joyously in the background.

'Merry Christmas, Kieran! Hey, kids, come and wish your uncle a merry Christmas and thank him for the presents. No, now – he's on the – I know, Roisin, but it will still be there when you get back. No, Rudolf isn't going to eat it, he's definitely gone to bed now, the poor f – the poor soul.' He rolls his eyes at me. 'Niamh's sister sent them each a variety pack of chocolate, and unfortunately the kids found them before we did. They're both as high as kites on sugar and E-numbers. They'll probably be sick any minute.'

'Ah, the true joy of Christmas.'

He manages to corral the kids into frame. They wave at me and blow kisses – Colm has already managed to smear the Irish rugby jersey I sent him with chocolate, but at least he's wearing it. A moment later they've wriggled out of his grasp and they're off again. Niamh appears and puts her arm around Brendan's waist.

'Happy Christmas from the madhouse, Kieran. How's Paris this morning?'

'Peaceful. Calm. I made myself cheese and mushroom croissants for breakfast and I might go for a walk in a bit.'

She laughs, shaking her head.

'You're lucky I love you so much, 'cos it would be really easy to hate you right now.' The noise from the kids ratchets up a notch. 'Ah, for the love of – Brendan, go somewhere quiet to talk to your brother. Have a great day, Kieran. Kids, how about we watch *The Muppet Christmas Carol* again?'

The cacophony diminishes as Brendan walks away from the open plan living-dining area at the centre of their house.

'How are Mum and Dad?' I ask.

'Not up yet, fortunately. I've taken them some tea. I think Dad had an okay night.'

'And how is his weight?'

'Better. Not where it should be, but better. I've been using those recipes you sent over. They're good. You should put together a cookery book.'

'Maybe one day.' I grin, remembering the phone call I had yesterday. 'Actually, I've a great opportunity coming up after Christmas. Arnaud is going into rehab.'

'Oh, that's brilliant news.' My brother grins back at me. 'So you'll be able to come home for a while.'

I stare at him, trying to work out how to tell him he's wrong. I stare for an instant too long. His grin fades.

'Is that not what it means, Kieran? I thought you said you couldn't take a break because Arnaud was determined not to close the restaurant, but surely, with him gone . . .'

The sentence hangs in the air.

'It's not quite that simple, Brendan,' I say. 'I'll be in charge for at least eight weeks. I can cook my own dishes. And if Lavigne comes back – that restaurateur who was here the other night – it could change everything.' I watch Brendan's face, willing him to understand. 'And Dad's going for the respite care next week, so—'

'The respite care is a great idea.' Brendan sounds irritated. 'We appreciate you paying towards it, we really do. But it's not the same, Kieran. We'd all rather see you. So would Dad.'

'But I can't close the restaurant now. I just can't. People are relying on me.'

Brendan shakes his head. 'There's always something, isn't there? Anyone would think you don't want to come back. That you're afraid to come back.'

'Don't say that. Of course I want to come back.' I open my mouth, about to say the same thing I said to Emma: six months. Give me six months, and it will all be different. But will it? If Lavigne does, by some miracle, want to set up a restaurant for me, he's not likely to open it in Cork. And if I'm working to set up my own business I'll have less time to travel, not more. Something else occurs to me: I've barely spent more than a year in one place since I was twenty. If I start a restaurant in Paris, how long will I have to stay?

'What are you running from, Kieran?' Brendan asks.

I'm asking myself the same thing.

'Look, I don't want to fight with you,' he continues. 'Today of all days. But just – think about it, will you? You don't even have to spend all your time with us. You could go to London. Or invite Emma here. I'd love to meet her. I know Niamh would.'

I nod. 'I'll think about it. I promise.' And I do mean to think about it. But Lavigne, if he should turn up again ... 'I'd better go. I'm cooking with Emma later, and I've some prep to do. I'll call back this afternoon to talk to Mum and Dad.'

'Of course. We'll be here. And I don't mean to be Scrooge. I miss you, that's all.'

'I miss you too. Hey, are you rereading—'

'Of course. He's just met the ghost of Christmas past.'

'I'm already up to the ghost of Christmas present.'

Brendan laughs.

'Wait until you have kids and see what they do to your reading speed.' Niamh calls from somewhere in the background, and Brendan groans. 'Once more unto the breach, I suppose.'

'Good luck, Bren. Speak later.'

I end the call. Hesitate, and video call Emma. Her voice is soft with sleep when she answers, her eyelids look heavy, and she's still lying down, head on her pillow.

'Happy Christmas, Emma! I didn't wake you, did I?'

'No. I'm awake. Merry Christmas, Kieran.'

She smiles, but she doesn't look as happy as I'd expected. There's a haunted look in her eyes I don't remember seeing before.

'What's wrong? Did you not get the book finished in time?'

'Yeah, I did. I sent it off to Lauren at six-thirty last night.'

'So what is it?' I frown. 'You're missing Daisy? Are you worried about the new housemate?'

'No. Well, yes.' She sighs and closes her eyes for a moment. Lying there like that, she looks so vulnerable that my heart aches; I want to fold her in my arms and kiss away her worries and look after her so that she'll never be worried again.

'Ems?' I prod.

'It's not just Daisy and the new person, though I am anxious about her. She doesn't like tea. But yesterday—' She draws in a quick, deep breath, as though jabbed by something sharp.

'What is it?'

'My dad turned up.'

For an instant, I don't know what to say.

'Your – your dad? But I thought he was dead. You've never mentioned a dad. I mean, I know you must have one, but it never occurred to me—' I realise I'm rambling. 'Sorry. You were saying. Your dad turned up.'

She gives a slightly bitter laugh.

'He may as well have been dead. I was thirteen when he fucked off. The last letter I had from him was when I was sixteen. The last birthday card came a year after that. He could have been dead, for all I knew. *I* could have been dead, for all he cared.'

We're both silent for a moment, taking in her words.

'What did he want?' I ask.

'I don't know exactly. He said he'd been wanting to get in touch for ages but that he hadn't been brave enough until now. I don't know why you'd need to be brave to come and see your kid.'

Brendan's words to me earlier echo through my memory. Maybe, sometimes, you do need to be brave to see your kid. Or your parent.

'So what happened? What did you do?' I ask.

'Nothing much happened yesterday. I've arranged to see him after Christmas, on the tenth of January.' She pulls a face like she's tasted something unpleasant. 'He messed up Christmas Eve. I don't want him to mess up any more of my Christmas.'

'And do you want to see him?'

She gives a one-shouldered shrug. 'What else can I do? He says he want to patch things up. He says he has something for me.'

You could tell him to fuck off, I think, *you owe him nothing*, but doubt keeps the words behind my teeth. I hardly think my own family life is in a fit state for me to be advising other people, especially someone I love. I don't want to advise her badly.

Emma sits up and gives herself a shake.

'I should get up. I'm sorry for putting a downer on Christmas morning.'

'Never apologise for that. I really care about you, Emma. If you've got problems, I want to know about them.'

'I do have some good news too, though.' She does an excited little wave with her fists. 'Mrs Farrell, the woman I started cleaning for in February – she's given me a cash bonus. Two hundred and forty pounds.' Her eyes open wide. 'Can you believe it? Maybe I actually can save up to get a cheap flight to Paris and book a hotel for a couple of nights.'

'You know you're welcome to stay here.' The words are out of my mouth before I've really thought them through. 'I mean, I can always sleep on the sofa. I don't want to assume . . .' I trail off.

Emma is blushing bright red. 'I wouldn't want to assume either. I mean, I want to. I think. But you know – we have actually only spent two minutes in the same physical space.'

'Of course. And I wouldn't want you to ever feel any pressure.' Now I'm blushing too, I can feel it, and we're gazing at each other like a couple of lovestruck, lust-struck teenagers. 'Well, the option is there. We can play it by ear. We're quite good at doing that, I think. But I'd absolutely love that, if you were to come for a visit. And maybe I can persuade you to stay longer.'

Emma smiles, and it's a beautiful smile.

'Maybe, if I can.' Suddenly, comically, her face changes to one of dismay. 'Oh, hell, am I supposed to have got the chicken out of the fridge, or something? What's the time?'

I laugh despite myself.

'Don't worry, we've plenty of time. You can get it out now and let it come to room temperature. Get the butter out too. And if you've white wine, stick it in the fridge if there's room.'

'Okay. Chicken, butter, wine.'

The view blurs a little as she gets out of bed, but I catch a glimpse of her long legs before she turns the screen so I can see her trajectory through the house: landing, stairs, kitchen, all resplendent with fairy lights. Then the fridge, opening.

'Right, here's the chicken. I'll just prop you up.'

My next view is of Emma holding the chicken.

'Do I need to wash it?' The anxiety in her voice makes me laugh again.

'No. That'll just spread the germs around the kitchen. Get the roasting tin out and stick it in there for the time being. Take the plastic wrapping off first, though.'

She follows my directions.

'Ugh, it's all clammy! Are you sure about this?'

'Don't worry, it'll be delicious by the time we're finished with it. Don't you trust me?

She hesitates – hesitates for a little longer than I'd like, to be honest. But then she nods, smiling again.

'You know what, Kieran? Actually, I do.'

Chapter Nineteen

Emma

I'm standing outside Claire's Accessories, wondering whether to go in and get a second piercing in my ears, when my phone buzzes. The sight of Kieran's name on the lock screen feels like a beacon in the gloom.

'I'm so glad you called,' I say immediately. 'But don't you have lunch service right now?'

'Just finished. The restaurant's closed and I'm letting my minions do the cleaning up.' He chuckles. 'One of the many advantages of being in charge.'

'So Arnaud is sticking it out at the rehab?'

'So far. What about you? How's your day going?'

I can't help groaning. It's the second Friday of the new year. January, damp and miserable, has been hanging around like a D-list celebrity willing to do anything for attention, and yet there's still so much of it to come. There's something about this month that seems to warp space-time. Thirty-one days in August zip by in moments. Each day in January moves like a funeral procession.

Or maybe I just am in mourning. Daisy has gone, and it doesn't really help that she's only moved to Fulham. Though her new address is still west London, still north of the river, this is the furthest apart we've ever been, except for a brief spell when I tried and failed to make a go of university. It's as if a bit of me is missing. And every time I catch sight of a dark patch on the wall where one of her framed anime posters used to hang, every time I notice the absence of the Japanese silk wash bag she used to keep hanging on the back of the bathroom door, my heart breaks all over again.

'It's alright,' I lie. 'I was cleaning this morning. Now I'm wandering around Westfield, killing time. I'm meeting my dad for coffee in a bit.'

'I know. Are you feeling okay about it?'

I smile despite my mood; he must have made a note of the date. 'I feel better now I'm talking to you. I don't know what to expect, that's the main problem. For someone who hates uncertainty and wants to know exactly what's coming next, it's not ideal.'

'It might be a good thing, though. He might want to make amends. Or . . .' Kieran gasps dramatically '. . . maybe he's found out that he's the next in line for the throne of a small European kingdom, and he needs to tell you that you're actually a princess.'

'First, I love that you know the plot of *The Princess Diaries*. Second, I doubt it. Though I suppose you could be right.' I sigh, my natural gloom reasserting itself. 'He probably wants something from me instead. Like a kidney.'

Kieran laughs. 'Well, you don't have to say yes to anything. Remember that. And I'm here for you, Emma. On the other end of a phone line, at least. You can call me whenever you need to. You know that, right? Don't worry about the time.'

'I know.'

Talking to Kieran feels like the verbal equivalent of a hug. I just wish that he were actually here to put his arms around me.

'How's it going with Smelissa?'

He means Melissa, my new housemate.

'You're going to get me into trouble. One of these days I'm going to call her that out loud, and she's going to give me one of her looks. One of her "disappointed but not surprised and actually quite glad because it gives me an excuse to be more of a bitch than I already am" looks.'

'What's she done now?' he asks.

'When I got home last night, I found all my work stuff – my dictionary, my notebooks, my index cards, my laptop – dumped in a pile on my bed. She's having a dinner party tonight so she needs the table. But instead of asking me, she just moved everything and left a Post-it note on my bedroom door. *Hope you don't mind, but the downstairs back room is a dining room, not an office.*'

'So the Post-it note thing is still happening?'

'It's her main way of communicating.' Ever since Melissa moved in on New Year's Day – who moves house on New Year's Day? – a steady stream of Post-it notes has appeared on my door.

Hope you don't mind, but I've taken an extra one of the kitchen cupboards; it only seems fair since I pay four-sevenths of the rent.

Hope you don't mind, but I've taken your cushions off the sofa, polyester isn't good for my skin.

Hope you don't mind, but I've drawn up schedules for using the kitchen and the bathroom and a rota for cleaning, and I've taken the times that work best for me since my work hours are a lot less flexible than yours.

Perhaps I wouldn't mind, if she actually were super-clean and tidy. As it is, she ignores her own cleaning rota – 'I'm just too busy at work!' – leaves her dishes in the kitchen sink for days and soaks her washing in the bathroom basin. The hallway is currently doubling up as an assault course because of her boyfriend's bike.

'Honestly, Kieran, I'm beginning to hate the sight of a sticky note. And I used to love the bloody things. They're so handy for plotting.'

'It's too bad this isn't a novel,' he says. 'You could bump her off. Make it look like an accident.'

'Don't tempt me.' I pause for a moment, unwilling to banish the image of Melissa somehow being crushed to death by an avalanche of little yellow squares. 'But I'd still have the same problem. I have to have someone to share the house with. I can't afford to live here on my own.'

'Unless you move,' Kieran suggests.

I hear him, but I want to pretend I haven't. The idea of that much change makes me catch my breath. 'What?'

'Move. Rent somewhere different. Your own space, maybe.'

'Leave the house? I don't know about that,' I say automatically.

'Worth thinking about, though, don't you think? Imagine: a studio flat, compact but bijou, all to yourself. Somewhere nearer to Daisy, perhaps. Or to me.'

For a moment, I allow myself to be seduced by the image. A bright, clean space filled with furniture that I've chosen. A desk by the window, my books arranged next to a vase of flowers. No saggy psychedelic sofa, no manky carpet in the bathroom, no lurid green feature wall, no Melissa. Somehow, I've drifted away from Claire's and towards Zara Home. I can almost hear the homewares displayed in the window calling to me.

But it's no good. Even if I would, I couldn't. Fulham is expensive. Paris, I imagine, even more so.

'I'll think about it,' I say to Kieran.

'Good,' he replies, though I'm not sure he believes me.

'I'd better go. I want to get to the café first.'

'Okay. Good luck, Ems. Love you.'

'Love you too.' I reply. Saying the words makes me shiver with some weird combination of pride and fear. I'm still not used to saying it, and it still sounds odd, even to me. *Can you really love someone you've only actually spent two minutes with?* Dan asked me on New Year's Eve, and I didn't blame him – but it's true. 'I'll let you know how it goes.'

A glance at my watch makes me quicken my pace out of the shopping centre and towards Café Olay. My father had suggested one of the posher venues in Westfield, but I wanted somewhere that feels like my turf. Ron promised to reserve a table for me, and he is true to his word: the table in the booth at the back bears a large, handwritten 'reserved' sign. He even brings me a mocha on the house.

I've only just started drinking it when the door opens. My father looks uncertainly around the room. When he spots me, he hesitates for an instant, as if he's debating whether to run away again.

'Emma.' His gaze drifts to my mug. 'Do you want another drink? Or—' he frowns in the direction of the counter '—or a cake, or something?'

'No, thank you.'

'Oh. Okay. I'll just . . .'

He goes to the counter – I can see Ron eyeing him up – and returns with a cup of tea. Takes off his coat and cap and slides on to the bench opposite me.

I take a sip of the chocolatey coffee.

'Well?' I ask. 'What did you want to see me for?'

Dad blinks at me. His eyes are the same shape and colour as mine. It's disconcerting.

'I'm sorry, Emma. I really am. I don't know what I was thinking. We were young, your mum and me, and I wasn't in a good place by the time I . . .' He clears his throat and stares at the cup of tea. 'I thought you'd be better off without me. I wasn't coping. I wanted security, but your mum was so unpredictable. Everything felt so, so out of control—' He breaks off again.

My fingers tighten around my mug. This is getting on to dangerous territory. Mum had problems. She was never easy to live with. But she was there for me for as long as she could be.

'If you've just come to make excuses,' I begin, 'I don't want to—'

'I've not, honestly, Emma. What I did was wrong. Terribly wrong. I've regretted it for years, but I've been too much of a coward up until now to try to set it right. Too afraid of what you might say. Of what might happen.' He leans his forehead against the fingertips of one hand. 'I didn't want to risk it.'

I shift uncomfortably in my seat. This is all getting too much. I don't want to look like this man I've taught myself to hate. I don't want to be like him.

'What changed?' I ask.

'My mother died.' He looks up at me. 'Do you remember her?'

'A little.' In truth, it's only images. Nana watching *Coronation Street*, or dancing at a family wedding, or playing ball with me in the garden of the house in Yorkshire. Kirkbymoorside. The place name comes back to me in a flash. Nana was the only grandmother I'd had; Mum left her family behind in Spain and never went back. Never even spoke to them. 'I thought Nana didn't want to see me any more. I thought that neither of you – that neither of you wanted me.' I have to force the words out as a surge of unexpected grief – for myself, for my barely remembered grandmother – threatens to choke me. The coffee is only lukewarm now, but I take another sip.

'I'm so sorry, Emma,' Dad repeats. 'We never stopped loving you, either of us. And Mam never forgave me for what I did. The breach with your mother was so . . .' He shrugs. 'Mam tried to get in contact with you, but your mum wouldn't have it. She said it wasn't fair on you to have it all raked up, since I had said that I didn't want to, that I couldn't—' Something like a groan escapes my father's lips. 'Perhaps she was right. But it broke Mam's heart. And then, when she died, she left a letter telling me I needed to at least try to heal things between us. She left something for you, too.'

I'm expecting him to hand me an object. Some piece of my grandmother's jewellery, or a framed photograph, perhaps. Instead, he slides an envelope across the table.

'A letter?' I ask.

'Open it.'

Inside is a cheque. A cheque made out to me, for two hundred and seventy thousand pounds. More money than I've ever seen.

My hands are trembling. 'I can't accept this.'

I won't accept it. Because how can I keep hating him if I let him change my life?

'Please,' he says, laying his hands over mine. 'It's all her money, not mine, though that'll be yours too, eventually, if you'll have it. Mam saved her whole life so she could pay her mortgage off, and she left you her house in the will. She wanted you to have it. I hope—' he draws back '—I hope I did the right thing, selling it so I could give you the proceeds. I didn't think you'd have much use for a bungalow in Yorkshire.'

I can't take my eyes off the cheque. With this amount of money, I could rent somewhere new. I could put a deposit on a flat. I could – I could visit Kieran in Paris.

Could I, though? It's one thing to say *I love you*, but to go there, to get in even deeper—

James's words from months ago float to the surface of my memory: *maybe it's easier* because *he's in Paris*. Is that what he really meant? Am I so terrified of commitment, so terrified of taking a chance, that I'd sooner break it off with Kieran than take the chance, now that I have it, of being with him?

I find my father's watching me.

'This doesn't make it okay. What you did, I mean.' I take a deep breath. 'I thought there was something wrong with me. Otherwise, how could you leave me?'

Tears well up in his eyes. 'I know this can't fix things. There's no magic wand that can undo the past. I wish there were. But at least . . .' He waves a hand at the cheque. 'Don't be like me, Emma. Don't settle for a small life. You're young. There must be something you want to do. Some adventure.'

Adventure. The word hangs there, strange and angular. And I don't quite know what to do with it.

Chapter Twenty

Kieran

I'm making myself lunch – toasted focaccia with mozzarella, sundried tomatoes and oregano, plus roasted broccoli drizzled with a tahini-based dressing – when the text from Brendan arrives, and my stomach drops through the floor.

> First session of immunotherapy done. Dad in good spirits and not too tired. Too early for proper results but consultant seems optimistic.

The message is followed by an entire two lines of thumbs-up emojis. I start breathing again.

> Thank fuck. Give Dad a hug for me.

> He says virtual hugs back at ya. Mum says please go and light a candle at the big cathedral.

> Notre-Dame? Will do.

> She says she'll know if you don't.

I laugh out loud, as much from relief as from the idea that my mum has some sort of supernatural candle hotline.

> Tell her I promise.

Okay. I need to let Niamh know. Speak later?

> I'll call when I'm on my break.

I return to my lunch prep with renewed enthusiasm. Once everything's plated and I've got myself a glass of water, I sit at the tiny table I've crammed in next to the window and call Emma, listening for the little catch of breath that still makes me smile at the start of all of our phone calls.

'Hey, Kieran!'

'You sound happy. Where are you?'

'Hammersmith Park. It's been so grey and horrible this last week. When I saw the sun shining this morning, I decided I had to get outside. It's glorious right now. Cold, but that kind of crispy cold that makes you feel more alive. Plus I'm feeding the ducks. They seem hungry.'

'Like me.' I tell her what I'm eating for lunch.

'Oh, that sounds so good! Maybe I'll treat myself to something delicious.'

'And what are the ducks having? Bread?'

'Definitely not! It's not that good for them. I had half a tin of sweetcorn sitting in my allocated three-sevenths of the fridge, so I'm giving them that. Did you know that ducks like sweetcorn?'

I grin. 'I did not. That's one of the many things I love about you. I'm always learning something new. I had some news about my dad, by the way.'

I read her my text exchange with Brendan.

'Oh, that's such good news, Kieran. I'm so happy for you.'

'It's very early days,' I caution.

'But it sounds positive.' I hear her sigh, but it sounds like a happy sigh. 'That's one of the things I love about you. You're optimistic. You see an opportunity where I see—' another sigh '—something to be scared of.'

'Speaking of opportunities, have you decided what to do with your windfall yet?'

'No. I just keep looking at my bank account. Reading the balance. Without wanting to sound like Scrooge, it gives me a lovely warm glow, seeing all that money sitting there. Though some part of me still thinks this isn't real, that it never happened. Especially since my dad's gone back up to Yorkshire.'

'Do you think you'll see him again?'

There's a silence on the other end.

'Ems?'

'I haven't exactly decided yet. Probably, I think. Right now, he's alive and healthy, but he won't be around forever. Part of me feels like I'm betraying my mum by even talking to him, but on the other hand . . . it'll be too late, eventually. I don't want to be left with a load of regrets.'

'Your mum would want you to be happy.'

'I know. There's a saying, isn't there: it's better to light a candle than curse the darkness? Something like that. I've no other family. Maybe making some sort of relationship with him is like lighting a candle.'

'My mum would definitely be in favour of that.'

Emma laughs. 'I'd like to meet her one day. I'd like to visit Cork. Though, right now, I have started looking into hotels in Paris. I don't want to splurge, but I reckon I'm allowed a short holiday. I'm desperate to get away from Smelissa. The amount of hair that woman leaves in the shower drain, I'm amazed she's not bald. And I've not heard anything yet about the edits for *Alien*. So, I was thinking . . .' She takes a deep breath. 'I was thinking that I could book something for two weeks' time.'

'That would actually be completely and utterly perfect.' I do a chef's kiss; she can hear the 'mwah', even though she can't see the gesture, and it makes her giggle. 'I had a message from Marcel, this morning. Kobe Lavigne has booked a table for lunch in just over two weeks. Fifteenth of February, I think he said.'

'No way! That's amazing, Kieran!' I can hear the pride in her voice, and my heart seems to swell in my chest.

'I'm so happy. I've not been out to talk to him yet, but I will next time, for sure. With a bit of luck, by the time Arnaud is ready to come back from rehab I'll be on my way to my own restaurant.'

'I'm so excited for you.'

'When you come over, we'll celebrate. I know – come on the fifteenth! I'll take the evening off and we'll have a night on the town.'

'I can't wait.'

I glance at the time. 'Ugh, I'd better clear up and get going.'

'You had. Aren't you supposed to be going to Notre-Dame to light a candle before you go to the restaurant?'

'Well remembered. Mum will be glad to know you're on her side.' There's been so much good news in the past hour that I can't stop grinning. 'Honestly, Emma, I'm so delighted that you're coming back to Paris. You have no idea. Even if it's only for a weekend. Even if it's only twenty-four hours, I'll take it.'

'I'm delighted too. We've been talking about it for such a long time. So I'm nervous, but delighted.'

'Don't worry. Just get yourself here, and I'll take care of everything else.'

My mood is lifted even higher by the cleaned and restored interior of Notre-Dame. After I've lit the candle – and sent my mum a photo by way of evidence – I linger as long as I can, basking in the vastness of the cathedral, breathing in the faint scent of frankincense and watching the stained-glass windows transmute daylight into rainbows, spilling across the stonework. Cycling to work, I return to my favourite daydream: imagining my future with Emma. The Gare du Nord is the place we met. Should I propose to her there? Or could we actually get married there? How far ahead would we have to book? I'm concluding that Brendan is right – I absolutely am an impulsive, hopeless romantic – when I push open the back door of La Reine.

Arnaud is there.

I stare at him, unwilling to believe my own eyes. Why has he left rehab?

'I don't understand,' I begin, then switch to French. *Je ne comprends pas. Pourquoi est-ce que vous avez arrêté votre cure de désintoxication?*' I can't hide my shock and vexation. 'They wanted you to stay for at least eight weeks – that's what you told me.'

My boss shrugs. 'Because they make the mistake in thinking I am an addict, *un alcoolique*, but I am not.' He glares at the rest of the staff before refocusing on me. 'You do not know the pressures of running a restaurant like this. It is *my name* that is at stake. I made some errors of judgement before Christmas, but it will not happen again. I needed a rest, that is all.'

'But surely,' I begin, 'it would be better to listen to the experts at the clinic and—'

'You are not my doctor,' Arnaud snaps, 'you are my employee, and we will not discuss this further.' He picks up a sheet of paper from the table. 'Now, I've made some changes to the menu you had proposed for this evening. And I see from the reservations list that Monsieur Lavigne is returning – I must think about what to cook for him. He must have the chance to experience La Reine with its founder at the helm, no?' Arnaud gives me the amended menu for this evening's service and claps his hands at the rest of the staff. Most of them have just arrived, and they've paused to watch this exchange. '*Continuez. Vous avez tous du travail à faire.*' You've all got work to do. They obey instantly. I'm left standing there like that saddo at the office party no one really wanted to invite.

The day goes from bad to worse. Arnaud is critical. Hectoring. Impossible to please. He finds excuses to throw perfectly good plates of food in the bin then roars for them to be remade. He reduces Fleur, one of our commis chefs, to tears. By the time the doors open for service everyone is on edge and frazzled, and the atmosphere in the restaurant has returned to what it was before Arnaud's pre-Christmas breakdown: tense and brittle. It's not until I take a short break, halfway through the evening, that I realise that someone is missing.

Ettore is standing in the courtyard behind the restaurant, dragging on a cigarette.

'Hey, Ettore, have you seen Chip?'

He blows a smoke ring and gives me a look. 'Fired. Just before you arrived this afternoon. Arnaud told him he was ...' he shrugs, '"surplus to requirements".'

'What? But we need a kitchen lad.'

Another shrug.

'I expect Chef would prefer a *garçon* who has not seen him passed out on the floor drunk.' He stubs out the cigarette butt and chucks it in the bin. 'The writing, as you say, is on the wall. Marcel and I are going to start the job search tomorrow. You should do the same.'

Ettore returns inside, leaving me to my thoughts. None of them is pleasant. If he's right, and Arnaud got rid of Chip because he was one of those who had seen him in the cellar that night, then the writing is indeed on the wall for both Ettore and Marcel, and also for me. For the entire staff, perhaps; all of them know what happened.

I'm wondering how long we've all got when my phone buzzes.

'Emma. Tell me something good. I'm not having a great evening.'

'Um ...' she begins. Her voice is off. As though she's trying not to cry.

'What's happened? Are you okay?'

'Yes.' I hear her sniff. 'Yeah, I'm okay. Nothing's happened, not really. What's going on with you?'

I move further from the kitchen door and lower my voice.

'Bloody Arnaud. He came back early from rehab. Says he's fixed. He's being a bloody nightmare.'

'Oh, no. I'm so sorry, Kieran.'

'I'll figure it out. I might just get in touch with Lavigne directly.'

'Yeah, that's a good idea.'

She still doesn't sound normal.

'Emma?'

A beat of silence.

'I've got work problems too, it turns out. Bit of a shock, really.'

'Tell me.'

'I had an email from Lauren. I thought it might be the edits, but – they've rejected the draft I sent them. Apparently, it wasn't "up to the expected standard", and they're not going to pay me for it. They're not going to commission me to write any more, either.' She laughs suddenly. 'Paige has fired me. She's actually fired me.'

'God, Emma. I'm so sorry.'

'Don't be.'

The edge of anger in her voice surprises me. 'You don't mind?'

'Of course I mind. Paige is an idiot. She can barely construct a sentence, let alone an entire novel, and one day someone's going to expose her. But – but – maybe this is a good thing. I've got some capital now. I can take a chance on finding another job. I can even take a break. Maybe I'll force myself to finish that novel I started last summer. Maybe I'll even submit the damn thing.'

She hiccups. A suspicion crosses my mind.

'Emma, my darling, are you drunk?'

'Not drunk. Bit tipsy, perhaps. I may have finished the rest of the Christmas Baileys after I read the email. And the end of the bottle of advocaat Daisy's mum gave us three or four Christmases ago.' She hiccoughs again. 'Does advocaat go off? It tasted very . . . yellow.'

'Were you keeping it in the fridge?'

'No. It was at the back of one of my three-sevenths of a cupboard. Three-sevenths of all the cupboards. You know what I mean.'

If it had been sitting there open for three years, it's no wonder it tasted yellow.

'Finishing the novel does sound like a brilliant idea, Ems, but perhaps you'd better have some water and a lie-down first of all.'

'It does sound brilliant, doesn't it? You know what, I'm not just going to finish the novel. I'm going to – I'm going to rent a studio in Paris for a couple of months.'

'Are you sure?'

'Yes. And it's not just the Baileys talking. Or the advocaat. I've been thinking a lot since I saw my dad, Kieran. It scared me, seeing him. I don't want my life to be small.'

'What *do* you want, Ems?'

'I want – I want my own space. I want a different future. And I want you, Kieran. I want you.'

Chapter Twenty-One

Emma

I strip the bedding off the bed. Duvet, pillows, sheet. Mattress topper – acquired half-price in the sale at Argos just after Daisy and I moved into the house. Revealing the mattress makes me wrinkle my nose; I'd forgotten how manky it is. Folded up, everything fits – just – into the last box. Or it will once the top is taped shut.

Now I just need to find the tape.

It hasn't rolled under the bed. Or beneath the now empty wardrobe. I check all the obvious places: my open suitcase, down the back of the chest of drawers, inside the bedside table, on the windowsill.

Bugger.

'Daisy!' I yell from the landing. 'Have you seen the tape?'

'The what?' she yells back.

'The tape!'

No response. I hurry down the stairs and find Daisy in the kitchen.

'This is your kettle, right?' she asks.

'Yeah. Melissa doesn't like tea, remember? That's hers.' I point to the large, chrome-accented coffee machine that takes up far more than its fair share of space, and means that Melissa's other stuff has inexorably crept over into my allotted three-sevenths of the work surface.

'Well, there's just time for me to descale it,' Daisy says, brandishing a box of citric acid that she must have brought with her, since I've never knowingly purchased any. 'Then I'll dry it up and pack it in the kitchenware box.'

I'm impressed. Also, surprised.

'Seriously? We lived together for five years.' I hold up my hand, thumb and fingers spread wide, by way of emphasis. 'Five. Our previous kettle literally burst at the seams from the amount of crap built up inside. Your response was to try to convince me that limescale in your tea is a good source of calcium. Now you've spent a few weeks with Dan and you're *descaling* stuff?' I narrow my eyes at her. 'Who are you, and what have you done with the real Daisy Takahashi?'

She laughs, managing to look smug at the same time. 'This is just what we engaged people spend our time doing, when we're not planning a wedding. I cleaned the inside of the washing machine last week. And the week before that, Dan defrosted the freezer.'

'No way! That is next-level adulting.'

Daisy grins, shrugs her shoulders and opens her hands wide in a kind of *look how fabulous I am* gesture. 'Now, are you done upstairs? The removal guys will be here any minute.'

'I just need the tape to close up the last box. Have you seen it?'

'You took it up with you.'

'Did I? I can't find it up there. I've looked.'

'Everywhere?'

'Everywhere.' I list the places I've searched. 'What am I going to do if I can't find it?' I wrap my arms across my stomach, trying to keep panic at bay, as visions arise of my unwashed bedding strewn across a motorway somewhere between here and Paris.

'Is it possible that the tape is inside the box?' Daisy suggests.

I stare at her. Race back up the stairs. Turf out bedding, towels, dressing gown and the fake sheepskin rug from Ikea – I think it was pink when I bought it. Underneath it all is the roll of tape.

I have the box sealed up and addressed just in time. The removal guys get here, and I direct them to the six boxes that – with the exception of my suitcase and backpack – represent the entirety of my worldly possessions. It doesn't feel like much to show for almost thirty years of existence. Still, if the removers think it's a bit pitiful, at least they keep it to themselves. Half an hour after their arrival, my boxes are on the way to Paris, together with a lorryload of other boxes headed in the same direction.

I close my suitcase and take a last look around the bedroom. Without its surface dressing of clothes and make-up and books and photos, without the lamp and rug and other knick-knacks acquired over the years, the room looks small and tired. Anonymous. I'd expected to find this moment impossible: so big a change, it would leave me in tears. But my world has altered over the last couple of months, despite my best efforts to prevent it. Daisy, my dad, my work; in the end, I couldn't hold back the tide. I can hear my mum in my head, fond, but laughing: *who do you think you are, my angel, King Canute?*

My life has, finally, moved on. And, perhaps because Kieran is part of what lies on the other side of the change, I think I'm just about okay with it.

'Thank you,' I murmur to the room, before closing the door behind me.

Downstairs, Daisy has packed a large carrier bag with the last few bits for the charity shop: some books I realised I was never going to read, and a couple of my mum's brightly coloured jumpers that I'd kept because they used to carry the scent of her perfume. That's long since faded. The jumpers don't fit me, but they're still in great condition. I've decided someone else ought to get some joy from them.

'We've got twenty minutes until Dan gets here,' Daisy says. 'Want a coffee?'

We look at each other, then at Melissa's fancy coffee machine.

'I don't know,' I say with a smile. 'Melissa told me on no account must I touch the coffee machine.' I press the on button and open the fridge. 'And I'm definitely not allowed any of her terribly expensive artisanal coffee.'

Daisy takes the tub of coffee, wrenches the lid off and inhales deeply. 'Now this really is the good stuff.'

While Daisy makes the drinks – luckily she knows how to use the machine, because Dan has an even larger version of the same thing – we run over the plan for the next twenty-four hours. I'm spending tonight at Dan and Daisy's flat, and this evening we're going out to dinner with James and Petros. I've already said goodbye to Ron at Café Olay and to the ladies I clean for. Then, tomorrow morning, Daisy is coming with me to King's Cross to see me off on the train. And tomorrow afternoon . . .

Tomorrow afternoon, Kieran is meeting me at the Gare du Nord.

Every time I remember – every time I realise that this is finally, really, happening – I get a tiny jolt of joy, a spark that reminds me of that moment when Kieran and I first met.

Daisy's phone buzzes. 'He's here. Ready?'

'As I'll ever be.'

I leave the mugs in the sink for Melissa to wash up.

Kieran

The evening service is just finishing – there's only one couple left in the restaurant, lingering over their coffee and cognac – when my phone buzzes. Emma has sent me a photo. A selfie of her and four other people, all waving and smiling broadly at the camera, clustered around a table laden with empty glasses. Daisy I recognise from the times she's bombed our video chats, and the other three must be Dan, James and Petros. The caption reads *Bonsoir from Fulham! Looking forward to seeing you very soon! Xx*

Ettore taps me on the shoulder. 'Kieran—'

'Just the lad. Quick selfie with my favourite sommelier?'

'For your Emma?'

I nod.

'In that case, allow me.'

We stand together and Ettore holds up the phone, grinning broadly and giving a thumbs-up as he takes the photo.

'Thanks, Ettore.'

'No problem. Marcel and I are looking forward to meeting her.'

He returns the phone to me, together with a small slip of paper. I'm guessing it's Kobe Lavigne's email address. Marcel, who unlike me is totally at home with technology, and more importantly has access to the protected data section of the bookings system, has come through for me.

'I owe both of you,' I murmur.

Arnaud is watching us. Ettore leaves and I make a show of checking the various stations before heading for the changing room; only there do I take out my wallet and put the slip of paper carefully inside.

With that email address, I have a chance. Even if Arnaud makes it impossible for me to leave the kitchen and talk to Lavigne tomorrow, I've a way to let him know that it's my food he's eaten on his last two visits. I add a caption to the photo Ettore took and send it to Emma. *Bonsoir! Me and Ettore, sommelier superstar and a true friend. Can't wait to introduce you! Literally counting the hours until you're here. Xx*

I am, too. I know she'll be stepping off the train in sixteen hours and twenty minutes, allowing for the time difference. My only wish right now is that it was sooner.

Emma

'So I've got my spreadsheet,' I tell Daisy for only second or third time, 'and I'm in touch with the venue, and the florist, and I'll chase up that photographer during the week. Okay?' I shiver in the damp chill of a February morning, despite my padded coat and the extra-long, vividly striped scarf – a present from James and Petros – looped around my neck. 'Everything's under control. My being in France for two or three months isn't going to make any difference. There's no need to panic about the wedding.'

'Mate, I'm not panicked about the wedding.' Daisy clutches my upper arms. 'It's not until December. You're the only one panicking. And you don't need to be.'

Displacement activity, that's what it is. If I'm stressing about Daisy's wedding – and let's face it, it is Daisy's wedding: Dan is getting next to no say in the whole thing – then I can't be stressing about the fact that I'm about to leave the city where I've lived my whole life for an entirely different country. A country where I know only one person – disappointingly, not yet in the biblical sense. Where I have no job and possess no discernible ability to speak the language. Old Emma, drunk on fear, is currently hyperventilating in a corner while simultaneously screaming *WTF, you crazy cow* at new Emma. New Emma has figuratively stuck her fingers in her ears and is saying *la la la I can't hear you* over and over again, in the hope that it will eventually be true.

'You're sure you've got everything?' Daisy asks. 'Purse. Phone. Spare phone battery. Passport.'

'Yes,' I reply. 'I've got it all. I've checked.' I've checked four times since leaving Daisy's flat this morning. It takes all my strength not to automatically check again.

'In a month's time, I'll be over to visit you.'

'I know.'

'And if it's not going well, I'll just help you move back again.'

'I know.'

'But if you need me, I'll drop everything and come and rescue you. Or I'll make Dan come.'

I throw my arms around Daisy and hug her tightly. 'I love you, D.' My voice comes out all weird and choked.

'Love you too. And I'm proud of you for taking a risk.'

'My second big risk in less than a year, if you count calling Kieran in the first place.' In the past, I've tried to limit risk-taking to a maximum of once every two years or so. 'I'm proud of me. I think my mum would be too.'

Daisy squeezes me harder. 'She definitely would.' I can tell by her voice that she's crying too.

'I'd better get going.'

'Okay. Call me when you get there.' She sniffs and winks at me. 'If you're not too busy with Kieran.'

'Hey, you know I'll call you, no matter how busy I am.' I smile back at her. 'Besties before testes, am I right?' Daisy cackles with laughter, but I really do have to go now, unless I want to dial the panic up to eleven. 'See you soon, Daisy.'

'Bye, Emma.'

I force myself to walk away and head for security. Thankfully it's well signposted, because I'm struggling to see through my tears.

Kieran

Come on, Kieran. You can do this.

I stare at the plate of food I've just made. Toasted brioche topped with smoked salmon, a poached egg, dill and a dollop of glistening, freshly made hollandaise. The plate of food stares back at me. Taunting me.

Come on. You've a lot on today. You need the energy.

My phone buzzes – it's Brendan. I give a sigh of relief and sit back in my chair.

'Hey, Kieran. Just calling to wish you luck today. Didn't interrupt your breakfast, did I?'

'No. Not really. To be honest, I've no appetite this morning.'

He frowns. 'Really? That's not like you.'

He's not wrong. I'm a big fan of breakfast. I'm a big fan of most meals. I can't think of a time of day that can't be improved by the addition of a hot or cold beverage and a morsel of something delicious, but breakfast is the best. Croissants, pancakes, crêpes, fry-ups, egg-in-the-hole – my grandad's speciality – *œufs en cocotte*, omelette, eggs Benedict, *pain perdu* – I'm partial to all of it. I sit with my coffee and a mouth-watering plate of something or other, and in that instant the day is still full of possibilities. Everything is peaceful, and I've not yet fucked anything up.

'You nervous?' Brendan asks.

'Yeah. I guess.'

'I get it. This Lavigne guy is a big deal, and you're cooking him lunch. But he likes your food, Kieran. He wouldn't be coming back again if he didn't.'

'Yeah, I know. And lunch will be fine,' I say, reassuring myself as much as Brendan. 'It's Arnaud's menu, but he's still a great chef. Nothing is going to emerge from the kitchen that's going to put Lavigne off, and at the end of service I'll have my chance. Hopefully. If not, I'll email him later this afternoon.'

'Seize the day,' Brendan comments.

'Exactly.'

'So . . .?' my brother prods.

'So?'

'Come on, Kieran. It's not just the lunch, is it? It would take something massive to put you off your food. An earthquake. Or an alien invasion. Or perhaps the arrival of someone you've fallen in love with despite having only spent two minutes in the same country.'

Brendan knows me too well.

'Fair play, Bren. I admit it: I'm nervous. Emma is going to actually be in the same city as me, and not just for a weekend either. I want it to be absolutely perfect. I want to meet her at the station and feel exactly that same gut-punch of attraction that I felt when she ran into me last year. I want everything to work out the way I've planned it in my head.' I gaze at my brother, but I'm not really seeing him, I'm seeing Emma. 'What if it doesn't? What do I do then?'

'Oh, Kieran.' Brendan is shaking his head. 'You're getting ahead of yourself. It might be weird at first, after all these months and months of virtual dating, but you have to give it some time.' He frowns at me. 'It's not like you to be worried. Your normal style is blind optimism, usually followed by stunned disbelief when it all goes to hell in a handbasket.'

'Yeah, okay.' I push my plate further away. 'This is different. She's my friend. My best friend, apart from you and Niamh. I really care about her, Bren. A lot.'

'I'm sure she cares about you too. She's moving to Paris, isn't she?' He grins at me. 'I honestly can't figure it myself, but there must be something about you she likes.'

I smile. 'Thanks for the vote of confidence. Tell Dad I'll call him tomorrow – Emma and I have plans this evening.'

'I bet you do,' Brendan replies suggestively.

'Feck off, you eejit.'

'Feck off yourself.'

He laughs and blows me a kiss and ends the call. My breakfast is still looking at me, all cold and reproachful.

'Sorry, lads. It's just not happening.' I tip the lot into my food bin and head for the door.

Outside, it's raining in a half-hearted sort of way, but I choose my bike over the metro: it's easier to think. I know what I want to say to Lavigne. I've checked Emma's train – on time so far – and I've booked a restaurant for this evening. The postcard – the third of the four I accidentally stole from her – should already have been delivered to the Airbnb Emma's staying at until she finds a longer-term rental. I toy for a moment with the idea of using the fourth postcard to propose, if everything goes well. Flowers. That's the other thing I need: a bunch of flowers for when I meet her at the station.

I'm wondering whether I'll be able to get tulips this early in the year when I arrive at La Reine, so it takes me a minute to notice the atmosphere. The music that's usually playing in the background while we do our prep has been silenced, and the early arrivals are moving mutely around the kitchen. Arnaud is in his office with the door shut. I go through to the restaurant and find Marcel, checking that every table has been set to his standard.

'*Qu'est-ce qui s'est passé?*'

He glares at Arnaud's office door. '*Quand je suis arrivé,*' he murmurs, '*Ettore et lui étaient en train de se disputer.*'

'What were they arguing about?'

'*Je ne sais pas. Mais—*' he leans closer '*—je crois qu'il recommence à boire.*'

'He's drinking again?' Fuck. 'Are you sure.'

Marcel takes a deep breath, like he's struggling to control himself.

'He fired Ettore.'

'He what?' I can hardly believe what I'm hearing. 'So now we've no sommelier?'

'No. Arnaud is either drunk or mad.' Marcel's voice has risen; a couple of the other staff look around. 'I am only still here because we've just put down the deposit on that new apartment I mentioned. Ettore is a genius, he will be snapped up, but . . .' There's a quiver of doubt in his voice. 'We cannot afford both to be out of work.'

'Arnaud has lost it if he thinks he can just walk out on the street and find someone with even a fraction of Ettore's talent.' I grip Marcel's shoulder. 'I'll go talk to him. If he's sobering up, he might already be regretting what he's done.'

Arnaud hasn't emerged from his office. I hesitate briefly – I've still not changed into my whites – and knock on the door.

'*Chef, je vous dérange?*'

Arnaud raises his head. His eyes are bloodshot, but his gaze is laser-focused. If looks could kill, I'd be no more than an unsightly smear across the tiles.

'*Qu'est-ce que vous voulez?*' What do you want?

Hardly inviting. Still, I have to try.

'Ettore. We need a sommelier, and he's one of the best. Are you sure that—'

'Whose restaurant is this, Monsieur Landry?'

'Yours, obviously.'

'I do not feel it is obvious. Not to Ettore, not to you.' He opens the desk drawer and pulls something out: the camera I hid in the cellar. 'I found this,' he continues. 'Ettore has been spying on me, the worm that he is. He was going to blackmail me.'

Cold rushes through me as if I've been dropped into an ice bath. The bloody camera. I'd completely forgotten about it.

'No. No, you've got it wrong.'

Arnaud gets to his feet and leans close to me. His breath reeks of alcohol.

'Wrong? In my kitchen, you tell me to my face I am wrong?'

'But it wasn't Ettore. I put the camera there. Wine was going missing and we wanted to find out who was taking it.'

Arnaud and I stare at each other. We've never talked about it, of course. He's never openly admitted that he was the one taking bottles from the cellar, despite the state we found him in. But I know it was him. And he knows I know.

His face purples with rage. 'Lies! *C'est – c'est de l'espionnage industriel!*' The words are accompanied by a shower of spit. 'You and Ettore were scheming to destroy me. To take away my reputation.'

'That's not true,' I reply, wiping my face. 'We were just trying to help the restaurant.' I reach towards him. 'Chef, you're a brilliant man, but you've a problem with drink, and you're blaming it on everyone else. First Chip, now Ettore—'

Arnaud pushes my arm away and bangs his fist down on the desk so hard that the papers spread across the surface jump.

'Enough! You are fired, Monsieur Landry. Get out of my kitchen and out of my restaurant.'

'But – but you can't—'

'This is my kitchen!' Arnaud bellows. 'I will do what the fuck I want. And you—' he jabs a finger into my chest hard enough to send me stumbling backwards '—you will never work again in this city. I will make sure of it.'

'You wouldn't.' My voice seems to be coming from a long way away. 'I'll talk. About Christmas, and the brandy, and—'

'And who will they believe? A nobody, from nowhere?' Arnaud sits back down at the desk, breathing heavily. 'Or one of the most respected chefs in Paris?'

I don't know how to answer him. Arnaud's mouth twists into a sneer. 'Get out. Now.'

My jaws are clamped so tightly together I've bitten my own tongue. The sweet-salt tang of blood fills my mouth.

'Lavigne is coming back here for *my* cooking, not for yours. And I'm going to make damn sure he knows that.' I croak the words out and fling the door open and stalk out before I do something worse, something I'll regret. The whole kitchen must have heard. No one is working; they're all staring at me.

'*Chef, s'il vous plaît*—' someone says as I stride towards the back door. Whoever it is, I don't stop to acknowledge them. My whole being is focused on getting out of there. On not falling apart. I have to hold it together, until—

Emma.

Christ, I'd almost forgotten. What am I going to tell her? She's moving her whole life to Paris for me, and now—

She's going to think I didn't say anything on purpose. That I want her here now because she's got some money.

My hands are shaking. The rain's got heavier, and it takes me three goes to unlock my bike. I drag it up the steps, blindly – one of the flowerpots crashes to the floor – and start cycling. Get away from here, get to the station – that's what I have to do now. Get to the station, and find Emma, and explain what's happened. She knows the problems I've been having with Arnaud. Meet Emma, then email Lavigne. Better still, I'll email him while I'm waiting for her. I'm going to be early. Fuck. The rain is dripping off the front edge of my hood. I can't believe this is happening. Everything I've been working for, all these years of effort, and now – and now—

The rain beats on my back like drumsticks, bouncing up from the pavements and slicking the tarmac into a mirror.

I put my head down and cycle faster.

Faster and faster.

Away from La Reine and the fight with Arnaud.

Away.

Emma

I press one hand to my stomach. I'm so hungry I feel faint, but the idea of eating anything makes me want to throw up. My coffee's cold. I drink it anyway and check my phone again. No messages, apart from the low battery warning. No missed calls. Nothing.

It's nearly six o'clock. In the four hours since I arrived at the Gare du Nord, I've watched countless people come and go. My legs have grown stiff. My fingertips are numb with cold, despite my gloves. The grey day has disappeared into dusk. And there's still no sign of Kieran.

What's that saying about trying the same thing over and over being the first sign of madness? Even so. I pull off my glove and hit redial.

'Sorry, this mailbox is full,' says the automated voice.

Did I honestly expect him to answer this time? Apparently so. A fresh surge of emotion – anxiety, anger, despair – makes my chest so tight that I can hardly breathe. I've called him and called him. I'm still calling, even though his phone stopped allowing me to leave a message nearly three hours ago.

Has something happened to him? Or did he just decide this was all a mistake? Could he not, at least, have told me to my face?

Redial.

'Sorry, this mailbox is full.'

Redial.

'Sorry, this mailbox is full.'

Redial.

'Sorry this mailbox is full.'

I jab the screen so hard my nail breaks.

I can't believe this is happening.

I don't know what to do. Stay? Or go? Maybe I should get on the next train back to London. Maybe I never should have left.

What's happened to you, Kieran? Where the hell are you?

Chapter Twenty-Two

Emma

There's a discreet notice stuck to the inside of the restaurant's rainwashed window: *On embauche* – we're hiring – followed by a list of jobs. I'm more concerned with the much larger sign that reads *Fermé*. I push against the door, just in case, but it is indeed closed. Still, a place as fancy as this must have a back door.

There's an antiques shop next to the restaurant, and beyond that a dank passageway that runs between this building and the next. The gate is unlocked, so I follow the passage to a small courtyard. A sign indicates the rear entrance to the restaurant: La Reine de la Nuit.

What if I actually find him here? What the hell am I going to say to him? The thought of a confrontation brings me out in a cold sweat. I start to catastrophise, following my fears into a rabbit hole. What if he's angry that I've found him? What if he's cold? What if he laughs at me? What if he claims we never actually met? What if, what if, what if.

And what if he's *not* here?

Before I can chicken out, I hurry down the steps, jerk the door open and walk into the kitchen.

There are three people in chef's whites prepping food. A couple of them look up when I enter, and I open my mouth to say the phrase I've made myself learn – *pouvez-vous m'aider, je cherche Kieran Landry*. I've only got out the first syllable when a man walks out of a side room.

He says something to me in French – all I catch is the very beginning, *Je suis Arnaud* – and looks at me expectantly.

'Er – *je ne comprends pas.* Um. *Est-ce que vous parlez anglais?*'

A scowl has settled on his face before I stumble the end of the sentence.

'You cannot work in a kitchen in Paris, *mademoiselle*, if you cannot speak French.' He turns away.

'I'm not here for a job. I'm looking for Kieran. Kieran Landry. He – he works here?' It's not meant to be a question, but I can't keep the uncertainty out of my voice. Three days after Kieran was supposed to meet me at the Gare du Nord, and didn't show up, I'm no longer certain of anything.

I went to his flat, yesterday and the day before. I went there seven times, over the course of the two days, from nine in the morning until after midnight. I leant on the buzzer and pleaded – and yelled – into the intercom. I begged him to answer me.

I've emailed, I've texted, I've called. Almost continuously. And I've got nothing.

Arnaud seems intent on ignoring me.

'*S'il vous plaît, monsieur,*' I add.

He turns back. 'Kieran Landry does not work here. I fired him.' The man's face reddens. 'Him, and the others who were conspiring with him to undermine me in my own kitchen. I will not have it, *vous comprenez?*' He breaks into a torrent of French, so loud and aggressive that I back away from him even though I've no idea what he's saying. By the time he stops, he's breathing heavily. 'He offered you work in *his* kitchen, I suppose?'

'What? No, I—'

Arnaud strides towards me, forcing me back towards the door. 'Pah!' I catch the smell of wine on his breath. 'Kieran Landry will never work again in this city. I told him that, and now I tell you. If you search for him, search outside Paris. I dare say he has crawled off somewhere like the – the rat he is. *Allez.* Get out.'

He manhandles me through the door and slams it behind me.

'You – you bastard!' I kick the door as hard as I can and beat my fists against the cold metal surface. 'You bastard! You utter,

utter bastard, Kieran, you – you—' Suddenly faint, I sit down heavily on the doorstep. Is that what really happened? Arnaud fired him, and he ran away? Could he really have been too embarrassed to tell me? Or was it just an excuse? A convenient way out of a relationship he'd actually tired of.

My legs are shaking. Still, I push myself to my feet and start walking. I'll go back to Kieran's apartment block again; maybe he'll have shown up by now. Despite the rain, despite the fact that I'm soaked to the skin, I have to keep moving. Part of me knows it doesn't make any sense. I can't actually hold off the pain and shock of this betrayal by trying to outrun them. But I have to try. Because if I give up – if I actually stop searching – then I've lost him.

And if I've lost him, I don't know how to carry on.

Daisy, peering at me from my phone screen, wrinkles her face as if faintly disgusted.

'You look terrible.'

'Thanks. I feel terrible.'

The no-show at the Gare du Nord was now four days ago. I spent yesterday afternoon visiting hospitals – pointless: I couldn't prove I was next of kin, so they wouldn't talk to me – and getting rained on. Again.

'Yeah, well, *quelle surprise*, you idiot. Seriously, what were you thinking? Running round Paris in the rain, not eating properly, not sleeping—'

'I wish I hadn't told you any of it now. I – I—' A huge sneeze sends me into a paroxysm of coughing.

'Oh, great, now you're going to die of consumption.'

'I'm not Victorian.' I manage to force the ghost of a smile. 'It's just a cold.' And at least now I can pretend that my reddened eyes and sore chest are down to being ill, rather than all the crying I've been doing.

'Huh. Well, I hope for your sake you're right.' Daisy wags a finger at me. 'And no doing anything stupid, d'you hear me? Or at least no more stupid than what you've done so far.' She pauses, pulling at her earlobe the way she does when she's worried. 'You'd better not go all Hamlet on me.'

I almost laugh. 'Hamlet thinks about killing himself, but he doesn't actually do it. 'Cos of, you know, existential dread, etcetera. And I'm not going to do it either.'

'Good. Because he's not worth it, Ems. No man is.'

'I know.'

She's still tugging on her earlobe. 'Look, why won't you come home? Once your boxes arrive, just send them back to London. You can come and live with me and Dan while you look for something else. Or let me come over there and look after you, at least. I can take a break from work. Why won't you let me do that?'

It's a fair question. Embarrassment, I guess. I can't stomach the humiliation. The idea of returning to London with my tail between my legs, like some prize idiot, sends a hot wave of shame prickling across my skin. I can't do it, even if I did have somewhere to return to. And I suppose that's why I won't let Daisy come here, either. I can't take the pity, even from her. Not at close quarters.

'I'll be okay. If I come straight back, I'm just allowing my life to revolve around Kieran. Just because he's apparently vanished off the face of the earth, that doesn't mean I shouldn't stay here. Maybe I'll enjoy it, eventually.'

Yeah, right. I'm kidding myself, and I know Daisy knows it. Still, she nods and gives me a thumbs-up.

'Too right! Who needs him, the – the arse.' She hesitates. 'Are you going to be alright next weekend?'

She means on my birthday.

Kieran and I had tentatively made plans. We were going to go to the Paris Aquarium. They've got thirty-eight sharks from four different species, as well as seven hundred coral colonies and the largest collection of jellyfish in Europe, and we were going to check it all out. Him and me. Me and—

I take a deep, jagged breath. Even thinking his name makes me want to curl back into a ball, holding my pain tight within my core. The worst thing is not knowing. Is he dead? Is he ill? Has he had to return urgently to Ireland because of his dad? That's possible. But surely – *surely* – he would have told me if he'd had to go home. More likely he's off somewhere else, congratulating himself on his escape, laughing at how he strung me along all those months. If he is alive, he'd better hope I never find him. I might just murder the fucker.

'I should go,' I say. 'I've got stuff to do.' Finding somewhere to live, for example. I have to be out of the Airbnb by the end of next week.

'Okay. Well, you know where I am if you need me. Speak in a couple of days?'

'Yeah. Sounds good. Thanks for calling, Daisy. Love you.'

'Love you too.'

I end the call and force myself to get up off the single bed-cum-sofa – bolted to the wall, like everything else in this rental. The postcard that was waiting for me when I arrived – one of the four that Kieran ended up with, and the third one he sent back to me – is on the floor nearby. According to the postmark, he sent it three days before I arrived in Paris. I snatch up the card, planning on ripping the damn thing into as many pieces as I can. But I pause, again. This isn't the first time I've tried to throw the card away. I know the inscription by heart. Still, I read the words over, tracing my fingertip across the slanted lines of his handwriting, trying to discover some clue hidden in the uneven surface.

Darling Emma,
 I'm so excited for you to be in Paris so I can conquer what's left of your heart! (Sorry, terrible pun, but I couldn't resist!) All my love, K. xxx

Despite myself, I smile a little: the postcard picture shows the statue of Napoleon Bonaparte at the Invalides, the complex of museums and military retirement home where Napoleon is also buried.

There must be an explanation. The man who wrote that card couldn't have just stood me up three days later.
Could he?

After three days registering with rental websites and looking at flats, I take the first one that seems halfway decent. A subdivided fraction of what was once a much bigger apartment, it has one bedroom, a kitchen/sitting room, and a shower room only marginally larger than a coffin. On the plus side are high ceilings, an attractive exterior of creamy stone and cast-iron balconies, and a safe-ish location – I hope – in the thirteenth *arrondissement*. The building has a live-in *gardienne*, Madame Pollie, who collects and distributes packages and generally keeps an eye on things. A week after I've moved in, I'm still not sure whether she counts as a benefit or not. On the one hand, I guess she offers some extra security. On the other, she's seventy years old if she's a day, and she's still way more fashionable than me. A typical outfit is black cigarette pants, a black sweater and black biker boots; it's hard not to feel frumpy in comparison. So far, she also insists on translating my surname into French, and calling me Mademoiselle Noël.

I'm too exhausted to argue with her.

I'm still searching for Kieran. Going online doesn't turn up much. I already knew he loathed social media – it was one of the first things we'd realised we had in common – and technology in general, but I didn't know how hard that would make it to find out anything about him, other than the stuff he's told me himself. There's a seven-year-old photo on Facebook in which he was tagged, and an article in an Irish newspaper about him winning some sort of culinary prize when he was twenty-two. But that's it. I don't know his parents' names, and searching for 'Brendan Landry' is also a dead end, though I think Kieran said they were half-brothers, so maybe they don't even share a surname.

I decide to try something more radical. Despite my lack of French – it's amazing what you can achieve when desperate – I manage to get some fliers printed: his photo, an email address I set up for the purpose, and '*Personne Disparue*' in big letters across the top. Missing person, if Google Translate is right. I spend the afternoon of my birthday handing them out near the Gare du Nord, but it's pretty dispiriting. Most people won't take one. Some take one and immediately chuck it in the bin. I give up when the police start giving me funny looks and head back to the apartment.

It's dark by the time I arrive. I open and close the front door of the block almost silently and start to tiptoe towards the stairs, and I'd be willing to swear that I haven't made a sound, but somehow Madame Pollie knows I'm there. She shoots out of her room before I can make my escape. It occurs to me that she might be an alien. Or, with her widow's peak and predilection for black, a vampire.

Though this evening, she's accessorised her long black dress, black wrap cardigan, black tights and black patent high heels with a metal pin badge about the size of a small plate. The badge displays the words '*C'est mon anniversaire!*', written in primary colours in a large, jokey font.

Madame Pollie hands me a small package. For an instant my heart races, but the writing on the address label isn't Kieran's. I turn the package over; my Dad has written his name and address on the reverse.

'Oh. *Merci. Et bon anniversaire*,' I squeak. The badge is so garish I can't stop looking at it. '*C'est mon anniversaire aussi.*'

Madame Pollie shakes her head. '*Non, non, c'est mon anniversaire.*' She points at the badge.

I give up. '*Oui.* It's very – *c'est très joli*. Pretty.'

'*Merci*,' she replies, inclining her head, seeming pleased at the compliment. Her gaze sweeps over me again, more thoroughly, and her eyes narrow. 'Hmm. *Vous avez une mine terrible.*'

'*Pardon?*'

Madame Pollie rolls her eyes. 'You. Look. Dreadfully.'

Was that all she wanted to tell me? Great. Thanks.

'Well, *je suis* knackered. *Fatiguée.* I have to – to sleep. *Dormir.*'

I start to edge towards the stairs, but Madame Pollie – lightning reflexes despite her age, *must* be a vampire – grabs my wrist. '*Un instant.*'

I wait while she disappears back into her lair. When she returns, she's holding a plate with a piece of cake on it. There's an unlit birthday candle stuck into the icing. She passes me the plate but doesn't immediately let go.

'*L'assiette*, the plate, *il faut me la rendre*. Give back.' She raises both eyebrows. '*Vous comprenez?*'

I nod. '*Je comprends*. I understand.'

'*Très bien.*' She releases her grip on the plate and tilts her head to look at me. '*Ne soyez pas vous, soyez Gloria Gaynor.*' Seeing my incomprehension, she sighs. 'Be. Gloria. Gaynor. I will survive. Hmm?'

How does she know? Tears fill my eyes.

'*D'accord.* Okay. *Merci, madame.*' A sentence resurfaces. 'Er, *vous êtes trop gentille*. Too kind. *Merci*.'

She smiles at me – a warmer smile than I've ever received before – and waves me towards the stairs.

Back in my apartment, I turn on a lamp and sit on the sofa. The exterior of the package from my dad is ninety per cent Sellotape, but it eventually gives way. The first thing I see is a letter.

Dear Emma,
 Hope this finds you well. Do let me know how you're getting on, if you want to.
 I thought you might like to have this.
 With love,
 Peter/Dad

I set the letter aside and pull out something wrapped in a tea towel. A framed photo: me, aged about eight, at a guess, and both my parents, smiling and squinting into the sunshine. I've not seen a photo of the three of us together since Dad left and Mum went to town on the family albums. We'd been to the seaside in Southend. I remember the taste of hot doughnuts, eaten on the pier. The smell of seaweed. Shrieks of excitement from people on the rides and tinny music from the slot machines.

My feet squelching in the cool, muddy sand. Dad must have asked someone to take a photo, though I don't recall posing.

They both look so happy.

On impulse, I set the photo upright on the table next to the birthday cake. Kieran sent me a photo of himself in a card only recently, and I've still not chucked it. *So that you'll recognise me when you get off the train – it's been a minute.* That's what he wrote inside. I retrieve the photo from my suitcase, fetch some matches and light the birthday candle.

The flame bursts into life, illuminating the photographs.

Dad definitely let me down. So did Mum, really: she took a stupid risk, and died because of it. Why would a woman who couldn't even swim decide it was a good idea to go mudlarking on the Thames foreshore, in the dark, without a permit and with no knowledge of the tides? What was she looking for? I never found out for sure: the brain damage meant that she couldn't really speak after the accident. She slipped on some steps, fell into the water and got hit by a passing boat, or that's what the police concluded. The last six months of her life were spent in hospital.

We never properly got to say goodbye.

And now Kieran seems to have let me down too.

He reminds me of my mum, a bit. The same ability to take chances without caring. Or thinking. The same magnetism. The same immense energy and optimism. He was – is – the type of person who attracts the eye and draws one's attention. Glittering. Shiny.

Trouble is, shiny people are dangerous. They mesmerise you. Suck you in and burn you up until you're nothing but ash. And you don't even realise it's happening.

I still miss my mum, though. I miss Kieran too, though I wish I didn't.

I blow out the candle.

I wish it didn't hurt so much.

PART THREE

Spring

Chapter Twenty-Three

Kieran

Someone is singing, though it takes me a while to figure that out.

I recognise noise, first of all. Something from outside my dark cocoon. Something melodic yet insistent, breaking into my sleep, dragging me back towards the surface.

Music. My brain eventually supplies the word. And with it comes a faint sense of recognition. Music that I've heard before, somewhere. And a man, singing. My – my father? Or my – my . . .

Groping for the word induces a wave of sickening pain. I relax back into the song, and slowly it carries me up, up.

I stumble through the landscape of our dreams,
Where everything is real, love,
But nothing's as it seems.

The shadows around me lift a little. I'm holding someone. I can feel the warmth of her in my hands, through layers of fabric. My fingers flex in response to the memory.

A name attaches itself to the memory: Emma.

And if you die in dreams you die for good,
Or so they say.
So hold me close and kiss me
Before we fade away . . .

From somewhere outside, a voice cuts through the music, loud enough to make me wince. I don't want the voice. I want to stay with the music and the memory in the dim warmth of my cocoon. But the voice won't let me. It gets louder still, repeating the same word over and over. I feel something warm grip my shoulder and the memory fragments and slips away.

Unwillingly, I open my eyes.

Light, so bright it hurts. The blur in front of me resolves a little. A face.

I blink. Try to focus.

My mouth is dry and foul-tasting. Another wave of nausea threatens to overwhelm me. But I recognise the face, finally. My brother.

'Bre ...' Barely a whisper. My throat, my tongue – nothing seems to work properly. I try again. Manage to croak out the word. 'Bren.'

'Kieran,' my brother exclaims, 'oh, thank fuck.' His voice sounds weird, though not as weird as mine. 'Hold on.' He retreats, and I close my eyes again, but I can hear him shouting. 'Hey, can I get some help in here? He's awake. He's finally woken up.'

I spend the next two hours being prodded and poked by doctors and nurses and told – repeatedly – how lucky I am. *Vous avez eu une drôle de chance!* By all accounts, I had a miraculous escape. The lorry that hit me knocked me off my bike but threw me out of the path of the bus coming the other way. Not that I remember any of it. The doctors explain about the various bones I broke, and how they've been pinned back together, and point out my good fortune in not ending up with serious internal injuries. Their main concern was whether I would wake up, and, if I did, whether I'd wake up with brain damage. However, so far – I look around for a piece of wood to touch, but don't find any – so far, everything seems to be working okay. The last thing I remember is the fight with Arnaud, but my memory before then seems to be intact. I remember my family, my work, my apartment. Emma.

Finally, the doctors leave. Brendan's been loitering outside, and I see him talking to them, frowning. When he comes in, he's shaking his head.

'You are one lucky bastard, you fecking eejit. What were you thinking, not wearing a helmet? They were convinced – *convinced* – that if you ever woke up you'd have lost most of your marbles. Seriously, Kieran. I can't believe you'd take such a risk. I can't . . .'
He sinks his head into his hands as he starts crying.

I've never made my brother cry before.

'I'm sorry, Bren,' I murmur. My right arm's in a cast, but if I reach out my left fingers I can just about touch the top of his head. 'I'm sorry. I just never got into the habit of wearing a helmet. And I didn't mean for this to happen.' He's pressed the heels of his hands into his eyes. 'If it's any consolation, everything hurts.'

This makes him look up. 'Good,' he snaps, before his face softens. 'Does it, so?'

'Yeah.'

'You're probably due more painkillers soon.' He gestures to the drip I'm hooked up to then grips my hand. 'I was so worried about you. I thought I'd lost you.'

'I'm sorry,' I repeat. I try to squeeze his hand back, but my muscles don't seem to have any strength in them. 'Can I ask you some things?'

'Fire away. Though the doctors told me you've to sleep, so they might come and kick me out in moment. And you're not to get worked up, okay? You've to stay calm.'

I nod my understanding.

'How long have I been unconscious?'

'Almost six weeks. The accident was on the fifteenth of February, and today is the twenty-fifth of March.'

Christ. Six weeks without moving or eating or drinking. No wonder I feel terrible.

'And you've been here the whole time?'

'I went back just after they'd finished the operations, to get some more clothes and things, but otherwise, yeah.'

'But what about Niamh, and the kids?'

'They understand. Niamh told me I needed to be here. Mum's been helping out with Roisin and the other parents have been great with helping to take Colm to school.' He shrugs. 'You couldn't be moved, and we weren't about to leave you on your own.'

I don't know what to say. All I can think about is how much it must have cost my brother to be away from his family for all this time, and how am I ever going to repay his kindness.

I replay his words in my head.

'So, if Mum's helping out with Roisin, does that mean . . .'

He smiles. 'Yeah. Dad is doing great, apart from worrying about you. The immunotherapy is going really well.'

'Oh, thank God.' I sip the water I've been given, still needing reassurance that everything I'm experiencing is real, not just a vivid dream. 'So everyone is okay? Mum and Dad, and Niamh and the kids?'

'They've been anxious enough over the past few weeks, but otherwise they're all good. And now they're all very relieved.' He reaches up to the wall behind me. 'The kids made you a card. I pinned it up for you.'

Colm has drawn a stick man lying on the floor in what looks like a pool of blood while another stick figure, with a horrified expression on its face, bends over him. Underneath is a large and roughly executed smiley face with two legs but no body or arms – Roisin's work, I'm guessing. On the other page is an inscription, also in crayon:

Der Uncul Keran
Get weel son
Lov
COLM

The signature takes up at least half the page. An adult has added 'and Roisin' underneath, plus some kisses.

I well up, overwhelmed with an urge to sweep up my nephew and niece and hold them as tight as I can.

'Sure, the art's not that bad,' Brendan observes. 'And we're working on the spelling.'

'It's grand. Put it where I can see it, will you?'

As Brendan places the card on the bedside locker, I steel myself to ask the last question that's weighing on my mind.

'Has anyone else been by to visit me?'

My brother sits down and takes my hand again, so I know it's bad news before he says a word.

'If you mean Emma, then no. But she couldn't have done.'

'What do you mean? Didn't you tell her?'

'I've had no way of contacting her.'

'But my phone—'

'You got lucky. Your phone and laptop, not so much. The bus missed you but crushed your bag into a pancake. We couldn't even extract the SIM card out of your phone. And why did you even have your laptop with you?'

'So that I could help her look for a longer-term rental.' I rub my hand across my face. No. No, this can't be happening. Not after all these months. Not after she finally made it back to Paris. 'She doesn't know?' I ask, horrified. 'She – she just waited at the station, and I never showed up?'

'I did try, Kieran. I tried to get the phone people to help. But they said you never set the automated back-up, so they couldn't retrieve anything. They wouldn't try anything else without talking to you.'

Fuck.

'I was going to do it. I just never got around to it. What must she think? That I just decided to dump her, or that I was playing her all this time, or that I got cold feet or—'

'Hey, don't panic.' Brendan is rummaging in the duffel bag again. 'I guess you don't remember her phone number?'

I give him a look.

'Right, right, no one learns anyone's phone number now. Luckily for you I've got my laptop here. You can just log into your email account.'

'Yes!' I emailed her too. I can send her an email. My heartbeat slows a little.

Brendan turns on the computer and types something.

'Okay. I've entered your email, so what's your password?'

'My password?'

He nods.

Shite.

My brother's looking at me expectantly.

I stare back at him. Stare, and think, and try to recall.

'Ah, bollox.' I shake my head. 'I can't remember.'

'You can't remember the password?'

'No.'

'Did you write it down somewhere? On a little bit of paper in your wallet, maybe?'

I smile slightly, despite the mixture of panic and grief and anger swirling around inside me. Brendan's main method of filing is little bits of paper; Niamh's efforts to introduce him to modern technology have, by and large, totally failed. Not that I can talk. All my passwords were saved in the notes app on my phone.

'Well, that's okay,' Brendan says. 'I'll just click on "forgot password" and you can set a new one.' He clicks. 'Oh. It says it's going to send a message to the phone number associated with the account.' The phone number that no longer works because my phone is in a thousand pieces and I didn't back it up. 'Tell me you added in a recovery email to your account?'

'What do you think?' I growl, furious with myself.

He brightens suddenly. 'Tell me her email address and I'll email her.'

'Right. Great idea. Emma's email address. Um . . .'

He frowns. 'Can you not remember that either?'

'It was something weird and complicated. Like, M, A, then a number, 62, maybe, then an X, and then some more numbers, or . . .' I groan and press my fingers to my temples. 'She thought it would be safer.'

'Shite,' Brendan comments. 'I'm sorry, Kieran.'

I gesture for him to put away the laptop.

'Did any of my stuff survive the crash?'

'Your wallet, mostly, and your keys. I booked into a hotel around the corner while they were doing the operations, but I've been staying at yours the past month.'

'Mostly?'

He produces a key, unlocks the bedside cabinet and hands me my wallet.

My bank card and drivers' licence have both shattered. The only other thing in there is a photo of Emma. The one she sent me in her Christmas card. I turn it over to inspect the back, hoping her phone number might magically appear.

Brendan yawns, and I notice how exhausted he looks. He badly needs a shave and some less rumpled clothing.

'I'm sorry, Bren. You've had enough to deal with. If only I hadn't been so ... so ...'

'Hey ...' Brendan grips my upper arm lightly. 'These things happen, and it could have been so much worse. It's almost been restful, sitting here with you. I read an entire book in one sitting for the first time since Colm was born.'

'And no one else has been to visit?'

'How could they? I've not been able to contact anyone to let them know you're here. I did go to the restaurant a few days after the accident, to tell them what had happened. It was your boss that I saw, I think – Arnaud? He seemed really shocked, actually. Went white as a sheet when I told him what day you'd had the accident. But he's not been in.'

'I'm not really surprised. Did he tell you that he fired me? Right before it happened. I remember being angry. And – devastated, I suppose. All that work. Maybe I wasn't paying attention.'

Brendan hesitates. 'Well, I wasn't going to say, but they didn't press any charges against the lorry driver. You just shot through a red light, apparently.'

A spike of pain makes me flinch and clutch my head.

'I've really ballsed everything up, haven't I?' I ask, once the pain has subsided a little. I'm alive, and I should be grateful, but I can't keep the bitterness out of my voice.

'It'll be okay, Kieran. We'll figure it out. But not now: you need your sleep. The doctors are talking about you starting physio in a few days' time, after they've taken the casts off.'

'I am tired,' I admit, fighting against the weight of my eyelids. Weak, too. I feel as if someone has removed most of my muscles for a joke and replaced them with flabby dollops of congealed rice pudding.

'I'm not surprised.' Brendan stands and pushes my hair back from my forehead. 'Maybe I'll see about getting you a haircut tomorrow, if you're feeling up to it.' He studies my face, then gently lifts my limp arm and fist-bumps my hand. 'Just . . . don't be sleeping for another six weeks, promise? I don't think my heart could take the strain.'

'I promise.'

He pushes the buzzer for the nurse then lifts up my shoulders, handling me as though I'm some fragile piece of antique china, so he can rearrange my pillows.

'I'll be back in the morning, and we'll talk about it all then.'

'Okay.' I'm losing the battle to stay awake. Brendan starts talking to someone, but I lose the conversation in sleep.

Chapter Twenty-Four

Emma

Daylight filters through the flimsy blind in the bedroom. With my eyes still closed, I grope for the switch of the old radio that came with the flat and flip it on. It only plays one channel: a French equivalent of BBC Radio 2, as far as I can make out. I quite enjoy the mixture of French chat and French and English pop, and at least I can pretend that I'm absorbing the language as I listen. My French is marginally better than it was when I arrived here six weeks ago – it could hardly be worse – but that's about all I've 'achieved'. My laptop is jammed beneath a pile of jumpers in the top of the wardrobe. Still, I can sense it judging me. I can't remember that last time I wrote anything longer than a text message.

The news bulletin starts on the radio.

Bonjour à toutes et à tous, il est 13 heures, mercredi, 30 mars ...

I swear. So much for getting out early and going for an invigorating walk. I guess I shouldn't have stayed up scouring back issues of *Taste of France* – a magazine dedicated to French chefs and French food – for any mention of Kieran. And I definitely shouldn't have spent another hour or so searching for his name online and scrolling through the photos he sent me. It was past three a.m. by the time I fell asleep.

A Den Mahoney song starts up on the radio and I swear again. I only recognise it because bloody Kieran – as he's now known – introduced me to the guy's music. I can't seem to get away from him.

Somewhere in my bed, my new phone – the roaming charges got too expensive to keep my UK number – starts buzzing. I find it, eventually.

'Guess where I am?' Daisy exclaims.

'Er, London?'

'Well, yes, but where in London? Guess!'

'Your flat?' I hazard. 'Buckingham Palace? Scotland Yard? Have they finally arrested you for being unreasonably and dangerously cheerful?'

Daisy groans.

'I'm at St Pancras Station! With James! And we're coming to see you today!'

In the background, Den is pleading.

So hold me close and kiss me
Before we fade away.
I'll follow you into the shadows,
Through the storm and through the rain,
Through the fire and through the pain ...

Daisy, however, is practically screaming with excitement, loud enough that I have to hold the phone away from my ear. 'For one night only: Daisy, Emma and James, live in Paris!'

If it was anyone else, I'd say they were drunk, but Daisy doesn't need to be drunk to be absolutely high with exhilaration.

'Hold on,' I begin, 'you're coming all this way for—'

'One night only, like I said! Live fast, die at home aged ninety, that's my motto. And yes, we are crashing with you. It's going to be brilliant!'

'It is,' I exclaim, laughing, catching her enthusiasm.

'I'm glad you agree, because we should be there by half past four.'

'I can't wait to see you, Daisy. Both of you.' My voice catches in my throat.

'I miss you, Ems,' Daisy says. 'And James does too. I know you've been saying you don't want to see anyone, but I'm not going to let bloody Kieran keep me away from my best friend. I've done the right thing, haven't I?'

Den is still singing.

We set a candle burning
And it's just a single flame,
But it's enough.

I don't reply to Daisy's question. I can't, because I've burst into tears.

'Ems.' Daisy nudges me at the same time as waving to the young waiter who's been saddled with looking after us this evening. 'Ems, how do you order more wine again?'

'*Une autre bouteille de vin rouge, s'il vous plaît,*' I remind her.

Always a bit of a lightweight, Daisy is looking at me hazily in a way that gives me zero confidence in her ability to speak English coherently, let alone French.

'*Une autre* . . . bottle of this.' Daisy shakes the empty wine bottle and grins up at the waiter, who gives her a charming smile and sashays away, obviously aware that Daisy is watching him go. Or at least watching one, very specific part of his anatomy.

She turns back to James and me.

'I could totally get used to it here. Every waiter I've seen is a total hottie. The men *and* the women. It's like – it's like . . .' She narrows her eyes, suddenly suspicious, as if she's stumbled upon a huge conspiracy. 'Uncanny.' A long pause. 'Maybe it's the government.'

'Shame on you, you almost-married woman,' James exclaims. 'You shouldn't even be looking at another man.' He drains his wine glass. 'But also, you're not wrong. They must put something in the water.'

I roll my eyes, laughing. 'Guys, they're not all that good-looking. Not, like, objectively. I think it's more to do with confidence.' I survey our fellow diners. 'Confidence equals hotness equals more sex. Maybe. Speaking of, did you find out about the new book Lauren wants you to write, James?'

The guy deserves a break. Daisy and I have been talking non-stop about her wedding since they arrived, so it's only fair to pick a different topic. As long as the topic isn't bloody Kieran.

James waits until the waiter has brought the fresh bottle of wine. 'So, on the basis of no knowledge whatsoever, Paige has decided to go into classical mythology for the new book. The King of Greece sends his daughter, Ixes, to be married off to the Prince of Atlantis, Ocean, but she also falls for his younger brother, Brine. Cue lots of mermaid sex, clamshell nipple clamps and inappropriate activities with tridents.' He pauses. 'And yes, Ixes is just 'sexi' backwards. Paige chose the names. She says they're evocative.'

'Yeah, evocative of complete idiocy,' Daisy mutters.

'Greece wasn't an independent, unified state until the 1832 treaty of Constantinople,' I point out. 'Ixes ought to be princess of one of the city states, like Athens or Sparta or somewhere.'

Daisy and James both look at me.

'This is Paige,' James replies. 'No one is going to care about the historical accuracy.'

'And what's going on with your crime novel?'

I regret the question as soon as it's out of my mouth: James's whole posture tenses.

'Oh, not much. I mean, it's going to be published, which is great.'

His tone is off. Daisy is about to congratulate him; I kick her beneath the table.

'It's my own fault really,' James continues. 'I should have checked my contract.' He laughs shakily. 'Probably shouldn't ever have signed the damn thing. But you know,' he picks at the edge of the paper tablecloth, 'it's still an opening for me. And hopefully, if it does well, I can get better terms on the next book.'

'What do you mean?' I ask. 'What should you have checked?'

'Anything I write while working for Paige, she automatically gets the option of having it published under her name. It was there in black and white, if only I'd spotted it.' He drains his glass and pours some more wine. 'But I was so excited to get the ghostwriting gig in the first place.'

'But that's outrageous!' I grip his empty hand. 'Lauren told you to send her the manuscript, and she must have known. What an utter – an utter—'

'Crook?' suggests Daisy. 'Liar? Fraudster?'

'All of the above,' I retort. 'Seriously, James, you need to get some legal advice.'

'I signed the contract. And I can't even go to the press, because there's a line in there about that, too. But it's going to be fine. Lauren's offered me more money than I get for churning out a PAP, and then hopefully I'll be able to get an agent for the next book and end the contract with Lauren. It's all good.'

It's obvious from the look in James's eyes that he's lying – none of this is good. At that moment, however, the waiter returns with our main courses.

'Oh, this looks fabulous,' James exclaims, focusing on his *filet mignon*. 'I cannot wait to tuck into this!'

Clearly the subject is closed.

The sound of snoring jerks me awake. The bedroom is pitch dark. For a moment I lie disorientated, trying to remember.

My head is throbbing. My mouth is coated with something evocative of municipal dustbins.

Oh . . .

Daisy and James. And the restaurant. And then the nightclub. And then, when we got back to the flat, that bottle of *crème de cassis de Dijon* that I picked up last week at the local Carrefour . . .

I swing my legs out of bed, wait for the wave of nausea to pass, then stumble to the window. Sunshine floods into the room and burns uncomfortably into my retinas.

Time. What's the time? My phone's lying on the floor, dead. I remember the clock in the wardrobe – I shoved it there because the tick is so loud.

'Daisy.' I shake her out of the middle of a snore. 'Daisy, what time's your train?'

She opens her eyes a fraction. Groans.

'What time's your train?' I insist, holding the clock up in front of her face.

She gazes vacantly at the dial for a moment, then her eyes open wide.

'Shit!' She sits up fast. Too fast. Our heads collide and I drop the clock as the nausea, now served with a side of agony, sweeps back with a vengeance.

I just about make it to the bathroom.

I go back to bed for a bit after Daisy and James have left. When I wake, in the early afternoon, I'm feeling well enough to be tempted outside. There's a list on my phone: places Kieran visited. Places he said he wanted to visit again, with me. I've decided to go and see them on my own. When I've crossed off the last place, I'm allowed to go home. And by then I'll be over him.

That's the theory, anyway.

I get ready and head to my local metro station. Next stop, Sacré-Cœur.

The white stone basilica is almost blinding in the spring sunshine. To my left, a flight of steps leads steeply down. Trees, pale green with new growth, cling to the slopes nearby, spreading towards well-tended lawns. The view from the top of the steps is breathtaking: a sweeping vista with the huge expanse of the city at my feet. Just before Christmas, Kieran sent me a photo he took near this spot. I perch on the edge of the top step – despite the sunshine, despite my coat, the stone is still cold – and scroll through the images on my phone until I find it.

He must have been sitting more or less where I am now. If I close my eyes, I can almost feel him next to me. Warm places where our upper arms and thighs and hips are touching. His arm heavy around my shoulder. All imaginary, of course. I never got the chance to sit next to him in reality.

My chest tightens, and the dull ache below my ribs returns. I hunt for a tissue in my bag and decide to skip the interior of the cathedral. Instead, I go to the shopping centre I discovered last week: the Forum des Halles. Once I realised it's operated by Westfield – *my* Westfield, the same Westfield that gives people who don't work at the BBC or support QPR a reason to go to White City – it became my new happy place.

My shoulders drop as I pass beneath the soaring glass canopy, and a sense of calm returns. There's a Zara, just like the one back home. A LEGO shop. Even a Claire's. The familiar names soothe me. And perhaps it's just part of the hangover guilt – I'm never going to drink again! I'll exercise every day! – or perhaps it's because spending the evening with Daisy and James really has restored a part of myself I was in danger of losing, but when I spot a Moleskine shop I decide to treat myself to a new notebook. I need to get off my arse – metaphorically – and start writing again. If I'm going to write, I need to plan. And, to plan, I need stationery.

There's a lot to think about. I mull over colour, size, type of cover and layout. I'm eyeing up the fountain pens when someone addresses me.

'Emily, is it not?'

'Hmm?' I tear my gaze away from something in rose-gold aluminium and look up into the face of a slightly older man with grey hair and a cute smile. He's giving George-Clooney-with-a-French-accent vibes. He's also giving me a nagging sense that I've seen him before.

'Err . . .'

'Jacques Toussaint. We met last year, at the exhibition.' He raises an eyebrow. 'Paris and the Printing Press . . .?'

My memory finally gets on board with the conversation.

'Oh – yes. Emma, not Emily. You gave a speech at the beginning.'

'And you were there as an official photographer.'

'Er, yes.' As in, I was officially pretending to be Daisy's assistant. 'It was a great evening. Very . . . informative. Are you still involved in, um, printing?'

His mouth quirks up on one side.

'In so far as I am involved in magazine publishing. You are here for more photography?'

'No. I'm not really doing that any more. I'm staying in Paris for a while because – because—' I can feel my face flushing. I cannot – *cannot* – tell Mr Almost-George-Clooney about Kieran and the whole has he dumped me or is he dead debacle. Fortunately, my mouth gives up waiting for my brain to come up with something and takes over. 'Because I've started writing a series of articles about dating in Paris.'

News to me, but okay. Luckily, Jacques seems to accept it too.

'Ah, because Paris is the city of love.'

'But *is* it?' I say. 'Or is it actually just as hard to meet someone here as it is in London? Does the city deserve its reputation? Or has online dating made everything as difficult in France as it's become in the UK and America?' I hope I sound more like a journalist than a slightly hungover weirdo. 'Are French men really better in bed?'

Fuck. Weirdo it is, then.

Jacques raises both eyebrows, as if giving my question serious consideration, then he laughs.

'As a Frenchman, I cannot be expected to give an unbiased opinion. But, the concept of the articles, it is interesting. You have a commission?'

'Er, no. I've been ghostwriting for the past few years. As well as doing the photography,' I add quickly. 'I'm taking a break from that, so this is just for fun, I guess. To see if anything comes of it. I'm writing in English, of course.'

'Brave, to take a chance. And Paris is very multicultural. How long do you stay here?'

'I'm not sure exactly.'

'Here.' He hands me a small oblong of thick card with his name and some other details printed on it. 'When you finish the first article, send it to me. I can promise nothing, but . . .' He shrugs in a very French way. 'I must go, unfortunately, but it was delightful to meet you again, Emma. *Au revoir.*'

'*Au revoir.*'

He leaves, and I study the card he gave me. *Jacques Toussaint, Éditeur, Maison Carnet Médias, S.A.* A quick online search tells me that his job title is the French version of commissioning editor, and Maison Carnet Médias is a big-time magazine and book publisher. And he remembered me.

Not that it matters, if I'm no longer capable of stringing a sentence together. I put the card away carefully and turn back resolutely to the notebooks.

The first thing I do, though, when I get home, before unearthing my laptop and making some notes in my new notebook, is open the one box from home I've not yet unpacked. It's got my paperwork in it. Everything that I've ever thought might come in handy, printed out and neatly filed. I spent too long watching Mum desperately searching for some vital document, like her passport or my birth certificate. Her 'system' was to shove anything important into some random drawers around the house and forget about it. Sometimes it turned up again, sometimes it didn't. Is Kieran as disorganised as she was? I push the thought away.

I doesn't take me long to unearth what I'm looking for: the contract I signed when I first started writing for Paige.

It's only two pages long. I was the first official ghostwriter Lauren employed; at that point she'd only just set up Anchor & Hope, and I think she'd unofficially been writing Paige's books herself. Or was at least responsible for turning them from 'sandpaper' – a draft so rough it could take your skin off – into something more readable. I skim through the clauses of the contract, then reread them again carefully. There's nothing here about Paige having an option on everything I write. Nothing about non-disclosure agreements, either.

Apparently, Paige and Lauren got themselves a better lawyer by the time James started working for them.

It makes me feel bad for poor James.

It also gives me an idea.

Chapter Twenty-Five

Kieran

Four weeks of physio, and it still takes me nearly four minutes to get up the stairs to my apartment. And that's with a crutch. And someone helping me.

'I used to be able to do all three flights in a minute and a half,' I complain to Brendan, who's come back for another couple of days to help get me out of the hospital and back home. 'Less than, on the way down.'

'Then I'm amazed you didn't break your neck months back,' he replies, shaking his head and smiling. 'Honestly, Kieran, I get that you're frustrated, but it's a long process. I know you heard what the doctor said when they discharged you. There's nothing wrong with your ears.'

One of the few body parts that didn't get a least a little damaged in the accident. At the moment, although the speed of my movement irritates me, I'm most worried about my right hand. As Brendan unlocks the door and takes my bag inside, I get the foam ball out of my pocket and start squeezing it, trying to regain the strength I once had. The strength I'll need, if I'm ever to work in a professional kitchen again.

Stepping into the apartment is like walking back in time, into a life that suddenly slipped away from me while I wasn't looking. Brendan must sense me taking a mental inventory.

'I tidied up when I first got here, and chucked out the old food, but I didn't mess with your stuff. I know how you feel about people messing with your stuff. I'll just go and unpack your bag.'

He disappears into the bedroom, and I advance further into the living area. My knives are still laid out on the countertop in the kitchen. My winter coat and scarf – no longer needed now, in late April – are still hanging on the back of the door. And the photo of Emma is still in a frame on top of the half-height wall that divides the kitchen from the living room. I lift my hand and skim my fingertips across the image of her face.

Brendan returns and he must see what I'm doing, but he doesn't mention Emma. Just goes to the fridge, opens the door and gestures inside.

'So, I followed your list, and I was able to get most of the groceries and the fresh food you asked for, but you've got the details of the delivery service. I got your man downstairs—' he means the building's *gardien* '—to recommend a couple of cleaning services, and I've texted you the numbers. He said they can take your washing to the launderette as well. And don't forget the physio will be here at ten tomorrow.'

I grin. 'Yes, Mum.'

'Oh, you think I'm being like Mum, do you?' He puts his hands on his hips. 'Just thank your lucky stars she doesn't want to leave Dad yet. Otherwise, you'd be spending the next month only allowed out of bed for the exercise, and living off of her idea of coddle.'

'Alright, alright, you're nothing like our mother at all.' I limp over to Brendan and put an arm around his shoulder. 'Apart from being unfailingly kind and self-sacrificing and an all-round great person.'

He blushes – my brother never was good at taking compliments – and wags his finger at me.

'*This* time I've been kind and self-sacrificing. But don't be making a habit of almost getting yourself killed. As soon as Roisin starts school, I'm back to work.' He grins. 'If I get any more calls from the emergency services after that, you're on your own.'

'Don't worry. I'm going to wrap myself in cotton wool, I promise. You've got the letter, right?'

It's a letter to Emma, addressed to her old place in White City. I'm hoping she might have some sort of post redirection set up. If such a thing works internationally.

Brendan pats his chest pocket. 'Got it here. Don't worry.' He glances at his watch. 'I'd better be heading to the station.'

'Too right. I don't want you to miss the train.'

Yet my brother makes no move towards the door. 'Are you sure you're going to be okay now?'

'I'll be fine. Let me know when you get home, will you?'

'Will do.'

I think for a moment he's going to ask me to let him know that I've managed to cook dinner, or take a shower, or get ready for bed – but he resists. Just.

'I'll be fine.' I push him gently towards the door. 'Go. Give them all my love.'

'Okay. And I will.' He pulls me, very carefully, into a hug. 'Concentrate on getting your strength back. There's no need to worry about the future right now.'

'I think there is a bit of a need, Bren. I can't be living off of you and Niamh forever. I need to get back into work—'

'And you will. But if you push yourself too hard you'll set back your recovery.'

I sigh. 'You're right, I s'pose.'

'I usually am. I'll call tomorrow.'

He slings his bag over his shoulder and leaves.

My brother's left my new laptop and phone on the coffee table. I lower myself gingerly on to the sofa and set aside my crutch. Our dad – who is somehow way more competent with technology than either Brendan or me – has broken it to me that I need to give up on recovering my email account. That ship has well and truly sailed. However, he reckons I might be able to persuade my old mobile phone provider to at least send me itemised bills. It will likely take a fair amount of time; I'll need the perseverance to get through to an actual human being at the phone company, for a start. At the moment, fortunately, time is something I have in abundance.

* * *

Apart from a daily break to chase up my phone records, I spend the entirety of the next two weeks working at my physiotherapy exercises as if they are the key to earning a Michelin star. No matter how tired I am, or how much everything aches, I do all the reps I've been told to do, and I never miss. Brendan, who at first calls me several times a day to check up on me, realises that I'm doing what I'm told. I think we're both relieved when he backs off a little from the mother hen role. I start venturing outside with my crutch. Though I flinch every time a lorry rumbles past, I still manage to get to the Airbnb Emma stayed in when she was first here. Of course I don't recall the exact flat number, and no one I talk to has a forwarding address, but at least I feel like I'm trying something.

My hand strength starts to return. I'm not up to my old speed and agility with the knives, but it's getting there. I've even made my physiotherapist a couple of salads for him to take away for his lunch. He's been timing me.

Today, he stops looking at his watch and nods his head.

'*Très bien! Je suis impressionné.* I'm going to miss your salads.'

I stare at him. 'Does that mean . . .?'

'*Oui, bien sûr.* You're doing very well, Kieran, *vous avez fait beaucoup de progrès*, which means you and I are finished. You must continue each day with the revised schedule I'm going to send you, then in two weeks you go to the clinic, and they check you over. *Ça marche?*'

'*Oui, ça marche.*' I give him a thumbs up. '*Merci, Jean-Luc. J'apprécie tout ce que vous avez fait pour moi.* Honestly, thanks for everything.'

'*De rien.* Take care of yourself. No more throwing yourself from bicycles, hmm?'

'My brother said much the same thing.'

Jean-Luc leaves, and I move slowly, carefully, towards the table. There are three emails open on my computer. Two are drafts. One, with my CV attached, is what I'm about to send to various Parisian chefs, in an attempt to get a job. The other is an email to my landlord giving notice on the flat; I'll need to send it if I don't get some work soon. The third email is one I received just as Jean-Luc arrived. It's from Lauren Carter, Emma's former editor. From her assistant, rather.

> Kay Phips <phips.k@anchorhopepublishing.com>
> Wednesday 7 May, 12.38
>
> Dear Mr Landry,
>   Thank you for your email addressed to Lauren Carter.
>   Emma Christmas no longer has a working relationship with Anchor & Hope Publishing, so we are unable to fulfil your request to pass on a message. Neither do we have any up-to-date contact information. In any case, to share such details would be in breach of data protection legislation.
>   Regards,
>   Kay Phips, assistant to Lauren Carter

In other words: fuck off. Mentally crossing Lauren off the list, I move on. My e-reader is now loaded with several Paige Adams Pereira books; my next plan is to discover James's surname and reach Emma through him. I pick up the e-reader – with some trepidation: Emma was always a bit vague about the level of spice in the novels – and open the first of the books, and then the entryphone buzzes. I guess Jean-Luc has forgotten something.

But it isn't my physiotherapist.

'Kieran?'

I recognise Arnaud's gravelly voice. My first instinct is to put the receiver down. Then I remember Brendan's comment about how shaken Arnaud was when he heard about the accident. Does he think I might sue him? Has he come here to dissuade me, or threaten me?

'What do you want?' I ask in English, not choosing to do him the courtesy of speaking in French. He gets the hint, and replies in the same language.

'To talk. To apologise. I will not take up much of your time, I promise.'

In all the months I worked for him, I never once heard Arnaud apologise. It's not something executive chefs tend to go in for, to be fair. Regret and humility are not good seasonings when you're trying to convince the world that you're God's gift to the art of cookery.

'Please,' he says. 'Just a few moments.'

He doesn't sound drunk, so I decide, on balance, that he's not likely to try to murder me. I press the buzzer for the door.

'Come on up.'

When he arrives, I'm shocked by the change in him. He's lost weight. Enough that he looks a little shrunken. On the other hand, his eyes and hands are steady, and his gaze doesn't dart suspiciously around the room the way it did the last time he was here. I gesture him to a seat.

'Thank you for seeing me,' he begins. 'I hope you are mending?'

'I am. I was very lucky.'

'Good, good. Me, I have been very lucky too.'

I don't understand what he means. Perhaps he's come to crow about Kobe Lavigne offering to open a new restaurant for him, though I've not seen any announcements.

'If you died in the accident,' he continues, 'I do not think I can cope. The accident is my fault. You are angry with me, and I do not blame you.'

I stare at him.

'You think I'm angry with you because of the accident?'

There's a flicker of uncertainty in Arnaud's expression. 'Of course.'

'No. I wasn't paying attention, and I was cycling too fast given the weather, and I wasn't wearing a helmet, so that was on me. I'm angry with you—' I jab a finger at him '—because of what happened before. The drinking, and the stealing, and the lying, and the – the sacking people who just wanted to help you. Not just me. Ettore, and that poor American kid too. And I dare say you got rid of others, after you'd kicked me out. Marcel? Alex?'

I try to calm down. Reigniting my rage is making me breathe hard, and the ribs I broke are still not healed enough for that to be a fun experience.

'And the porter you got rid of back in early December. That was you too, wasn't it? The missing wine.'

Arnaud nods his head and slumps forward, leaning on his knees. 'There is nothing I can say. No excuse to offer. But I have, finally, accepted that I need help. The rehab, as you say, pff . . .' He pulls a face. '*Mais Alcooliques Anonymes*, so far, it is saving me.' He looks up at me. 'The day your brother told me you nearly died, that was the last day I drank. I had been drinking that morning. I was drunk when he arrived. The next day, I found a meeting. Now, I go to the meetings without fail. I have people I can call when I am tempted. Every day is a struggle. But so far—' he takes a deep breath '—so far, every day, I succeed.'

'What about La Reine?' I ask.

He shrugs. 'I shut it down. Too many bad memories, and I cannot concentrate on it. To be a great chef demands great focus. You know that.'

No job going there, then. Not that I'd have taken it.

My gaze drifts to the photo of Emma, and I think about what might have been, until Arnaud drags me back to reality.

'Kieran, is there anything I can do? I cannot fix the past, but perhaps the present? I do the Twelve Steps. One of the steps is making amends.'

Part of me is tempted to tell him to go to hell, that I don't want his help, or his apologies. Then I hear Emma's voice in my head, repeating some questions she'd asked me once. *Do you always rush into things? Doesn't it ever go wrong?*

I'd said no, at the time.

Not entirely true.

'Maybe,' I say to Arnaud. 'There might be some things you can help me with.'

'Name them.'

'I need a job, and you know every chef in Paris. If any of them are thinking of hiring . . .'

'Of course, of course,' Arnaud says eagerly. 'I will put out the feelers, as you say. As soon as I get home.'

'Also, I lost my phone and laptop in the accident. I'd like to get in touch with Ettore and Marcel. Do you still have their numbers?'

His brows draw together in thought.

'Perhaps, yes. Not on my phone, but maybe *sur l'ordinateur* – the, uh, computer. I will search.'

'Thank you. And the last thing . . .' I point to Emma's photo. 'Do you recognise her? She might have come to the restaurant, just after the accident. She might have been looking for me.'

Might have. The words piece my heart. I wish I knew. I wish I could say for certain that she was trying to find me.

Arnaud fetches the photo and stares at it. His face flushes. 'Yes. Yes, I remember her.'

'You – you do?'

'Yes. She came into the restaurant.'

'When?' I demand.

'Well . . . two or three days after your accident, I think. As soon as we were open after the weekend. I was drunk, of course.' He pats at his thinning hair, puts the photo frame down and picks it up again. 'She asked about you. I told her I had fired you. That you would never work in Paris again. I told her . . .' His voice falters for a moment. 'I told her to look for you outside the city. Then I threw her out.'

My hand has moved to the walking stick that's resting against the sofa, and I'm gripping it so tightly that my knuckles are white. I can't move. If I do, I fear I might lash out at him.

He threw her out.

But then . . . but then, she *was* looking for me.

Arnaud stands.

'I will take no more of your time – thank you for seeing me. And the things you have asked, I will do my very best to help you.'

I nod – that's all I can manage – and he holds out his hand, and for the second time – the last time, I'm guessing – we shake hands.

Chapter Twenty-Six

Emma

'*Joyeuse fête, madame!*' I hold out a slender bunch of irises to Madame Pollie, the vivid purple petals flaring against the shady, monochrome entrance hall. '*J'ai appris le*, um, I mean *la coutume*, the custom, *pour célébrer* . . .' I give up. 'I learned about the French celebrating name days, and since your first name is Désirée, I realised that today is your special day. *Bonne fête!*'

Madame Pollie, quickly covering her surprise, inclines her head and accepts my offering with a smile. I've been working hard to restore my relationship with the fearsome *gardienne*, somewhat damaged when Daisy, James and I stumbled in drunk at half past one in the morning (Madame Pollie apparently *never* sleeps – more evidence for my vampire theory.) Over the past five weeks or so, I've asked her advice on cleaning products, changed a light bulb in the hallway that she couldn't reach, and gone to the supermarket for her a couple of times. A few days ago, I even made a cake – my very first. She was pretty critical, but she ate it. And at least the criticism made it plain that her English is quite a lot better than she's been letting on. My French has improved, too, thanks to my new neighbour, Agnès; the same neighbour who told me about the name day custom. I give English lessons to Agnès's ten-year-old daughter, not that she really needs any, and in return I get to inflict my French on Agnès. As a result, Madame Pollie and I can now stumble through a basic conversation without too much difficulty. Which is just as well. Because I'm hoping that the flowers and my recent good behaviour will be enough to persuade her to give me some help.

'*Alors, madame,*' I begin, '*est-ce que vous êtes libre? Je . . .*' I pause to give my brain time to get up to speed and to remember the sentences I've carefully worked out. '*J'ai besoin de votre aide. C'est pour un article que j'écris pour un journal.*' I've told her I need her help for an article I'm writing for a magazine, or that's what I hope I've said.

She gives me a hard stare.

'*Vous êtes journaliste?*' she asks.

I stare back at her.

No, you're definitely not a journalist! You can't say you're a journalist when you've not had a single article published.

'*Oui.*' I can hardly believe that I've ignored myself. 'Yes, I am. *Je suis journaliste.*'

'Ah . . .' Her eyes gleam with excitement, and to my surprise she gestures that I should follow her into her apartment.

I've never been invited in before. Once through the door I look around surreptitiously, but the room is reassuringly lacking in coffins, candles and gothic décor. Madame Pollie points at an overstuffed floral armchair.

'Sit. I bring coffee.'

'*Oh, non, merci*, I just wanted to—' Too late. She's already disappeared into the kitchen. I get out my notebook and pen and review the notes I've made for the article on dating in Paris. It's almost written, and I just want one more source.

Madame Pollie returns with two espressos.

'*Vous voulez écrire sur ma vie?*' she says, miming the action of writing. 'About my life?'

'Er . . . not exactly. I'm writing about the dating scene in Paris. Um, *j'écris sur . . .*' What the hell is French for dating? '*Un moment.*' I get out my phone and pull up Google translate. '*La scène des rencontres*. Do you know anyone who is trying to date? Who wants to go out . . . *qui veut sortir?*'

She raises both eyebrows. 'Someone who wants to date with *you?*'

The tone of surprise does not make me feel good.

'No, not with me. I mean in general. I'm looking for people to talk to. Lots of people, who want to go out. *Je cherche beaucoup de gens qui – qui veulent sortir.*'

The eyebrows elevate even further. 'You want to date lots of people?'

'No!' I say quickly, shaking my head and Google translating 'interview'. 'Okay. *Je veux*, I want, *interviewer des gens*, to interview people, *sur les rencontres*, about dating.'

Madame Pollie relaxes.

'Ah . . . why did you not say so?' There's just enough hint of amusement in her eyes to make me suspect that she's been winding me up this whole time. 'Well, I know someone you can interview. Me.'

'You?' I raise my eyebrows right back at her.

'*Bien sûr*. Just because I have seventy-eight years, may I not have the dates? May I not have the sex?'

There's an edge to her voice that suggests that, now, she's being deadly serious.

'Oh – yes. I mean, of course you may.'

'Well, then, I will tell to you all the problems of trying to find *un homme tolérable à Paris*. I will also tell you *la verité* – the truth – about the French men. But first, you will tell to me why *you* are not dating.'

Her bargaining takes me by surprise.

'Me? I'm dating. Definitely.' She can't know, after all. She doesn't have X-ray vision.

'If you date, where is the man?' she demands. 'Hmm?' There's a pause, while she watches my discomfort. 'I see everything. You arrive, you are sad, you stay in your room for weeks. Only now you come outside, but you bring no one here apart from those two—' her mouth twists in distaste '—*Anglais*. You have no ring on your finger. So, I tell you, you are not dating, and you will tell to me why, and then I will help you.'

Madame Pollie sits back in her chair and gazes at me expectantly. And it dawns on me that talking through the past almost three months with someone who doesn't know me, who has no stake in my life, might actually be just what I want right now. What I need, even.

'*D'accord.*' I clutch the warm coffee cup and take a moment to get my thoughts in order. 'Okay. So, there was a man. Someone I fell in love with, even though I never even kissed him.' I laugh. Saying it out loud … the whole thing seems insane. But that doesn't make it not true. 'His name was Kieran …'

My first feeling on waking up, surely, should be excitement. Or dread. Or some combination of the two. With Madame Pollie's help, I finished the article and sent it off yesterday afternoon – from my new, more professional/normal-looking email address – to Jacques Toussaint, the editor at Maison Carnet Médias. It's the first time I've ever submitted work in my own name to someone who might be interested in publishing it. I should be obsessing about when – whether – he's going to reply.

In fact, after checking my email once, I get showered and dressed and revert to my usual morning routine: drinking tea and Googling.

Kieran Landry death.
Kieran Landry restaurant.
Kieran Landry marriage.
Kieran Landry alien abduction.
Kieran Landry bigamist fraudster.
Nothing shows up.

Talking about him to Madame Pollie yesterday has definitely not helped me move on. If anything, it's just made me more desperate to find him. Describing to her how we met and recalling all the little details – the messaging, the phone calls, the photos of random body parts – he told me he found the photo of my clavicle 'disturbingly sexy' – has only intensified the ache that drives through the centre of my chest whenever I think about him. I feel like a butterfly pinned to a collecting board. Perhaps I could free myself, if only I knew why he disappeared. Why he stood me up.

I dreamed that we were together last night. That I was lying in bed with my back against his chest and his arm draped across my hip. I could feel his breath, warm against my earlobe. My feet were cold, and he let me warm them up against his legs.

It was so ... real.

Even now, sitting on the sofa with sunshine streaming into the room, if I close my eyes, the dream is waiting to reclaim me. The skin on the back of my neck prickles, as if he's standing just behind me ...

I need to get out of the flat. Besides, I might not have much time left here. It's the ninth of May, and I've promised myself that, if Toussaint says no, I'll return to London at the end of the month. If he says no, I doubt I'll ever return to Paris. I'll have no reason to.

I grab my list – I've still got five places to visit – and head out.

It's a beautiful day, so I walk the forty minutes or so from my flat to the Île de la Cité. I take the scenic route and stroll through the city's botanic garden, the Jardin des Plantes, before heading through the Jardin Tino Rossi with its collection of modern sculpture. Bloody Kieran still manages to distract me; every time I catch sight of a man with approximately the right height and colouring, I think it's him. Sitting on a bench or striding along the paths or wheeling a bike, Kieran seems to be everywhere.

My ultimate destination is the cathedral of Notre-Dame, but once I reach the Pont de l'Archevêché I keep going, seduced into browsing more of the second-hand books on offer from the green-painted *bouquinistes* boxes. I snap up an old French edition of Richard Scarry's Best Word Book Ever – *Le Grand Livre des mots*. It's probably just about the right level of French for me. Passing the turning for Rue de la Bûcherie, I think about going into Shakespeare & Co., but there's a long queue outside. And another Kieran lookalike, drinking coffee, hunched over his phone. Despite the warm sunshine I shiver, as my brain starts chattering about ghosts and haunting. With an effort, I turn my back on the stranger, walk to the Petit Pont and cross the river.

In the square outside Notre-Dame I find a relatively uncrowded spot to stand and crane my neck, gazing up at the façade and the restored spire. I remember the fire. The shock of it, when Daisy gasped and turned her phone so I could see what she was seeing. All that history going up in flames. And now, with the restoration, they've engineered a fresh start.

Sunlight catches the golden rooster on the top of the spire. The sudden brilliance is dazzling, but I don't look away.

A fresh start – that's what I need to try for. This morning has proved that I'm not over Kieran. Perhaps I should stop trying to be over him.

I find somewhere to sit down, bring up on my phone the list of places Kieran visited, and force my finger down on to the dustbin icon.

There. That wasn't so bad.

Next, I go into my internet browser and delete my 'Kieran Landry'-themed search history.

Work. That's going to be my new obsession. I'm going to focus so hard that I won't have time to dream about Kieran. The article was a start, but the new novel is what I need to throw myself into. My story – James's story really, and I've started planning it with his blessing – about a put-upon writer who slaves away ghosting novels for an erotic novelist. James's contract stops him talking about his work with Paige, but there's nothing in *my* contract to stop me doing whatever the hell I like. The irony is, if I hadn't come to Paris, if I hadn't fallen for Kieran and survived losing him, I'm not sure I would ever have been brave enough to do any of it.

I open my documents and re-read my title and opening lines. Lauren and Paige are both going to be in there – disguised, of course, but they'll know. Everyone will know. A surge of excitement bubbles up through my veins. Is this what people mean when they talk about being drunk on power? Before I know it, my mind has slipped seamlessly from completing the book to sending out queries to the important question of what I should wear for my book launch.

A text from Daisy pops up on my screen.

Been up since 6 making up 30
extras to look like Regency gentry
this morning – not sure how long
I can keep this up! On a break
now. Tell me something fun.

                    I was just planning what to wear
                    for my book launch. I think I'll
                    have it at Hatchards'. Oldest
                    book shop in London – fact!

Wait what???????? You
got a book deal?

                    I wish! Have to write it first. Sent
                    in article to Jacques, though.

🍆
BTW you should totally seduce
him. I've been Googling him.

Of course she has.

                                    And?

He's loaded. Descendant of
French aristos who managed to
avoid getting heads chopped
off AND kept hold of all their
loot. As all the characters in this
production keep saying, he is
totally an eligible bachelor.

As I'm typing my reply – a whole line of laughing face emojis – a notification pops up. My stomach backflips. Sweat, cold and clammy, drenches my armpits.

OMG – just got an email from him.

Open it! Open it now!

Hold on.

The last thing I want to do is open it.

He's emailed back really quickly. That means it's going to be bad news.

There it is again, that negative bit of my brain. The bit that seems to want me to fail just so it can say 'I told you so'. And the worst thing is, I can't think of any positive response. But maybe – maybe – I don't have to. I just have to open the email.

Or you could not. You could never open the email. If you don't open the email, then it won't count as a rejection.

Bloody hell. I really have spent too long being frightened of failure.

Okay, okay, my negative half says. *Go ahead and open it. But when it turns out to be a rejection, we go to La Maison du Chocolat in the Carrousel du Louvre and get something nice to help us feel better.*

Or, what if we go to La Maison du Chocolat either way. It's kind of spendy, but we might want to celebrate.

My dark side doesn't reply, so I open the mail app and click on the email and scan Jacques's response.

Then I read it again, more slowly. Delight wells up inside me, taking my breath away, so fierce it almost makes me cry. He loves the article, and he wants to publish it, and he thinks he knows where to place it. He'll be in touch before the end of the month.

I'm actually going to be published.

And I get to stay in Paris, if I want.

Maybe my fresh start is about to materialise after all.

Chapter Twenty-Seven

Kieran

I've not slept well. I'd like to blame it on my aching leg, the one which now has five pins in it. Truthfully, though, the leg aches most nights, especially now I'm trying to wean myself off the painkillers. The calendar on my bedside table – a gift from my auntie, who has sent me a calendar every Christmas since I was ten – displays the real reason I lay awake for hours in the dark: the date.

The thirty-first of May.

A year to the day that Monsieur Arnaud offered me a job. A year to the day that I met Emma.

All night long, I've been trying to work out what to do today. There's something I could try that would almost certainly work, if Emma and I were characters in a romantic comedy. In real life, I suspect it's likely to end in tears. No good will come of it, as my mother is fond of saying.

Still, I think I'm going to go for it.

It was eleven-thirty in the morning when I first saw her. I remember because the Gare du Nord has a clock high up on the façade, and that's what I was looking at when she ran into me. I was angry at first. Who wouldn't be? Then she almost fell over, and she looked so mortified, and was so apologetic, and so striking with her dark hair and green eyes and pale skin . . .

I remember the way my heart leapt. That sense, like a fizzing excitement coursing through my blood, that this was important. That *she* was important.

I still can't believe I've lost her.

It's nearly eight-thirty. Plenty of time yet. I check my phone. My cyberstalking of James, Emma's friend, has been successful . . . sort of. Once I found his full name – in very, very small print at the back of one of Paige's books – it was easy to find him on social media. X, Instagram, Threads, Bluesky, Mastodon, Discord, Facebook: you name it, he's on it. I spent a fair amount of time setting up profiles and figuring out where he was most active before I DM'd him. I told him about the accident and begged him to let Emma know what had happened, and to put me in touch with her. I'm pretty sure he's read the message, but he's not replied.

Scrolling through James's Instagram also led me to a photo in which Daisy was tagged. I messaged her yesterday. No response from her either, so far.

In the meantime, I'm going to get ready, buy some flowers and go to the Gare du Nord.

She might turn up.

She might.

Emma

The cereal in my bowl – never very appetising in the first place – has disintegrated into mush. Good job I'm not actually hungry. I scrape the remnants into the bin and think about making myself another coffee, but I'm already pretty keyed up. So far, my attempt at pretending this is just a normal day is not going that well.

Because it isn't a normal day. Even though it's over three months since I last heard from Kieran, it's also a year since I nearly ran him down outside the Gare du Nord.

My eyes flick to the time on my phone.

At eleven-thirty it will be exactly a year.

Tea. That's what I need now. I make myself a fresh mug, sit down at my desk and spend a minute reorganising my space: dictionary, pens, highlighters, notebook, Post-its. A copy of the *Writers' & Artists' Yearbook* – it lists every literary agency in the

UK – to act as motivation. I adjust the angle of my desk calendar, open the lid of my laptop and bring up the chapter I'm currently working on.

My phone starts buzzing. My heart races.

But it can't be Kieran, I remind myself. *He only ever had your old UK number. Not your new French one.* Besides, I don't recognise the number.

'Hello?'

'Emma? It's Jacques Toussaint. Is now a good time for you?'

Jacques Toussaint. And he's actually calling me.

'Yes, definitely.'

'*Bon*. I need you to come to our offices. One of my colleagues is going to launch an online magazine aimed at Parisian residents whose first language is not French, and she is interested in taking some articles from you, but she wishes to meet you first.'

'Oh, that sounds absolutely amazing!' I squeak. I take a breath and try to sound less overexcited and desperate. 'When – uh, when would she like me to come in?'

'She leaves for Toulouse in a couple of hours. Can you come now?'

'Yes, of course,' I say. The novel will still be here when I get back. And there's nothing else I have to do today. Nothing at all. Just an ordinary day.

'*Très bien*. You have my card still? We are on Rue La Pérouse; the nearest metro is Kléber. Ask for Sylvie Klein when you get to reception.'

'Will you be there too?'

'I wish I could, but I have another meeting. Don't worry, Emma. I'm sure she will be impressed with you.' He sounds more convinced than I am. 'I will be in touch later. *À bientôt*.'

'*Au revoir*.'

I check the directions – twenty minutes to Kléber plus a short walk – then grab my bag and keys. If I leave now, I can be relaxed about the journey and I'll still easily be there by ten-thirty. It'll be a short meeting, if she's got to get away. She probably just wants to check I look vaguely normal.

Normal. Right.

I glance down at what I'm wearing – leggings, socks and a faded T-shirt, accessorised with no make-up and a scrunchie around my wrist – and realise I have a maximum of ten minutes to transform myself into a glamorous, professional and above all Parisian-standard journalist.

Fuck.

Kieran

I lean more heavily on my walking stick, wincing. It's okay when I'm moving, but even with a detour to the Marché aux Fleurs, on the Île de la Cité, I got to the Gare du Nord early. I've been standing outside the main entrance since ten past eleven. The bouquet of lilac I'm clutching seems to be getting heavier and heavier. My leg is aching something fierce. I look down at my watch and then up at the clock that's in the centre of the station's façade.

Eleven-forty. No sign of her, so far.

Turning slowly, I scan the area around the station, peering through the crowds, murmuring to myself as if I can summon her into existence.

'Come on, Emma. Be here. Please.'

Someone is calling my name. I spin round so fast I almost tumble. There's a woman, waving at me.

But even as I open my mouth to call out her name I realise – it isn't her. It's Marianne. Marianne from the restaurant in Roubaix. What on earth is she doing here?

For an instant, it's as if the last year never happened. As if Emma is just a figment of my imagination. Then Marianne is in front of me, and I have to smile and pull myself together and try to follow what she's saying.

'. . . and I thought you hadn't got my message; it's been so long since I've heard from you, so to find you waiting is such a wonderful surprise.' She kisses me on the cheek and takes the flowers. 'Ah, *elles sont magnifiques* – you shouldn't have.' Stepping back, Marianne spots my walking stick and gasps. 'But what's happened?'

Her smile fades.

'You didn't get my message, did you?'

'No. Sorry.' Another ripple of pain makes me flinch. 'I couldn't. I haven't even got the same phone number any more.' I try to smile. 'It's a long story.'

'You are very pale, *mon ami*. Do you need to sit down?'

It's nearly eleven forty-five. Emma isn't coming.

'Yes,' I reply. It's hard to keep my voice steady. 'Yeah. Let's sit down.'

Emma

I'm getting déjà-vu – which I now know means 'already seen'. The meeting with Sylvie Klein seemed to go well. I left their offices at eleven, and I was going to go straight back home. Go home and carry on writing. That was the plan.

Until, somehow, it stopped being the plan. Because meeting Kieran became the plan instead. And now I'm sprinting along the Rue du Faubourg Saint-Denis towards the main entrance of the Gare du Nord on Place Napoléon III. I'm hot and sweaty and I'm trying to run in high heels and I feel as if I'm about to lose my mind. I'm not dragging my little wheely suitcase, and I'm not wearing a trenchcoat, but otherwise it's almost exactly like it was a year ago.

Apart from the fact that I'm late.

I swear as I leap out of the way of a woman walking while staring at her phone and risk another glance at my watch.

Eleven-forty.

Slow down! You're going to have an accident. He's not going to be there anyway. Why would a guy who stood you up, who's ghosted you for over three months, suddenly decide to do something super-romantic like show up to the place where you first met exactly a year later?

I ignore myself and speed up.

Because Kieran was – is – the most romantic man I have ever met. And, despite everything, I can't give up on what we had.

Finally, gasping for breath, I reach the front of the station and scan the crowds desperately.

And to my utter disbelief, I actually see him.

He's right there. Sitting down on a bench just outside the station. And this time it's really him, not a figment of my imagination, or a ghost or – or—

The crowd thins.

He's sitting on a bench, but he's not alone. He's talking to a woman who's clutching a bunch of flowers. There's a little wheely suitcase next to her. As I watch, she reaches across and puts her hand on his shoulder.

A sharp pain wells up in the centre of my chest. I'd almost convinced myself he had to be dead.

The tears come suddenly and without warning, blinding me.

But I won't let him see me cry. I won't give him that satisfaction. Turning away, I stumble into the shadowy entrance of the station.

Kieran

Marianne gave the flowers back to me. She didn't think it was right to take them, once I'd explained; in any case, there'll be nowhere to put them in her hotel room. She's here for an interview at a restaurant, funnily enough.

Though my instinct was to dump the lilac boughs, I end up taking them all the way home. Once I've trimmed the stems I put them in a jug with some water. Turns out I don't actually own a vase.

My phone pings. It's an email from my old phone provider.

Dear Mr Landry

After further review of your case and the documents you recently provided, I am pleased to tell you that we can release your mobile phone records for the past six months, as

requested. The file is attached below. We apologise for any
inconvenience and . . .

I click on the file without bothering to read the rest of the message. My heart is racing so fast I can hardly breathe. Emma's number. I scrabble around for a pen, write the number down and dial it.

'Please, pick up. Pick up. Pick up.'

'This number is no longer recognised.'

What? I stare at the phone. Hit redial.

'This number is no longer recognised.'

No. This can't be happening. Redial. Redial. Redial.

I get the same message every time.

Maybe she's blocked me. And, if so, I can hardly blame her. If she is still in Paris – and that's a big if – I'm now just the guy who never showed up and never called. After months of trying to persuade her to come here. She probably thinks I'm a massive arse, at best. Or possibly a psycho. So why would she take my calls? Why would she go anywhere she was likely to meet me? It's far more likely she'd stay the hell away.

I take some painkillers and slump down on the sofa, planning to drown my sorrows with daytime TV and a multi-pack of Keogh's Cashel Blue cheese and caramelised onion crisps – part of the 'care package' Brendan brought me on his last visit. Marianne and I are going to meet for a coffee tomorrow, after her interview, but right now I've nothing to do.

I'm about halfway through the first packet, and still channel-hopping, when the entryphone chimes. I groan, and push myself up off the sofa to answer it.

'Yeah?'

'Monsieur Landry? Kieran Landry?'

'That's me.'

'I'm glad I found you. My name's Lavigne. Kobe Lavigne. I'd like to talk to you about opening a restaurant.'

Emma

The last thing I want to do is go home and sit on my own in the flat. Instead, I head to Galeries Lafayette. Once I get to the toilets, I lock myself in a cubicle and cry as quietly as possible.

Eventually, the sobs subside. I'd stay here for the rest of the day if I could. But I'm hungry.

Outside, I splash some cold water on my face and try to wipe off the mascara that's smeared around my eyes. Another woman silently passes me a travel pack of make-up-remover pads. Her kindness almost makes me cry again.

I head upstairs to Café Coutume, and purchase a coffee, a cookie and a grilled cheese sandwich. I manage to grab a seat at the long, sinuous counter that offers a view of the glass dome and the gilded arches and the tiered balconies that encircle the central space, like so many boxes at a fancy opera house. I eat, I suppose; when I next look at my plate the food is gone, though I've no memory of the taste.

I should never have gone to Gare du Nord this morning.

I try to tell myself I'm glad he's not dead. That it will be easier now. Easier simply to hate him than to grieve.

Except that I don't think hearts work like that. Even now, if he showed up here and told me he was sorry – even now, I have a horrible feeling I'd forgive him.

And I can't convince myself that everything we had, everything I felt, was a lie.

I take a few sips of coffee. My meeting with Sylvie Klein feels like something that happened weeks ago. I try to remember exactly what she said. Yes, she loved my article and was certainly willing to pay to use it – I should give my details to the secretary before I leave. And yes, she liked my ideas for ways to follow it up, but how quickly could I write them? And would I be willing to travel to other parts of France to gather information or carry out interviews? And did I want to publish under my own name, or use a pseudonym that might fit with the slightly *drôle, effronté* style of the piece? Overall, she seemed enthusiastic. Though I guess it's possible she was just being polite.

I check myself.

She likes your writing. You sold her one article, and you can definitely sell another. This is the start of something new, so just enjoy it, for fuck's sake. You need something good to be going on right now.

You know, you're absolutely right.

Well, that's something. I'm in agreement with myself, for once. On the metro on the way home, I decide to divide the rest of the day between drafting the novel and making notes for the next article.

Madame Pollie is lurking in the entrance hall.

'Mademoiselle Noël.' She still refuses to use my actual surname.

'Madame Pollie, *comment allez-vous*?' I smile brightly, hoping she won't notice – or at least won't comment on – my puffy eyes. '*J'ai une bonne nouvelle* – some good news. The article I wrote is going to be published in a new magazine. *Un nouveau journal.*'

'*Ah, c'est bien.*'

I was expecting a more enthusiastic response than 'that's nice.' But the *gardienne* has turned her back to me to pick up a large bunch of ivory-coloured roses.

'*C'est pour vous.*'

For me?

Madame Pollie is holding out one of the yellow cards that she uses to leave passive-aggressive messages for the block's inhabitants, sliding them beneath our doors. *Please do not walk about your apartment so heavily, you are waking the dead. Please clean your shoes, you are leaving mud on the stairs and this is not a forest. Please talk less in communal areas.* That sort of thing. They remind me unpleasantly of Melissa.

'*De la part du monsieur qui a apporté les fleurs.*' From the gentleman who brought the flowers.

My hand is trembling as I take the card and read the name at the bottom.

The flowers are from Jacques Toussaint. I don't know whether to laugh or cry.

Dear Emma,
Sylvie's secretary gave me your address - I hope that is acceptable. You made a hit with Sylvie, as I knew you would. May I buy you a coffee to celebrate?
Amicalement,
Jacques

Madame Pollie is watching me. There's a sly smile on her face.

'*Il est charmant, cet homme.*'

'Yes, he's very charming.' She obviously wants something more, so I add, 'He's a work contact. At the magazine publisher.'

'*Et maintenant*, you can go on the date.'

'No, there's not going to be a date. It's a work thing, that's all.'

Madame Pollie is still smiling as she turns away. '*On verra bien.*' We'll see.

I take the roses upstairs. They really are beautiful, their petals like cream-coloured velvet. Scented, too.

Maybe I should say no to the coffee and just keep things professional.

But on the other hand, I'd like to be able to ask Jacques to read my novel, at some point.

And he is, as Madame Pollie pointed out, *charmant*.

By the time I've arranged the roses, I've decided. Kieran has clearly moved on, the bastard.

So why shouldn't I?

PART FOUR

Autumn

Chapter Twenty-Eight

Kieran

'Kobe, great to see you!' Seeing him in the flesh again, after three months of online meetings, I'm hit again by the full force of my business partner's personality before he's even opened his mouth. Physically, he's not a particularly big guy. His appearance isn't striking. His clothes don't shout. His jewellery – a signet ring and a St Christopher on a chain around his neck – is expensively discreet. Yet he fills every room he enters. Or distorts the space, somehow; inevitably, everyone gravitates towards him, like ball bearings rolling down a slope.

I lead him through the kitchen, a gleaming stainless-steel oasis since it was finished two weeks ago, and into the dining room, still full of dust and busy with electricians and decorators.

'How was the holiday?'

He pulls a face. Not the reaction I'd expected from someone who's just spent a month on a northerly German island that is – apparently – a magnet for the jet set.

'Well, you know. Pretty good. Restful, and the kids loved it.' Despite having lived most of his adult life in Paris, Kobe sounds one hundred per cent American. At least when he's speaking English. 'The great thing about Sylt is you don't get the heat of the Côte d'Azur, and it's super-quaint. Kind of like the Hamptons. But—' Kobe shrugs '—you know me. The French half of me is totally into taking the whole of August off. The American half of me, not so much. I spent most of the holiday wondering how to persuade the hotel to let me invest in their restaurant. And I was desperate to get back here, of course. What about you?'

'It was good to be back. I'd missed it more than I realised.'

An understatement. A few days after accepting Kobe's offer at the end of May, I had gone home. It was the first time I'd spent more than a week there since I was eighteen. Two months with my family turned out to be just what I needed: I was able to help build up my dad's strength, I gave Brendan and Niamh a proper break, and I healed.

More or less.

My bones are fully fixed. My heart . . . not so much. I don't know exactly what Emma did to me that day at the Gare du Nord, but I can't seem to get over her. Her voice, her face, the way she used to press both hands to her face when she was worried – time hasn't erased a single detail. I'm beginning to believe that I might forget every recipe I've ever learnt, yet still remember her.

Kobe is nodding.

'I get it. I'll probably never live in New York again, not full-time, but it's always going to be home. And hey, if this goes well, you never know. Dublin could be a good second opening.' He rolls his sleeves up – literally: Kobe is a guy who likes to get in on the physical labour of opening a restaurant, and he's picked up a surprising number of skills – and looks around the dining room. 'Boy, this is looking good. A month makes a big difference.'

'You're not wrong. I was well impressed when I got back at the start of August, but they've done wonders since.'

'And you're happy with the kitchen?'

'More than happy.'

'Good, good.' He surveys the dining room again, tapping the toe of a probably handmade leather shoe against the floor. 'The wood works well. And the tables and chairs are arriving from Italy next week. That green marble . . . mmm. *La couleur est parfaite.*'

'*Oui, je suis d'accord.*' I gesture at one of the delicate hand-blown glass lamps that are being installed to hang above the tables. 'And I love these. The lighting concept is going to work brilliantly.'

The site manager comes in, spots Kobe and hurries over to greet him. Dispensing with pleasantries, Kobe fires off a bunch of questions in rapid, flawless French. *Have the electricians been meticulous in checking the table layout? When will they be finished? When is the lighting designer back to sign off on the work?* We're opening in twenty-one days, so his intensity is understandable. I leave them to it and head back to the kitchen.

It's been a strange three months. Though the restaurant, nominally, is going to be mine, the money is all Kobe's. And as far as the look of the place is concerned, I've been consulted, but he gets the final say. Fortunately, his taste is exceptional. When it came to the kitchen, however, I was given free rein. Choosing the equipment and the cabinetry and planning the layout was like being a kid in an enormous toy department who's been told he can have whatever he likes. And now I'm sitting in *my* complete professional kitchen. I still can't quite believe I get to say that.

The draft menus for the opening weeks are in front of me. I spread them out and start checking the detail, making sure everything hangs together, and noting alternatives if for some reason the seasonal produce we're aiming for isn't available. My focus isn't exactly laser-sharp, though. The envelope Ettore dropped off this morning keeps tugging at my attention. Eventually I give up, slide the contents out again and re-read the note he's stuck on top. *When I saw this I thought, could it be her?*

The note's pinned to a printed-out page from a magazine called *Notre Ville*. There's an article in English about the dating scene in Paris, written by someone called M.A. Noël.

M.A. Noël. Emma Christmas.

It doesn't take long to find details of the magazine online. There's a street address and an email. Generic, though, that's the problem: one of those 'info@' emails. I've no confidence anything I send that way will actually reach her. After a moment's deliberation, I make a note of the street address. I've got meetings with suppliers all afternoon, but I've plenty of time tomorrow morning. If I can talk to someone, explain in person, maybe I can get a message to her. For the first time since I realised Emma's friends weren't going to reply — and had in fact blocked me — hope makes me grin.

Kobe walks in, slightly spattered with paint and wiping his hands on a rag. 'Everything's on track. How's it going with the staffing?'

'Getting there. I've hired a pastry chef and he's already given me input on the dessert menus. And Ettore and Marcel have started to interview the waiting staff.' My old friends handed in their notice as soon as I told them about Kobe's plans.

'Excellent.' Kobe claps me on the shoulder. 'Efficiency, that's what I like.' He checks his watch. 'I've got someone coming in to meet you shortly, but there's something I want to show you first.' A wide grin lights up his face. 'It's gonna make your day. Here you go.'

I take the phone from him to look more closely at the image he's showing me, and the reality of what we are doing is suddenly borne in on me in a wave of delight.

'Is that . . .?'

'Sure is. The name of the restaurant, all ready to go up above the door.'

Le Bon Frère. The Good Brother, in gold letters on a green background. A name I hope says something about my cooking, and how it is rooted in love and in family, even if you do happen to live 521 miles apart. As the crow flies. Emma told me that fact once, and I still remember it.

'Kobe, this is perfect.'

He laughs. 'Knew you'd like it.'

'*Like* is not a strong enough word. Can you send me the photo? I've *got* to show my brother. He'll be made up when he sees this.'

Kobe taps his phone screen. 'Done. Oh, and before I forget, we'll need something stylish and kind of —' his face scrunches in thought '—poetic, to put in the fronts of the menus. Something about what inspires your cooking, and so on. See what you can come up with. But don't sweat it; I've got some buddies in publishing and I can always send it to them for a polish. Some of them are coming to the opening, so they definitely owe me.'

This puzzles me. 'Don't we owe them, if they're going to potentially give us a review?'

Kobe winks at me. 'I've tasted your cooking, Kieran. Believe me, we are doing them the favour.'

The site manager sticks his head around the door. '*Votre invité est là, Kobe.*'

'*Merci. Demandez-lui d'attendre un instant, s'il vous plaît?*' He turns back to me. 'You're about to meet one of those publishing buddies, actually.'

'A journalist?'

'Kinda. His name's Jacques Toussaint – we studied together at ESCP.'

I'm impressed; the École Supérieure de Commerce de Paris is one of the oldest and most prestigious business schools in the world.

'Strictly he's an editor, not a journalist,' Kobe continues, 'but he has a side gig – and I'm telling you this in confidence – as the restaurant critic for *La Capitale*.'

I give a low whistle. *La Capitale* only launched a couple of years ago, and it's now the most popular lifestyle magazine in Paris. As for the restaurant reviews … they're penned by an unnamed reviewer who styles him or herself *Le Gourmand Anonyme*. Or perhaps that should be poison-penned; the critiques are nothing if not razor-edged. According to rumour, a review in *La Capitale* can make or break a new restaurant within weeks.

'You mean he's …'

'Yep. He's LGA.'

'Shite. Are you sure this is a good idea?'

'Hey, you trust me, don't you?'

'Well, sure, but—'

There's no time for my concerns. Kobe is already opening the door into the dining room and ushering me through.

'Jacques, I'm so glad you could make it. This is Kieran Landry, soon to be one of the most renowned chefs in Paris. Kieran, this is Jacques Toussaint.'

I don't know whether to throw myself at Toussaint's feet or smack him one; chefs pretend to like restaurant reviewers, but we all secretly loathe them. I settle for shaking his hand.

'So,' Kobe continues, 'Jacques has some contacts in radio, and he's managed to get an interview set up with Ici Paris – it's a big local station. They're interested in your story: the journey from Cork to Paris, the family angle, the accident. It's pencilled in for the sixteenth of October. Sound good?'

'Er, sure.' I nod more enthusiastically than I want to, because Kobe is clearly keen, even if I'm not. I want people to come to the restaurant for the food, not because they're interested in my 'story'. 'Thanks, Monsieur Toussaint. I appreciate the opportunity.'

He inclines his head. '*De rien*. You're welcome. Though I do have a favour to ask.'

'Of course.' What is he going to want in return for the interview? I wonder. I've heard about chefs getting asked for anything from a permanently reserved table to private cooking lessons.

'I am not able to attend the opening, unfortunately: I go away on business that morning. But I would like very much to be able to publish a review sooner than this.'

'That would be awesome,' Kobe observes. 'We'd love that.'

Would we, Kobe? Personally, I'd be happy to skip a review from *Le Gourmand Anonyme*.

'Then, may I dine here the night before the opening?' Jacques asks. 'The twenty-fifth of September? I would be happy to choose from a limited menu. The, um, journal I write for goes on sale the day after you open.' He smiles at me pleasantly enough. 'I cannot guarantee what my review will say, but I can at least guarantee that it will be included in that week's edition, if I am able to eat here that night.'

'Of course, of course,' Kobe says instantly. 'Kieran, you can make that happen, right?'

He's not exactly leaving me a choice.

'Definitely.' I return Jacques's smile. 'And of course we'll offer you the full menu. Would you perhaps like to bring a guest?'

He would, it turns out. Kobe decides that he and his wife will also eat at the restaurant that evening, so I'm left with nothing to do but inform the staff that some of them are going to need to be available for an evening shift one night earlier than they'd expected.

Nothing about the situation feels quite right to me, and the feeling hasn't faded by the time I leave my last supplier meeting and start walking home; like my confidence, my fondness for cycling took a hit in the accident. It's a lovely evening, warm for the time of year, and the streets are bustling. As I walk, I remind myself that Kobe is funding the whole enterprise, and resist the temptation to call him to ask about the economics of having the restaurant open to accommodate just four diners. At least his friendship with Jacques might mean we're more likely to get a good review. Maybe.

As for the interview ... perhaps, if going to the offices of *Notre Ville* doesn't work out, I can use the radio platform to appeal for information. I've no idea how many people are likely to tune in to hear me banging on about my so-called story, but one of them might have come across Emma. Especially if she's still in Paris.

I'm not planning on walking all the way home – it'll take me the best part of two hours. Yet, somehow, I keep passing one metro station after another. When my stomach starts growling I pick up a deliciously cheesy pizza from a tiny Italian place near the Sorbonne and eat it in the Jardin Tino Rossi, overlooking the river. It's dark by the time I finish. I decide to head across the river and pick up metro line one from Bastille to Porte de Vincennes, but I'm using back roads, and I guess I get turned around somehow. Stepping back to check what street I'm on, I realise the tall glass windows opposite belong to a restaurant, its name so discreetly displayed as to be almost invisible. There's a small red plaque displayed on the restaurant's frontage: it's got a Michelin star.

My interest is aroused; every high-end restaurant in Paris is shortly going to become the competition. I edge forward to peer into the windows. Stripped floorboards, tastefully subdued lighting, arty, abstract photos in black and white—

For a moment I stare, unblinking, disbelieving, shocked into immobility.

It can't be.

My brain races. Calculating. Comparing. The hair is shorter. The clothes subtly different.

It can't be, but it is. Emma.

'Oh, my God.'

She's sitting at a table right in front of one of the windows, looking down at a menu, wearing a wide-necked sweater that's sliding off one shoulder.

As she turns her head I leap backwards, stumbling off the kerb, holding my breath until I'm sure she hasn't seen me. She won't be able to, I realise; from inside the lit restaurant the dark street is invisible. All she's seeing is her own reflection in the window glass.

Joy warms me just as suddenly as shock chilled me. I decide instantly – I'm going to go in, sit down at the table, and beg her to listen to me for just a moment. I'll tell her everything, and she'll understand, and we'll be together again. Everything's going to work out just as I imagined. Everything's going to be brilliant.

I'm about to turn towards the restaurant's front door when Emma looks up and smiles at a man approaching the table.

Not a waiter. Not the maître d', though that's the hope I cling to for an instant when I see the man's dark suit.

Emma picks up her bag and stands at the same moment that I recognise him.

Jacques Toussaint. The guy I just met a few hours ago.

He says something, smiling, and Emma laughs, tilting her head back and narrowing her eyes in the same expression of amusement that I've seen so many times. His puts his arm around her waist, pulls her close, and kisses her.

Jacques fucking Toussaint.

With my Emma.

I should go in. I should go in and confront them, and – and deck the bastard, and tell Emma that it was all a horrible mistake, and – and . . .

The fire dies out of me. My hand, already reaching for the door, drops back to my side. What right have I, after all this time? God knows how much I've already hurt her.

My Emma. But she's with someone else. And she seems . . . happy.

Chapter Twenty-Nine

Emma

I'm still in bed, enjoying a good stretch – toes and fingers pointed, spreading myself out like a starfish, basking in the luxury of space and the bliss of a sunny Thursday morning – when my phone starts ringing: Daisy wants to FaceTime.

I hit 'join'.

'Morning!' she trills. 'What are you up to?'

Daisy is also in bed, but the floral silk pyjamas and the huge pile of pillows and throw cushions behind her make it look like she's in a newspaper supplement lifestyle shoot.

'I'm taking a day off: my next article isn't due for three weeks. You?'

'Also taking a day off. Me and Dan are going to the big John Lewis to do our wedding gift list.' She gives a little scream of excitement.

'Fun! I wish I could come with you.'

'I wish you were coming, too, but you know, I guess Dan's got to have some say in what we ask for.'

'Yeah, fair enough. Besides, I've got a date with James later on to parallel-watch *Desperate Housewives*, so you know, plenty of excitement this side of the Channel!'

Daisy takes a sip of her tea. 'And, er, any more news?'

She means news about my book. Finished – I basically locked myself in the flat all summer, only emerging for dates with Jacques – and now awaiting judgment from the first batch of literary agents I sent it out to.

'Another rejection. This one "didn't connect with the main character". So that's eight rejections so far. And one full manuscript request, though I've not heard back from her since I sent it.'

'You will. And you only need one "yes", am I right?'

'Yeah, you're right.'

'And, in the meantime, there's sex with Jacques.'

I laugh. Sex with Jacques. Sounds as if it should be a TV show, like *Cooking with Jamie*. 'That's true.'

Daisy pulls a face. 'Ugh, my mum's calling. Another fifty people she wants to add to the guest list, probably. Call you later?'

'Great. Enjoy the shopping!'

I drop the phone and close my eyes, but, before I can snuggle back under the duvet, a volley of knocks shatters the peace. Someone is hammering loudly on my front door.

'*Mademoiselle Noël, ouvrez la porte! Ouvrez-moi, ouvrez-moi!*'

Madame Pollie. I swear and pull on my dressing gown and stumble through the living room to open the door. '*Bonjour, madame. Qu'est-ce qui se passe?*'

Rather than replying, she thrusts a stylishly wrapped bouquet of at least forty roses into my arms. An intensely sweet scent rises from perfect, velvety petals of deep cerise. Instinctively I bend my head over the blooms and inhale deeply.

'Another gift from Monsieur Jacques,' she comments. '*Un très joli cadeau, n'est-ce pas?*'

I should have remembered. Jacques timetables his entire life, from meditation to calls with his parents to trips to buy birthday presents for his two nieces. We've been dating for over three months now. He doesn't stay over – my flat clearly isn't up to his standard, though he's never said so – but, since we've started having sex, flowers invariably arrive the morning after. He must have some kind of scheduled service with the high-end florist he uses.

Madame Pollie is holding out the card that's come with the flowers. The bouquet is so huge that I have to shift the weight of it on to one hip to take it. When I turn away to put the roses on to the table, she follows me inside.

The envelope the note comes in isn't sealed, which means that Madame Pollie has one hundred per cent read the contents. She's looking around the room with interest. Is she hoping to discover Jacques himself, lounging on the sofa in leopardprint underpants? Maybe holding another rose between his teeth? Her expression sinks into slight disappointment as she takes in the total absence of men, partially clothed or otherwise. She's even more invested in our relationship than I'd realised.

'*Alors, merci, madame.*' I open the door wider, inviting her to step back outside. '*Je dois prendre* a shower – *une douche.*'

'*Et ce soir, vous allez encore sortir avec Monsieur Jacques?*'

'Yes. This evening I'm going out again with Monsieur Jacques. For dinner.' I look pointedly at the clock on the wall. 'Oh, is that the time?'

'*Ah, c'est tellement romantique! Et après …*' Madame Pollie winks, slowly. 'I put some candles in the apartment, yes? *Et du vin. Une bouteille de champagne.*' She gasps. '*Et, des nouveaux sous-vêtements.* Something in silk and lace. Something sexy. This – this is the worst.' The disgust on her face as she gazes at my faded Hello Kitty dressing gown, a present from Daisy's mum about five years ago, suggests someone's just asked her to take a swim in a sewage treatment plant. 'No woman should wear this. But do not worry. I will arrange all.'

'No. No, you don't need to do that.' What the hell did Jacques write in the card? 'No candles, no champagne. Definitely no new lingerie. Thank you, Madame Pollie.' I basically shoo her out on to the landing. '*À bientôt.* See you later.'

The roses are filling the entire room with their fragrance.

I close the door and lean against it and open the card.

My dear Emma,
  I enjoyed yesterday so very much – it was a delight to share with you my favourite parts of Paris, and to share the evening with you too.

I wish I did not need to go away tomorrow; never has a business trip been worse timed! Yet tonight, I know, will be very special. And dare I hope, when I return, that I might whisk you away? Just the two of us, somewhere romantic.
Jacques

Yet tonight, I know, will be very special ... That's the phrase that's set Madame Pollie's knickers smouldering. However, unlike Madame P, I know that Jacques is talking about the restaurant we're going to. He has a flight at six-thirty tomorrow morning; we've an early booking so that he can get back and pack at a reasonable hour, and he made it clear when we were discussing the evening that shenanigans would not be on the table. Or up against the wall. Or even in the bed.

I get into the shower, set the temperature to cold, and force myself to turn on the water.

Before Jacques, I hadn't had sex for almost two years, give or take. At least, no sex that involved another human being instead of something motorised from the Ann Summers catalogue. And Jacques, despite our age gap, has turned out to be exceptionally good in bed. All that extra experience and exercise, I guess. He prioritises my needs over his. He knows exactly where to touch me. He's even found that spot on the side of my neck that seems to have a direct connection to 'the naughty nodule that is climax-control central', as Paige once insisted on it being described. I hadn't realised how much I'd missed it. The first time we did it, we barely made it through the front door. I think he quite enjoyed me attempting to yank his trousers off without undoing his belt first.

Of course, I've not told him that, while he's busy screwing my brains out, I'm busy imagining I'm having sex with Kieran.

The shower is not really helping.

After I'm dressed, I re-read the card. Perhaps a mini-break with Jacques is exactly what I need. We can get away from Paris to a place where the image of Kieran that I carry around with me isn't so solid. Some place he never went. Some place my brain can't constantly conjure him out of thin air. Maybe there, I'll be able to be with Jacques without getting ... distracted. I pick up my phone.

Thank you so much for the roses – they are truly stunning! And they smell gorgeous. And yes please to the trip away when you get back.

Jacques replies to the text instantly.

Formidable! While I am away, we will plan where to go. I am looking forward to seeing you this evening. I have meetings until six. The car will pick you up at 5.30 and we can go from here.

His assumption that he is the only one who is busy irks me just a little.

Actually, I have some work to finish up. What's the address of the restaurant? I'll meet you there.

61 Rue de Varenne. Le Bon Frère. Xx

Merci! Xx

Once I've made myself a cup of tea, I open my laptop and type in the name of the restaurant; I want to see how fancy it is so I can decide what to wear. The website is listed near the top of the page, and I click on the link.

'Shit!' The tea goes everywhere. 'Shit, shit, shit!' I grab the throw off the sofa and start frantically dabbing at my keyboard. 'Fuck.' Bloody Kieran, staring out from my laptop screen, looking all moody and gorgeous. If I've wrecked my keyboard because of him I'm going to – I'm going to ...

I'm going to be eating at his restaurant this evening.

I drop into my chair as the realisation sinks in.

Cancel. I'll just tell Jacques I can't make it. I grab my phone and start typing in the message.

But I don't send it.

I showed up. I moved country for him. Why should I be the one who hides?

There's nothing on the restaurant's website about him being a two-timing bastard who stands people up. There is, however, a little section in which he talks about the inspiration behind his cooking: love, family, friendship.

Well, you could have fooled me.

A plan crystallises in my mind as I delete my message to Jacques, put the phone down and walk into the bedroom. Not only am I *not* going to cancel, but I'm going to stride into Kieran's restaurant with my head held high.

I open the wardrobe and survey its meagre contents.

I'm going to face Kieran on his own turf, looking utterly fabulous.

First, however, I'm going to go shopping.

It turns out that achieving utter fabulousness is pretty time-consuming. And expensive. Maybe because all I've ever done in Galeries Lafayette up until now is drink coffee and admire the glass dome – I've never actually bought anything – a sort of madness takes hold the moment I step inside Agnès b. I buy a little black dress in merino wool, the pockets and neckline trimmed with white, and barely look at the price tag. The sales assistant recommends a pair of heeled black and red ankle boots to go with the dress, and I snap them up. After that, it seems completely reasonable to buy a fringed leather clutch – bright red – and a black cashmere jacket to sling over my shoulders. As the assistant – aka my New Best Friend – points out, the evenings are a little cold at this time of the year. At least, I think that's what she says, and it seems to make sense. At this point I lose all restraint. When my New Best Friend recommends a facial and a manicure – she now knows all about the importance of me looking good this evening – I carry my purchases off to La Wellness Galerie in the middle of the shopping centre. Luckily they're not too busy to fit me in, and it turns out that facials and manicures aren't the only thing on offer. I never expected, when Madame Pollie woke me up this morning, that I'd end up having my eyebrows threaded.

Has it all been worth it? I think so. The woman gazing back at me in the mirrored wardrobe door looks more elegant, certainly. A little more poised in her mostly monochrome outfit. I take a selfie to send to Daisy, but I don't send it. If she calls, if I actually talk to her, I don't trust myself not to burst into tears and ruin my make-up. Despite my new clothes and new eyebrows, I feel like very much the same person inside.

I'm still the woman who fell in love with a man who stood her up at a railway station and never even told her why.

Even worse, I have a horrible feeling that some part of me is still in love with him.

Well, fuck that. I'm going to go and confront him.

He'll probably be stunned to see me. He probably thought I'd just run back to London, but I'll show him. And when I see him in real life for the first time in almost sixteen months – when I see him next to Jacques – I'll probably realise that he was never that amazing in the first place.

In the rush of shopping, I forgot to eat lunch. Definitely a mistake. The combination of hunger and nerves means I'm not feeling my best when I get to the restaurant.

Jacques is already inside when I arrive, waiting in the bar area. Apart from him, the bar is empty. So is the restaurant. For an instant I feel bad for Kieran, but I push the thought away.

'Do you think it will get busier later?' I ask Jacques after the maître d' has seated us. 'I suppose we do have quite an early booking.'

'Oh, no,' he replies, smiling. 'The restaurant is not actually open.'

'You mean it doesn't open until later this evening? Have they opened a little early just for us?'

'Not a little early.' His smile widens. 'An entire day early. The official opening of the restaurant is not until tomorrow evening, but since I am away by then, and since I would like to write an early review, and since they would like to receive one . . .' He laughs and shrugs.

I'm stunned. I know Jacques is a heavyweight in Parisian publishing, and I know he writes restaurant reviews on the side, but I had no idea he was important enough to swing something like this.

'I wanted to do something special, before I have to leave you for two weeks. Also, I thought it would be a good opportunity to introduce you to my friends. They should be here soon.' He looks over my shoulder and stands up. 'Actually, they are here now.'

The maître d' ushers over a man and a woman, both about the same age as Jacques.

'Emma, may I present Juliette and Kobe Lavigne? Juliette is an artist, and Kobe is a restaurateur. He helped the chef set up this place.'

'Oh—' I exclaim, before biting my tongue.

Kobe smiles and looks puzzled. 'Hi there, Emma, Emma. Have we met?'

'No. No, I've heard your name, that's all. I have – had – a friend who was, um, he was into cooking. Restaurants, I mean.'

Way to sound like an idiot, Emma.

We sit down. Kobe and Juliette both seem charming, and we talk for a little about books, and they ask me to describe my novel to them. Juliette and I start to discuss art, but her English is about as good as my French, and I get the feeling that she doesn't share my view that pictures should be of recognisable things, not just blobs of paint on a canvas. When Kobe and Jacques start discussing local Parisian politics, and the state of the housing market, and how to get teenagers off their phones – Jacques's nieces are the same age as the Lavignes' children – she joins in their conversation. I don't have a lot to contribute to any of those topics, particularly when the others slip into colloquial French.

At least the food is, predictably, outstanding. Jacques orders for me, citing his need to try a certain number of dishes for his review. My entrée is an artichoke soup with white truffle, served with a delicious sundried tomato brioche. For the main course, Jacques chooses me Bresse chicken – only in France would chickens come with the same sort of regional designation as wine – served on a bed of creamy, caramelised chestnuts. Between each course we get an *amuse bouche*, presented with 'the compliments of the chef'. I'd choke on them if they weren't so tasty.

Kobe orders wonderful wines to go with each course. I drink more than I'm used to – certainly more than I've drunk since that evening with Daisy and James back in March. The conversation drifts past me; I laugh when the others laugh and try to at least look as if I'm following along, but discussions about pension taxation leave me cold. I haven't even got a pension. I've never had enough money to start one. This evening, the fifteen years dividing Jacques and me are starting to feel like an ocean, not a brook.

The maître d' – no mere waiter for us this evening – is handing me the dessert menu. I let my gaze drift down the page, translating the French as I go, until I see the last item.

La Reine de l'amitié, inspirée d'un dessert anglais traditionnel et d'une amitié.

I read it again: the Queen of Friendship, inspired by a traditional English dessert and by a friendship.

Queen of Puddings. I remember telling him how much I loved it. Did he remember too?

'Emma, *pour le dessert*,' Jacques says, 'I will order you the *mousse au chocolat*.'

'*Non. Je voudrais la Reine de l'amitié, s'il vous plaît.*'

The others laugh – I'm English, so no doubt that's why I'm ordering an English-inspired dessert – but I don't care. I want to see what Kieran, or his pastry chef, has done with my favourite pudding.

What he's done, it turns out, is elevate it into a work of art. The bronzed peaks of the snowy meringue are highlighted with gold. A delicate drizzle of poached plum sits in the folds. And the whole thing is encased in a heart-shaped basket of spun caramel. I can hardly bear to eat it.

I do, of course. Every last mouthful. Jacques looks up from his own dessert – an almond *dacquoise* – to find my plate completely clear. He looks a bit put out that I didn't leave him some to review.

'Marcel,' Kobe calls the maître d' over, 'ask the chef to come out. We need to compliment him in person.'

My heart starts thumping in my chest, and my stomach twists so tightly, I think, for one horrible moment, that I'm going to throw up everything I've just eaten. I'm not ready – I can't see him yet. Not yet. The words leap into my mouth, but I clamp my lips shut.

Marcel bows and disappears into the kitchen.

When the door swings open again, it isn't Marcel.

It's Kieran.

Chapter Thirty

Emma

Kieran hasn't changed a bit. Tall and commanding in his chef's whites, he walks unhurriedly over to the table without catching my eye. We all get up to greet him, and Jacques and the others are congratulating him, and suddenly I'm back at the Gare du Nord in the bright sunshine of late May, but this time I feel as if I've slammed into a brick wall, not just run into a person. I can't catch my breath. My head swims.

As I clutch the edge of the table Kieran grabs my upper arms to steady me. '*Madame, ça va?*'

The same words. The same spark of physical connection, of deep, unsatisfied longing, making me gasp. His voice cracks and he clears his throat, but he doesn't let go of me.

'*Mademoiselle*,' I hear myself correct him as if from a great distance. A voice from the past.

Kieran releases me and steps back as Jacques hurries to my side of the table. '*Emma, tu ne te sens pas bien? Tu as une mine terrible*, ghastly. *Il faut que tu* – you must sit. Sit.' He pushes me back down on to the chair.

'*Ah, j'ai mal à la tête*. A migraine.' I've only had a migraine once in my life, when my mum died. It was awful. This isn't remotely as bad, but the waves of queasiness when I move my head certainly remind me of it.

Jacques is already on the phone to his driver.

'The traffic is bad. He will be here in twenty minutes or so,' he says. 'Do you want some water? A cold towel *pour ta tête*, your forehead? Painkillers?'

'Just some more water, please.' I can't swallow anything else at the moment.

Someone – Juliette, I think – pushes a glass into my hand.

'Let's give her some space,' Kobe suggests. 'Jacques, shall we show you the kitchen? Juliette hasn't seen it either.'

'That's a good idea.' Kieran's voice. 'I'll stay out here just in case Emma needs anything. Marcel, show our guests around. Be sure to take them into the wine cellar too.'

Another moment, and we're alone.

Kieran

Emma is sitting with her head in her hands, breathing rapidly, as if she's trying to ride out waves of nausea. I pull up a chair next to her.

'Emma? Emma, I think you're hyperventilating. You need to take slower breaths.'

No response.

I reach across and tentatively touch her shoulder. She shrugs my hand away. I can hardly blame her.

'Emma, I know this must be a terrible shock. Me suddenly walking out, and—'

She straightens up and looks at me. There are tears in her eyes.

'I knew. I knew you were here. I found out this morning, when Jacques told me the name of the restaurant and I looked it up. And I saw you. I saw you at the Gare du Nord. A year to the day after we met. I saw you with someone else.'

For a moment I can't think what she's talking about. I just stare at her. 'But I went there to—'

Oh. Marianne.

Fuck.

'How could you, Kieran? How could you do that to me? I thought—' The tears spill across her cheeks, and she scrubs them away with her napkin. 'I thought you wanted me to come to France. I thought you loved me.' A sob shakes her. 'I can't do this. I need some air.' Grabbing her bag, she leaves the table and practically sprints to the front door of the restaurant.

I follow her outside. The narrow street is deserted.

'What you saw, that wasn't – it wasn't what you think. Marianne is an old friend, that's all. I didn't even know she was going to be there. I went to the station because I was looking for you. I was so desperate, I hoped that . . . but I couldn't, I . . .'

I'm not making any sense, and Emma won't look at me. I take a deep breath. I have to force my racing brain into some sort of order. I have to try to make her understand.

'I did want you to come to France. And I do. I do love you, Emma. I've never stopped loving you.'

'Then *why*? Why didn't you show up? Why did you leave me standing there, not knowing if you were – if you were dead – or – or . . .' She stifles a sob with the back of her wrist.

All I want to do is pull her into my arms and comfort her.

'I did try to find you, Emma. To explain. You see, the day I was supposed to meet you, I had an accident.'

Emma

Kieran tells me about being fired by Arnaud, and cycling too fast through the rain, and waking up in hospital weeks later with his brother next to him. About his phone and his laptop being destroyed. About the painful sessions of physiotherapy. He tells me that Marianne, a colleague from another restaurant, just turned up that day at the Gare du Nord by chance. He offers to give me her number so I can call her myself. He shows me the scars on his arm.

Is he telling the truth? I've only ever seen his arms on a screen, up until now. He was wearing a long-sleeved jacket the day I ran into him at the Gare du Nord. The scars don't look old, though. Even in the glow of the yellow light spilling through the restaurant windows, the skin still shows up pink and puckered.

Kieran gets out his phone and shows me an email from Lauren's assistant – a reply to his email asking for my contact details – and watches me read it.

'Please, Emma, you have to believe me. Once I was out of the hospital, I tried so hard to find you. I went to the Airbnb you stayed in, to see if you'd left a forwarding address. And then earlier this month Ettore saw the article you wrote and guessed it was you, and I was going to go to the publisher's offices. I'm doing a radio interview in a few weeks, and I planned to put out an appeal.' He smiles, uncertainly. 'You know: *have you seen this woman?* That type of thing. Then, when I saw you three weeks back, in that restaurant near the Opéra, I just . . .' He puts both hands behind his head and turns, slowly. 'I thought I was going mad, for a moment.'

I replay the last couple of sentences in my head.

'Hold on – you saw me?'

'Yeah. I just happened to be passing. I was lost, actually. Restaurant Vie, that was the name of the place. When I spotted the Michelin star on the façade, I peered in the window. And there you were.' He reaches towards me then drops his hand back to his side. His laugh has a bitter edge to it. 'Sure, if Fate is trying to get us together, her timing is terrible.'

Restaurant Vie is the place Jacques took me to on the fifth of September.

'You saw me,' I ask, 'but you didn't come in? You didn't even try to attract my attention?'

His mouth drops open. 'Well, I was going to. But you and Jacques . . . I saw him kiss you. And I knew who he was because Kobe had introduced him to me that morning, and he'd asked if he could come to the restaurant a day early so he could write a review.'

Shock sends another wave of nausea through me.

'So I'm less important to you than getting a good review from Jacques?'

Kieran raises his hands, fingers spread wide. 'What? No! No, that's not it – not at all—'

'I can't believe you, Kieran. You saw me sitting there, and yet you walked away.' The shock on his face makes me want to laugh and scream at the same time. 'And don't tell me I should have come over to you when I saw you with Mariela or whatever her name is. I'd pretty much convinced myself you were *dead* when I saw you that day.' Tears threaten to choke me; I have to force the words out. 'If you'd just opened the door, Kieran. Hell, if you'd just waved at me through the window—'

Movement inside the restaurant catches the corner of my eye. Jacques and the others, plus the maître d' and the head sommelier, are walking back to our table.

Kieran

Emma pushes past me and opens the door of the restaurant.

'Emma,' I whisper, 'just let me explain—'

She ignores me and walks quickly back to the others.

'Emma, *ma chérie*, are you feeling better?' Jacques asks.

'A little. The cold air helped.'

Jacques's phone buzzes. '*Bon.* The car is here.'

'Good. I just need to go home and lie down in the dark.' She turns to Kobe and Juliette. 'Thank you so much for this evening, it was wonderful. I'm so sorry I broke up the party early.' And then she's holding out her hand to me. 'Thank you, Kieran. Good luck with the restaurant. I'm sure it's going to be an amazing success.'

And that's it. She's walking away from me, and I can't even watch her leave because Jacques is claiming my attention.

'I think I can promise you a review you will be delighted with, Kieran,' he says, smiling. '*Chaque bouchée était exquise.* Exquisite.'

He shakes my hand.

I want to rip his head off.

Kobe claps me on the shoulder and says something congratulatory which I barely even hear and then, thank God, he and Juliette follow the others out of the restaurant and I'm alone.

Marcel pushes me into a chair. He and Ettore look at each other.

'Your Emma, *non*? Why did you not say?'

'Because she's not my Emma any more. She's with Jacques Toussaint, the – the bastard.'

'You are wrong,' Ettore declares. 'I watch them when I serve the wine. There is no *chimica* there, no chemistry. If you fight for her, if you—'

I raise a hand to silence him. 'Ettore, I know you mean well, but not now, please. I'm in no mood.'

Ettore looks as if he's about to argue, but Marcel shakes his head. 'Shall I fetch you a cognac, chef?' he asks. 'Or a glass of champagne? After all, this evening was a success, at least for Le Bon Frère. We will get a *très bonne* review in *La Capitale*.'

The cognac is tempting. A little something to dull the agony that stabs at me with every in-breath. Trouble is, I reckon once I start, I won't want to stop.

All I wanted to do tonight was make sure Emma was okay, and to apologise. I believed she'd moved on, and that I was alright with that. Maybe neither of those things is true. Still, I thought maybe we could be friends. Yet somehow I've managed to hurt her even more. How did it go so badly wrong?

And was she right? Did some part of me not want to go in and break up her dinner with Jacques because of the power he has to thrust Le Bon Frère into the limelight – or into oblivion?

'Chef?' Marcel murmurs.

'No cognac, thanks, Marcel. Though I wouldn't say no to some coffee. Come on.' I get up and tuck the chair back where it belongs. 'Let's make sure the kitchen's been put to bed, then we should all get some rest. We've still got a restaurant to officially open tomorrow.'

I don't sleep well. In my dreams, I keep replaying my conversation with Emma. The way she looked at me when I first walked in from the kitchen, as if she was seeing a ghost. Her expression when she'd understood that I'd known she was definitely in Paris for the past three weeks.

I could have got her a message. Once I knew about Jacques, I could have found out where he worked. I could have sent her a letter, care of his offices. I could have carried out my plan to go to the magazine office and tried to get someone there to help. I could even have probed Kobe for some information.

Why didn't I?

I'm still no nearer to an answer when I drag myself out of bed, head pounding, at eight the next morning. Turning on my phone, I find a message from Marcel.

> I asked Kobe to ask Jacques for Emma's details. I told him the restaurant would like to send some flowers to wish her a speedy recovery.

The next message contains an address and a mobile number. I text Emma before I can talk myself out of it.

> I'm so sorry about last night. I don't think Jacques and the review was the reason that I didn't go into Restaurant Vie that evening. I hope not. But I can truthfully say that when I watched you through the window you smiled at Jacques like you were pleased to be with him. You looked – happy. And for you to be happy is all I've ever wanted, from the moment you first ran into me. I hoped – I still hope, I guess – that I would be the one to make you happy. But to break up your relationship with Jacques, just because I wanted you, and didn't want him to have you – I couldn't do it, Emma. Review or no review. I'm not that kind of guy. And you deserve better than that kind of guy.

Once the message has sent, I set my phone to Do Not Disturb. The restaurant opening is going to take all my concentration and energy today, and I can't deal with any more pain.

The opening is, according to Kobe, 'a fucking raging success, man'. I'm happy. Really I am. I'm delighted for Kobe and for my amazing team. Yet I feel it all at one remove. Every reaction is slightly deadened, as if I'm underwater.

I don't check my phone until I'm home. There are two messages from Emma.

> I thought I'd lost you for ever,
> and now you're back, but I'm not
> sure I can do this again, Kieran.
> I'm not sure I can take the risk.

> I'm leaving tomorrow and going
> back to London for a couple of
> weeks. Please, don't message me.

What does she mean? Don't message her while she's in London? Or don't message her ever again?

It's late, almost one in the morning. I call Brendan anyway.

He answers, his voice groggy but also sharp with anxiety.

'Kieran, what's wrong?'

'Nothing. Not really.'

'Then why the hell are you calling me at – at midnight?'

'It's Emma.' Trying to hold back the tears nearly chokes me. 'I found her, Bren. And I think I'm about to lose her all over again.'

Chapter Thirty-One

Emma

Another message from Daisy pops up on my phone.

> Dan says he can come and pick you
> up from the station. It's no trouble.

I break off from packing to reply.

> Don't be daft – I can get on the tube.
> I won't have that much stuff with me.

> Okay, if you're sure. The spare
> room is all ready. New scented
> candles and everything! xxx

> Literally cannot wait! I'll message
> when I get off the Eurostar. xxx

My trip back to London was planned weeks ago, so Daisy doesn't need to know about the latest in the Kieran saga. Neither does James: he and Petros have just got engaged, and they've set a date for next March. I'm a bit worried that hanging out with both Daisy and James is going to turn into some sort of competitive wedding planning event, but I'll live with it. I want them both to be happy. Hence my resolution: for the duration of my trip, I'm going to keep the whole Kieran thing shut inside a box. A very inaccessible box. A box that is, metaphorically speaking, locked inside a tall tower on an island, protected by a moat and a thorny hedge, in the middle of a poisonous swamp.

I'm going to put Kieran inside that box. And then, for good measure, I'm going to throw away the key.

I put my laptop charger into my suitcase, cross it off my packing list, and go back into the living room to fetch the laptop itself from my desk.

An email's arrived since I last checked.

> Virginie O'Keefe
> Re: Submission: THE GHOSTWRITER'S GUIDE TO MURDER

My hand flies to my mouth. Virginie O'Keefe. The agent from the Delamere Agency who asked me to send her the complete manuscript of my book.

As I click to open the message, I'm shaking.

> Dear Emma,
> Having read the full manuscript, I'm delighted to offer you representation . . .

It's not until I've read it three times that it begins to sink in. I've actually done it. I'm going to have an agent. An actual, real-life agent who will try to sell my book to publishers. I've cried so much over the past twenty-four hours that I'm surprised there's enough water left inside me, but still – the very next thing I do is burst into tears.

After a very quiet summer in Paris, the first few hectic days in London feel like falling asleep in a Jane Austen novel and waking up in an Ibiza nightclub. Bridesmaid's dress fittings. A wine-tasting at the caterers. Meetings with the florist and the band that Dan's booked for the reception. Shopping with Daisy for honeymoon clothes. Shopping with James for a hen night present for Daisy. James takes me to a spa and asks me to be his best person on the same day that Daisy and I spend the evening at a karaoke bar in Holborn with Daisy's twin cousins – the other two bridesmaids. We bond over a shared teenage obsession with Justin Bieber; by the end of the evening, all four of us are drunkenly declaring how much we love each other.

I try to throw myself into everything with enthusiasm. I guess I succeed: Daisy tells me more than once how well I look, and James tells me he's relieved that everything in my life has fallen into place and is going so smoothly.

Nobody mentions Kieran.

When it feels as though Petros, James's fiancé, *is* about to bring him up, I drop the news about me signing a contract with Virginie O'Keefe.

Despite all the rushing around – despite the fact that I'm acting a part – it is good to be back. Dan is easy to be around, and Daisy is Daisy. Watching them is the first chance I've ever had to see what a really good romantic relationship looks like up close. It's obvious that Dan adores Daisy; he says outright that making her happy is his number one priority. And I can see how Daisy's respect and admiration make Dan feel good about himself. They bring different strengths to their partnership, though I struggle to pin down exactly what the strengths are. Maybe Dan is more organised. Perhaps Daisy has greater emotional stability. In the end, I decide, they just . . . fit. As one of those corny inspirational posters might say, they are better together.

I realise that I want the same thing.

And who's to say that Jacques and I don't or can't just fit?

I message Jacques, currently on business in America, with a list of possible locations for our mini-break. And I don't think about Kieran at all.

Well, not more than a couple of times every hour.

By the last full day of my visit, I'm feeling pretty smug. I've succeeded in keeping my two closest friends totally in the dark about my real emotional state. I'm going to get back on the train tomorrow, and neither of them suspects a thing.

James and Daisy and I are sitting in the living room, drinking tea and eating our way through a box of M&S Outrageously Chocolatey Biscuits and discussing seating plans. Daisy's wedmin collection – now running at seven absolutely rammed A4 ring-binders – is laid out on the coffee table. Daisy flicks through one of the binders, pulls out a sheet of paper and hands it to me.

'That is the right spelling of Jacques's name, right?'

I check the list.

'Yeah, that's right. What's it for?'

'This is the list I'm sending to the printers for the place cards.' I must look blank, because she adds, 'You know, on the tables at the reception. So people know where to sit. His card was going to read "Emma's plus one", but that was before. We know who he is now, so I may as well get it printed properly.' She grins. 'I can't wait to meet him.'

My appetite evaporates. I put the biscuit I just picked up back in the box, untasted.

My first mistake. From the corner of my eye, I see James frown and lean forward.

'Have you not invited him to the wedding yet, Ems?' he asks.

'Er, no,' I reply. 'Not yet.'

'He'll want to come, though, right?' Daisy says, the inflection of her voice conveying the unspoken next sentence: *after all, my wedding is going to be fabulous, what kind of idiot would turn it down?*

'I'm sure he would. Will, I mean. I just, haven't mentioned it yet, that's all. We've only been dating, like, four months.'

'But you'll have been together nearly seven months by the time of the wedding,' Daisy insists, 'and he's just so perfect for you.'

I don't reply. I can't – I'm trying not to cry.

'I mean . . . isn't he?' Daisy asks.

What is it they say, about pride going before a fall? With an explosion of sobbing on my part, Kieran bursts out of his box.

I try to explain what I've been feeling since the night at Kieran's restaurant. Perhaps I'm not as coherent as I might be, because it seems to take both James and Daisy a while to understand exactly what I'm upset about and why I'm so very upset. When the pair of them finally get it, they both look surprised.

But not as surprised as I expected them to be.

'All this time,' I repeat, 'I thought he was dead, or that he'd just dumped me. And then I thought that he'd gone off with someone else – the woman I saw him with at the Gare du Nord, the one I told you about. But actually, it was just a – a maelstrom of facts and events.' Is maelstrom the word I want? I try again. 'A convergence. If he hadn't had an accident, or if he hadn't broken his phone, or if he'd left his laptop at home, or if he'd actually backed up any of the tech he owned, the utter dimwit . . .' I shrug and sip the fresh cup of tea that James has made me. It makes me wince; he must have put about five sugars in it. 'I don't know. If it wasn't for the fact that when he *did* finally see me in that restaurant he didn't do anything about it . . .'

I tail off. Daisy and James are both watching me like I'm a pot that might suddenly boil over.

Come on, Emma. You're meant to be a writer, for fuck's sake. How can you be finding it this hard to express yourself?

I take a deep breath.

'I guess what's bothering me is this: did he *really* want to find me? I traipsed round Paris searching for him. When he saw me, literally sitting on the other side of a window, he immediately gave up. So, what does that mean? Perhaps it means that he didn't really want us to be together again. Do you get what I'm saying?'

They both nod.

'Yeah, yeah,' James says. 'I get it. And I guess, um . . .' He puffs out a breath and drums his fingers on the arm of the sofa. 'Well, you know . . .' A flush rises up James's neck and into his face and he sort of wriggles about in the seat like a toddler who needs the toilet.

I frown. 'James, you're squirming. Why are you squirming?'

'I'm not squirming,' he insists, squirming even more. 'Daisy, tell her.'

'Tell me what?' I demand, turning to Daisy.

My best friend is not squirming, but her left eyelid is twitching, and I've known her too many years not to know what that means.

'Daisy,' I say, trying to keep my tone calm and polite, 'what exactly have you done?'

'Done?' she exclaims. 'I haven't done anything! What makes you think I've done something?'

The calm and polite thing evaporates. 'Because you look exactly the same as you did when you let Simon "Not Remotely" Sexey copy my English coursework in year eleven and we all got into massive trouble!'

James lets out a kind of strangled moan and he and Daisy glance at each other with something approaching desperation.

I put down my tea.

'You're both hiding something, so come on. Spill. Now.'

'Look, Emma,' James begins, 'we weren't deliberately not telling you. We only found out just before you did, back in May, I think. And then—'

'And then we talked about it,' Daisy interrupts, 'and we both agreed that it was best just to . . .' She holds the nearest binder up like a shield. 'Just to . . . not . . . bother you with it. Especially after you told us you'd seen him with another woman.'

I can hardly believe what I'm hearing.

'Let me get this straight. You're telling me that both of you—' I jab my finger at each of them in turn – 'found out that Kieran was alive, but you decided, without asking me, that I didn't need to know? How the hell did you find out?'

'Well – well—' James stutters. 'He contacted us! He wanted us to tell you!'

'Wait, what?' My hands are shaking.

'We just thought that it might not be true.' Daisy rushes the sentence out. 'I mean, sure, he *says* he had an accident, but we thought he might be making it up, just to get sympathy. We thought he'd dumped you and then maybe he'd changed his mind. And then you saw him at the station, and we thought he was like, a romance scammer, or something. And Jacques seems so great. So perfect . . .' The praise withers in her mouth at my expression.

'You don't know that he's perfect. You don't know anything about him, not really. You've never even met him!' I explode. 'You've never met Kieran either.' I'm so angry I can barely get the words out. 'Seriously? You knew – you *knew* – not only that Kieran was looking for me, but that he'd had an accident. And you still didn't think I deserved to be told? Show me,' I demand, holding my hands out to Daisy and James. 'Show me the messages he sent you.'

Unwillingly, they both get out their phones, unlock the screens and hand them over.

The DMs they show me are hard to read.

Hi James, it's Kieran Landry here – we've never met but you might remember me from Emma talking about me, and I think we waved at each other on a video call once. I'm sure Emma has told you I stood her up, but please let me explain. On the day I was due to meet her I had a really bad accident. When I woke up in hospital a few weeks later, I discovered that my phone and my laptop and all Emma's contact info had been destroyed. I've been trying to find her ever since and I'm hoping you'll be willing to help me get back in touch with her. I can't stand the thought that I might have lost her forever, and if you can help me, I'll be so very grateful . . .

Hello, Daisy, this is Kieran – we spoke a couple of times when I was video chatting with Emma. I've been trying to find her for months. I had an awful bad accident the day we were supposed to meet – my phone and my laptop got destroyed at the same time, so when I woke up in hospital I had no means of contacting her. I know she must think I changed my mind, at best, or that I was playing some horrible game, but please believe me when I swear that

isn't true. I would be so very grateful if you'd tell her I'm
searching for her, and give her my new number. I can't
imagine my life without her . . .

Neither James nor Daisy had replied to the messages.

I sniff, and wipe a tear away from my cheek.

'*Why?*' I ask. 'I'm not a child. I'm not an idiot. Why didn't you let me decide for myself?'

My friends don't seem to have an answer. I give them back their phones and get up.

'I'm going for a walk.'

It's cold outside. Cold enough that I shiver and pull my coat closer across my chest. Of course, it's October, so I suppose I shouldn't be surprised, but Paris hadn't felt quite so autumnal when I left. Withered leaves are blowing across the path and crunching beneath my feet. I'm walking by the river, through Imperial Park, heading in the direction of Battersea Railway Bridge, but I might as well be on a treadmill for all the attention I'm paying to my surroundings.

I just can't *believe* that Daisy and James didn't tell me. Abruptly, I realise that Kieran didn't tell me either. The other night, standing outside his restaurant, he mentioned contacting Lauren. But he said nothing about messaging my friends.

A fresh lump forms in my throat. He was protecting them.

'I'm going to kill him. And Daisy, and James. I'm going to kill all three of them. Really, really slowly.' A passer-by gives me a strange look as I fumble in my pocket for a tissue. Ordinarily if I were feeling this miserable I'd call Daisy, but right now . . .

I sit down on one of the benches. My list of friends and acquaintances has shrunk since moving to Paris and becoming a full-time writer. I need to fix that, whatever happens with Kieran.

I find myself staring at a number in my contact list.

Well, why not? There's a first time for everything.

I hit dial. The call connects.

'Emma?'

'Hey, Dad. Um, do you think I could ask you for some advice?'

'Financial advice? Yes, I'd be happy to—'

'No, not financial. Like, relationship advice.'

'Oh.' He pauses. 'Well, I can't promise it will be good advice. I'm hardly an example of outstanding success when it comes to relationships, as you know. But of course – anything I can do to help you, Emma.' Another pause. 'Perhaps – perhaps if you tell me what the problem is?'

So I tell him. I tell him from the beginning. Running into Kieran, literally. The spark I felt when he touched me. The awkward first call, the months of video chats, the voice messages, the cooking lessons, the late-night text exchanges. I describe how I felt when he didn't show up at the Gare du Nord, and how I trawled Paris searching for him, how I almost convinced myself he was dead, until I became certain that he was just a player. How I tried to make myself accept that he wasn't coming back. Until, of course, he did.

'And now I've discovered that Daisy and James knew, and that Kieran knew that they knew, but still – he didn't come into that restaurant, when he had the chance. He didn't *fight* for me.'

As soon as I say the words, I realise that *that*, right there, is what's been eating me.

He didn't fight for me. And I wanted him to.

There's a silence on the other end of the phone.

'Dad?'

'Sorry, love. I mean, Emma. I mean, I'm sorry that you've been going through such a rough time. I wish you'd told me. Though I understand why you didn't.'

'What do you think I should do?'

'About your friends, or about Kieran?'

'About all of it.'

'Well, your friends were in the wrong, there's no doubt about that. But they thought they were protecting you. They love you, by the sounds of it.'

'Yeah.' I sigh. 'I know.'

'As for Kieran . . . how do you feel about him?'

'I think . . .' I hesitate, trying to untangle the cat's cradle of emotions in my core. 'I think I love him. Even now. We – we clicked, somehow, the moment we met. We just slotted together, like two bits of a jigsaw puzzle.' No question of trying to make it fit. 'When I imagine my life with him in it, it just makes more sense. On the other hand, he takes chances, and he gets swept away by things and he's not . . . predictable. And maybe I want predictable.' Or if I don't want it, maybe I need it.

I can almost hear my father mulling over what I've said.

'You know, love, I felt I took a risk when I married your mother. But if I were to list all the things I regret in my life – and there are plenty of things I regret bitterly – that is not one of them. My only regret when it comes to your mother is not being stronger. Not being braver. She needed me to help her, and instead I ran away. And that was the worst mistake I ever made. I don't know Kieran. Only you can decide if he's right for you. But it sounds like you love him. Like he loves you. And if it comes down to a choice between love and safety, well, if had my time again, I know what I'd choose.'

Chapter Thirty-Two

Kieran

'Dad – come on in. I'm so sorry I couldn't meet you at the station. It's just been crazy at the restaurant.' I give my father a hug, relieved to find that he feels more solid than he did when I said goodbye to him at the end of July. His face has filled out a little, too. 'You're looking grand.'

'Thanks. Your mother made me get a haircut and buy some new clothes before she'd let me come. She always has had excellent taste, I'll give her that.'

'She does indeed. In clothes and in husbands.'

That makes him laugh.

'I am quite glad to be getting away from her cooking, though. I've just about persuaded her that I'm well enough now to start making dinner again.'

'Is the hotel okay? Kobe recommended it so I'm hoping it's good.'

'It's very fancy. I might never want to leave.' He takes off his coat. 'Mind if I have a look around?'

'Of course.'

I return to sautéing the potatoes. After taking a tour of my flat – less than two minutes, since it's not exactly Versailles – Dad comes to stand next to me. He has something in his hand.

'Cousin Pete emailed this to me and I printed it out for you. You remember Pete, right?'

'Sure. Are they still living in Montreal?'

'Yeah, still there. Anyway, he saw this online.'

I take the piece of paper. It's an article in French from *Le Quotidien de Montréal*, a newspaper I remember from the few times we've visited Dad's family in Canada. I don't bother to read the article. The contents are pretty obvious, given the title – '*Le Prochain chef célèbre?*' – and the photo of me that's stuck next to it. It's the same photo we've used on the website of Le Bon Frère.

'Your mother was made up when she saw it,' Dad chuckles. 'I think she wants to get a large copy of that photo and hang it over the mantelpiece.'

'Dear God, please don't let her do that. It makes me look like a right piece of work.'

I'd wanted to smile, for the photo. The photographer Kobe hired, however, had other ideas. He told me I was to 'glower sexily'. Apparently, the current vibe is for a chef-patron to look like a superhero who's just put in a long day saving humanity from aliens and/or itself and is feeling pretty worn down by it all.

'Tell her the photos has too many pixels to be blown up, or something.'

Dad grins and shakes his head. 'That's not exactly how pixels work, son. On the other hand, if you cook me enough delicious food to make it worth my while . . .' He sniffs the air appreciatively. 'Ah, that smells amazing. What are we having?'

'*Blanc de poulet aux champignons sauce vin blanc*. In other words, chicken breasts and mushrooms in a creamy white wine sauce. To be served with sautéed potatoes and a green salad.'

'I've really missed your food over the past couple of months.' He starts fiddling with the herbs I've left out on the counter. 'Your mother and I were so sorry not to make the opening.'

'Don't be. The hospital appointment was more important. And you're here now.'

'I am.' He pats his stomach. 'And I've been saving myself, the past couple of days.'

'Don't worry, you won't have to wait long – it's a quick dish. The chicken is done, and the salad is made. I've just to reduce the sauce and finish these.' I wave my father's hand away as he tries to snatch one of the sizzling golden cubes of potato from the frying pan. 'Careful! Why don't you pour us some wine? There's a bottle of champagne in the fridge.'

His eyebrow goes up. 'Are we celebrating?'

'Of course. I'm celebrating you being here.' In more ways than one.

We finish the meal sitting on the sofa, eating Brie de Meaux spread on very thin crackers.

'That was delicious, Kieran,' Dad says, picking up his wine glass and leaning back against the sofa cushions. 'Best thing I've eaten since last time you cooked for me.' He raises the glass in a toast. 'We're very proud of you. You know that, don't you? Your mother's already been on to the local radio station about interviewing you when you're next home.'

'Seriously?'

Dad nods, and I pull a face, torn between gratification and embarrassment. My expression makes him laugh.

'There's no point trying to avoid it. If Mum has her way, you'll be on *Today on RTÉ One* as well as *Morning Ireland*. The Irish chef making it big in Paris. Who'd have thought it, given what you used to eat when you were a kid.'

'Hey, I didn't eat anything that weird.'

'That's not how I remember it. You ate a pair of your mother's contact lenses and most of a box of crayons. And some of Nana Foley's rheumatism cream.'

'It was *one time*,' I protest. 'I was only four. It looked like icing, so I wanted to see if it tasted like it too.' It did not, for the record. 'At least I wasn't like Brendan, the world's fussiest child.'

'Well, I'll give you that. Do you recall his "plain pasta" phase? Was that one year, or two? Are you old enough to remember when we were in that restaurant on holiday, and someone dared drizzle it with olive oil and he went absolutely—'

'Yeah, I remember.' Brendan, about six years old, staring at the glistening pasta as if it had been laced with arsenic, before completely losing his shit. 'It was hilarious.' The memory makes me laugh properly, for the first time in what feels like ages.

'It was mortifying,' Dad corrects, though he's laughing too. 'Your poor mother looked like she wanted to die, especially since you'd already complained very loudly about the Caesar salad you'd insisted on ordering – she'd forgotten to ask them to put the dressing on the side. We pretty much threw some money on the table and ran.'

'I'd forgotten the salad. Poor Mum. We did give her a hard time.'

'Occasionally. But you've always been good lads, and worrying comes with the territory for parents.' Dad tilts his glass so that the pale golden liquid catches the lamplight. 'We still worry about you.'

His tone is unmistakable.

'Brendan told you, then?' I swear under my breath. 'He wasn't supposed to, the eejit. I told him not to. You've got enough on your plate and I—' I break off and force myself to relax my grip on the stem of my wine glass. 'I'm happy. I've got a brilliant family and my own restaurant and I've no right to be sad. No right in the world.'

'And yet . . .?' Dad questions.

'And yet nothing. I'm over her. She's moved on, and it's just as well. I've no time for a relationship at the moment.'

Dad just smiles. 'Sure, you're a terrible liar, Kieran.'

We stare at each other for a moment, but his gaze doesn't falter.

'Tell me something I don't know.' Irritated, I pick up our plates and take them to the sink. 'Exactly how much information did Brendan give you?'

'Enough, but not a lot. He said you finally found Emma, but she's dating someone else, and that you had a row, the night you saw each other again.' Dad brings the wine glasses over to the kitchen and leans against the countertop. 'Did she not believe you? About the accident and your phone and everything?'

I think back over what Emma said.

'I reckon she did believe me. It wasn't that.' As I jam the plug into the sink, dump in some washing-up liquid, turn on the hot water and start scrubbing the plates aggressively, I find myself telling my dad about the fight Emma and I had. I tell him how upset she was that I *hadn't* busted into the restaurant, that night I saw her, and tried to break up the date she was on with Jacques. Suddenly, I'm back at home in Cork, thirteen years old again, and going to my dad for advice on why my first girlfriend had dumped me. 'I told her I loved her, Dad. So why didn't she immediately break up with Jacques? Why did she tell me not to contact her?' I grip the edge of the sink. 'Did I do the wrong thing?'

Dad picks up a tea towel and starts drying.

'No, for sure you didn't. You'd no idea whether she was really into this fella or not, the first time you saw them. You'd no call to be barging in. Having said that . . .' He puts the first plate carefully back in the cupboard. 'Having said that, it's understandable that she would want to know that you really want to win her back. She might want that certainty. That commitment. It's not your fault, but she's been through a lot, one way or another. What with the accident, and everything.'

And everything. He means me being a complete and utter thicko who never thought to take five minutes to avoid losing the phone number of the woman he'd fallen in love with.

The threat of tears chokes me; I hadn't realised how close to the surface all of this still is. I take a deep breath and try to sound normal.

'I have no idea if she wants to see me any more. Neither do you.'

'No, I don't. But I do know that you're not as happy as you should be.' He puts his hands on my shoulders and forces me to look at him. 'Your body has mostly recovered from the accident, Kieran. But your heart hasn't.' He studies my face for a moment before dropping his glance towards my dripping wet hands. 'And unless you want to ruin your skin you should be using rubber gloves for that washing-up. Maybe I'll get you a pair for Christmas.'

Despite myself, I smile. The tension breaks.

'You're right, Dad. As usual.'

My father picks up the next plate and dries it up.

'As usual, Kieran. As usual.'

I ask Kobe to come to the restaurant early the next afternoon. Emma will be back in Paris in a couple of days, and I want to try to see him before the rest of the staff turn up to get ready for the dinner service. As it is, Chip, the college kid Arnaud fired, is already waiting outside when I arrive. He got in touch after seeing the restaurant advertised, and I've hired him as a kitchen assistant.

'Hey, Chip. You're early.'

'Hey, Chef. You don't mind, do you? I've brought some carrots.' He stands to one side as I unlock the door, and holds up a paper bag. 'I need to practise my julienning and I don't have any good knives.'

'You should ask for some for Christmas. Every chef needs a good set of knives.' I glance at my watch. 'Kobe's going to be here shortly. When he arrives, d'you mind running out and fetching us a coffee from the place on the corner? I don't dare turn on the machine in the restaurant before Marcel gets here.'

Chip beams. 'No problem, Chef, whatever you need.'

Chip is a good as his word. Once Kobe arrives, he practically sprints to the coffee shop, brings back our order then makes himself scarce.

'How's my favourite chef?' Kobe takes a sip of the coffee and nods appreciatively. 'We should find out where they get this blend. Have you had any thoughts about the Christmas menu yet?'

'Not yet, but there is something I need to run past you. A personal matter.'

He frowns. 'Your father's not worse again, I hope?'

'No, no, nothing like that.' I decide to get to the point. 'It's Emma.'

Kobe looks blank.

'Emma,' I say. 'Who came to the restaurant with Jacques.'

'Oh.' He drinks some more coffee. 'What about her?'

I launch into the story from the beginning. A summarised version: Kobe is a busy man. When I'm finished, he picks up a pencil and starts doodling on the edge of a receipt from our wholesale fruit supplier.

'So, let me get this straight. You and Emma had a thing, then you had your accident, and now she has a thing with Jacques, and you both just pretended not to know each other that night.'

'Basically. I wasn't trying to be deceitful. I didn't know whether she'd want to acknowledge it, or whether she'd said anything to Jacques . . .' I crumple up an old menu and aim it at the recycling bin. 'Sorry.'

'Hey, don't worry. I remember being young and single. This stuff can get complicated. And you guys—' he whistles '—boy, you've had some bad luck. But why are you telling me this now?'

'Because Jacques has a lot of influence, and he's a friend of yours, and because I owe you a huge amount. I would never do anything shady. But, I am going to tell Emma – again – that I love her and that I want to be with her. Whether she wants to be with me . . .' I throw up my hands. 'Well, that's her choice.'

Kobe focuses on his doodling. 'So . . . you're asking my permission?'

'No. I just thought you should know, in case.'

He glances up at me. 'In case Emma chooses you, and Jacques decides to take it out on Le Bon Frère.'

'Basically.'

'Okay. Well, I appreciate your honesty, Kieran. And I don't think you should worry – Jacques's reviews can be harsh, but he's not an a-hole. And he really does love your cooking. On the other hand, he is rich, cultured, good-looking, and he has a lot of influence in the publishing world.'

Kobe drums his fingers on the table as if weighing up what to say next.

'You know Emma's just getting started as a magazine journalist, right?'

'Yeah. Ettore sent me that article she wrote, about dating in Paris.'

'Sure, sure. Did you also know that she's written a book, and is hoping to get it published?'

The news hits my stomach like a extra-large helping of suet pudding.

'No. I did not know that.'

'Well, I'm just saying. I wish you luck, man, but Jacques has got a lot going for him. Don't be too gutted if she doesn't play ball.'

'Okay. Thanks for the heads-up.'

'No sweat.' Kobe smiles. 'You're a good guy, Kieran. More importantly, you're worth a lot of money to me. I don't want anything to upset your cooking. I guess what I'm saying is, if she chooses Jacques over you, keep it out of the kitchen, *capiche*?'

I raise my empty coffee cup to him.

'*Capiche*.'

That night, tired as I am, I send a message to the family WhatsApp. Mum, Dad, Brendan, Niamh. We never have had any boundaries, so I may as well use it to my advantage.

> Hey, everyone. I need ideas, please. I want to convince Emma that dumping the guy she's with and taking a chance on me, despite the whole never-turning-up-after-having-convinced-her-to-move-her-entire-life-to-France thing, is a sound and sensible thing to do. Just so you know, the other guy is rich, influential and looks kind of like George Clooney. I am definitely the underdog here. Any thoughts? Any ideas for romantic gestures that say 'pick me!' without crossing

the line into being that guy who sneaks around smashing up other people's relationships? Should I tell Parisian George Clooney what I'm doing??? Any suggestions gratefully received. I'm too stressed out to come up with anything remotely sensible. Love you guys. K

I hit send.
Now all I have to do is wait.

Chapter Thirty-Three

Emma

I make the decision on the train home. Jacques will be back in Paris in two days. We're both proper adults. Well, he definitely is, and I'm working on it. So I'm not going to dump him over text, or ghost him, like some pathetic twenty-year-old boy who's just playing at dating. No. Jacques is a decent guy who helped me get into journalism and has taken me out to lots of lovely places. He's done absolutely everything right. His only failure is not being Kieran, which is hardly his fault. I owe it to him to break up with him face-to-face, and to break up with him before he books any of the luxury resorts he's been suggesting for our mini-break. And definitely before I get in touch with Kieran. If I get in touch with Kieran.

What if he was right about fate, but wrong about the outcome? What if we're just not meant to be?

Part of my brain starts reminding me about Jacques's financial stability and all the great sex. Before I can change my mind, I type a message, asking if we can meet for coffee late afternoon the day he gets back, and hit send.

I cross 'initiate breaking up with Jacques' off my mental to-do list and get out my laptop. The next article for Sylvie is due in just a few days. I open the document that has a list of ideas, several of which I've already started researching and drafting. French versus English pop music – I'd discovered that France has quotas to ensure that thirty-five to forty per cent of the songs played on the radio are in French. French versus English tourists – my theory is that being a tourist automatically makes you really annoying, regardless of nationality. Where to spend an evening in Paris if you want to avoid seeing other people's romantic success – top tip: an out-of-hours pharmacy in a particularly dodgy area. Trouble is, nothing on the list is really speaking to me at the moment.

I open up a new document. Stare out of the window for a bit and drum my fingers lightly against the keyboard.

Come on, Emma. You can't let Sylvie down. Not if you want her to make your articles a regular feature.

I drum my fingers a bit more, then type a few words.

Recipe for the ideal boyfriend.

Not much, but it's a start.

It's early evening by the time I get back to the flat. I'm tired, but in a good way. The article is mostly done – at least a sandpaper draft of it – although, worryingly, the ideal boyfriend sounds a lot more like Jacques than Kieran. At least on paper. Still, I'm more convinced than ever that breaking things off with him is the right thing to do. It feels as though a weight is off my shoulders, despite the extra weight of my suitcase – several weeks' supply of Marmite, some boxes of tea, and a large tub of my favourite unavailable-in-Paris peanut butter.

I've lived here long enough that I'm no longer surprised when Madame Pollie materialises as soon as I step across the threshold.

'Mademoiselle Noël!'

'Madame Pollie, *comment allez-vous?*'

She ignores my question, disappears beneath her counter and reappears with another vast bunch of flowers. Dahlias, I think: vivid scarlet petals shading towards yellow at the centre. They remind me of a sunset. There's a card, too. *Ma chérie, j'ai hâte de te voir. Avec tout mon amour, Jacques.* He can't wait to see me, and he sends all his love. Boy, but his florist must be working overtime. And his assistant too; Jacques himself doesn't even land until tomorrow morning.

I hand the flowers back to Madame Pollie. '*Pour vous*. For you. I can't . . . *je ne peux pas les accepter.*'

Her eyebrows fly up. 'But why? Why may you not accept them?'

'Because I'm going to break up with him. *C'est fini*. Finished.'

Madame Pollie breaks out into a torrent of French, the gist of which is, I think, that I must be terminally stupid to be making such a stupid decision. She was really keen on Jacques. I find myself apologising.

'*Désolée, Madame. Mais, il n'est pas le . . . le bon.*' Not the right one – I think that's what I've said.

'*Mais il est si riche, si charmant!*'

'He is rich and charming, you're right.' An idea occurs. 'He will also, once I've broken up with him, be single again. *Célibataire.*'

Madame Pollie's eyes light up. '*Ah, oui. C'est vrai.*' She nods. '*Pauvre Monsieur Jacques*. I will console him.'

'Excellent idea.'

'*Alors*, I must arrange these flowers.'

I leave her to it and make my escape.

I push open the door of the café, close my umbrella and look around. Jacques being Jacques, when I suggested meeting up for coffee, he didn't just reply to my suggestion of meeting with a thumbs-up emoji, or even a '*great idea, I'll call you*'. He replied with a scheduled invitation – 5.40 p.m. – to a meeting at an elegant, mirrored, Viennese-styled coffee shop, where his assistant has booked a table.

I spot him in a booth at the far end. He waves and stands up as I approach.

'Emma, I have missed you.' He leans in for a kiss. I turn my head at the last moment so his lips land on my cheek, then start unbuttoning my coat and taking off my scarf. Easier than looking him in the eye.

'Thank you for meeting me, Jacques. Especially in this horrible weather.' I wave vaguely towards the rain-soaked streets on the other side of the windows.

'But of course. You received my flowers?'

'Yes. Yes, they were beautiful. As always.'

I can tell from his expression that he knows something is wrong. A waitress approaches and I ask her to give us a few minutes. He knows I know he knows. Still he doesn't say anything.

'How was your trip?' I ask, playing for time, scanning the menu without really reading it. This is much harder than I'd expected it to be.

'Fine. Successful, for the business. And London?'

'Oh – busy. But it was good to be back, to catch up with my friends.'

'*Bon, bon.*' He takes a sip of his coffee. And waits.

I shut the menu and launch into the explanation I've been trying to prepare and perfect since I got back to Paris.

'The past few months have been amazing, Jacques. Really special. And you're amazing. Any woman would be lucky to have you. Ought to think herself lucky to have you, I mean. You're – you're clever, and kind, and handsome, and I mean, you know, the sex is just—' I mime having my mind blown. There's a sudden, noticeable cessation of conversation from the next table. I lean forward and lower my voice. 'And this whole thing, on paper, is just ridiculous. I'm being ridiculous. But I just – I can't—'

Jacques's reading glasses are folded on the table next to his menu. He's tapping his forefinger on the bridge, over and over. Otherwise, he's immobile. No indication that he's listening to me at all.

'You deserve better, Jacques. You deserve better than someone whose heart isn't fully free. And when we met, my heart wasn't free. I thought it was. I tried to convince myself it was, but . . .' I shrug and look down at my hands, clasped together in my lap. 'We shouldn't see each other any more. It's not fair on you.'

'There is someone else?' he asks.

'Yes. For a long time. When we met in the Moleskine shop, I actually thought he might be dead.'

'But he is not.' Something in the tone of Jacques's voice makes me glance up.

'You know?'

'The, er, hot young chef, *non*? I suspected, that night at Le Bon Frère, that you had met before.'

I half-reach my hand towards him. 'Don't take it out on him. It's not his fault. Once he found out about us – he didn't try to – to barge in—'

'"Barge"?'

'He didn't try to break us up. He stopped looking for me.'

Jacques nods at a hovering waitress. '*Un autre café, s'il vous plaît*. In what way do you imagine I would "take it out on him"?'

The question throws me.

'Well – you might give him a bad review. Or you might tell Kobe to fire him, or—'

Jacques laughs, almost. '*C'est drôle*. He has asked me almost exactly the same thing. *Do not take it out on her*. Such an odd phrase, when one thinks about it.'

I know my mouth is hanging open.

'What?' I manage eventually. 'I mean, *qu'est-ce que tu dis*?'

'I had a message from Kieran Landry waiting for me when I returned yesterday. He . . .' Jacques waits as the waitress places the fresh coffee down in front of him. 'He was worried, I suppose, that your behaviour at the restaurant would make me suspicious. He told me that you had both concealed the fact that you already knew each other, and asked me to direct my anger at him, not at you.'

I grip the edge of the table. 'What else did he say?'

'I think that was all, as far as I recall. I had a great deal of correspondence to catch up on.' He drinks the espresso and sits back, sighing. 'He does not need to worry. Neither of you do. I am not a vindictive man. Nor am I an idiot. Kieran Landry is a great chef, and Kobe has allowed me to make a small investment in Le Bon Frère. You are an entertaining writer, and you will increase advertising draw for the magazine.' Jacques puts his reading glasses away and catches the eye of the waitress. '*L'addition, s'il vous plaît.* I am not in the business of destroying things of value, my dear Emma.' He pays the bill. 'Will you go back to him?'

'Yes. I mean, probably.' Thinking about it makes me smile. 'It could be a disaster, of course. I might find he picks his nose at the breakfast table or leaves toothpaste in the basin or communicates half the time through passive-aggressive Post-it notes like my last housemate, but I think I have to try.' I put on my coat, and we walk towards the exit. 'Are you – are you going to be okay?'

Jacques smiles, this time.

'I will survive. At my age, I no longer believe that there only exists "the one true love". I have enjoyed our time together, but I will meet someone else. And you are young. Possibly too young for me, as Juliette suggested. You have time to make mistakes.'

'You think I'm making a mistake, then?'

He shrugs, still smiling. '*Au revoir, Emma. Et bonne chance.*'

Jacques disappears into the crowds. I put up my umbrella, turn the other way and hurry towards the metro.

I still can't believe that Kieran got in touch with him. Did he really do it for me? Or was he just trying to protect the restaurant?

I'm still no nearer to figuring it out when I get back to the flat. Madame Pollie is too busy berating one of my neighbours for traipsing mud across the tiles to do anything other than wave at me as I pass. I call out a compliment on her new outfit – chunky-soled, knee-high black boots, black sparkly tights, a black leather mini-skirt and a Chanel-coded black bouclé jacket – and head upstairs.

As soon as I'm inside, I check my phone. No messages from Kieran, though I know he now has my new number. No voicemails. No emails. No missed FaceTime calls.

What did you expect? You told him not to contact you. You told him you thought he was too big a risk.

Damn.

I make myself some tea, get out one of my notebooks and open it to a new page.

I figure I should make the first move and contact him. Is that enough, though? Do I need to make some big romantic gesture?

At the top of the blank page, I write a title. *Big Romantic Gestures.*

I pause, then underline it carefully.

Trouble is, I'm not good at being romantic. Never have been. I suspect I take after my dad.

Writing, though ... that's something I know. And my next article, if Sylvie likes it, will be published online at the end of the week. Kieran and I have been waiting long enough. A few more days won't make any difference.

I cross out *Big Romantic Gestures* and start again. *Soulmates.*

The article I've already drafted, the one about the ideal boyfriend – that will keep. This is what I want to write about: is the concept of a soulmate totally ridiculous, or is there really one person who's more right for you than anyone else on the planet? And I've already got the opening line.

> Imagine this: it's a gorgeous late spring/early summer morning in the most romantic city on earth, and you've just run into the person with whom you're destined to spend the rest of your life.

Chapter Thirty-Four

Kieran

I haven't heard anything back from Jacques Toussaint. Not surprising, perhaps. He's hardly going to wish me luck. Given he was the guy who set up the interview with *Ici Paris*, I'm a little surprised when the reporter actually shows up to the restaurant with her photographer.

Surprised, but relieved. And nervous.

Make a public declaration – that was Brendan's suggestion. If he had his way, I'd have paid for billboard advertisements across Paris by now: *Emma Christmas, will you marry me?* I've told him no, of course. I would think that kind of public declaration, especially when we've never been on an actual date, might feel like quite a lot of pressure. It did get me thinking about the interview, though.

The reporter is checking over her notes. Our conversation is going to be recorded, then broadcast tomorrow lunchtime.

'So, Kieran, we are going to talk about your journey to becoming *chef-patron* of Le Bon Frère. The interview will be in French, but if you want me to clarify something in English, just raise your finger. We can edit out any breaks in the flow.'

'Great, no problem.'

'And you do not mind personal questions?'

'Not at all.' Here goes. 'I'd quite like to talk about the love of my life, actually.'

The photographer stops snapping the interior of the kitchen and stares at me.

'The . . . love of your life?' the reporter questions.

'Yep. I'm not giving you her name, obviously, but I'd like to talk about how we met. And how I lost her. And how I hope to find her again.'

'No problem. No problem at all.' She picks up her phone and types rapidly. 'I've just messaged my boss – we might run some additional trailers. I have a feeling our listeners are going to really love this.'

I just hope Emma loves it.

Emma

The message is from James.

> I have NEWS. Call me. Call
> me NOW. NO EXCUSES!

So I do.
He picks up instantly. 'Guess what?'
I'm about to guess when an email arrives.
'Hold on – email from Sylvie. Just let me check.'

> Emma,
> 　Merci pour cet envoi.
> 　C'est génial, encore mieux que le précédent. L'article suivant à la même heure le mois prochain. Toujours du point de vue des rencontres/relations amoureuses.
> 　Amicalement, SK

My shoulders relax. I hadn't really expected her to dump me, not after Jacques making a big thing about not being vindictive, but it's still a relief.

'Well?' James nudges. 'What does she say?'

'Er . . . she likes it even better than the last article and wants another one next month. And I'm to stick with the dating/romance angle.'

'That's brilliant news, Ems! But back to me. Guess! Guess what's happened?'

'Let me think . . . Virginie O'Keefe likes your sample chapters and has asked to see the rest of the manuscript?'

James gasps. 'You knew?'

'She told me how much she was enjoying reading what you'd already sent. I'm pretty sure she's going to offer to represent you.'

'Shut up!'

'No, seriously.'

'Well, I don't want to get ahead of myself, but—' I hold the phone away from my ear as James shrieks. 'Sorry. I'm just so happy!'

'You deserve it. I couldn't have written *The Ghostwriter's Guide* without your inspiration.' I check my watch, swear, and start shrugging myself into my coat. 'I have to go or I'll be late for the hairdresser. Have you booked your train tickets yet?'

'I'll get on it this afternoon.'

'Good. I want to celebrate with you!'

I close the flat door as quietly as possible and tiptoe down the stairs, but Madame Pollie – preternaturally sharp hearing, so I'm back on my vampire theory – practically leaps out of her room as soon as I'm on the top stair.

'Mademoiselle Noël, *vous avez entendu?*'

'*Bonjour*, Madame Pollie. Have I heard what?'

Madame Pollie gives a theatrical gasp and her hand flies to her chest. She is literally clutching her pearls.

'*Attendez* – wait!' She rushes back into her room, returns with a TV and radio listings magazine and slams it on to the counter. '*Voilà!* This is him, *non*? Your chef, the one you tell me about? I listen to his interview just now.'

She taps one nail against the page. There's a blurry little black and white photo of Kieran, the same photo he's got on the restaurant's website. Had he mentioned that evening that he was going to be on the radio? I don't remember.

'*Oui, ç'est lui.*' I nod.

More pearl-clutching. '*Oh, c'est tellement romantique.* It was you he describes. His lost love.'

I snatch up the magazine.

What exactly did Kieran say?

Kieran

Marcel looks up from the laptop as I walk into the kitchen and shakes his head. There's a slight smile playing on his lips.

'Seriously?' I ask. 'There are more?'

'Another twenty-five overnight. On the positive side, seventeen of them have also made reservations. We are now fully booked up until the January closure. There is a saying, *non*? About publicity.' His shoulders are shaking slightly because he's trying not to laugh.

'There's no such thing as bad publicity.' I guess it's true. And the publicity I've been getting from that radio interview isn't exactly what you'd call bad. More . . . embarrassing. Emails have been arriving in the restaurant inbox. Most from women, a few from men, telling me how romantic my story is, and offering to take the place of my 'lost love', with varying amounts of graphic detail. I've been offered everything from a romantic dinner – though that might also have been a ploy by an aspiring chef to get me to taste their food – to a night in a 'sex dungeon' guaranteed to make me forget all about the woman who broke my heart.

Marcel loses the battle and bursts out laughing. He makes a strategic exit into the dining room before I can think of anything to say.

Instead, I get out one of my knives, move to a chopping board and start taking out my emotions on some defenceless mushrooms.

The emails will die down, eventually. Hopefully. In the meantime, will the interview help? It was meant to be a grand gesture. A way of reassuring Emma of my seriousness and commitment through a public statement. What if she thinks it's lame?

What if she never even hears it?

I get my phone out and bring up her number. Perhaps I should just have kept it simple and called her. Perhaps I should call her now.

The back door of the restaurant opens and Ettore stomps in, removing his motorcycle helmet and shaking himself like a wet dog.

'The rain,' he exclaims. 'We might as well be in Inghilterra.'

'What are you doing here?' I ask. 'You're not due for another two hours yet. Not that I don't love having you around, but—'

He holds out his iPad.

'*Regarde.* The new issue of *Notre Ville*. There is another article by Emma.'

I take the tablet and read the opening line. Then I read it again. Ettore is watching me, a big grin on his face.

. . . and you've just run into the person with whom you're destined to spend the rest of your life.

I read the whole article and hand the tablet back to Ettore, but I can't stand still. 'When did she write it? Did she hear my interview first, or – Ettore, do you think—'

'Kieran, *il y a un problème.*' It's Marcel. He looks unusually harassed.

'Oh, for—' I bite my tongue. 'What's wrong now?'

'A woman, banging on our door. An elderly woman. I tell her we are closed, but she will not depart.' He swears. 'She insists she must speak with you. She says she has—' he exchanges a glance with Ettore and almost starts laughing again '—information.'

I rub my hand over my face. 'Christ. If I ever talk about doing an interview again, just sedate me until I've come to my senses.'

I follow him through to the dining room. A woman of around seventy is seated at one of the tables, very upright, dressed entirely in black and holding a large handbag in front of her like a shield. When she sees me, however, her scowl disappears.

'Ah, Monsieur Landry! I come with news. Wonderful news.

Emma, she is free. *Elle a rompu avec Monsieur Toussaint. Il faut aller la voir.*'

I understand, but I don't believe what I've heard. 'What?'

The woman clicks her tongue with annoyance, and huffs.

'Emma. Is. Free. Monsieur Toussaint, he is FINISHED.' She speaks very slowly with sudden, explosive emphasis. 'They are BROKEN. UP.'

Broken up? My heart leaps. But why hasn't Emma told me?

'How do you know?' I ask. '*Comment savez-vous ça, madame?*'

The woman draws herself up. '*Je suis Madame Pollie*. I am the friend of Emma. She tells me everything. I show her your interview. Also, I am the *gardienne* of her building.' She breaks into a peal of laughter. 'Hah ha. A *gardienne* angel, ha!' Mopping her eyes with a handkerchief, she adds, 'I am a genius. I make the jokes in English and in French.'

I find myself laughing as if the woman is the muse of comedy personified.

'*Madame*, I don't know how to thank you.' I look at my watch: nine-thirty in the morning. Lunch service starts at twelve, but I've got time. '*Est-ce que je peux vous offrir un petit quelque chose? Du café et des gâteaux, peut-être?*'

She inclines her head, graciously accepting.

'Marcel, look after Madame Pollie, would you? I'll be back shortly.' I lean in and whisper in his ear. 'Whatever it takes – don't let her leave.'

Emma is single again.

And this time, I'm going to do everything right.

Emma

I know something is up when I come back to my apartment for lunch. Madame Pollie has been – weird, that's the only way to describe it. She's been weird since yesterday, when she came back from wherever she disappeared to. When I returned yesterday evening carrying a takeaway burger she started scolding me about my figure, then grabbed my face and told me how pretty

I was. Now, as she hands me my post, she doesn't say anything, but she gives me a look. The kind of look that would be described as 'arch' if I were living inside a Regency romance novel. The look that tells me she has information, and I don't.

Well. I'm not going to give her the satisfaction of asking for an explanation. Instead, I take my post upstairs and close the door behind me and make myself a sandwich before I look through it.

There's a letter that seems to be from the local council, giving notice of the renovation of the civic offices. Other than that, it's all circulars.

Almost.

A jolt of recognition jerks me upright as soon as I see the postcard. The Eiffel Tower at night. It's the last one of the four postcards I bought that first weekend I spent in Paris – the postcards Kieran accidentally picked up after I ran into him. There's no stamp; it's been hand-delivered.

Hardly breathing, I turn the card over.

Emma

You're no longer with JT, or so I've been told, and you can't know how happy that makes me. Can we start again? If you want to, please meet me at the top of the Eiffel Tower tomorrow at 5pm. I've booked you a ticket, in hope - just ask at the ticket office.

Know that I love you, whatever you decide.

Kieran xxx

PS - I read your article on soulmates, and it was wonderful. Not that I needed to be convinced. You already know I believe in fate.

He was pressing so hard when he wrote the kisses that they've indented the card. Flipping back to the picture of the tower, I run my fingers over the raised marks.

Is he right? Is fate finally going to be on our side?

Chapter Thirty-Five

Kieran

Saturday evening dinner service is over, thank God. I've been wishing the day away since I woke up this morning. I finish saying goodbye to the last of the diners – we've been open just long enough now that we've started to accumulate regulars, and this particular guy always orders the very best – and race back into the kitchen.

'Thierry?' I look about for the *pâtissier*. He can't have left already, surely? 'Thierry! Damn it, where is the—'

Thierry emerges from the staff locker room and raises one eyebrow. 'You bellowed, Chef?'

'Sorry. I'm just – I really need your help.'

His eyes narrow a little. 'Another "English pudding"—' he actually makes the little quotation marks '—that you wish me to elevate into cuisine?'

'Are we or are we not getting rave reviews for *La Reine de l'amitié?* Didn't one of the reviews personally congratulate you for being brave enough to attempt something completely different?'

He has the grace to look a little embarrassed. '*Oui*, Chef. You were right, of course.'

I know what that must have cost him.

'Thank you. Now, you can make chocolates, right?'

'Of course. I make exquisite chocolates.'

'Great, I need your help. I need chocolates, for Emma.'

There's a flash of comprehension. 'Ah, you wish me to make *une petite boîte* of the most delicious creations to win her back.'

'Almost. I want you to teach *me* to make a box of delicious creations. And to help me make them. Tomorrow.' The restaurant is closed on Sundays. 'I'll pay you overtime for the whole day, of course.'

'Tomorrow? A single day?' Thierry's hand waves in a wide, dismissive arc. 'In a year, I could not teach you. You hate the chocolate, and the chocolate will know this. It will not co-operate.'

I pinch the bridge of my nose. It's been a long day.

'Please, Thierry. Could we just try? I'd really appreciate it.'

He glares at me for a moment, then softens. 'Very well. I promise nothing, but, since it is you, and you are a genius, we will try.'

'That's grand, thank you. I'll see you back here tomorrow at . . . ?'

'Eight a.m.' He almost groans. 'We will need all the time we can get.'

Emma

'What about this one?' I stand as far back from the laptop as I can manage and twirl around. 'I don't want to be cold.'

Daisy covers her face with her hands.

'Seriously? Whatever happened to suffering for the sake of fashion? The other dress is much sexier.'

'But it's sleeveless. And it's October. And I'll be wearing a coat, anyway, and—'

She throws up her hands.

'Fine. You still look cute. But add the belt. And pin up your hair and wear the dangly earrings.'

I hold up a pair for approval.

'No, not those ones. The others – the ones with the blue flowers.' Daisy leans forward to peer at my next offering. 'Yeah. Those ones. You should have told me. I could have come over and helped.'

'I only got the postcard yesterday. Besides, you're on a film shoot in Scotland. I'm sure they'd have had something to say about you just disappearing.'

Daisy waves a hand, dismissing my concerns. 'Lipstick?'

'I've got a new favourite. Le Rouge français.'

'Apply,' Daisy orders. I pick up my hand mirror and slick some on. 'Yes. Yeah, that looks great. Good choice.'

'Thanks.'

Daisy turns her head, nods and gives someone a thumbs-up. 'I have to go. Our lead actor has smeared his eyeliner.' She makes a heart shape with her fingers. 'You've got this. And tell Kieran I'm sorry about blocking him and not telling you he was alive, yeah? Because I am. I really am. You know that, don't you?'

'Course I do. Don't worry, D. If I could give you a big hug right now, I would.'

'Right back atcha. Have an amazing time, okay?'

'Will do. I'll call you tomorrow. Love you.'

'Love you too.' She blows me a kiss and ends the call.

I bring up the chapter of *A Ghostwriter's Guide* that I'm supposed to be editing and stare at it for a bit.

Pointless, really. I can't concentrate. I can't think about anything but five p.m. and getting to the Eiffel Tower.

At three-thirty, I give in. I can either spend the next hour pacing up and down in my apartment, or I can leave now and walk all the way there.

No choice to make, really.

I slip the postcard into my bag, grab my gloves and scarf and set off.

By the time I reach the tower, I've walked off some of my energy but none of my ridiculous anxiety. Even after I queue up and find that there is indeed a ticket waiting for me, the voice in my head is still whispering in my ear.

What if he's changed his mind since he sent the postcard?
What if it's a trick?

What if he just wants to tell you to your face that he only wants to be friends?

What if, what if, what if . . .

Until I want to scream.

I guess that bit of me is never quite going to go away.

Still, it doesn't stop me taking one of the glass-sided lifts up to the highest floor. There are two floors, in fact: one enclosed, one open-air. The enclosed space feels a little claustrophobic, so I head to the open area, find an empty spot on the balcony and look at the view.

It's dark now, but Paris lies below me, ablaze, and so heart-stoppingly beautiful I can't tell if the tears in my eyes are caused by the wind or the gratitude swelling inside me.

'Emma.'

I turn around, and he's there.

'Kieran.'

We stare at each other as the crowd moves around us.

'I wasn't sure you'd come,' he says.

'I wasn't sure you wouldn't have changed your mind. Jacques told me that you'd contacted him, that you'd told him about us knowing each other and asked him not to hold it against me, but I still wasn't sure.'

'Huh.' Kieran gazes out across the city for a moment. 'So he didn't tell you the rest of what I said?'

'The rest?'

'I didn't just tell him we knew each other. I gave him notice that I was going to fight for you. That, unless you told me that it was over, that you didn't love me, didn't want me any more, I wasn't going to give up.'

Jacques lied. I can't quite believe it. 'He said he told me the whole message.'

Kieran shakes his head. 'I guess I can't blame him. Maybe he hoped you wouldn't contact me. That I'd never get to tell you that I loved you from the moment I saw you.' His voice breaks. 'I'll never change my mind about you, Emma. Losing you nearly destroyed me.' He steps forward, closing up the distance between us, allowing me to look up into his eyes. 'I can't believe this moment is finally here. I can't believe – I can't believe I finally get to kiss you.'

In response, I close my eyes and lift my mouth to his. His lips move against mine, soft and warm, and the electric spark that I felt the day we met shoots through my core, stronger than ever before, heating my blood and setting my skin tingling.

The perfect kiss. I don't want it to end.

When we do break apart, breathing heavily, he smiles down at me.

'I've got a gift for you. It's my first attempt, but I hope you'll like them.'

Keeping one arm wrapped around me, he manages to extract something from his bag: a small golden box.

'I'm learning to make chocolates.'

I open the box, still standing within the arc of his arm. Six beautifully decorated dark chocolates gleam in the lamplight.

'Do you like them? I mean, I know you've not tasted them yet, but—'

I silence him with a kiss, then grin. 'You had me at chocolate. Hell, you had me before then. You had me that day I nearly scythed you down with my suitcase at the Gare du Nord.' I press my fingertips to his cheek. 'I love you, Kieran Landry.'

We kiss again, and I lose track of time.

'What now?' I ask eventually.

Kieran pulls me closer, and I rest my head on his chest, and he kisses my hair.

'Now, Emma Christmas, what I really want to do is finally take you on a date.'

I sigh, filled with too much happiness, if that's possible.

'That sounds perfect. Let's just take one last look at the view.'

Hand in hand, we gaze out across the city, then turn away towards the lifts. I know we'll come back here soon. And Paris will be waiting for us.

Acknowledgements

Attempting something new is always scary, so up front I'd like to thank you, the reader, for picking up *We'll Always Have Paris* and giving it a chance. Writing this book was a joy, and I hope at least some of that experience has come across in its pages.

WAHP is my first contemporary romantic comedy, the first book I've written without my sister, and my adult debut. Those mentioned below gave me the confidence, support and means to make it happen, and I'm so very grateful to all of them.

(By the way, they are all living, breathing people: this book is entirely the result of human, not artificial, intelligence.)

First, I need to thank my utterly brilliant friend and agent Kristina Pérez of Pérez Literary & Entertainment. It's not an exaggeration to say that this book would literally not exist without her. A big shoutout too to Isabel Lineberry and Jack Mozley, also of PLE, for all their support.

Thank you to everyone at Hodder & Stoughton who has helped make WAHP into the best book it could be, in particular Kit Nevile, for bringing his keen editing skills to bear on my manuscript, Tallulah Lyons, Linda McQueen and Jon Price.

I'm also grateful to Linda McQueen and Virginie Busette for correcting and polishing my stilted French. Any errors that remain are mine and mine alone.

Thank you to Daisy Woods for providing me with the romance cover of my dreams – I'm still not over how pretty it is!

I owe a huge debt to all the friends I've made since I started in this industry, more years ago than I care to remember! Publishing is sometimes harsh, and it would be nigh on impossible to survive without friends who know exactly how harsh it can get. I'd especially like to thank Perdita Cargill, Alexa Casale, Anna McKerrow, Chris Moore, Mich Kenny, Holly Race, Ava Eldred, Gill Perdue, Clare Harlow, Lorraine Brown, Anna Bell, Tina Orr Monro, Josh Winning, Andreina Cordani, Bex Hogan, Kat Ellis, Sinéad O'Hart and everyone in the UKYA authors chat. I'd also like to give a big virtual hug to all the super wise women of Fem 2.0.

I'm writing these acknowledgements several months before WAHP is due to be published, but I'd like to thank in advance all the people at Hodder who will be involved in the book's marketing, publicity and audio production. My thanks also to all the booksellers, booktubers, bookstagrammers, booktokkers and festival organisers who will be helping to put WAHP into the hands of readers; I'm so appreciative of everything you do. I'd especially like to mention Beth, Sifa and Gary for their generous ongoing support.

To my non-writing friends, especially Sophie, Guy and all the lovely ladies of the adult ballet class, thank you for the gift of your company.

Finally, my family: you are the best and most important part of my life, and I love you all dearly. Extra special big hugs to my husband Neill, who deserves the title of husband-of-the-year every year forever, and to my daughters Georgina & Victoria for making me laugh and generally being wonderful. And for Lizzie, who has spent more time than most talking me out of my imposter syndrome: this is for you.